BOOK THREE IN THE DAN

EL ALAMEIN

JACK MURRAY

LUME BOOKS

LUME BOOKS

Published in 2022 by Lume Books

ISBN 978-1-83901-444-4

Typeset using Atomik ePublisher from Easypress Technologies

www.lumebooks.co.uk

For Monica, Lavinia, Anne and our Angel, Baby Edward

PART 1: OPERATION THESEUS

31st Dec 1941–Jan 1941

Operation Crusader had come to an end. Although Crusader had failed in its original objective of crushing the Axis forces, the Eighth Army had, at least, pushed them back some 500 miles (805 km) to El Agheila in western Libya. The Axis garrisons at Bardia and Sollum in eastern Libya had surrendered but the cost had been high for both sides. The Allies lost 17,700 men, the Axis around 37,000. Tobruk had been relieved, and Cyrenaica recaptured along with many airfields, which was good news for the convoys supplying Malta. They would receive more air cover while they supplied the besieged island.

The armies of both sides were exhausted, and winter had set in. However, from late December, the impact of bombing the Allied-held Island of Malta began to tell. Malta had been a thorn in the side of the Axis powers throughout the war. Damaging the island's capacity to attack Axis convoys meant that more reinforcements were getting through to the Axis-held Tripoli. Meanwhile, the Eighth Army supply lines were badly stretched and their forces dispersed across hundreds of miles in the western Libya desert.

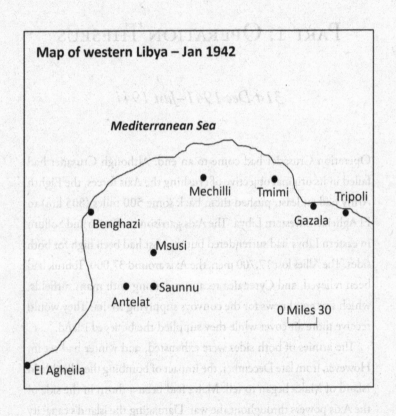

Map of western Libya – Jan 1942

Mediterranean Sea

Tripoli

Gazala

Tmimi

Mechilli

Benghazi

Msusi

Saunnu

Antelat

El Agheila

0 Miles 30

CHAPTER ONE

New Year's Eve, 1941

An hour after sunrise on New Year's Eve and the enemy was already tearing into Danny Shaw. They were numerous, more relentless, and crueller than the Germans. They never surrendered and came back each day, every damn minute, undeterred by the anger of their victim, unvanquished by the violence inflicted upon them; immune to the hatred and the vitriol directed towards them.

'Feckin flies,' said Gerry 'Fitz' Fitzgerald, echoing Danny's thoughts. 'Whatever possessed anyone to fight a feckin' war in this godforsaken place I'll never know. Militant little bastards.'

'At least you know how your old editor felt,' observed Danny. He'd heard countless stories from the former newspaperman of his run-ins with his boss while working on the local newspaper in Galway.

'Shush, you two, I can see Jerry coming now,' said Sergeant Adam Gray, squinting through a pair of binoculars.

All Danny could see was a mid-morning haze. It made his eyes water to stare at the horizon too long. The presence of the enemy had the usual impact on the men crouched behind the slope of the wadi overlooking the road leading to Agedabia in western Libya. Finally, he saw some shapes emerge from the shimmering haze. It was too far for him to tell if it was the enemy. He turned to Gray.

'What are they, sarge?'

Gray waited a moment before replying. 'Might be part of the supply echelon. Let's hope so anyway. I don't fancy tangling with any Panzers today.' He might have added 'any day'. They were not equipped to deal with tanks. The job of the Jock column was harassment. Direct confrontation with heavy armour was not recommended.

Danny glanced at their six-pound guns. They were dug into the side of the ridge; impossible to see from the road. Alongside them was a battalion of infantry and a half a dozen mortars. All was still. No one moved, not even to swat the malignant plague of flies that buzzed unwelcome around each soldier. Some held their breath.

Danny felt a tap on his shoulder. It was John Buller, the gunner. He nodded towards the shells. Nothing was said. Slowly Danny ducked down and lifted one of the shells. Behind him he sensed someone clambering up the slope.

Keeping his eyes on the road, Sergeant Gray said to the new arrival, 'It's definitely a German supply column, sir. They'll be here in two minutes.'

'Very good, sergeant,' said Lieutenant Blair. 'Make ready, gentlemen.'

Danny levered the breech open and heaved the cartridge into the jacket of the barrel. He closed the block quickly while Buller adjusted his aim.

'One minute, wait until we can see all of the echelon. Don't fire until they are completely side on. Wait for the order,' added Blair unnecessarily. 'Pass it along.'

The instruction passed along the line.

4

Then silence.

Gradually the hum of the convoy became louder. An endless line of trucks. There were no tanks. The column snaked along the desert road watched by a hundred pairs of eyes.

'Let's give Jerry a little present for New Year,' said Blair to no one in particular.

Danny held his breath and looked across the ridge. Dozens of bodies lay against the face of the slope. Waiting. The sound of the motor convoy grew louder.

'Wait for it,' said Blair. His eyes were no longer on the echelon driving near them but on Captain Arnold nearby who had his hand up.

Even though they were in the middle of the desert, Danny felt a chill descend on him like a curtain. For the last month he'd been involved in a number of these ambushes. He shivered from the cold but there was excitement, too. A voice nearby said, 'Nearly there. Come on, Fitz. Get a move on.'

Danny smiled. That used to be what Tom would say to him every morning before they went to the forge. Get a move on. Bit by bit the echelon moved past them. It was a few hundred yards long. The lead elements were past when Arnold's arm descended like a guillotine.

'Fire!' shouted Blair.

Guns chattered and explosions detonated nearby. But Danny was no longer listening or even thinking. He was loading the next cartridge into the breech.

'Get a move on,' said Tom Shaw. He was staring down at the can of water. It was sitting on top of another can filled with sand and oil which had been lit. Urging it to boil with various expressions of profanity did not seem to speed matters up unfortunately. He was dying for a brew. By the looks of the men around him, so were they.

5

'I can't make it boil any faster,' moaned Morris, the young man tasked with making the tea. He held his arms out in supplication. This was met by an all too predictable volley of abuse from the three men sitting around the fire.

A few minutes later Tom stood up and walked over towards a man standing piquet. Without saying anything, Tom tapped him on the shoulder. The man nodded and went over to the campfire to get his brew. A minute later he was back. They stood together and looked out at the flat, barren landscape, empty save for the barbed wire. For hundreds of yards directly in front of them were mines lying waiting for the return of the Afrika Korps. Neither man doubted they would be back.

A companionable silence followed. The two men warmed their hands on their cups. It was mid-morning and a hint of rain lay in the air.

'How long do you think it will be, Bert?'

Bert Gissing didn't have to have the question explained. It was the thought uppermost on all their minds. The Germans had been pushed back to the west of the country, but they hadn't been defeated. Nor could they be. The Allies had simply stretched themselves too far to inflict any real damage now. If anything, the greatest risk lay in the possibility of a counter-attack.

'Not long,' concluded Bert. He was as tall as Tom but much broader despite the rather limited diet forced on them. They'd grown up together, gone to school together, fought against each other and then fought together against the Axis.

Neither said anything for a minute as they watched a plane overhead. Each man tensed. The plane was not yet visible. When you cannot see, you hear. Their ears blocked out all sound except that of the brittle clatter of the engine. One of ours.

'Wouldn't catch me up in one of them things,' said Bert before laughing at the ridiculousness of the statement. As if the danger in the air could anyway be more than what he'd faced over the previous eight months. Tom wasn't going to let him get away with this.

'Aye, you're right there, Bert. Much better facing Jerry here at the seaside.'

In fact, they were a little too far inland to see the coast now. Tobruk was a few miles away. They were at the inner perimeter. Then the mines. Then Jerry. The thought of this made Tom glance towards the jeep nearby.

'Even Jerry must celebrate New Year, right?' offered Tom, hopefully.

'What's to celebrate?' replied Bert. He could feel his eyes sting as he said this. Tom glanced at him. An apology was in his eyes. Bert shook his head.

'Sorry, mate. Here's to Hugh,' said Tom and held his cup up.

Bert nodded and they clinked cups.

'To Hugh. Happy New Year up there,' said the two men in unison. A eulogy for a fallen comrade, a friend, a brother.

They were silent once more and remained so for some minutes, lost in thoughts that were not of the present but of green countryside, of stolen apples and of wrestling matches by secluded, shady brooks.

Their reverie was broken by the arrival of a jeep. A corporal hopped out clutching mail. Tom and Bert went towards him.

'One for you, Bert and a couple for you, Tom,' said the corporal.

Tom glanced at the first letter and recognised the elegant handwriting of his mother.

Kate Shaw felt satisfied that the rain had stopped. She gazed up at the liquid sky, the grey cloud moving like treacle; she would risk it. Throwing a coat on she stepped over a puddle at the front door and wondered why she'd bothered. She was wearing wellington boots after all.

The garden gate led directly onto the high street. Behind her she could hear Stan beating the hell out of some metal. She glanced back at him, but his attention was focused solely on the job. He was bathed in the orange glow of the forge.

She walked along the street in the direction of 'Nettlestone's Village Store'. Lottie Gissing was on the other side of the street. Lottie waved to her and smiled. Kate was on the point of wishing her a Happy New Year when she remembered and stopped herself. Poor Hugh. She felt her stomach tighten.

Just behind came the sound of horses' hooves clopping on the cobble stones. Kate turned around just in time to see a young woman hop gracefully down from a beautiful chestnut horse. She saw Kate and smiled. It was clear something was on her mind, so Kate waited for her to come over.

'Good afternoon, Mrs Shaw,' said Sarah Cavendish.

'Hello, Lady Sarah,' said Kate.

'I'm sorry we didn't have a chance to chat on Christmas Eve,' said Sarah. 'I wanted to ask you about Tom and' – she paused for a moment, a hint of red blushing her skin – 'Danny.'

Kate needed no invitation to talk about her sons. Alas what was there to say? Letters from them were infrequent.

'I had a letter from them both around the middle of November. It was just before the last push. They were both well. Tom is still in Tobruk as far as I know and…'

Kate caught her breath. Sarah instinctively grasped her arm and Kate could see there were tears in her eyes. News of the battles had gradually filtered through.

'I suppose no news is good news,' said Kate.

Sarah nodded, unable to speak. The two women looked at one another for a moment and then they heard a man's voice just behind.

'Hello, Lady Sarah,' said Stan Shaw. 'I thought it was you.'

Stan Shaw was tall and rangy, with grey-flecked black hair and haunted eyes. He smiled at Sarah, but she could sense the fear within him.

'Hello, Mr Shaw,' replied Sarah. 'I was just hearing about Tom and Danny. I sent them, and the other boys from the village, letters. It's not much, I know. But they are all in our thoughts.'

Kate smiled at Sarah. It seemed conspiratorial, not that Stan would have noticed. Then Kate saw Sarah take something out of her saddle bag.

'What's that? A camera?' asked Kate.

Sarah's grin lit up her face as she showed off her new Eastman Kodak Ektra camera.

'Father Christmas was very generous this year,' replied Sarah with a wink. 'I thought that it would be nice if I could take a photograph of you both to send to Tom and Danny.'

Kate smiled and responded, 'I'm not sure he'd not prefer a photograph of someone else, Lady Sarah.'

Sarah pretended not to hear but the reddening face told Kate that the message had been received. Then she started to organise the Shaws. It took four photographs and a large amount of good-natured abuse directed at Stan's inability to smile before Sarah was happy that she had a good shot.

'I think I've just seen Father Christmas,' said Kate, motioning with her eyes towards a point over Sarah's shoulder.

Sarah turned and saw her father, Lord Henry Cavendish. He was with another man at the centre of the village. They were standing by a monument to the fallen from the Great War. When Henry saw his daughter, he waved. He touched the arm of the man he was with. They both started to walk towards Sarah and the Shaws.

'Good afternoon, I'd like to introduce you to Stan and Kate Shaw. Their boys Tom and Danny are over in North Africa.'

'How do you do?' said the man holding out his hand.

Stan's eyes widened in shock. The accent was not what he'd been expecting. The man before him was German. There was a moment of hesitation from Stan. Henry quickly realised that explanations were necessary.

'This is Max Kahn. He's a refugee from the Nazis. How long have you been working for me now, Max? Five, six years?'

Understanding broke like a wave over Stan Shaw and he held out his hand.

'I've heard terrible rumours about what the Nazis were up to, Mr Kahn. Are they true?'

Kahn's face changed immediately. He nodded and replied, 'Sadly, the rumours probably don't come close to telling the full truth, Mr Shaw. Jewish people have been sent to camps. Imprisoned without trial. I have many friends who've lost everything. Britain must defeat this man. He is evil.'

'We shall,' said Henry. 'With the Americans in the war now, Germany can't win.'

The talk of the war cast a pall over the group. Recognising the awkwardness of the moment Kate changed the subject.

'We've just had our photographs taken.'

Henry laughed but there was more than a tinge of fatherly pride when he replied, 'Yes, Sarah's photographing anything that moves. The dogs are hiding in fear now.'

The group laughed and Stan felt relaxed enough to speak to a German, perhaps for the first time in his life.

10

'Where are you from, Mr Kahn?'

'A small town near Heidelberg. Ladenburg.'

Geschäft Ladenburg, read the sign over the shop. It was late afternoon. The sky was gradually darkening and there was a bite in the air. Peter Brehme made his way past a group of soldiers chatting by a fountain and into the grocery shop. The shop was empty save for a middle-aged man and his Labrador.

'Hello, Otto,' said Peter, bending down to give the dog a pat on the head. 'Hello to you too, Felix.'

Felix jumped up and put his paws on Brehme's thighs, tail wagging furiously. Otto Becker smiled nervously at the police chief and told Felix to get down. Brehme could see there was some anxiety in Manfred's old primary school teacher's eyes. Perhaps it was his police uniform. People instinctively were on their guard these days. Brehme felt sad about this but recognised it was a sign of these times.

'How is Agatha?'

'Very well, Herr Brehme. Have you heard from Manfred?'

Brehme tried to smile but the effort proved too much so he reverted to the neutral mask that he wore most every hour of the day. He was neither happy nor sad now. The despair of losing his wife, Renata, had transformed into a detachment that he tried to veil behind a smile or a joke. It rarely worked; every day was the same now. The work he hated was an escape from the loneliness he felt. He was caught between two worlds, neither of which he liked; his friends had stopped calling. This was a relief, but he recognised how little sense of purpose he had now. A glance out of the window to a street full of soldiers told him he was redundant. He no longer cared as he once had. Crime had been legalised, murder industrialised, and it had a black uniform. One such man, clad in black, came into the shop behind Brehme.

Just at that moment Arnold Weber, the shop manager, appeared from the back. He held up a bag.

'Here you are, Otto. I knew I had some sardines in the back,' said Weber. He was a big man and widely liked in the town. He grinned at Brehme and said, 'Your usual?'

'Yes thanks,' replied Brehme. The big shopkeeper took down several packs of cigarettes and handed them to the policeman. Brehme paid for the cigarettes, nodded to Weber, and followed Otto Becker out of the shop. The little man, he noticed, was carrying two large bags.

'Otto, wait,' called Brehme. 'You seem to be feeding the five thousand. Let me take one of those.'

There was reluctance in the eyes of the little schoolteacher. He smiled and handed Brehme one bag. It was full of potatoes.

'I hope you're not distilling alcohol,' laughed Brehme.

Becker paused a moment but then his face broke into a grin.

'I hadn't thought of that. Perhaps I should.'

'Let me know, I'll come and drink a shot with you.'

They walked along the street. There was music coming from somewhere. It was a Christmas carol. The two men trudged along, their feet crunching through the dirty snow. Neither spoke as they passed a group of soldiers. They were loud and clearly in good humour. Brehme looked at them with barely concealed distaste.

'Any former pupils of yours there?' asked Brehme to the schoolteacher.

'I don't recognise any of them,' said Becker. Brehme wasn't sure if this was because they'd grown up or something else. The changing face of youth in the country had been more than physical. He barely recognised what they'd become. And what he saw appalled him. There were a few other young people in the street. Interestingly, the younger people were in casual clothes. It seemed odd not to see them in some form of uniform. Perhaps the fashion for dressing up like a soldier was passing. A good thing, too, thought Brehme. They arrived at the large house belonging to Becker that he shared with his wife.

'Well, I suppose this is you,' said Brehme.

'Would you care to come in and have a drink with us?' asked Becker.

Brehme was policeman enough to recognise that Becker did not want him to accept and polite enough to decline in a manner that gave no offence. They parted company and Brehme returned to his own empty house. The sound of his boots on the wooden floor echoed harshly in the permanently dark hallway. He saw a note from Leni, his housekeeper. She'd prepared some food that needed to be heated up in the oven. For a moment he felt a swell of anger. What was he paying her for if she was not here to cook? Then he remembered it was New Year's Eve. The anger dissipated in seconds to be replaced by a feeling of ennui. He took off his coat and walked into the kitchen. A quick look inside the oven confirmed the presence of something to eat.

He shut the door of the oven and left the kitchen. Maybe later. He went to the front door remembering that he'd forgotten to check for post. There was none. He exhaled and went into the living room. He flopped down in his armchair and stared out of the window to the back garden. The day slowly gave itself up to the darkness of night. The snow provided a purple glow that Brehme found oddly comforting. It was hypnotic and he sat for a while absorbed in the strange lilac light. How long he sat he could not tell but he was jolted awake by the sounds of revelry on the street.

Leaning over the chair he switched on the radio. A voice that he knew so well was speaking to Germany.

'German Volk! National Socialists! Party Comrades! For the third time, destiny forces me to direct my New Year's Proclamation to the

German Volk at war. It is clear to the German Volk that this fight, which was forced on us by our old greedy enemies, as so many times before in German history, is truly a question of life or death.'

A dozen people crowded round the radio to listen to the speech. The Fuhrer spoke about the rightness of their fight and the inevitability of victory. The Mayer household and their guests listened mostly in silence.

'Perhaps this year you will have a chance to face those enemies, Erich,' said Mayer.

'I hope so, Herr Mayer,' replied Erich without flinching at his outright lie. Erich was dressed in a black uniform. There was a strip of medals emblazoned on his chest. He had yet to face the Allies.

'Then after the war is over and our enemies are defeated…' Mayer left the sentence unfinished. He glanced meaningfully at his daughter and then at Herr Sammer who was standing beside his son.

'I hope the war will be over soon, Herr Mayer,' replied Erich with a smile. 'But not so soon that I can't get at them myself.'

'Well said, young man,' replied Mayer, nodding in approval. Gerd Sammer clapped his son on the back, pride leaking from his eyes. And he was proud. His son had met a young girl as beautiful as she was dutiful. She would bring many fine young men into the world. He'd done well. A son to be proud of. The match between the Mayer and the Sammer households would cement his position both within the town and the party. He felt so happy that he barely listened to the rest of the speech from their leader.

Anja Mayer had only just turned eighteen. She would leave school at the beginning of summer. Then she felt Erich take her hand. It felt cold. She turned to her fiancé and smiled dutifully.

When the speech drew to its uplifting conclusion there was spontaneous and excited applause in the room.

14

'Time for some music, I think,' announced Mayer. He leaned over towards the radio.

Captain Johannes Kummel, commander of the first company in Regiment 8 of 15th Panzer Division switched off the radio. He was with the heads of the other companies in the tank regiment.

'So we're going to win the war this year, apparently.'

'That's good to know,' replied Lieutenant Stiefelmayer, in a voice that was barely audible. 'I was worried for a while.'

Kummel looked at the drawn features of the man before him. Grime-encrusted hands rubbed sunken eyes. His face was buried into his chest. Silence fell on the group. Kummel listened to the sounds of the regiment. It was eerily quiet as midnight and the New Year approached. In place of high-spirited chat or the sounds of engines being made ready, there was, instead, a low murmur.

The head of the regiment, Lieutenant-Colonel Hans Cramer, appeared in front of the group. Red, inflamed eyes on a bloodless face gazed down at men as exhausted as he was.

'It's nearly midnight. We should announce the award,' said Cramer.

His voice was stronger than he looked. Vertical lines were carved like canyons into his cheeks and on his forehead. He'd never fully recovered from his wounds of the summer, and it showed. Yet his presence was appreciated deeply. There was an impalpable force within Cramer that lifted them all.

They sat in mute exhaustion, unable to respond. Then, one by one, each of the senior officers rose. First Kummel, then the others raised their heavy bones; every man creaking like a wooden door with rusted hinges. How could the act of walking be so difficult, thought Kummel? Moving one step after another was its own triumph of will. He, and the other officers, walked along the centre of the leaguer. They nodded to the men they passed. All were sitting around campfires by their tanks. Some nodded back. Most were too exhausted to speak. Others had already fallen asleep, uninterested in waiting until midnight to bring in 1942. There was no shame in this. They were all at the edge of a precipice.

All along the rank of tanks, men climbed wearily to their feet as the officers of the 2nd Battalion of Regiment 8 came towards them. Kummel, Cramer and the other captains walked the full length of the leaguer and back again. The men began to follow behind Cramer and the other company commanders.

'What's happening?' asked Manfred. He was sitting beside his friend, Gerhardt Kroos, near his Mark III tank.

Gerhardt looked at the unshaven, hollow-eyed face of his friend and shrugged wearily. They rose slowly to their feet and started to follow behind the other men. They weren't sure where they were headed. It hardly seemed to matter. Finally, Manfred spotted Colonel Cramer. He nudged Gerhardt and pointed towards him.

'Not another bloody attack,' commented Gerhardt. The thought of this gave him the energy to be angry. What was left of the tank regiment was a mockery of what they had been only a month previously. Damaged tanks, damaged men. All numbed by physical and mental fatigue. Few, if any, were in a fit state to fight.

They, and dozens of other crewmen, finally reached the colonel. Cramer stood erect, feet shoulder width apart. At that moment it seemed like a caricature of military discipline. Everyone knew he was as exhausted as they were. He began to speak.

'We have heard our Fuhrer speak. We know what is demanded of us. We know what is at stake. Victory in this war will only be achieved if we can take Cyrenaica back and then Egypt. This year has been hard for all of us. We have come close to victory, but we have also lost friends and comrades. None braver nor dearer to us than Major Gunther Fenski. I received news earlier this week that Major Fenski has been awarded the highest honour that can be bestowed upon a soldier, the Knight's Cross. He is the third member of our regiment to be so honoured. He receives this for the bravery of his actions, and sacrifice, on 23rd November 1941. We give thanks that we had such a man amongst us. A man who led us, who inspired us, and whose memory this nation will cherish as long as soldiers gather together to remember those who have fallen.'

Cramer stopped for a moment and gazed out at the sea of exhaustion that faced him, and his throat tightened. He thought once more of the courage shown by his dead friend and comrade, Fenski, and how proud he was to serve with the men in front of him who had given so much. He nodded to the men and then turned towards the senior officers. The speech, if that's what it was, had finished. There was only an odd silence. Applause seemed inappropriate. Then, from somewhere in the ranks, a voice began to sing.

Manfred and Gerhardt turned around but could not see who was singing. The words cut through the cold night air like an electrical current. Soon other voices joined the lone singer. And then the two boys began to sing. Nervously at first and then, quickly, it became full throated, like the cry of a wounded animal.

Deutschland, Deutschland über alles, Über alles in der Welt, Wenn es stets zu Schutz und TrutzeBrüderlich zusammenhält. Von der Maas bis an die Memel, Von der Etsch bis an den Belt

CHAPTER TWO

Wadi Faregh, south of Agedabia, Libya 21st January 1941

Manfred finished shaving and wiped his face with a dirty damp towel. It was five thirty in the morning. Despite the early hour, he felt curiously rested. A break of two weeks from the fighting had been enough for him to recharge. A couple of days in Tripoli had helped too. Upon his return he'd been assigned to a new tank to make way for the reinforcements to the regiment.

He drained the rest of his coffee and cleared up just in time to see his new commander come round the corner of the tank. He stood up immediately. Alongside him the other members of the crew also rose.

Hans Kummel nodded to Manfred and the others.

'Any coffee left?' asked the commander of the 1st Battalion. Kummel had been put in temporary command of the battalion following the death of Major Fenski the previous month. There was no better man to lead them, thought Manfred. That said, there was no worse one to be in the tank with. This was not a comment on his leadership. He was rightly adored by the men. However, 'the Lion of Capuzzo' had a nasty habit, observed Gerhardt drily one day, of always being at the head of a charge.

'He's suicidal,' said Gerhardt. 'Or mad.'

'Maybe he thinks death is inevitable and he just wants to get on with it,' suggested Manfred.

The conversation with Gerhardt had occurred a week previously when Manfred had heard of the transfer. It was an honour and clearly a reflection of the fact that he was well thought of. The news of his actions on *Totensonntag* had clearly made it all the way up to senior command. As with many things in life, Manfred was learning that glory and honours were not bestowed freely. A price was always paid further down the line. For now, Manfred enjoyed special favour by being in the tank of the regiment's figurehead. The toll would be demanded soon.

Kummel ran a hand through his dark hair and leaned forward. Ernst Hubbuch, the tank driver, handed Kummel a coffee. He took a swig and imparted the news they'd all been expecting.

'We leave in three hours. We are to take Agedabia and push forward from there. Rommel thinks we can catch the British out before they can reinforce. He's right. They're stretched over half of Libya.'

'I'm sure our leader will be delighted that you concur, sir.'

Kummel grinned at Sergeant Franz Beer, the tank gunner. Beer had ridden with Kummel since their arrival in North Africa. He'd earned the right to be freer in his conversation than the others. Still, it surprised Manfred just how far he could push it with the captain. He wished he could enjoy a similar level of confidence as Beer. Perhaps one day. For the moment he was the new boy in the tank. A loader once more after a brief spell as a driver in another tank. He didn't mind. The men he was with were the best of the best. But always at the back of his mind were Gerhardt's words.

19

'Your perceptiveness does you credit, Beer. Perhaps you would like to hear what our leader has written?'

Beer and the others nodded. Kummel extracted a piece of paper from his pocket. He took a sip of coffee and ignored the impatient sigh from Beer. Manfred smiled at the little man from Berlin. He was heavyset but nearly a foot shorter than Kummel and Manfred. A few more moments of silence followed as Kummel pretended to study the note. Beer began to whistle. The radio operator, Igor Siefers chuckled. He was relatively new to the tank but was around ten years older than Manfred, like the other members of the crew.

'It says, as you're so interested… actually, assemble the men, Beer, would you?'

Beer sighed while Manfred and the others, Kummel included, laughed.

'German and Italian soldiers!' read Kummel to the assembled 1st Battalion. 'Behind you lie heavy battles with a vastly superior enemy. Your morale remains unimpaired. At this moment we are considerably stronger than the enemy facing us in the front line. Therefore, we shall proceed today to attack and destroy the enemy. I expect every man to give his utmost in these decisive days. Long live Italy! Long live the great German Reich! Long live our Fuhrer!'

Kummel raised his voice at the end and was rewarded with a full-throated cheer from the assembled ranks. Then, as quickly as they had gathered, they dispersed to their tanks. It was almost 0830. The morning was cold and greyly uninviting. The order to move from Cramer came across the radios.

The tanks rolled forward as sand began to blow into their faces.

'That's all we need,' said Beer. 'As if fighting the British isn't enough, we have the bloody weather to cope with here.'

Manfred couldn't agree more. He detested the desert. He knew

20

why they were here but could not fathom what would make anyone want to live in such a pitiless land. As if to validate Manfred's feelings, the desert threw up a sandstorm almost immediately they had left the leaguer.

They drove forward blindly. Shutting all hatches didn't matter. The sand still found a way through, caking their sweat-stained faces with grit and oil. In these conditions they were forced to use periscopes to guide them forward. After half an hour, Kummel called a halt.

'We've reached sand dunes. We'll have to give the trucks a tow. The sand is too soft. Wheels will never be able to climb these.'

Kummel glanced down at Manfred, the most junior member of the crew. Manfred smiled ruefully and put goggles on. Then he wrapped a scarf around the lower part of his face. To the sound of laughter from Beer, he opened the lower hatch and climbed out.

The sandstorm was not as bad as he'd thought. He'd been in worse. Manfred walked forward towards a group of men standing near one of the large number of trucks.

'We can help tow one of you,' said Manfred to an infantry captain. The captain nodded and went to the side of the truck and banged it. Within moments soldiers came pouring out of the truck. A grappling hook was attached to Manfred's tank.

In all the time Manfred had been out, no words were exchanged. The operation to hitch the truck to the tank took less than a minute, much to Manfred's relief. The sandstorm was not the strongest he'd encountered, but it could still sting.

Three minutes after leaving the tank, Manfred was back inside. He nodded to Hubbuch who started to move the tank forward and up the sand dune. The engine coughed and spluttered like a bronchial old man all the way up the hill.

'Let's hope there are not too many of these ahead,' commented

21

Kummel grimly. He looked at his wristwatch and then switched his attention to the periscope. He heard Hubbuch cursing below as the engine protested. They crested the dune. There was another just ahead but not so high. To his right and left, he saw other tanks similarly engaged. What are we doing? he thought. Madness.

The next set of dunes proved to be the last. Soon they were back on the flat and pushing on against the sand lashing the front of the tank. Manfred was miserable. He could feel sand all over his body and it had already begun to prickle. Beer looked across to Manfred, a ghost of a grin appearing on his face. He watched as Manfred's body contorted in an effort to find some relief against the itch.

'Don't,' warned Manfred, spying the direction of Beer's gaze. 'It's not funny.'

Of course, this was as likely to stop the torrent of laughter that followed as a hand shielding against rain. The whole tank erupted at Manfred's discomfort, even the normally serious Kummel.

'If you keep on like this, I will leave the tank,' said Manfred in the manner of a dissatisfied worker handing in his notice.

The sand rattling against the tank was drowned out by the sound of five men laughing as they headed towards war.

Around ten in the morning, having travelled thirty kilometres, the tank was woken up by the crump of a gun.

'Who was that?' shouted Kummel into his mic.

The voice of Lieutenant Stiefelmayer replied calmly, 'That was me. British tanks sighted.'

Kummel looked through his telescope but could see only the backs of the tanks belonging to the 4th and 8th Panzer companies. It was too hazy ahead as the sandstorm rendered the British tanks indistinct shapes.

'How far?' asked Kummel.

'Seven hundred metres,' replied Stiefelmayer. There was more gunfire as the rest of the 4th and 8th Panzers opened fire on the enemy tanks.

Hubbuch raced the tank up to the others, but Kummel held his hand up. They would allow the others to fire.

'Two hit,' came Stiefelmayer's voice. 'No, three.'

This brought a cheer inside the tank and a 'well done' from Kummel. The tanks pushed forward. Within minutes they were at the point where they had intercepted the British tanks. There were eight burning tanks but no sign of any others.

'What can you see?' asked Kummel on the mic.

'Sand,' came the reply from Stiefelmayer. 'They're gone. I can't see anything now.'

'Drive on,' ordered Kummel. 'We have to reach Saunnu to block off any Allied retreat from Agedabia.'

The engagement was over and already forgotten in the minds of the crew. Only the next objective counted. Manfred settled down and tried to make himself comfortable. Another few hours driving on the road lay ahead. The heat of the tank, now more than one hundred degrees, meant they were all thirsty. But there was to be no break.

23

CHAPTER THREE

Nr Saunnu, Libya, 22nd January 1942

It was just a handful of black specks at first in the clear late afternoon sky. You could see them before the cackling engine stretched your nerves to breaking point. The column stopped on the order of Captain Arnold. He didn't have to say battle stations. They already knew the drill.

Arnold was just thirty years of age and seemed as if he'd been born to be in the army. In fact, he had been. His father and his grandfather had both been lifers. There was never any question of where young Arnold, or Arnie as his friends in the 'Mess' knew him, would end up. He took to this sort of command easily. Men followed him willingly. He made them feel like schoolboys playing pirates again.

For over five weeks they'd been a scourge to German supply columns; contributing to the slow strangulation of the Axis forces during the Crusader operation. With each raid, the element of surprise was diminishing. Arnold stood in the front of the jeep with binoculars pinned to his eyes.

'Yes, it's Jerry all right. I wondered when they would find us.'

Corporal Barnes gripped the steering wheel nervously.

'I suppose we've had a good run, sir. It was bound to happen.'

Arnold felt a sudden rush of fear surging through his body. Against the echelons they ran into, Jock columns were deadly. They always stayed clear of tanks but the risk from air attack was a constant waking worry. It was a big desert. The chances of being found by air were remote. The vast emptiness was their salvation and their nemesis. It looked as if their month-long run of luck was coming to an end. They were no longer on their own.

Instinct told Arnold that the prowling Luftwaffe patrol would see them. Arnold waved his arms. This was the order for the column to disperse to make life difficult for the approaching planes. No one was in any doubt that they were German.

Danny held onto the side of the vehicle for dear life as it tore away from the column. Sergeant Gray drove like he was at Le Mans. Within half a minute they were two hundred yards from the rest of the column. He drew to a halt inside a small depression.

'Emergency action. Don't worry about the pedestal,' shouted Gray.

Danny, Corporal Buller and Fitz hopped out of the vehicle and quickly unhooked the trail of the two-pound gun from the truck. They swung it in the direction of the planes while Gray drove the truck out of the way. Buller sat in the gunner's seat while Danny and Fitz raised the shield.

Then they all turned towards Lieutenant Blair for an instruction on when to commence firing. He was staring at the sky, hypnotised. The three men exchanged looks. Then Sergeant Gray jumped out of the driver's seat.

It was something of a long shot that they would hit the fast-moving planes as this was not an ack ack gun. At best, it would give

25

the enemy pilots pause for thought on how many runs they would take at the column. The drone of the aircraft grew louder. They were unquestionably going to intercept the column.

'Heading this way,' said Fitz glancing up at the sky.

'Sounds like the Bf 109,' said Buller. No one argued because no one was listening. Danny was too busy mounting the gun on the incline of the depression to compensate for the limited elevation. The gun was now facing in the direction of the approaching Messerschmitt fighters.

Gray shot a glance in the direction of Lieutenant Blair.

'Sir?' said Gray in a steady voice.

Blair turned round and seemed to wake as if from a dream. He nodded to Gray and took his place behind the gun screen. Danny knelt by the gun and took a shell from the emergency ammunition box. Buller, on the other side of the gun, was busy peering through the telescopic sight, aiming for a spot half a mile ahead of the approaching fighters. Behind him, Fitz was busy removing the hand spike and inserting it into the socket of the trail leg to ensure the gun stayed rooted to the spot when it fired. The operation had taken less than thirty seconds.

Danny's heart was racing. He risked a glance at the scene around him. The trucks were now dispersed. All the machine guns and field guns were manned and ready for action. This gave him some cause for reassurance. The Messerschmitt fighters were going to have a warm reception.

Captain Hans-Joachim Marseille couldn't believe his luck. Whether it was good or bad luck remained to be seen. Days of patrols had failed to find any enemy. Now he had, at last, come across a column. Not quite the easy pickings of a supply train but it would do. He glanced down at his fuel gauge. This was not the time he would have chosen to find this column. A voice on the radio broke into his thoughts.

'Blue leader, are you receiving? Hans, have you seen?'

'Yes, I can see. Prepare to engage. Two passes. No more, we can't risk the aircraft.' Marseille pushed the stick forward and began to descend. Eyes focused, unblinking, behind tinted goggles. His machine began to shake. Marseille knew his mind would soon close off. His body and instinct would take over. He trusted these instincts. They'd kept him alive through countless sorties, dozens of engagements with fighter aircraft and perhaps one hundred kills.

In those moments of frenzied action, Marseille was at his calmest. His thumb came to rest on the gun button. The column was scattering now. This made sense and he acknowledged the presence of mind of the commander. They would not be able to rake the whole convoy with fire. His mind's eye picked out the guns, the trucks with the machine guns and the supply truck. He would target the latter. If he couldn't take out any guns, he could certainly put a dent in their water and petrol. In the middle of the desert, this would soon tell.

'Concentrate on the covered truck,' said Marseille. He pushed the stick further forward. He was diving into an attack. Eight thousand feet soon became two thousand feet. Then one thousand. He was quarter of a mile away. And then the firing began.

Danny closed the breech and Buller fired without waiting for Blair to give the order. They both glanced over the top of the shield, but a burst of gunfire sent them back under cover.

'I think we missed,' said Danny speaking the obvious. It would have been a miracle shot if they'd hit.

'Load,' ordered Sergeant Gray but Danny was already opening the breech. They fired at the third plane. Missed again. The whole column was firing on the air patrol. There were five planes. Each had come down, one after another, raking the column with gunfire.

27

Bullets lashed the sand around them. Danny was dimly aware of an explosion nearby. This was unusual. The 109s didn't normally carry bombs. He stopped thinking about it and concentrated on loading the next cartridge. From somewhere nearby he was aware of shouting and intense heat.

'A beer for whoever hit the truck,' said Marseille.

Three pilots immediately jammed the airwave trying to take credit. Marseille laughed at their shamelessness. He was ecstatic. It was too late for them to knock out the column but unless he was mistaken, they'd done the next best thing. Black smoke was pouring from a truck. With any luck this would cripple them at some point.

'Enough, I think we've all earned a beer. Let's go home. No need for another pass. I think Tommy will have to hitch a lift home.'

This was greeted with relieved laughter. No one had been hit but there was always a risk. He pulled the stick back and slowly began to rise. As he did this, he simultaneously began to veer the plane away from the soldiers down below. Why give them a second chance? The five planes departed the scene as quickly as they'd come.

Danny and the other men watched the planes change course. He turned around and saw the reason why they'd decided to knock off work early. He tapped Buller's shoulder and pointed to the burning supply truck.

'Bugger,' said the big Liverpudlian.

'That's torn it,' agreed Danny.

Gray ignored the conversation and kept his eyes focused on the sky until their visitors were no more than dark specks. Then he turned to the truck.

'Get this gun back on our truck,' said Gray irritably.

Fitz took out the spike and soon they were pulling the gun and attaching the trail leg back onto the truck.

Gray and Blair went off in search of Arnold while Buller drove the truck back towards the centre of the convoy. The soldiers all climbed out of their vehicles and looked at the burning mess. It was a write off and with it, gallons of fuel and water. Although each vehicle had its own supply, this was an important reserve.

Danny watched the lieutenant and the sergeant join Arnold and the other senior officers in a rapid conference. It looked as if it might take a while, so he turned to the others and said, 'Anyone fancy a brew?'

'Better make enough for the sergeant and Lieutenant Blair too,' suggested Fitz. 'I suspect they'll be wanting something.'

'I'll help,' said Evans, grabbing a tin of tea and some cups.

Ten minutes later the men were sitting around the fire drinking tea and eating some biscuits. The mood was despondent. For five weeks they'd managed to avoid serious damage to man or vehicle. For Danny, it had almost been enjoyable. Fighting an enemy who could not fight back on equal terms had been a damn sight easier than being a sitting duck in a tank. The jackboot had, for a while, been on the other foot. Now they faced an uncertain reality. They were at least fifty miles inside German lines. There was no guarantee that there was enough petrol for all to get home. Nor was there any certainty they had enough water either.

They were soon joined by Sergeant Gray who accepted a mug of tea from Evans with the hint of a nod. He sat down. Nobody said anything. Something on Gray's face suggested a man torn between anger and worry. He drained the cup in a single gulp. It was clear that the news was not good. Danny held his breath and watched the sergeant wipe his mouth with his sleeve. Then he looked round at the group.

'So there's bad news and very bad news. Take your pick.'

Silence.

'Very well. The bad news is we've lost our reserve of fuel and water. We have what we're carrying.'

'Isn't that enough? We can't be more than half a day's travel from Agedabia even allowing for looping around wide,' pointed out Buller.

Gray smiled grimly and shook his head. Danny interjected at this point.

'Is the really bad news, sarge, that our boys are no longer there?'

'Correct, Shaw,' said Gray. 'They're no longer there.'

'What happened?' asked Danny, trying not to sound alarmed.

CHAPTER FOUR

Antelat, Libya, 22nd January 1942

Mid-afternoon Kummel finally ordered a halt to the battalion. He could see the crew were badly in need of a break. They'd been on the road since morning and covered over one hundred kilometres.

'The British can wait until I've had a coffee,' said Kummel dusting half a desert from his uniform.

'I need something more than that,' added Beer rushing quickly to the hatch.

'Perhaps if we could point his ass at the British, we could end this war at a stroke,' shouted Manfred to the departing gunner. He waved his hand in front of his nose. 'Who knew the smell of petrol would be a break from a human being.'

The others laughed in sympathy. The humour to be extracted from one man's flatulence was an ongoing source of release. The increasing frequency and virulence of Beer's expulsion of unwanted gastric gas had eroded any sympathy they had for the Berliner's extraordinary capacity to create, store, then expel the olfactorily, deadly combination of methane, carbon dioxide and hydrogen sulphide.

'And don't come back,' shouted Manfred which brought a round of applause from Siefers and Hubbuch while Kummel merely chuckled.

Thirty minutes later they were on the move again. During this time, they had refuelled and taken on some fresh supplies of food and water. They were past Agedabia and heading for Antelat, a town further on up Via Balbia, gradually moving north-east on a path that would take them back near Tobruk. The whole of the 15th and 21st Panzer divisions were on the move. Past Agedabia, Manfred noticed that the pace was faster now. Congestion had slowed progress throughout the last two days as the vehicles bunched through bottleneck gaps in the mines left over from the December offensive. The voice of Colonel Cramer on the radio put an end to their break; soon they were on the road again.

'1st Battalion has been assigned to a Battle Group,' said the colonel. 'In their wisdom they've called it Battle Group Cramer. Rather inspiring, I think. Maybe they'll write an opera about us one day. We're to engage the British armoured formations in Saunnu. To save you consulting your maps, that is thirty kilometres east of Antelat. They want us to destroy them. I think we can do that, don't you?'

Kummel smiled and nodded down to Hubbuch. The Battle Group veered off Via Balbia in a wide arc.

'It sounds like he wants us to surround the British forces within the area,' said Kummel by way of explanation to the crew.

'That was my guess, too,' said Beer, earning a light clip round the head from his captain.

As the light was beginning to fade, Manfred's hopes grew that they would get through the day without seeing the enemy or being seen. It had been a long march and he suspected it just might continue through the night. Kummel grabbed his binoculars. This meant he intended sitting outside the cupola of the tank. They continued in silence for another twenty minutes, then Manfred heard it.

'Enemy tanks in front of us,' said Kummel.

A voice crackled on the radio. It was Cramer.

'How many do you see?'

'It's difficult to say; at least a company,' said Kummel simply. 'They are directly ahead to the east of the road to Giof el Mater.'

'How far?' pressed Cramer.

'Three, maybe four kilometres,' replied Kummel. '4th Company attack frontally. All others turn towards Giof el Mater. We must take the airfield.'

Lieutenant Stiefelmayer replied immediately, 'Engaging.'

The radio went quiet. Manfred found his heart racing. No one spoke in the tank. All were waiting to hear what the 4th Company encountered.

The next few minutes flew by in seconds. One moment Manfred could hear the crump of tank guns from both sides. The next he heard Kummel calmly announce that he'd seen anti-tank guns.

'Range six hundred metres, twelve o'clock. Armour-piercing shell.'

Manfred was already loading it into the breech.

Kummel ducked his head back into the turret. He put his mouth to the mic. 'Companies one and two, frontal assault. Three, work your way around to the west, and take the guns from that side. We'll swing round from the east. Oh and Beer...'

'Yes, sir?' said Beer looking up at the captain.

'You can start firing.'

A grin broke out over Beer's face. 'Yes, sir.' He put his eyes on the sights and his thumb over the button.

33

The fighting resumed once more. An unequal fight that did not last long. The British were sent in headlong retreat.

The next morning began, as it usually did for Manfred, at five thirty. He had just about enough time to shave when he saw the others in his crew beginning to stir. Even Kummel was still sleeping when the smell of coffee woke him.

'Is the war over yet?' asked Kummel, rubbing his eyes.

'No, sir,' replied Manfred, 'but I think Churchill wants to meet you to discuss terms.'

'Send Beer, I want to sleep longer. Beer's farting will soon have Churchill suing for peace.'

Manfred's muscles ached. So did his bones. Yet he felt oddly elated. The fighting yesterday had been one-sided. They had, quite simply, pummelled, then overrun the enemy. This was so different to only a month ago.

The morning of the twenty third was inactive but reports filtered through that the 21st Panzer division was in heavy fighting. Kummel listened intently to the radio for any news on their progress.

Manfred studied him closely. The captain was often good-humoured but for much of the time he was frighteningly intense. Every fibre of his being was engaged in a way that Manfred found unlike anyone he'd met, save for Sergeant Overath. They were both fighting men. They understood war with an insight that Manfred doubted he would ever gain.

As much as he had excelled in training, the real thing was altogether different. The difference between Kummel and all the other men, save for the exceptional few like Basler and Stiefelmayer, was the ability to find clarity in the confusion that surrounded them. He had that rare quality which allowed him to think, and then communicate coherently and succinctly, ideas that grasped the situation they faced, distilled what action was needed and then directed men towards achieving success. To Manfred, Kummel represented the highest level of leadership. He doubted he could ever be like this man.

Survival, as Manfred had come to realise, was a matter that went beyond mere capability. It was a function of luck. Neither seniority nor proficiency was a shield. No rank was immune from death. Capability was no guarantee either. Overath and Kastner had been minced by fragments from an explosion inside the turret. Kummel seemed to be blessed with the twin qualities of luck and capability. Manfred believed his chances of surviving were greatly improved if he stayed with this man.

Kummel's clear blue eyes fixed on Manfred. Even first thing in the morning he looked immaculate. His hair combed back from his forehead like a matinee idol. His strong, aquiline nose led down to a mouth that rarely smiled. While the eyes appeared cold, Manfred sensed humour lurked somewhere deep behind them. Someone had told him that the captain was thirty-three. He seemed older. His leadership aura added years to him.

'Are you ready, Brehme?'

'Yes, sir,' replied Manfred. Kummel looked at him for a few moments then nodded. Manfred had the uneasy feeling the question was about something else. He thought about it for the next few minutes as he packed their cooking tins and utensils away. All along the line of the leaguer, men like him were engaged in the same activity.

Soon the battalion was ready to move. Manfred assumed they would head directly north of Saunnu to contain any breakout from the enemy. Instead, the morning was a relatively quiet affair despite the distant sound of explosions.

'Why aren't we supporting the 21st?' asked Kummel at one point.

'I'll go ask Rommel, shall I?' responded Beer before bumping into Manfred to avoid the kick aimed at him by Kummel.

'Be careful what you wish for,' said Hubbuch, as cynical as ever. Hubbuch was permanently grouchy. Manfred enjoyed his downbeat view of the world. It never quite crossed the line into either surliness or disobedience but rarely showed much respect for, or confidence in, authority either. He seemed like an antidote to the penetrating focus of Kummel. Manfred believed Hubbuch was like a weathervane for Kummel, an ongoing dialectical conscience for the single-minded captain.

Around three in the afternoon, Kummel came striding back to the tent. He'd been away for the previous half hour with Colonel Cramer and the head of the 2nd Battalion, Captain Josef Zugner. Manfred glanced at Beer. The Berliner threw the remains of his coffee into the fire.

'I think we're on our way.'

Kummel confirmed this when he arrived at the campfire.

'The 21st Panzers are engaged with British armour. They need support.'

'What about the Indian division that was supposed to be moving south from Beda Fromm?'

Kummel shrugged. They were no longer a concern. Instead, Rommel and Cruwell believed they had an opportunity to defeat the British in detail.

'Make ready,' ordered Kummel and he left to speak to Lieutenant Basler. Within seconds, like a wind blowing over a wheatfield, rows of men rose to their feet to make ready for the march.

The tanks set off soon after three, led by Cramer. Behind the tanks were the trucks carrying infantry and artillery. Manfred was sitting up top marvelling at the sight of a division on the move. Despite all they had been through, seeing so many men and armour never failed to thrill or scare him in equal measure. Yet he knew now that the armour, far from being a shelter, could also be a coffin. Against anti-tank guns they were vulnerable and, if it was true, the British had new tanks with bigger guns that could match the firepower of the Panzers.

Kummel exuded his usual certainty. Yet this was no longer sufficient to quell the fear Manfred felt. Manfred sensed the eyes of the captain on him, and he turned towards Kummel.

'What do you see, Brehme?' asked Kummel.

Cannon fodder, thought Manfred. That's what I see.

CHAPTER FIVE

Forty miles south-east of Saunnu, Libya, 23rd January 1942

The column made camp following the air attack. They needed to tend to a few of the men who had been wounded. In addition, they had to salvage what they could from their supply truck. There was nothing for Danny to do while this happened so he, Buller, Evans and Fitz went for a walk.

'After all,' said Danny when he made the original suggestion, 'there's so much to see.'

Fitz and Buller stared out at the beige nothingness. An endless sand carpet broken up by scrub and distant hills. The sky was pale blue, laced with white clouds here and there.

'You're right, Danny,' said Fitz. 'You know we never really take time to stop and enjoy the beauty of nature.'

Buller looked at the two men and shook his head.

'You two are losing it.'

'And you, my friend, are a philistine,' replied Fitz with an air of superiority.

They sat on top of a low ridge and resumed a conversation that had started the previous evening.

'Blair's getting windy,' said Buller. 'I don't like it. He's going to cause us trouble, you'll see.'

'Do you think?' asked Evans.

Danny and Fitz agreed and turned in surprise to Evans. Perhaps he'd simply not been in North Africa long enough to see the signs that the others recognised. He would have had less exposure to seeing how men could be affected by the relentlessness of the fighting, moving, fighting again, and running. He trusted the instincts of his companions and remained silent as they discussed what they should do.

'Do you think Arnold knows?' asked Danny, his eyes fixed on the horizon.

'Aye, he knows,' replied Buller. 'I saw him taking a long look at Blair yesterday. He saw him freeze. It was Gray who was running the show. It's depressing, boys. I don't like it. C'mon, Fitz. Give us a story.'

'You've heard them all,' complained Fitz.

'I don't care. I need something to take my mind off things. What about the theatre one? You've never told Danny that one.'

'Haven't I?' asked Fitz.

Danny shook his head and made himself comfortable. Fitz's stories, whether true or not, were always great value.

'Here, Danny, you'll like this. So I was asked to review a performance of Hamlet at the town hall in Galway. I was theatre critic as well, I might add. I heard this afterwards from the lad, and it explained a lot. Anyway, this young lad had just joined the theatre company staging the performance. He told me the leading actor playing Hamlet was very English and had a real attitude towards we Irish. Called us 'Paddies' and 'Micks'. Thought we should be carrying spears. You know the type. By the end of the rehearsal period, he hated him. So did the rest of the cast. Anyway, not sure if you've read Hamlet, but, in the middle of the play, he does his famous soliloquy. You know the one. This actor's been aching to say this famous speech, Jayz, he can't wait. Meanwhile, this lad's thinking, I'll get you back. I'll fix you on the opening night. So here it comes. The posh English actor's standing there, looking magnificent, heroic even, with his crown and he shouts, "To be or not to be?" in his posh English accent. This lad wanders on stage as he's saying this and says, "Well that's a stupid question." Then he gives him a salute and walks off the stage to absolute silence. The last thing I hear is the lad shouting for a taxi outside the theatre.'

Danny erupted into laughter, as did Buller who acknowledged he never tired of hearing that story.

'I met the lad the next day and he told me the full story. Of course, the moron running the paper wouldn't let me print it.'

An hour later the entire column was sitting in a semi-circle. In front of them were Captain Arnold, Lieutenant Blair and two other lieutenants named Jepson and Barrett. Danny kept his eyes on Blair. There was no question he seemed fidgety. His eyes shifted in a manner that contrasted with the fixed stares of the other senior officers. Danny wasn't sure if he was now just seeking evidence to convict Blair or if he really had lost his nerve.

Captain Arnold stepped forward after a few moments and addressed the men. The only sound anyone could hear was the light wind blowing in their ears. And perhaps their hearts beating. Danny could sense that everyone was on edge. Facing the enemy was bearable compared to the uncertainty they now felt.

'As you know, we were due to rendezvous with the division at Antelat tomorrow. But they've moved back due to a surprise attack from Jerry. This puts us in a bit of a pickle. Yesterday's attack has destroyed a significant proportion of our fuel. In short, we may not have enough petrol to get back to the division. This means we must find some petrol and water from somewhere. Now the chances of running into a fuel dump in this wilderness aren't good. Our best bet is to reach an oasis thirty miles march from here and hope to God that Jerry has left some supplies there.'

Arnold paused for a moment to let this news sink in. Danny noted how calmly Arnold spoke. It all seemed like a bit of an inconvenience to him rather than the catastrophic situation that it might otherwise have seemed to Danny.

'I think the only way for it is to send a small group of men to find the oasis, take what we need and return here. Now, I know that every man jack of you will want to volunteer so I have been consulting with Jepson, Barrett and Blair on this. We will pick a handful of infantry and take one gun crew on this mission. I intend to lead the mission. Lieutenant Blair will accompany me.'

Danny looked at the other men in the crew. 'That means us, doesn't it?'

Buller turned to Danny and smiled mirthlessly. 'That it does, son. That it does.'

The new group consisted of Danny's gun crew, a jeep containing half a dozen infantry, and an infantry truck that would be loaded with any jerricans of fuel and water they could steal, assuming they were able to locate them. Captain Arnold rode in the truck while Lieutenant Barrett rode in a jeep with the other members of the infantry.

The group set off late afternoon. The intention was to reach the oasis before dark. Along the way they left flags to guide their return.

The moon would be a waxing crescent. Even without cloud it would be dark. With cloud there was a serious risk of getting lost even with the flags they'd laid out. This made the journey of thirty miles a much longer affair as Captain Arnold was not prepared to take chances on the smallest of details. That Arnold was leading gave Danny some hope. Confidence in Blair was almost non-existent.

After a couple of hours, the truck drew to a halt. Arnold climbed out and quickly convened a conference with Blair and Barrett. The result of the conference was clear when Blair walked back to the jeep. Behind him, Barrett took off in the infantry jeep.

'The oasis is a mile north-east from here, towards those hills in the distance,' explained Blair, pointing. 'Barrett has been tasked with reconnaissance. I think there's time for a brew up.'

This was always music to Danny's ears even though it was usually his job. Light was just beginning to fade. Barrett would need to be quick. He didn't know the lieutenant well, but he always struck Danny as dependable. Like Blair he was young and most likely from a public school. So many of the officers seemed that way to Danny.

Having grown up in the country and got to know the family of the lord of the manor, he was curiously unresentful about this. A Liverpudlian like Buller, on the other hand, was never likely to accept how the class system dictated the ranks within the British Army. In his view, the Germans were a professional army. They were not organised like a cricket team with demarcation between the gentlemen and players.

Of late Danny had begun to wonder if Buller was not right. He'd witnessed how men of the sort he would have looked up to had led them into the murderous fire of the enemy. Men like Arnold and Turner at least, exuded a professional authority. Even Captain Aston in the tank regiment had enough sense to question the point of cavalry charges with tanks. Danny wondered if the captain had survived Operation Crusader. He suspected the answer was yes.

Danny took a jerrican and filled it with around three inches of sand. He poured petrol down a stick into the sand and stirred it so that it had the consistency of porridge. Striking a match, he threw it on the petrol and sand mixture causing a small explosion. He placed a second tin, full of water, on the flame and prepared the brew. It lacked the ceremony of Japanese tea-making that Fitz had once talked about, but it was a welcome break from the toil.

The sound of a jeep returning broke into Danny's thoughts. He heard Blair telling them to follow him over so they could hear, first-hand, the results of the reconnaissance.

'Well?' asked Arnold.

Barrett jumped out of the jeep and reported what he'd seen.

'There's a company of infantry at the oasis. At least two hundred men. I don't think we can overpower them, sir. I didn't see any guns or tanks, but they have a couple of nasty looking half-tracks with mounted machine guns.'

Arnold nodded as if he'd expected this. He seemed remarkably sanguine given the odds they were facing.

'To be expected, I suppose. Did you see if they had petrol?'

'Yes, sir, lots of it,' replied Barrett with a grin. 'It's not fenced off. Just sitting there. Stacked very neatly, too.'

'At least that's something. How is it guarded?'

'They have set up a picket at four points, sir,' replied Barrett. He used his stick to draw a rudimentary map in the sand. 'The guards are here and here, around forty yards from the main group. The supplies are here, right beside the oasis. There was a hill about fifty yards from where the pickets are stationed. We were able to get a good view of the layout from there. I left Johnson behind to keep a check on how frequently the guard changes.'

Arnold nodded while studying the rough map.

'Good work, Barrett. A direct assault is clearly out of the question. They won't be expecting us, that's for sure. Very well, here's what we'll do.'

CHAPTER SIX

Antelat, Libya, 23rd January 1942

The sound of explosions grew louder with each passing minute, or was it his heart? Manfred felt his skin prickle with each blast. Even Beer, who was normally blackly composed, looked on edge. His hands gripped the rail as the tank bumped along. The frequency of the fire suggested there was one almighty battle going on. Kummel unerringly read the mood of his crew.

'It sounds like there are a lot of tanks. No wonder the 21st wanted help.'

He peered into the telescope just as the voice of Cramer crackled over the radio.

'Attention. Orange 2. Attack enemy tanks on the left.'

'Remind me, who is Orange 2?' asked Beer.

'Stiefelmayer,' cut in Kummel, swinging the telescope to see what Cramer was looking at. He gave a low whistle. 'Interesting.'

This was too much for Beer. He stared through his own sights and let rip a volley of oaths. Manfred watched as two flank Panzers peeled off. In the distance he saw an enormous number of dark shapes. These were the British tanks. The British were probably too far away to do much damage.

'Eleven o'clock. Engage enemy armour,' called Cramer. Hubbuch responded without waiting for Kummel's order. The tank immediately altered course.

'How far?' asked Kummel.

'A kilometre?' suggested Beer.

'Yes,' agreed Kummel. 'Bring us a little closer, Hubbuch.'

The tank was moving forward towards the mass of British tanks. Manfred glanced at Beer and received a nod in response. In a moment, Manfred had reached down and opened the breech. Hubbuch brought the tank to a halt.

'AP armour piercing,' said Kummel, his eyes fixed against his telescope. 'Fire.'

Manfred loaded the cartridge. Beer pressed the electronic firing button.

'Short,' announced Kummel. 'Up fifty. Reload new range and fire.'

The angle of the turret gun was immediately altered by Beer. Manfred opened the breech and quickly loaded another armour piercing shell. Beer pressed the firing button again.

'Yes,' shouted Kummel. 'Right on target. Up another twenty-five. Reload.'

Exhilaration swept through Manfred. After a month of running and fighting this felt like they were back in control. He loaded another armour piercing shell and heard Kummel yell in triumph. The tank was now under attack, too. Shells hit the tank and bounced off like rain on a pavement. The enemy was still too far away to do damage. The radio crackled with communication.

'Ninety tanks.'

'Five hit.'

The British were taking a beating and, all at once, thoughts of the heat, the smell and the sand disappeared from Manfred's mind. He became part of the tank. His arms pumping cartridges into the breech like pistons. It seemed almost effortless the efficiency with which this machine unleashed its deadly intent.

Kummel was standing in the cramped space. Manfred could see his face muscles working as he chewed gum. Spitting out orders.

'Up fifty. Load. Fire.'

Despite the noise of explosions outside, he wasn't shouting. This was more like a conductor of an orchestra. The musicians knew their job. The job of the leader was to set the tempo, control the direction and listen for the key moments which would determine their next actions.

The engagement lasted a matter of minutes. Even so, Manfred was bathed in sweat; his heart was beating rapidly although his breathing remained controlled. Kummel was standing motionless now, eyes fixed on the viewfinder of the periscope. He held a hand up to halt the firing.

There was silence in the tank although explosions continued outside. The silence was enough to send Manfred's imagination racing.

'British are pulling back,' said a voice on the radio. It sounded like Stiefelmayer.

'I'm not surprised,' commented Kummel.

Manfred looked through his periscope. There was too much smoke to have any real sense of the damage they'd inflicted but he could see black smoke and red flame engulfing a couple of the enemy tanks.

Cramer called a halt. Manfred looked surprised which Kummel noted with a smile.

'We don't want to be drawn into the range of their anti-tank guns. At least not yet.'

47

The roar of explosions lessened to such a degree that Manfred had to strain his ears to gain a sense of where they were detonating. They sounded distant as if the Panzers were giving the British tanks a send-off.

'Forward,' said Cramer, after a few minutes.

Hubbuch grumbled into his mic, 'Here we go again.'

The tank rumbled forward and then was ordered to stop. Kummel looked down into the tank and said, 'Everybody out. Get some air and see what we can find in the British tanks.'

Manfred and the others hesitated a moment and then Beer kicked open the hatch which allowed the acrid smell of cordite-infused air to flood into the cabin. They exited the tank and Manfred took a few steps forward to view the landscape.

All around were the smoking hulks of British tanks. Manfred stopped counting them when he reached forty. The smell that greeted him was more than just cordite. Manfred didn't want to think about that. Perhaps one of the reasons why Kummel and the other senior commanders had ordered them out onto the open was to remind them of what the price of failure looked like. It was littered all around them. Black twisted shapes of metal that had once been tanks and the charred bodies of the men inside. Dozens of British soldiers wandered with their hands up. Manfred ignored them and joined Beer who was scavenging inside a British tank.

In the gathering gloom, Manfred and the others took what they could. It seemed like a competition with the other Panzer crews. Just before Kummel called for them to return, Manfred ran into Gerhardt who was laden with two jerricans of water. They smiled at one another.

'I wish it was always as easy as this,' said Gerhardt as they stopped and shared a cigarette. 'We stopped at least six of their tanks.'

'We destroyed seven,' said Manfred. Any sense of triumph at having outscored his friend was quietened when he heard a small explosion inside a burning tank. They looked at one another, a trace of guilt in their eyes. There was no goodbye, just a nod and they returned to their respective tanks.

At the tank, Siefers was busy tying down the jerricans containing fuel and water. The tank seemed to be weighed down by their haul. Nearby, Kummel was talking to Cramer. Manfred watched them and the other company commanders in conference. It was quite animated, but this was normal. Disagreement and debate were not frowned upon. However, once a decision was made, obedience was demanded. Kummel returned to the tank and gathered the crew together.

'We do not have a clear idea of enemy numbers, but we've made a dent today. The British forces are still in and around Saunnu but they seem to be retreating. The intention is that we move at first light towards Msus and then the coast at Benghazi. If the British are retreating, then we will help them. Just to warn you, we have a long journey ahead of us.'

CHAPTER SEVEN

South-east of Saunnu, Libya, 23rd January 1942

They waited until midnight before setting off again. In the meantime, Arnold insisted that everyone rest. The reduced column followed flags left by Barrett on his initial reconnaissance. In the darkness it was difficult to see the faces of the other men. They drove in silence. Danny's nervousness was exacerbated by the chill of the cold night air. He was glad it was dark, and that conversation was forbidden. Despite having been with the Jock column for over six weeks, this was their first night mission. There was a hint of desperation in the air. Previously they were like pirates. The hunter preying on slow moving echelons. They could wade in and create all manner of hell before running away knowing that the enemy could not catch them.

Now it felt different. This was not about harassing the enemy. It was about survival. For the first time since joining the group, Danny felt a prickle of real fear.

Half a mile from the oasis they stopped. Barrett and a group of infantry soldiers set off to their objective with orders to send a runner when the guard changed over. For an hour they sat in this position. Danny's muscles were beginning to lock into place when they heard the two messengers return. They went straight to Arnold. Danny was too cold to listen to what was being said.

Arnold called Blair over and quickly gave some orders to the lieutenant. One of the infantry men hopped into the back of the truck. When Arnold had finished issuing the orders, Blair returned and joined Sergeant Gray in the front.

'We are to drive to within four hundred yards of the oasis,' announced Blair. 'We think that the hills will help muffle the noise of the engines. The infantry will look to take out the pickets. Meantime, the truck will circle around and wait for a signal once the pickets have been removed. It will freewheel into the oasis, and we will load as much as we can, hopefully without attracting the attention of Jerry. If for some reason Jerry catches us in the act, then, clearly, we're in a bit of a pickle. This is when you men come in. We are to keep Jerry interested by hitting him with all we've got while our men make their getaway.'

Danny didn't need to look at Buller to feel that this was a plan full of risk.

'What are we aiming at?' asked Buller.

This was no small matter. It was dark; they could not be sure of distance or direction. They couldn't get close enough to see.

'We could try to get closer,' suggested Gray, trying to keep the edge out of his voice.

'Out of the question,' said Blair. 'We'll have someone on the hill giving us guidance via radio. Shaw, you've had experience with radio.' Then he ordered the truck to turn to allow the gun to face in the direction of the oasis.

Danny accompanied a young infantry man to the hill overlooking the oasis. He carried a small radio set on his back. He could feel its weight digging into his shoulders.

'I'm Danny Shaw,' he said as they walked towards the oasis.

'Lenny Piper,' said the soldier who was a similar age to Danny. He sounded like he was from London. 'What do you think of the plan?' asked the young soldier nervously.

Danny was tempted to say 'the same as you probably' but decided not to sound like a bellyacher.

'It's a risk. But we need the petrol.'

A couple of minutes later they were sitting on a ridge overlooking the oasis. It was larger than Danny had imagined. A thicket of palm trees surrounded the water on one side. Across the oasis, on the other side, were a couple of dozen tents. Set off from the tents was a compound containing the fuel and, presumably, the water. A dozen trucks were lined up near the fuel dump. Soldiers milled around but, for the most part, none seemed particularly on the lookout for the enemy.

Two hours passed, mostly in a brooding silence. There was nothing they could think to talk about. Danny glanced at his watch. It was now close to two in the morning. There was little or no moonlight. The desert was a dark blue sea behind them, with a few palm trees and a company of Germans in front of them. Nothing to worry about, thought Danny grimly.

With each passing hour, the camp emptied with soldiers going to their tents. The only soldiers that Danny could see were two guards on each side of the camp. They were sitting on makeshift wooden benches, smoking. Neither appeared interested in looking out into the night. Across from them, fifty yards to the other side of the camp, the other two German soldiers were also smoking. Danny watched them both for a few minutes and wondered when they would strike.

They waited.

Just before three in the morning, Danny felt a tug on his elbow. Dark figures were approaching the German soldiers who were standing picket. Two soldiers had met on the middle for a chat, leaving one of their comrades alone. Seconds later there was a noise which attracted the attention of the soldiers. They both walked forward.

From his vantage point on the hill, Danny saw that the lone soldier was looking in the direction of his comrades. He didn't hear the two Allied soldiers rush towards him, one of them brandishing a knife. It was over in seconds. Danny felt a rush of sympathy for the young German whose life had been taken so clinically. But it was momentary. The other soldiers would soon be aware. The operation hinged on them not warning the rest of the camp.

The two Germans continued forward. One of them took his gun off his shoulder. Both were staring into the darkness, unaware that the two Allied soldiers were racing towards them.

Another noise from the shadows. The two German soldiers turned to their right, too late to react to the two soldiers behind them and two coming in from their left. Danny was impressed with the deadly efficiency of the British soldiers but shivered involuntarily from the adrenalin surging around his body.

The pickets dealt with was the signal for the British truck to roll silently towards the oasis, partly freewheeling, partly pushed by the remaining infantry. It drew to a halt and quickly the infantry men began to take jerricans of petrol from the store and load it onto the truck. Danny watched the operation spellbound. It was freezing now but perspiration dripped from his forehead. Fear gripped him as he watched the petrol being quietly loaded onto the truck. It seemed impossible that they would not be discovered.

Minutes passed in agonising slowness. Danny wanted to shout down to the men to hurry up or stop. How much was enough?

Then he saw the flickering torches. These were followed by shouts. Danny knew the men had been seen. He quickly grabbed the radio, switched it on and began to transmit.

'Operation is compromised. Repeat compromised. Begin to fire.'

Just as he said this, he heard the first gunshots. A few cracks at first and then more. Half a dozen British soldiers were streaming towards the truck. The engine of the truck kicked in but around twenty or thirty German soldiers, many half-dressed, were running towards the truck firing.

The truck began to reverse at great speed but in its haste the wheels began to spin without traction. Danny looked on helplessly and yelled 'fire' into the mic.

At that moment an explosion landed forty yards to the left of the compound.

'Traverse right forty yards. Distance is good,' shouted Danny.

The Germans were firing at the truck which had managed to start moving. A second explosion landed on one of the armoured cars. A blossom of flame erupted from it as the fuel caught fire.

'Faster,' shouted Danny but he wasn't sure who he was talking to.

The truck was now widening the gap with the Germans chasing it. And then Danny saw a German soldier with a mortar.

'Look,' he said to Piper.

Piper nodded and directed his rifle towards the soldier with the mortar. He fired. The soldier fell wounded, but two others grabbed the mortar. Some of the soldiers turned their attention to where Danny and Piper were positioned. Bullets began to lash the sand around them.

'You have to get them,' said Danny. 'They'll hit the truck.'

Piper leased off another shot, but the intensity of fire was such that both boys had to keep their heads down.

'We can't stay here,' said Danny. 'There's too many.'

He risked a glance at the truck just as it exploded in a deafening roar. Bits of metal and canvas flew fifty feet into the air.

'What happened?' shouted Piper anxiously.

Danny couldn't speak. They were all dead. The mortar had been a direct hit. The fuel exploded. No one could have survived such an explosion. He shook his head and grabbed Piper. They stumbled down the back of the slope just as a mortar landed where they'd been sitting. Other mortars were now being launched and blasting plumes of sand into the air on their left and right. Whatever Piper might have been saying was lost in the hail of fire.

Overhead, Very lights were launched lighting up the area in a bright white light. Shouts behind them; the Germans were closing in. Danny, weighed down by the radio, fell behind Piper. They were now on the flat and running much faster now. The white light died, and Danny changed direction just as shooting started from the top of the hill.

Danny was now thirty yards to the side of Piper and at least twenty yards behind. He dived into a hollow as another light went up illuminating the area all around him. Piper was still running, seemingly unaware that every German could see him.

'Get down,' shouted Danny. Piper was now bathed in light. Danny saw sand fly up behind his feet. Then he saw Piper fall. A few seconds passed. The young soldier did not move. And then darkness returned. Danny stood up and began running again. He heard a shot and then another light went up. He dived to the ground. Shots raked the ground nearby. There were shouts now as the Germans soldiers began to race down the slope, confident that they were not going to be shot.

When the Very light went out, Danny got up and began to sprint again, switching back towards where Piper lay. He arrived at Piper's body. He was dead. Shots pinged a few yards away. He grabbed Piper's rifle and stumbled forward a few yards before diving to the ground when another Very light lit up the night.

The light revealed to Danny that half a dozen soldiers were in pursuit around forty yards away from him. They had fanned out and were walking slowly. Danny took aim and fired. One soldier was down forcing the others to hit the ground. By firing he had effectively given away his position. Moments later he heard a mortar being launched. It landed twenty feet behind him.

Darkness returned. Danny stayed where he was. Another light soon went up. A German soldier risked standing.

Danny shot him. He fell and did not move.

'Stop firing,' ordered Blair gazing at the Very lights going up five hundred yards away.

There had been no more wireless contact since the firing had started. Buller looked at Blair and then to Gray. He wanted to keep the barrage going. Gray stared at Blair.

'Shouldn't we keep firing, sir? We don't know what's happening…'

'My point, Gray. We don't know what's happening. Captain Arnold was specific. If a firefight develops use your own initiative.'

That doesn't mean running away leaving the men behind, thought Buller. He shot a glance at Fitz. The Irishman's face was a mask of anger. Gray pressed again.

'Can't we just keep the volley going a bit longer, sir?'

Blair shook his head.

'What about Shaw and Piper, sir?'

'We have to assume they're dead, Corporal. There's been no contact. Now pack up. That's an order.'

'But what about the Very lights and the gunfire?'

Blair wasn't listening. He turned around and stalked back to the front of the truck. There was no choice. The chain of command brooked no argument. Buller's training kicked in and he, Fitz and Gray quickly reattached the gun trailer to the back of the truck.

Buller glanced at Evans who was manning the radio. The Welshman shook his head. Gray climbed into the front of the truck and started the engine. He put the truck into gear and began to turn away from the oasis. Just then the radio crackled in the back of the truck.

'Shaw here. Operation has failed. Repeat, Operation failed. I'm pinned down about four hundred yards from you on the other side of the hill. Piper is dead. All the others, too.'

Gray stopped the truck and looked at Blair. The lieutenant's eyes were wide with fear. Then they hardened for a moment.

'We can't stop. Drive on, Gray.'

Danny finished his message and switched off the radio. He didn't want a reply to give away his new position. The situation was now impossible. Behind him was a hill. On the other side of the hill, some three or four hundred yards away, was the truck. The Germans would easily pick him off as he went up the hill. He couldn't stay there as they would soon overwhelm him. His ammunition was almost spent even though he'd been careful.

It was hopeless.

He thought about surrendering. But what would be his chances? He'd probably be killed. The enemy soldiers would want to take full revenge for the men he'd killed or wounded. Another light went up. Indifference replaced fear now. In front of him the landscape seemed empty, but he knew they were there. Someone would be acting as spotter. Then the others would either attack or they would mortar him to smithereens. Just as the Very light started to dim, the mortar bombing started. They were closer now. The light went out. He rose to his feet and sprinted directly towards the hill, then dived into a depression.

There was darkness for a few seconds. Danny heard muffled footfalls on the sand and fear gripped him. He listened as they grew more numerous. The Germans were using the cover of darkness to encircle him. He felt his despair growing; his hand rooted around the bag for ammunition. There was none. He was down to his last few bullets now. Somewhere in the distance he heard a motor engine. They were bringing up the armoured car with its machine gun.

Twenty yards to his right he caught sight of a shadow. It was rushing towards him. He fired at the shadow. It dropped. Having revealed his position, a volley of bullets threw up sand in front of him, which forced him to duck. A grenade or mortar would follow soon, he knew.

Resignation swept over him. It was over.

An explosion, then another and then an even larger one rocked the earth around him. Danny looked up. He was alive. How could they have missed? A Very light went up revealing close to a dozen Germans standing less than fifteen yards in front of him. Gunfire erupted from somewhere and the Germans began dropping.

Danny turned around just in time to see Fitz and Buller with the big gun unleashing another shot at the Germans. He ducked his head and heard its crump. The explosion rent the earth apart just as the Very light faded. In the darkness Danny could make out the more advanced German soldiers retreating. The gunfire ceased and Danny risked standing up.

He made a beeline for where he'd seen Fitz and Buller.

'Don't shoot. It's me,' he shouted, fearful of surviving one firefight only to get killed by mistake.

'Get a move on, ya eejit,' said Fitz. 'Help us get this thing back onto the truck.'

58

'Took your bloody time about it,' said Danny.

'Bloody lucky we came at all,' said Buller but did not expand further on the point. They hauled the gun down the hill towards the truck. Blair was manning the wheel.

'Hurry,' ordered Blair, somewhat unnecessarily. In less than thirty seconds the gun trailer was attached, and they tore off into the night. Gray turned around to Danny.

'What happened?'

CHAPTER EIGHT

Between Antelat and Msus, Libya, 24th January 1942

Danny and the remaining member of the party drove through the rest of the night and arrived back at the camp just before first light. There were no guards on picket duty. All was silent. Something was most definitely wrong. Danny glanced at the others. Everyone seemed on edge.

'What on earth's going on here?' asked Lieutenant Blair. There was just a hint of hysteria in his voice. He was close to cracking.

They drew to a halt. Sergeant Gray leapt out of the front and began checking the camp for signs of life. The trucks in the camp were empty. The others slowly climbed out of the back, joining Gray in the search for the soldiers who'd stayed behind. Danny switched on the wireless set to contact the others. There was no response. Gray reported back to Blair after a few minutes of searching fruitlessly.

'No one, sir. They've all gone. A number of vehicles are still here but one of the trucks and one of the guns is missing.'

'What do you think has happened?' asked Blair, trying to keep the edge of fear out of his voice.

'Hard to say, sir. We avoided radio contact for fear that the Germans would intercept. Perhaps they came under attack again from the air and had to take evasive…'

'Look over here,' said Buller, thirty yards away.

The others went over to join him. Buller was standing near a cluster of mounds. Guns were stuck in the ground and helmets draped over the top of them. There were a dozen mounds in total. One of the mounds had a beret draped over it. Blair went over and lifted the black beret up.

'Jepson,' said Blair. He turned to Gray. 'There can't have been more than half a dozen others. They've been taken prisoner.'

Gray nodded in agreement. It made sense. Why else would they have buried the bodies? There was just a hint of light now and they could see better the signs of explosions pitting the landscape either side of the camp. There was no question they'd come under attack from either guns or tanks. Any survivors would have been taken as prisoners of war.

Blair sat down and stared at the ground. It seemed like a good idea in the circumstances. The others joined him.

'I think it unlikely Jerry will come back,' said Blair after a few minutes. 'We'll rest here for today.' He fell into a sombre silence.

Gray took charge. He looked at the group and said, 'See if there's any petrol we can siphon from the two trucks. We'll need everything we can lay our hands on. And check if there's any ammo or food, water left. Anything.' There was no hiding the resignation in his voice. Or was it tiredness? They'd all gone without sleep. He looked at Blair and added, 'But first we should get an hour or two sleep. Then when we're rested, we can find everything we need.'

Blair nodded mutely. Danny glanced at Blair and saw a man who was utterly crushed. Without hope. Whether this was in memory

61

of his fallen comrades or something else, he didn't know. Danny felt sad for the men that had fallen but he felt something else, too. Elation. He'd survived a situation in which he was convinced he would die. The euphoria had lasted for as long as the journey back to the camp. When he finally bedded down for the night, he succumbed immediately to a dreamless sleep.

Danny woke up with a start. An engine was coughing to life nearby. Bright light blinded him although he was lying in shadow. His eyes focused on his watch. It was just after two in the afternoon. He'd been asleep for eight hours. He rolled away from the truck and staggered to his feet.

'Tea?' shouted Fitz.

'Yes, thanks,' said Danny.

'Go and bloody make one then,' added Buller. The old one-two. Danny groaned as Buller and Fitz laughed at him. He went over and sat near them. Danny nodded towards the lone figure standing at the edge of the camp. They all looked in the direction of Blair.

'What do you think, Danny boy?'

'I can't think without tea and something to eat. But if pressed, I'd say we were fairly buggered.'

'That would be my assessment too,' agreed Fitz. 'Buggered with plums on top.'

This stopped Buller mid-sup of his tea. He looked at Fitz. The Irishman merely shrugged.

'What does Gray think?' asked Danny.

'Ask him yourself,' replied Buller. This was a standing joke about the notoriously tight-lipped sergeant. 'While you're at it, you should thank him.'

Danny turned and looked questioningly at the Liverpudlian.

'Blair was all for leaving you to Jerry. Gray somehow got him to make that last attack.'

'Bloody hell,' replied Danny.

That was the consensus on their mood. Danny made a brew for himself and the others. They sat drinking it in silence wondering what they were going to do now. As far as Danny could see, their options were limited. With limited fuel, food and water there was only so far they could travel and so long they could live without any fresh supply.

The next few hours were spent draining water and fuel from the engines of the vehicles that had been disabled by bullets and bombs. There was no ammo left. The Germans had seen to that. They had one truck and a two-pound gun and enough fuel for a day's travel at most. With careful nursing they could make the water and food last a little longer. But there wasn't much left. Hunger would be as much a companion to them as the man next to them. They needed to return to their base. But where was their base now?

Blair strolled over towards Danny and the others. He called Gray and Evans over, too. Both were taking spare parts from one of the other trucks. Everyone sat down and looked without any great sense of expectation towards Blair. His authority had been on the wane for a couple of weeks now. Sergeant Gray was their leader in all but name. Throughout their time in the harassing of the Axis troops, his manner had never changed. He remained coolly professional throughout the close calls they'd experienced. If what Buller said was true, he'd effectively overruled Blair and insisted they return to rescue Danny. For Buller that had almost been the final straw in his view of the lieutenant.

'We're in a pretty rum situation, boys. There's no use in hiding it,' began Blair. His manner remained despondent, and it was influencing the others.

63

'Our choices are limited. None of them good. All, in their own way, wrong. For this reason, I think we forget for a moment chain of command and discuss, as men, what we do next. I want you to feel free to express an opinion. Everyone's opinion is valid. Who's first?'

Danny nodded and all eyes turned to him.

'We should drive towards Saunnu. We should have enough fuel to take us there. It's a risk we'll run into Jerry, and we'll have to take our chances. If we're smart and travel by night, perhaps we can either find a way of getting through, finding fuel and supplies, or maybe we'll even run into some of our boys, who knows?'

'Anyone else?' asked Blair.

'I'm with Danny,' said Buller. Fitz and Evans both nodded in agreement.

All eyes turned to Gray. The sergeant fixed his eyes on Danny. For a moment he was silent, then he spoke in his usual measured way.

'Heading towards Saunnu is suicide. It will be crawling with Germans if the last radio contact we had was any guide.' Danny's heart sank and his face reddened. He should have stayed silent. The folly of youth. 'Unfortunately, Shaw is right,' continued Gray. 'The Germans are to our south. The desert is to our east and west. There may be a chance of running into our boys if we head north-west. We have no other choice, sir.'

Danny tried to hide his delight at being proven right. The words of Gray, not just the words, his manner of speaking made any alternative inconceivable.

'Saunnu it is then,' said Blair. 'I hope to God we're right.'

'One other thing, sir,' added Gray. 'We've lost a lot of good men and I think when we've finished our work here, and before we leave, we should spend a few minutes commemorating them.'

There were nods from the others. They hadn't spent any time thinking about those who'd fallen. It was the least they could do.

'Anything on the radio?' asked Blair for what seemed like the twentieth time. Buller turned sharply towards the lieutenant and seemed on the point of telling him to shut up when Fitz nudged him. Buller nodded sullenly.

'Nothing, sir,' replied Danny. They'd been driving for three hours, and darkness shrouded the road ahead. Blair touched the arm of Sergeant Gray, and the truck slowed to a halt.

Blair looked around and then fixed his gaze on a point off the road. He turned to the others in the back of the truck.

'I think we'll stop here for the night. Pull off the road and we'll camp fifty yards over there. Evans, Shaw, can you take a recce? No point in falling into any soft sand.'

'Don't worry about the mines, Danny boy,' chipped in Fitz.

'Thanks for your concern,' replied Danny, laughing. This obvious danger had occurred to him as it had the others before Fitz gave it a voice.

Danny and Evans fanned out ten yards apart. In theory, they were unlikely to upset any mines. The intent was to blow up trucks rather than individual soldiers. Each walked slowly forward, testing the ground, lightly, with their feet. Danny found himself holding his breath. He inched forward, eyes staring at the ground in what remained of the light. From the corner of his eye he saw Evans stop suddenly.

'What's wrong?' asked Danny urgently.

'I have a stone in my boot,' came the reply.

A volley of abuse was hurled in the Welshman's direction which he dealt with by lying on the ground and laughing.

Twenty minutes later they had a small fire going. They put

sheets up to hide its glow. The land around them was as flat as it was featureless. A fire would be seen from miles away. The risk of attracting the attention of any German patrol was uppermost in their minds.

They pooled a couple of tins of bully beef and Evans made a stew of sorts. As soon as they could, the fire was extinguished. Some blankets had been rescued from the original trucks, but they were barely enough to keep warm in the freezing cold of night.

After such a long sleep that day, Danny found it hard to settle and barely slept an hour or two that night. Instead, he listened to the loud snores of Buller and a distant hum.

Around midnight, still unable to sleep, Danny stood up and went for a walk. Away from the snores of Buller, the hum he'd heard earlier grew louder. He walked a bit further and listened.

There was no question that there were vehicles out there. The question on Danny's mind was whose they were. They were too far away to make out anything distinguishing about them. The noise grew louder now. They were closer.

Ten minutes later, he saw them. The unmistakable outline of Mark III Panzers. He counted forty of them rumbling past, half a mile away. They seemed so much larger and fearsome than the British Crusaders. He looked at his watch. It was ten after midnight. In all his time in North Africa he could only remember one night march in a tank. Yet he knew the Germans did this as a matter of course. No wonder they were so difficult to defeat. They were relentless. He watched the column recede into the distance and then he returned to the camp. A voice whispered to him.

'Jerry?'

It was Gray. Danny nodded and then settled back down into his makeshift bed. He fell asleep an hour later.

The jeep set off early next morning. The news that they had nearly been run over by a convoy of German tanks was greeted with dismay. It increased their sense of vulnerability without providing any reassurance that where they were headed was in British hands.

'What's that saying?' asked Evans as the truck bumped along the endless road.

'Between a rock and place?' suggested Fitz.

'No, not that one. But that's good.'

'Out of the frying pan?' continued Fitz.

'No, not that one either.'

'Caught between the devil and the deep blue sea?' asked Danny.

'No,' replied Evans.

There was silence for a few moments. Then Fitz found the waiting unbearable.

'And?'

'Oh nothing. I was just trying to remember it,' said Evans with a wistful smile.

Fitz stared at Evans and then looked over to Buller.

'Buller.'

Buller took off his beret and proceeded to beat the Welshman with it. His laughter suggested that the punishment was not quite as painful as Fitz would have liked. They were several miles south of Saunnu when they saw dark shapes in the distance. The consensus was to keep going. From this distance it was impossible to tell if it was friend or foe. If it was the latter, they could certainly get away, but their limited supply of fuel was unlikely to keep them safe much longer. With each mile, it became apparent that the shapes in the distance were not moving.

'Perhaps it's a leaguer,' suggested Buller.

Danny looked at the way the shapes were arrayed across the horizon. They were tanks. All stationary.

'No. Stop,' said Danny. 'They're all dead.'

They drove over towards the shapes with only Danny confident about what they were. The scene that greeted them was horrific. Less than twenty-four hours earlier this had been a battlefield but now it was a graveyard. There must have been twenty tanks littering the desert over a couple of square miles; none were German or Italian.

'Bloody hell,' said Buller. Everyone else was silent as they drove past one blackened hulk after another. It was nightmarish. The twisted metal was still smoking. One tank was glowing red in parts. The air was rank with the acrid smell of cordite. Danny felt tears sting his eyes. He wondered if he knew any of them. Finally, Gray stopped the truck and they all climbed out. Buller lit a cigarette while Blair walked forward twisting his head left and right like a tourist in an art gallery.

The initial sadness and inertia gave way to something else within Danny. The desire to survive. He went over to Gray.

'Sarge, we should see what we can salvage from the tanks.'

'I agree, Shaw. You, Buller, Fitz and Evans each take an area. Search the tanks and find what you can. Anything that might be useful.'

'Perhaps we can get one of the tanks working again.'

Gray looked dubious about this but nodded anyway. He watched Danny detail the others and the search of the tanks began. It was only as he approached the first tank that Danny realised just how heart-rending a task this would be. Inside many of the tanks lay what remained of young men just like him. The blackened exterior still had wisps of smoke floating gently upwards. On the other side of the tank were two charred figures that had been caught in an explosion. Danny fought back the urge to be sick.

He pushed on towards another tank that had been crippled but was not burned out. The crew had clearly been able to evacuate in time. On the side were jerricans. He lifted one. It was half full of petrol.

'Over here,' shouted Danny. A minute or two later Gray drove up in the truck and they loaded the jerricans. There was no water or food to be found. This set the pattern for the rest of the afternoon. They identified tanks that had been crippled and took what they could from them.

Lieutenant Blair surveyed their haul as the light began to dim and the sky turned from a blue to a pastel mauve, laced with pink-tinged cloud. There was little by way of water or food, but they managed to find sufficient petrol to take them at least as far as Tobruk which was around three hundred miles away.

'Were you able to identify any tanks that might be repaired?'

Danny shook his head.

'Jerry is usually pretty good at locating and repairing any of our tanks that might still run. Damn sight better than us if truth be told.'

Blair nodded but seemed unperturbed by the news.

'Very well. We'll camp nearby tonight then make a start tomorrow for Tobruk. I suspect we will run into Jerry at some point, but we have two things on our side. The desert is a big place, and a division of Germans is hard to hide; we'll see him before he sees us. Also, we now have enough fuel to get us to where we want to go and, if we can ration sufficiently, enough water, too. I think by the time we hit the coast we'll be fairly hungry, but we'll be alive.'

A melancholy peace descended with the sun. Nothing could be done for the men who lay like charred statues in their metal coffins. There was little said as they ate. The sights and the smells they had encountered were too vivid, too raw to countenance the idea of the usual ribaldry that threaded their conversation. They munched solemnly. Each alone in his thoughts. Danny's stomach ached at the thought of how men had died screaming trapped inside their metal coffins.

The thrill of the adventure, begun just over a month ago, had been replaced by a vision of a future they all faced. They could see it in detail: black, arbitrary and indiscriminate. Death was a remorseless hunter, and they were the prey. Danny thought of his father that night. He thought of the tortured guilt he'd lived with after seeing the carbonised bodies of men he'd fought with. Alone, under his overcoat, he wept for his father and for the men who'd died in terror and indescribable pain.

CHAPTER NINE

South of Msus, Libya, 25th January 1942

For two days the Regiment 8 tanks of the 15th Panzer division travelled over flatter land; then it grew hillier. The British were like a boxer facing a heavier opponent. They would trade punches then retreat. Stop, fight, retreat. It was so different from just a month ago. Then the Afrika Korps had been worn down by the relentlessness of the attacks. Now they were the ones who had the tail wind. It had all happened so quickly. The ground they'd fought for, died over and lost during December had been recovered in a matter of days. Manfred could barely believe how fortunes could change so quickly in war. He wanted to ask Kummel why the initiative had shifted so dramatically in favour of the Afrika Korps. His throat tightened, squeezing the life out of the question he wanted to ask. The desire not to seem naïve outweighed his need to learn.

None of the other men in the tank questioned the situation. They seemed happy that they were the ones dishing out punishment rather than being on the end of a beating. So they pushed on. A feeling nestled in Manfred that was somewhere between rejoicing at the reversal they'd engineered and fear, too. This slight tremor in his otherwise good mood was rooted in the suspicion that even Kummel did not know why they were making such rapid progress through Libya again. One could speculate, of course. No one did. They were winning. What else was there to know?

When things are going well you notice fatigue less. Success and failure affect your body as much as your mind. One is invigorating, the other draining. The march forward had been far less wearying than the retreat in December. He'd never liked chasing back playing football either.

The morning of the 25th of January began as so many others had in the last week. The regiment marched behind Kummel's tank for eighty kilometres, utterly unopposed. It was as if the British had melted into the sand. Near the Msus airfield, which the British had captured a few weeks previously, they finally encountered some cursory fire from artillery.

'What's that?' asked Hubbuch, almost affronted that they should be attacked.

Kummel called a halt and raised the binoculars to his eyes. His head and body were sitting on top, outside in the open. An explosion ripped the earth twenty yards away. He ignored it. Half a minute later another shell landed well in front of the tanks.

'They're running away,' said Kummel. There was a hint of disgust in his voice. The Tommies were at an advantage at this range, yet they chose to run. He wondered what kind of men were leading the army opposing them. They seemed to have lost their stomach for a fight.

Manfred gazed through his periscope. He could see lots of dark shapes on the horizon, but it was difficult to tell what they were and in which direction they were moving. The radio crackled. It was Cramer.

'Attack them.'

Hubbuch needed no second invitation. The tank leapt forward with all the speed and grace of a hunting tortoise. This fact was noticed by Kummel.

'Can't you go any faster, Hubbuch?'

'Come down and see if you can do any better,' came the reply.

Kummel ignored him and they pressed on through the softer sand.

'How far, sir?' shouted Beer. He was looking through his viewfinder but the dust being thrown up by the escaping British vehicles made distance judgement a challenge.

'Seven hundred metres at least. Send one over. They're within range,' responded Kummel laconically. The captain stayed seated on top. Fire from the enemy had noticeably diminished. Manfred loaded the first shell. Beer fired immediately.

'Short. Fifty metres at least.'

By now, the other tanks were also firing and scoring hits on the retreating artillery trucks. Suddenly an explosion rocked the tank. Manfred glanced around and saw that it had not caused any damage.

'Traverse left. British tanks eleven o'clock.'

Another explosion sent a jet of sand shooting up into the air. Kummel jumped down into the tank. Outwardly he was as unruffled as ever, but he seemed angry.

'I don't know how we missed that. He's just destroyed one of our tanks.'

Manfred spun his periscope around and saw the burning Mark IV. They were now in position to fire at the British tank. Manfred hurled another cartridge into the breech. Beer fired.

'Yes!' exclaimed Kummel. 'Direct hit.'

'Good shooting,' said Manfred.

73

Beer grinned and shrugged like it was all in a day's work. Manfred risked a quick look through his periscope. He saw the British crew escaping through hatches. Another shell hit it moments later. Manfred could not see if this had killed the escaping crew. They pushed forward. The going was better, and they were approaching something like full speed.

The firing had stopped now. Manfred could not see anyone defending the crest of the ridge that they were heading towards. The question on his mind and, he suspected, everyone else's was what was on the other side. Was this a trap? He glanced towards Beer. The Berliner appeared nervous. At least I'm not alone, thought Manfred. His heart was beginning to race now.

'Keep going, sir?' asked Hubbuch as they approached the ridge.

'Of course,' snapped Kummel irritably.

Manfred switched his attention to what lay ahead. Their tank was at the head of the regiment racing forward. The ridge was only a few metres high. But it was enough to hide what lay behind. Thirty metres. Twenty metres. Ten metres.

'My God,' exclaimed Manfred as they crested the ridge.

Even Kummel was shocked by the sight that greeted them. Hubbuch began to laugh. Beer joined him moments later. The laughter of men given a reprieve from a firing squad and then told they were free to leave.

'Airfield directly in front,' intoned Kummel.

'Armour?' asked Cramer.

There were no tanks. No guns. Just a dozen fighters sitting undamaged on the airfield. Kummel reported what he could see but by then Cramer was also over the ridge.

'Looks like they left in a hurry,' exclaimed Cramer. There was no hiding the hint of jubilation in his voice. Relief, too.

Manfred walked around the Msus airfield in a daze. It was becoming apparent that the capture would prove to be a coup for the Afrika Korps, and one obtained at little cost. Aside from the dozen or so working fighters there was a large fuel dump and supplies. These had been brought to the airfield by the Allies with the planned assault on Tripoli in mind. Manfred felt like laughing at the hubris of the enemy.

Something shiny caught his eye around fifty metres outside the perimeter. He walked towards it. A cloud slid in front of the sun and he lost track of the glinting metal. He pressed on towards where he'd seen it last. Just ahead was a slit trench. He stopped. It seemed unlikely there could be any Tommies left. He turned around and saw the airfield swarming with Afrika Korps men. A few were also taking the opportunity to stretch their legs and smoke.

Manfred decided he was worrying about nothing. He continued walking over to the trench. From about thirty metres away he could see a metal object lying on the other side. It looked like a small knife. The closer he got to the trench the more he became aware of a smell. The smell of death. It became so overpowering he felt he might gag.

He reached the trench and found a dead soldier. He looked away, unable to stomach the horrific injuries that were plainly visible. Nausea swept through him. He grabbed the Lee-Enfield rifle and helmet from the trench and then began to kick sand over the dead soldier. It wasn't much of a grave, but he did what he could, then planted the gun at its head and draped the dead soldier's helmet over the barrel. A small knife lay there gleaming in the sun. He lifted it up. It was too small to be a bayonet, but it was more than a penknife. He put it in his pocket and returned to the airfield.

* * *

Colonel Cramer was everywhere. Barking orders to anyone that would listen, which was everyone. Manfred could hear him ordering that the food supplies be handed over to the support echelon. This was a disappointment. They would have provided a welcome alternative to the universally despised food rations that the German crews had to live on.

The airfield was proving a veritable gold mine. Not only had they captured vital additional food supplies and dozens of Crusader, Stuart and Valentines but also the workshop and tools which had been repairing the damaged tanks.

'Christmas is a bit late this year,' said Manfred coming alongside Gerhardt. The day was just beginning to give way to night. They went for a walk up onto a ridge to get a better view of the airfield and the activity.

'Have you tried this yet?' agreed Gerhardt, biting into some chocolate Manfred had seized before the arrival of the supply echelon.

Manfred grinned and replied sardonically, 'Is there any left? That was for sharing.'

Gerhardt ignored the barb and replied, 'A few days' rest here will do us good.'

'More than that and you'll be too fat to get into the tank,' said Manfred, deliberately focusing on the chocolate.

Gerhardt rubbed his stomach with pride. There was not a spare kilo on his frame. He, like most of the Afrika Korps, had lost weight since arriving in North Africa. Poor diet, irregular meals and the heat inside the cabin meant that what they ate in no way replenished what was lost. He sat up and scanned the scene below. Dozens of trucks were dotted around the airfield. Hundreds of men were busy recording what they'd captured and loading it onto the trucks. 'I wonder if our Field Marshal will make an appearance to look at our haul.'

'He's probably chasing the British himself. He doesn't stop.'

Other groups of men were using the time to do as they were, catching up with friends from other tanks. The fluid nature of crews often meant that they could be in one tank for a period of weeks or months and then, without warning, moved to another. The period in which you were together, however short, saw extraordinarily deep friendships forged in the intense heat of battle.

Manfred saw Lieutenant Basler joining Lieutenant Stiefelmayer and Captain Kummel nearby on the ridge. He drew Gerhardt's attention to this.

'To be honest I don't know why we just don't send those three to fight the Tommies on their own. They'd kick them out of Egypt in no time.'

'Our Supermen,' said Manfred grinning but there was an underlying respect, too. They were commonly considered to be the outstanding commanders in Regiment 8.

As darkness fell, they headed back towards their vehicles. Manfred helped prepare food for the rest of the crew. When they'd eaten, Kummel returned from a meeting with all the battalion commanders. The news was positive.

'It looks like the British are in full retreat. We could continue to chase them, but Rommel wants us to take Benghazi first. I suspect he wants us to have a harbour closer to Egypt to land more supplies and reinforcements.'

'Who holds Benghazi now?' asked Manfred.

'The South Africans are there and in some of the outlying towns.' Kummel looked up at the clouds rolling over the darkening sky. One by one they all did.

'Let's hope the weather holds,' said Hubbuch.

'Let's hope the weather holds, he said,' sneered Manfred a few nights later. The crew erupted into laughter. 'Why didn't you keep your big mouth shut?'

Hubbuch's response was drowned out by the fury of hail, wind and sand buffeting them from outside. The weather had worsened to an alarming degree. Travel through the rain-sodden sand was proving impossible. Their skin was stinging courtesy of the moments each of them had been exposed to this particularly nasty sandstorm.

The mist of sand caked their clothing and bodies making it as physically an uncomfortable few days as Manfred could remember. An added element to the irritation of their skin was the drop in temperature. All wore their overcoats throughout the days and nights of travel towards their objective. The one positive in all of this for Manfred was that, for once, they were not leading the assault on Benghazi and the outlying towns.

One by one they heard of the towns falling. First Er Regima fell early morning on the 28th of January. Manfred and the 15th Panzers waded through the sandy morass to arrive that evening.

The next morning, they heard that Benghazi was under siege. The news brought with it a temporary abatement in the poisonous weather they'd suffered over the last few days. In the distance, Manfred listened to the sound of the shelling, expecting at any moment that Kummel would arrive and order them forward.

It wasn't until midday that the order came and, by then, the large coastal city had fallen. The news was greeted by conspiratorial smiles between Manfred, Siefers and Hubbuch. They'd formed a close bond united by the cynicism of Hubbuch towards the heroic 'Sigmund' Kummel and 'Wotan' Cramer.

The sky remained ominously dark as the 15th Panzers trundled along the rocky path that led to Benghazi. It wound around the hilly jebel country surrounding the coastal port. Manfred sat on top of the cupola and looked around.

'How could the Tommies not defend this?' he asked Kummel whose eyes, as ever, were fixed to binoculars and scanning the horizon like an anxious meerkat.

'Be thankful that they couldn't or wouldn't, Brehme.'

The road leading into the city was somewhat better and they progressed more quickly. Finally, the sea came into view and the white buildings of the city shining against the dark grey of the sky.

The order came for them to stop near the edge of the city. The Panzers grouped themselves into a hedgehog position while the support echelon drove into the city in search of stores the Allies would have stockpiled for any future push. Manfred sat beside Siefers and watched the convoy of trucks push ahead in search of supplies. Siefers handed Manfred a cigarette.

'What will we do now?' asked Siefers.

Manfred looked up at the dark clouds overhead and replied, 'Well I, for one, will not be going to the beach.'

CHAPTER TEN

One hundred miles south-west of Tobruk, Libya, 28th January 1942

The overcoat was providing little protection against the biting cold wind stinging the faces of those on the ridge. Danny was hungry, too. Their food supplies had dwindled over the last two days and the rationing was barely enough to cover a poor breakfast never mind a full day. Sand whipped up into Danny's face to add to his misery.

He gazed out at the arid expanse through a pair of borrowed binoculars. About a mile away he could see a vast number of dark shapes. They had been stationed there for a day and had not moved.

Danny heard feet crunching over the rocky incline. Fitz joined him at the top.

'Are the Italians still there then?'

'See for yourself,' replied Danny handing him the binoculars.

Fitz took the field glasses from him but, in truth, they were unnecessary. He could see the encampment clearly without them.

'The lieutenant's getting windy again,' said Fitz.

To be fair, they all were. Hunger and cold were gradually chipping away at their willpower. They were still a hundred miles away from Tobruk and the only clear road was blocked by the Italians. They couldn't risk the desert as the rains had made much of it impassable. They were as stuck here as if they were in quicksand.

Danny stepped down carefully from the incline. There was no brew waiting for him, only silence. It would be hours before they had anything to eat. In the meantime, he had a pint of water to last him through that day. Discussion on their options had long since faded.

The wind was growing stronger now increasing the chill and discomfort felt by all. Danny looked around at the beaten faces. They'd travelled over one hundred miles in two days, stopping often and for long periods to avoid enemy patrols. Night drives were frequent, but progress was paralysingly slow. Yet they were so close. Tobruk was a matter of hours away. But one thought hung in the air like a nasty odour: was it still held by the Allies?

Danny watched Fitz scramble down the rocky slope clutching the binoculars. His face was a mask.

'Are they moving?' asked Blair, a little too hopefully.

'No, but I think there's a sandstorm coming this way,' replied Fitz. 'It might be an hour or two.'

'Great,' said Blair in a whisper. 'That's all we need.'

Danny looked at Fitz and then Gray. Both were frowning.

'Isn't this an opportunity?' asked Danny.

Gray shot Danny a look. Danny shrugged in reply. There was a palpable sense of nervousness in the camp, much of it stemming from the silent inertia of Lieutenant Blair. He was, once again, caught in his own world of despondency. Rather than communicate this, he chose silence. In the vacuum that followed, tensions escalated. Buller's temper was increasingly frayed. It was manifest in his humourless jibes at the Welshman Evans and, less vocally but certainly through eye-rolling gesture, at Blair.

Buller was listening and saw the exchange between Gray and Danny. He glared at Blair. The lieutenant's eyes were fixed on the small campfire. Seconds passed and no response was forthcoming from Blair.

'It's worth considering making a run for it if the sandstorm comes this way. It'll give us cover,' suggested Gray.

Blair didn't move and instead kept staring into the fire.

'Sir?' pressed Gray.

'I heard you, sergeant,' said Blair dismissively.

More silence followed this. Buller stood up. Gray turned sharply towards Buller. The eyes of the Liverpudlian were filled with rage. He ignored the glare of Gray and spoke directly to the lieutenant.

'We can't just stay here and starve.'

It wasn't just what he said. The tone strayed beyond insubordination. This was close to mutiny.

'Corporal,' said Gray. His voice was raised and there was an edge to it. This stopped Buller for a moment. As little as he thought of Blair, he had a high regard for the sergeant. It was too late. Blair shot to his feet, face red and eyes blazing.

'Have you something to say, corporal? Say it.'

This stopped Buller immediately, but his anger remained. He glared at the lieutenant.

'Sir, both Shaw and the sergeant have made suggestions. You haven't responded.'

Blair stepped forward and stood inches away from the tall Liverpudlian. He glared up at him and said, 'Do you agree with them?'

'I do,' replied Buller before adding, 'sir' a moment or two later. The delay was enough to further inflame the lieutenant.

82

'You disagree with my decision?'

This was very dangerous territory now for Buller. Recognising it as such, Gray stepped in.

'Sir, what Buller is saying is that we don't know what your decision is.'

Blair turned slowly to Gray. This was a different proposition and Blair knew it. His face reddened with the humiliation and fear he was feeling.

'I think I know what Buller is saying, sergeant. Am I to understand that you all support this foolish idea of heading into the teeth of a sandstorm?'

Silence followed this question. Finally Gray spoke.

'Yes, sir. We do.'

Then Buller nodded and said, 'Yes.' The others followed suit. Impotent with rage, Blair stood and looked at the men who were effectively conducting a mutiny. He spun around and walked away from them. All eyes turned to Gray.

'Start clearing up. Whenever the storm reaches the Italian camp, we'll start towards it.'

'What about the gun, sir?' asked Danny. 'It'll slow us down.'

Gray studied Danny for a moment and then nodded.

'Disable it.'

An hour later Gray came down from the ridge. He asked Buller if the gun had been put out of operation. Buller looked crestfallen at having had to do such an act of vandalism. Gray's attention shifted to Blair. The lieutenant was sitting alone in the truck, waiting.

'He's been there for the last half hour,' said Danny.

Gray didn't react to this. He pointed to the truck which was the order for them all to board. The sky had darkened considerably now although it was still only early afternoon. The wind had whipped up and sand was now beginning to sting their skin enough to remind them that the next few hours would be deeply uncomfortable, never mind enormously risky.

The men trooped up to the top of the ridge and looked at the approaching hell. A brown wall was approaching the Italian camp. It was at least a thousand feet high. Danny took the binoculars from Gray. He could make out Italian soldiers scurrying around trying to batten down anything that could get carried away or destroyed in the maelstrom.

Then they skipped down the hill and boarded the truck. Blair sat mutely sullen in the passenger seat. Gray ignored him and jumped into the driver's seat. He started the engine.

'Ready?' He didn't wait for an answer. Everyone pulled a scarf over their faces and the truck set off over the rocky ridge onto the road. The wind was blowing strongly. A mile ahead they could see the brown-orange leviathan beginning to engulf the Italian camp. Any guards still outside would be forced under cover.

Danny wrapped his overcoat around himself tightly. He pulled his beret low over his head. The scarf he wore around his neck to protect him from the sun now became like an outlaw's mask covering everything except his eyes. They drove slowly forward. It was evident that Gray was as concerned about maintaining direction as he was speed. The sound of the engine was soon drowned out by the high-pitched whine of the wind.

The truck pitched along unsteadily. The turbulence rocked them while at the same time throwing up scurrying grains of sand. What at first were thousands of individual particles soon became like a thin fabric of sand, stinging their faces. Underneath the mask, Danny found the hot air oppressive. Visibility declined to a few yards and the sky disappeared under the angry dust blanket. The sand transformed into lashing sheets of larger, coarser grains.

Danny and the others ducked down under the full assault of the storm's rage. They were probably travelling at no more than ten miles per hour yet the sand blowing in their faces and the rocking of the truck made it feel as if they were hurtling through a vortex signalling the end of time.

No longer able to open his eyes, Danny ducked his head into his chest and waited. He wasn't sure if they were even moving now, such was the fury of the storm and the loss of any sensory cues to guide him.

How long they drove for he could not tell. The drive seemed to take an age. Miraculously, no one stopped them. The Italians were sheltering in their tents from the raging force of nature. Then, suddenly, the storm ceased to be raging. Danny raised his head and lowered the sand-encrusted scarf from his eyes. He could not focus initially. His eyes stung from the sand particles that had embedded in his skin. He couldn't rub them as his hands were covered in sand. This would only make matters worse.

Finally, vision slowly returned. His eyes watered and focus was lost for a minute before shapes became more defined. Much to his amazement he realised that Gray was still driving. However, the sergeant was struggling now, and the truck was about to veer off the road. Danny saw that they risked crashing. He pushed Buller out of the way and leant over the sergeant's shoulder to correct the steering wheel.

'Stop the car,' shouted Danny.

'All right, all right,' replied Gray. 'You don't have to shout. I'm not deaf.'

The car came to a stop. All the men jumped out and tried to rid themselves and the truck of the excess sand. They had reached the other side of the camp, but they were still dangerously close to the enemy. Elements of the camp were now visible.

'Hurry,' ordered Gray. He didn't have to worry on that score. They could all see that they were very exposed. Within a matter of seconds they were back on board. Buller took over the driving to give Gray a break. The sergeant had borne the brunt of the storm and was clearly suffering. His eyes were caked with sand. Danny marvelled at the resilience he'd shown to keep pushing through despite the onslaught they'd faced.

Evans used up some of their precious water supplies in clearing Gray's eyes. It was tempting to give some to everyone to do this, but the risk was too great. They had no idea how many other delays they would encounter on the road to Tobruk. For now, though, they were making progress.

Around a mile past the Italian camp, they saw a lone figure walking along the road. As they drew closer, they could see an Italian uniform peeping out from underneath a coat of sand. His head was down, and he was plodding back to his camp.

He heard the approaching vehicle and glanced up. Danny and the rest of the truck looked back at him. A faint smile appeared on his face, and he saluted. Everyone in the truck, except Blair, saluted back.

Bert Gissing was enjoying a cigarette when he saw the approaching truck through his field glasses. He called over to Tom.

'We've company.'

Tom grabbed his Lee Enfield and brought over Bert's. They watched the truck for five minutes as it drew nearer. The truck looked in bad shape, the individuals inside, even worse. Everyone, truck included, was caked with mud and sand. As it approached the checkpoint, Bert stepped out and pointed his rifle at the vehicle.

Sergeant Gray was back driving. He looked at the two soldiers standing picket. Beside them was a sign that read 'Tobruk: 5 miles'.

'Who are you?' asked Bert.

Danny could not believe his eyes. Hidden behind Buller, he watched in amusement as Gray explained who they were.

Bert listened intently and nodded. Then he grinned and said, 'Well, I'm guessing you don't know the password then.'

Danny hopped out at this point and said, 'Beer. And make it sharp.'

Bert and Tom looked askance at the tall figure with a face that looked like it hadn't been washed in months. The men on the truck gawped at their grinning comrade.

'Well, I'll be,' said Bert.

'Danny,' shouted Tom in delight, throwing down his gun and rushing towards his brother.

PART 2: THE GAZALA GALLOP

31st Jan 1942–June 1942

The German operation, Theseus, had succeeded in pushing the Allied Eighth Army back towards the Gazala Line just in front of Tobruk. The German offensive destroyed seventy-five Allied tanks, against a German loss of twenty-nine tanks (out of one hundred). The Allied defensive line encompassed a series of 'boxes' at Knightsbridge and Bir Hacheim.

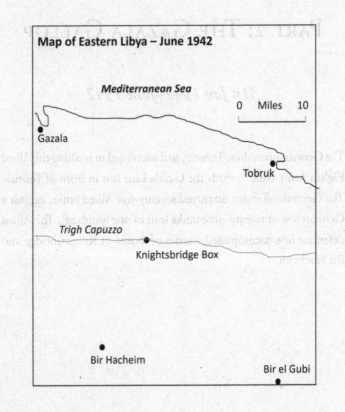

Map of Eastern Libya – June 1942

Mediterranean Sea

0   Miles   10

● Gazala

● Tobruk

Trigh Capuzzo

● Knightsbridge Box

● Bir Hacheim

Bir el Gubi ●

CHAPTER ELEVEN

Tobruk, Libya, 31st January 1942

If it wasn't much of a bar, then at least it had the benefit of reducing expectations for the quality of the beer. This subsequently proved to be a pleasant surprise. Danny sat with his brother and Bert Gissing at a table already crowded by empty glasses. Danny greeted the arrival of Fitz, Buller and Evans in the bar with a wave. The three men found seats and sat down.

'Sort out the drinks, Danny lad,' said Buller. The idea was received with acclaim from the Little Gloston boys. Danny rolled his eyes and dutifully organised the drinks. The discussion centred around the inevitable parting of the ways.

'We've been told we're heading out tomorrow,' explained Buller. 'Holiday's over.'

'Where are you going?' asked Danny. He felt a wave of sadness pass through him. He'd always accepted that they would have to part at some point. The knowledge did not diminish the sense of anxiety that he would feel at not having such men at his back. Over the two

91

months they'd grown as close as brothers. It felt as if the breath had been crushed from his chest. It was as bewildering to him as it was painful.

'Knightsbridge,' announced Buller grandly. 'They know class when they see it.'

Fitz shook his head and laughed at the look on Danny's face.

'Not that Knightsbridge. They've set up a series of defensive boxes. Our one is Knightsbridge. You can tell the type of people leading us, can't you? Won't be for long. The colonel suggested we'd return to our battalions by Easter.'

'When do you leave?'

'Tonight.'

There was a hint of sadness in Fitz's voice. He, Buller and Evans would have to go their separate ways. Danny realised at that moment how war was not just a clash of opposing armies but also a coming together of disparate people within an army. They formed units and, within those ad hoc groupings, deep friendships were forged in the heat of battle. But war had a habit of tearing these apart. They drank to a future that would see a victory over Nazism but more than that, they drank to the hope that they would all meet up one day in England. And drink some more.

Captain Stanton barely glanced up when Danny entered his office. He was scribbling on a sheet of paper. He made a signature with something of a flourish and handed it to a lance corporal. He dismissed the lance corporal and finally turned his attention to Danny.

Stanton was, like so many of the captains he'd encountered, surprisingly young and unsurprisingly from another social class. His hair was the colour of the sand and thinning around the temples.

'Shaw, thank you for coming. Sit down.'

Danny sat down facing Stanton and decided there and then he would never grow a moustache. Stanton had a thin moustache that was probably an attempt to look like David Niven or Ronald Coleman. It made him look like Anna Neagle in panto. His soft, feminine features were unlikely to be disguised by such a limp attempt at facial hair.

'We've located your regiment. They are in the Quassassin Camp which is near the Suez Canal. It would be fair to say that many of the people you knew in the regiment are no longer there. Like yourself, they were dispersed amongst other regiments following the encounter at Sidi Rezegh.'

Stanton, who'd been studying a piece of paper while he spoke, looked up at Danny at this point.

'Were you part of that?'

'Yes, sir,' replied Danny. He felt his heart lurch as the faces of Phil Lawrence and Sergeant Reed came to his mind. Stanton could see the colour drain from Danny and he nodded. His voice changed from the rather clipped business-like tone to something more sympathetic.

'That was quite a show, I gather.' Danny nodded but did not trust himself to speak. Sensing this, Stanton glanced down at the sheet in front of him and continued. 'A number of the regiment have been transferred to the Third Royal Tank Regiment. Perhaps a similar transfer might be of interest to you? I'm not sure there's much choice. They're badly understrength and it looks like Jerry is going to take another crack at us.'

Stanton handed Danny a sheet of paper. There was a list of names. 'These are some of the people who've been transferred.'

Danny ran his eyes down the sheet. His eyes lit up when he came to one of the names.

'I'll go, sir,' said Danny.

Stanton looked relieved and smiled. 'That's the spirit, Shaw. You'll leave for Egypt in a few days; 3 RTR is at Beni Youseff undergoing a refit and taking new tanks and men.'

'Thank you, sir.'

'Thank you, Shaw,' replied Stanton. He emphasised 'you'. Danny left the office and wandered down towards the harbour. It was a bright morning. White buildings were scattered like shells on a beach. The harbour area was unusually quiet. Many of the Royal Navy vessels had departed leaving just a few fishing boats bobbing about on the deep blue Mediterranean. Fitz, Buller and Evans had already left while Tom and Bert had returned to the outer perimeter. He strolled along the seafront and stared at the sea. A fresh breeze caressed his face. It seemed so peaceful. How much longer would this last, he wondered.

For those few moments he escaped the flow of time. His mind cleared itself of any thoughts of the future or memories of the past. Instead, he let his senses take over. He drank in the blue of the sea, listened to the coughing engines of cars and vans, and the cry of the birds overhead. A fishing boat chugged out of the harbour. It looked like there were three generations of fishermen on the little vessel. He recognised the life that they led: its simplicity, their unvarying routine, and he envied their freedom. He watched them sail out until they were barely a speck on the horizon.

A light drizzle fell on the garrison, but few seemed to notice. Soldiers were rushing between the dozens of vehicles lining the road for as far as the eye could see. It looked like an army on the retreat. While the sun sulked behind the steel grey clouds, Danny walked with Tom and Bert Gissing towards the truck that would carry him back to Egypt and his new regiment. It was an oddly British level of noise, somewhere between loud murmur and an embarrassed grumble.

'So this is it, then,' said Tom.

'Again,' pointed out Bert.

The two brothers laughed but there was more than a tinge of sadness. Nearby the motor of a truck was idling as a dozen men made ready to leave Tobruk.

A sergeant made his way through the crowd of soldiers and began to bark orders. He added, rather unnecessarily, that they were a horrible lot. Danny rolled his eyes.

'I can see this is going to be a fun trip.'

Danny turned to the tall figure of Bert Gissing. They shook hands. Anything else would have been uncomfortable despite the genuine warmth between them.

'Keep your big head down,' said Danny.

'And you. I doubt they'll get any nearer you than I ever did,' said Bert with a grin.

'I mean it, Bert. And look after this dreamboat.'

'The girls of England will demand it, Danny boy,' laughed Tom.

The two brothers looked at each other as the sergeant's tone became angrier due to the realisation that he was being ignored. Engines began to roar as the convoy slowly departed.

'Better go, kid,' said Tom trying to smile. 'You won't be too far away from what I hear.'

'Just down the road,' agreed Danny. 'I'll see you soon hopefully. As soon as I have a day off, I'll pop back.'

'Yes, you do that. Bye. Take care.'

Danny shook hands with his brother, then picked up his kit bag and threw it onto the truck. In one swift movement he jumped onto the truck and swivelled over the back. Within moments the truck was on its way, forcing a couple of soldiers to have to run and catch it up, much to the amusement of the others in the back and onlookers. Danny watched Tom and Bert for as long as he could and then they disappeared into the dust cloud thrown up by the departing truck.

A day and a half later, the truck arrived at a camp near Beni Youssef just south of Cairo. The camp stretched for miles. Hundreds of vehicles were lined up in neat rows. Among them Danny could see the familiar shape of the Crusaders and even some of the new tanks he'd heard about but not seen before. Their official name was the M3, but they were unofficially known as the Grant.

Even from a distance, Danny could see how much bigger the gun was. Its length and girth seemed to dwarf the fifty-seven-millimetre gun of the Crusader. At last, they would have something that would match the German Mark III and IVs. He felt empty rather than elated. For so long he and the other crews had been fighting with inferior tanks armed with popguns. It had taken too long to learn the lessons from defeat. So many men had been lost in this unequal fight.

It was late afternoon when Danny jumped down from the back of the truck, his feet landing on a thin layer of sand over rock. There were at least a hundred men disembarking at that moment. Danny's body ached all over from the long drive. He stretched his stiff limbs. All around him were young men who'd grown up, like him, in a matter of months. The sounds of joints cracking were like rifle shots at midnight.

'Bloody hell,' said one boy to Danny. 'When did I grow old?'

'The moment you arrived here,' replied Danny with a half smile.

The sergeant, who considered them a horrible lot, appeared not to have changed his opinion much on the trip from Tobruk. He shouted at them in a tirade that was only intelligible when he swore. Which was quite frequently. The gist of his request was that they should stand in ranks. The soldiers wearily complied despite the high decibel urgings of the sergeant.

'Hope I don't have him after today,' whispered Danny.

'Hope you do,' laughed the boy.

The two boys lost out on the battle to be in the second row and reluctantly stood at the front, in the centre. This was always likely to be a prime target for the martinet sergeant. So it proved. An inspection turned into something of a bath for several of the young soldiers at the front as the sergeant stood inches away and yelled at them for the most minor of offences.

'What are you smiling at?' demanded the sergeant to a young man who'd probably seen action a dozen times in the last few months.

'Nothing, sir,' came the sullen reply.

'What?'

The young man was clearly a heartbeat away from rolling his eyes. Instead, he repeated what he'd said at a similar level of intensity as the sergeant. The sergeant walked past Danny glaring malevolently before continuing to the end of the line without any further casualties. A corporal approached the sergeant and handed him a clipboard.

'Answer up when your name is called.'

For the next few minutes, the sergeant went through a long list of names. By the end Danny and a few of the others were shuffling. This brought a further wave of disapprobation from the sergeant.

'Ten shun.'

The men responded in a single movement. As they did this, two officers appeared to inspect the new arrivals. The sergeant saluted them dramatically. The first officer returned the salute and then ordered the new arrivals to stand at ease.

Danny estimated him to be in his mid-thirties. Yet he was already a lieutenant-colonel. His clean-shaven face was certainly younger looking than many of the senior officers he'd encountered. In this regard, he looked more like a captain. He walked up the line not so much to inspect the new arrivals as to allow them to inspect him.

'Stand at ease,' screamed the sergeant.

'Thank you, sergeant,' said the lieutenant-colonel wearily. 'Stand easy, men. My name is Roberts. Welcome to your new regiment. You've come to replace men we've lost. Some of you are new to this war. Some of you will have already seen action, seen men die. Over the next few weeks, you will train like you've never trained before. You will hate me, the sergeant and every senior officer in this regiment. But you will be ready to face the enemy. You'll sweat blood, believe me, but it may just keep you and your comrade's alive.'

Roberts finished on this note and then began an inspection of the men before him. He stopped every few soldiers and said a few words to the man before him. Coming before Danny, he asked, 'Where are you from?'

'Sixth Royal Tank Regiment, sir.'

Roberts nodded. There was a sadness behind his eyes. An understanding that both recognised. The moment passed and then he replied, 'Well, you're in the 3 RTR now.'

As they would not be assigned their tanks and responsibilities until the next day, Danny had some free time on his hands. He started his search. Spotting a few mechanics working on a truck, he went over to chat. They sent him to a sergeant standing over by one of the new Grants. The sergeant pointed him towards the other end of a long line of tanks.

Walking along the rows of tanks gave him an opportunity to spy the Grant up close. The new gun was certainly impressive, albeit strange. It was not actually part of the turret. Instead, a thirty-seven-millimetre gun occupied this position. The bigger gun was lower down to the side. Danny wasn't quite sure what the designers were thinking. The position of the big gun was limited in its ability to traverse right or left. It would require the tank to change direction to target an enemy tank. Mid-battle, this was not ideal as it would not only give Jerry a bigger target to aim at but also one with far less protection than the front plating usually offered. Danny had immediate misgivings about what he was looking at.

He walked along the line looking at groups of men sitting huddled around small campfires. It was getting colder, and night would soon draw in. He hurried his step, fearful of missing his quarry.

He heard the laugh before he saw the man. His back was to Danny, sitting with two other men drinking tea. Danny made his way quietly towards him, leaned over the man's shoulder and stole his tea.

'Oi, what the bloody hell,' exclaimed the soldier spinning around angrily.

'Hello, Arthur,' grinned Danny before necking the rest of the tea. 'Nice cup of tea, that.'

'Danny,' yelled Arthur leaping to his feet. 'What the bloody hell are you doing here? I thought you were off swanning around the desert like Lawrence of Arabia or something.'

'Been a right old holiday,' laughed Danny.

The two friends sat down and Arthur introduced Danny to the other members of the crew. Don Mitchell was the gunner. He was not much younger than Arthur. He was also a Glaswegian. When he spoke, Arthur erupted into laughter at the look on his friend's face.

'Don't worry, Danny boy, none of us understand him.'

Jim Compton was closer to Danny in age and a Londoner.

'No relation,' said Compton by way of introduction.

'Danny doesn't know anything about cricket,' said Arthur. 'A complete heathen if you ask me. I don't know why I let him hang around me.'

Another round of tea was served. It was getting dark just as the evening calm was broken by the sound of gunfire. Danny was startled but the others took no notice. Arthur smiled grimly at his friend.

'They're shooting the dogs,' he explained.

'Tomorrow's dinner?' asked Danny.

'Rabies.'

CHAPTER TWELVE

Tmimi, 30km east of Derna, Libya, 27th February 1942

Manfred sank to the ground. His sweat-stained shirt stuck to him like wet flannel and he desperately wanted to weep. It was his fault. All his fault. He knew it. Around him voices were shouting at him. Angry voices. He couldn't blame them. One person laughed. It was Gerhardt. He waggled Manfred's hair as he jogged past.

'Never mind, old friend. It's only a game.'

Only a game?

The match between the 1st and 2nd Battalions was more than that. It was the very stuff of life and death. Manfred's mistake would not only rankle with him it would provide endless opportunity for both his friend and half the battalion to mock him over the coming weeks. Months probably. The ignominy of it all was beyond words and could only be understood through feeling. And that feeling was pain.

Manfred rose slowly to his feet. They were now three goals to one down with barely a handful of minutes left to play. The match restarted. Gerhardt jogged forward. He grinned once more at Manfred.

'One more goal and I have a hat trick. Can you gift me another pass?'

Manfred's reply was drowned out by the shouts of encouragement from the side lines. Or was it abuse? It was good-natured, ribald and insightful in equal measure. His team were mounting an attack but, as ever, they failed to penetrate a defence every bit as stout in football as they were inside twenty tonnes of armour.

The 2nd Battalion had the ball now and passed it around like professionals. Some of them had played semi-professionally. They knew what they were about. There was no panic. Just control mixed with awareness as they picked out passes to their team. By comparison, the 1st Battalion could offer only enthusiasm, limitless energy and, in Manfred's case, suicidally risky play. That he had the ability to carry this off ninety-nine per cent of the time was immaterial. Gerhardt had only needed Manfred to lapse once, and he punished him severely.

The 2nd Battalion were on the attack. Manfred back pedalled to his position at the centre of the defence. The ball came across into his box. He didn't make the same mistake this time. He headed it away, just managing to outjump his friend.

'Bastard,' exclaimed a grinning Gerhardt, frustrated at missing out on his hat trick.

The ball moved forward again but not for long. Soon Manfred was racing out to the wing to tackle the tricky winger who'd twisted the spirit of his team inside and out. Another corner to the 2nd Battalion. Manfred had a feeling he knew how the Tommies felt at Tobruk. It felt like he'd spent most of the match under siege. The ball whizzed over and was met powerfully by the head of Gerhardt. Manfred stretched a leg out and hooked it away from the line. The groan from Gerhardt offered him a degree of satisfaction.

The 1st Battalion chased the ball up the pitch as the whistle blew for full time. Cheers and boos rang out around the makeshift pitch. Gerhardt came over and shook hands with Manfred. The grin was smug, and the words were cruelly designed to offer the least amount of comfort possible.

Manfred's teammates were good sorts. To a man they came over and consoled him. First over was Lieutenant Stiefelmayer.

'Brehme, that was unlucky. You played well.'

'Thanks, sir,' replied Manfred gloomily. Stiefelmayer patted him on the back and stood back as his other teammates joined him.

In their actions was the painful acknowledgement that they had been beaten by a better side and that without Manfred the score could have been considerably worse.

Inevitably, sympathy was always going to be in short supply from his friend and rival from yesteryear on a football pitch.

'Hard luck. You played really well,' said Gerhardt. The sentiment was somewhat undermined by a delighted grin that seemed to stretch all the way to Tripoli. The laughter that followed these words further bellied any hint of magnanimity. Gerhardt's sympathy was rewarded by Manfred throwing him to the ground. He stayed there. Laughing. A few of the other opposition were a little bit more understanding to Manfred's plight. In truth, he'd played a great game. One mistake can often eradicate memories of the honest effort expended; this was life, not just football.

Manfred helped the still helpless Gerhardt to his feet. His laughter stopped suddenly. The two boys paused for a moment and looked overhead. There was a lone aeroplane. It took a moment or two to register that it was one of theirs.

'I wonder what's wrong?' said Manfred.

By now most of the players and spectators were looking up at the sky. The plane began its descent. Landing gear and flaps became extended. After a few minutes, engine turning over more slowly, the plane landed on the pitch, much to the amusement of all the onlookers who began to flock towards it.

A familiar figure emerged from the cockpit. A smile erupted over the sweat-stained face of Hans-Joachim Marseille. His newly awarded Iron Cross glinted in the early afternoon sunlight but there was no mistaking how haggard he looked. It was clear he'd had a busy day. The bullet holes in his fuselage confirmed this.

He was helped down from the plane and all but carried to a hospital tent. This was the first time that either Manfred or Gerhardt had seen the famous air ace up close. Both felt a stab of guilt. While they had been enjoying the football, many of the Luftwaffe were flying sorties and patrolling the skies against the ongoing aggression from the RAF.

'He looks done in,' commented Gerhardt.

'What's he saying?' asked Manfred as there was too much hubbub to hear.

Finally the word came back. Two more kills. Cheers went up all around the flyer. When they subsided, both Manfred and Gerhardt heard him ask, 'Who won the match?'

The first hint of spring was in the air and flowering on the ground. There were wisps of colour in the unremitting sand and rock. In early March and April the desert was almost bearable. Since the end of February, life had transformed itself. No more marches. Better still, there was no more fighting. They were to stay in one place for the foreseeable future. The repairs taking place now were for more than just armour and machinery. The Afrika Korps was, at last, having a long overdue rest. The enemy, apparently, were mostly of a like mind. Only the RAF seemed intent on poking the wasp's nest.

There was renewed energy in everyone. The camp at Tmimi was

humming with new arrivals, both men and machines. Manfred was now one of the more experienced crewmen in the regiment. He had a new tank commanded by an old face. Lieutenant Basler had, as usual, been handed a few rookies. In return he'd requested an experienced crew member. He wanted Manfred. Kummel, reluctantly, released Manfred to join the lieutenant.

Moving from the captain's tank proved not to be a step down. He was to become a gunner. Manfred's experience of two battles was always likely to be too important to waste as a loader. The move to gunner was a promotion if not in rank, then in responsibility. It was recognition that he had performed well in the past few months and could be trusted with more advanced duties. Unfortunately, it meant that he would be leaving Hans Kummel's tank. This was a pity as he not only liked the captain, but he'd also learned a great deal from him. More importantly, he viewed Kummel as lucky. This was something all the soldiers understood but rarely spoke of.

Aside from Basler, his new crew consisted of one veteran driver, Klaus Jentz, and two newly arrived men, Thomas Keil, who would operate the wireless, and Gerd Kleff who would be Manfred's loader. Both were from Bavaria but could not have been more different from Manfred's old crew mate, Andreas Fischer. Manfred looked at them both on his first day in the new tank and wondered how he must have seemed to Overath and Kastner, when he'd first arrived. Back then he'd tried to mask his nervousness, not through the swagger that Fischer used, successfully he realised, but through a combination of seriousness and competence.

The two young men, and they were both younger than Manfred, seemed more like puppies: a combination of eagerness to please and enthusiasm. They used this to mask the fear they were feeling. Manfred felt some sympathy for their plight yet was happy to leave them to it. He couldn't be their nursemaid. If anything, this would be counterproductive. This was the army. They were in a war. They would have to figure it out for themselves. Only three things were needed from the two boys. A willingness to learn; a willingness to obey and, unspoken, a willingness to march towards death.

There was also a return. Manfred awoke one morning courtesy of a cup of cold water poured liberally over his head. Just as he was about to lay into the culprit, he saw who it was. Fischer beamed down at him seemingly none the worse for his wounds.

'You're back,' exclaimed Manfred, leaping to his feet. He stopped himself for a moment before adding, 'Holiday over, then?'

Fischer grinned and replied, 'Alas, yes. I don't know who was sadder. Me or the nurses.'

Some things clearly hadn't changed. Fischer's ego had avoided any long-term damage from his brush with death. If anything, the scar tissue only added another layer of thickness to his skin. What several months ago Manfred would have found irritating, he now enjoyed immensely. Adding to this peculiar pleasure was seeing the impact that a fully recovered and unconstrained Fischer had on some of the new recruits. Manfred's implied promotion had one other benefit that only occurred to him as he chatted with his friend.

'So you'll be loading then, Andreas?'

'Bugger off,' replied Fischer.

'I think you've a lot of experience you can bring to this position,' continued Manfred.

'Bugger off,' responded Fischer his eyes inspecting the engine of Manfred's new Mark IV.

'Perhaps one day you'll be my loader.'

That was the final straw and moments later Manfred was being chased round the tank by a spanner-wielding Bavarian intent on murder.

Other changes were less welcome. The news that the regiment commander, Lieutenant-Colonel Cramer, was to return to Germany was greeted with universal sadness. Manfred liked the gnarled veteran immensely. Like Kummel, he was a man that believed in leading from the front. He didn't ask the men to do anything that he was not prepared to do himself. This had nearly resulted in his death the summer before when the Allies had made a major push to relieve Tobruk. Any hopes that Kummel would replace him were dispelled by the news that the new commander would be Lieutenant-Colonel Willi Teege.

The new commander was an unknown quantity, but the reports were good. Quite a few of the men knew him from Panzer Troop School. Cramer's leaving speech confirmed what they all knew. He turned to Hans Kummel at one point and said, 'I know that it was you who led our regiment to victory. And I ask that you maintain your attitude and aggressiveness, which I have always admired, even under a new commanding officer.'

Cramer was given a rousing send-off from the regiment. He wiped a tear away then ducked his head into the car. Soon he would be on a plane back to Germany. Everyone envied him but there was no hint of begrudgery. He'd earned it. Probably they all had.

As soon as he was gone, life resumed its slow pace. A curious calm had descended on North Africa. The drum and the trumpet of battle lay ahead. For now, the drooping clouds and intermittent showers were giving way to a belligerently blue sky, sun and the first hints of the heat that would burn and blister and brutalise the senses of all who toiled underneath it.

CHAPTER THIRTEEN

Ladenburg (nr. Heidelberg), 1st March 1942

Another day passed in the gradual erosion of Peter Brehme's police powers. The day began normally enough. Crime in the town was at an all-time low. The Nazis, thought Brehme, had devised the perfect way of reducing crime. Force all likely criminals into the army and give them a war to fight. Amid some of the hardest years the country had ever experienced, Peter Brehme had never had it so easy. Nor had he ever been so bored.

The first inkling that this might be coming to an end came when he received a call from the mayor, Stefan Lerner, to meet him at his office. This was a monthly affair normally when Brehme gave his report which, of late, had lasted a few minutes, and then they had a few drinks. It was as convivial as it was absurd. Brehme looked forward to these meetings. He rarely socialised.

There were fewer soldiers in the square now. Even the Hitler Youth were less visible these days. It wasn't difficult to understand why. The country was fighting across two fronts. The '*volk*' required every able-bodied man to do his duty. No doubt boys, too.

He thought about Manfred and felt a stab of pain. His son had been swept along, like all his generation, by the fantasy propagated by the Nazis. The youth had rebelled against the misery and the discipline of post-war Germany. This was a rebellion not just against the situation but also against another generation: Brehme's generation. The harsh discipline of their elders had sown seeds reaped by the Nazis. Brehme recalled not only the severity of his own upbringing but also Manfred's. Had it been effective, or had he merely created the raw material that would ultimately be moulded by a man like Hitler? He knew the answer to this question, and it made him sick inside.

Brehme wondered how much Manfred still believed in the ideals indoctrinated by his surrogate parents in the party. Was it still possible to believe in a Fatherland and Fuhrer as he bore witness to the death and maiming of friends and comrades? If he did then his son was a fool. This thought, as much as any other, pained him. Life was the best teacher a man could have. Perhaps even he could still learn something new. And change.

Decades of service in the police force meant that Brehme could not stop himself noticing things. He stopped in the town square and looked around. Everything that was there was meant to be there. Something was missing, though, and it irked him. He could see no one from the Hitler Youth. Not one solitary member. When had they stopped being so visible? Perhaps their absence was a sign that the younger generation was waking up to the reality of Nazism: the horrifying prospect of being sent to some foreign field. And dying there.

Perhaps, instead, young people were merely doing what young people do. Rebelling against the older generations. Brehme smiled grimly at the thought that the older generation would be, by definition,

Manfred's. What remained were the old, the infirm or those too smart or too rich to get swept away by the waves of war.

Brehme nodded to a few of the townsfolk as he walked to the appointment. Otto Becker's wife said hello to him as she scurried along the square carrying a large bag of food.

'Feeding the five thousand?' laughed Brehme but she had already passed him.

He arrived at the town hall and bounded up the steps to Lerner's office.

'Just go on through,' said Heike, Lerner's elderly secretary.

Brehme gave a brief rap on the door and then entered. Lerner was behind a large mahogany desk. Another man was in the room. He was in his thirties and dressed smartly in a grey suit. Brehme recognised him as Gestapo immediately.

Overlooking the scene like a mother hen was a large portrait of the Fuhrer gazing into the distance like a seer. He would have made a good fish wife, thought Brehme. It was clear that neither he nor Lerner would be able to toast their leader in their usual barbed fashion.

'Peter,' said Lerner somewhat nervously. 'Thank you for making time.'

Brehme almost yelped in laughter at this. It was their private in-joke for a policeman who no longer had much to police. The look on Lerner's face put Brehme on his guard. This late afternoon chat was unlikely to end in a shared whisky, a bit of gossip about the latest idiocy of the Nazis and a few ribald tales.

'May I introduce Herr Keller.'

Tellingly he left the introduction at this. Keller, unlike many of the Gestapo he'd met, smiled and stood up. He held out his hand.

'Please call me Ernst. I try to ensure that working relationships are as cordial as they are professional. After all, we are on the same side.'

'Of course,' replied Brehme sitting down and already concerned by the use of the word 'working'. He shot a glance in the direction of Lerner. It was clear he was uncomfortable and somewhat put out that Keller had taken the liberty of breaking news to his police chief that, by rights, was his prerogative.

'So we will be working together?' asked Brehme, attempting to keep the tone light.

'Yes. From tomorrow. Herr Himmler has decided that our network should expand to towns which either have, or are near to, universities.'

Brehme was incredulous. Ladenburg was a small town with a population that had declined by a fifth because of the war. There were few if any students here as most were living in nearby Heidelberg. He hid his surprise. Years of interviewing suspects, listening to lies, had given him a face that any poker player would have killed for. It made him able to ask the most outrageous questions and make the most ironic comments without the listener realising where his true thoughts lay.

'There is a belief that Ladenburg is a centre of treason or espionage?'

Lerner almost choked when he heard Brehme ask this. Not because the question was absurd, which it certainly was, but because Brehme had made it sound like he was asking about the likelihood of rain that night. At that moment, Lerner understood just why Brehme had been such an effective policeman over these years.

'This is a very good question,' said Keller, getting serious.

No, it's not, thought Brehme: it's a ridiculous question and you are a moron.

'Thank you, Herr Keller, sorry. Ernst. I've often felt that we must give greater attention to the smaller towns in this country. Spies and troublemakers are not going to parade themselves in big cities. No, it

111

is the small towns of Germany which can become a hotbed of trouble if we are not careful.'

Keller slapped the table in a manner of someone who had just been validated.

'I knew that you were just the man, sir, to understand the challenge we face.'

Lerner was, by now, gripping the table to stop himself laughing at the young Gestapo man. As ludicrous an individual as he was, Lerner had no doubt he would be dangerous if crossed. He exchanged glances with Brehme and the message was understood. Don't push this too far.

For the moment, though, Keller was oblivious to the tacit understanding between the two older men.

'Have you heard of the Edelweiss Pirates?' asked Keller.

'Yes, of course, everyone has. But they are just adolescents rebelling against their parents. They're only good for getting young girls pregnant,' said Brehme perhaps more dismissively than he'd intended.

This was perhaps a slight exaggeration, acknowledged Brehme to himself, but not too far from the truth. He didn't like what they appeared to stand for, but he doubted they existed in the town.

'You must not underestimate these young people, Brehme. They are numerous, they are everywhere, and they are against the Fatherland. We know for a fact that they conduct violent attacks against the Hitler Youth. We also know that they help deserters and Jews and seek only to undermine our country. They cannot be allowed to flourish.'

'So we will be working together?' asked Brehme again.

'Yes. From tomorrow. Is there an office that I can use?'

'I'm afraid there's only the one office, Ernst.'

'Then we shall be like flatmates,' said Keller brightly.

Brehme wasn't sure if his own attempted smile didn't look more like the grimace of a man who has just stubbed his toe. There was

112

little point in trying to object. All he could do was to make the best of a bad situation. Keller was an idiot. A dangerous one, undoubtedly, but an idiot all the same. He, Brehme, had nothing to fear. His attitude towards the Nazis was one of forbearance and hope that it was a period that would one day pass in the nation's history quickly enough for him to enjoy retirement, more time with his son and whatever grandchildren God would bring him.

It was almost six in the evening. There seemed little point in returning to the police station. Instead Brehme walked home. The house echoed to his footsteps. He glanced down, as he usually did, at a photograph of Manfred in his Hitler Youth uniform. He'd insisted on having a portrait taken much to Manfred's embarrassment. A reminder to his folly. He went into his office to finish off the letter he'd started.

For a few minutes he sat and thought about what to write. There was no doubt the letters were being censored or, at the very least, read. He decided against mentioning his new 'work mate'.

There was a news broadcast on the radio. He turned it up. They were describing a successful engagement in North Africa. He wasn't sure how much he should believe about what was said. In the absence of anything else, at least it gave him reassurance that Manfred was alive and well. He took an atlas from the bookcase and opened it at North Africa while he listened to the broadcast.

One item piqued his interest. The news announced that Lieutenant-Colonel Hans Cramer was to return to Germany. Manfred had written about Cramer in glowing terms several times. The return of such a man to Germany was a worry. He wanted Manfred surrounded by the very best leaders. This was his best chance of surviving the war. He wondered what was to become of Cramer. Would he be sent on that fool's errand in Russia?

Brehme sat back in his chair. He felt impotent. Restless. There was a war going on to which he was contributing nothing except cynicism and doubt. His son was fighting for an idea of nationhood that appalled him. It was all wrong and he could do nothing about it. From tomorrow he would, effectively, become subordinate to a young idiot who represented everything that had gone wrong with his country. Something on the radio broke into his reflections.

The radio announcer was mocking the Americans at this point in the broadcast. This blackened Brehme's mood further. History would repeat itself; he was sure. No country could take on the British Empire, Russia and the United States and expect to win.

His thoughts turned to the Edelweiss Pirates. He doubted they had much, if any, presence in the town of Ladenburg. Of their political philosophy he knew little. This wasn't good enough. His curiosity was getting the better of him. He resolved to find out more.

At that same moment he realised, with some shock, that he would do as little as possible to hamper them in their programme. The enemy wasn't across the channel or the Atlantic Ocean. It was here, within. Sitting in power. Once more a wave of frustration engulfed him. He hated his own weakness. He wanted to act but knew not what he could do. But he had already started. The first act of rebellion always begins in the mind. Peter Brehme was about to embark on something his upbringing, his culture and his profession had trained him to abhor.

CHAPTER FOURTEEN

Tobruk, Libya, 23rd May 1942

'Good Lord,' said a voice just in front of Danny. 'Danny? Danny Shaw?'

Danny was lying on the beach alongside his brother Tom, and Bert Gissing. He looked up and saw a man standing over him. The man was silhouetted against the sun; the face was indistinct, but the voice was familiar. Danny shielded his eyes and slowly the features of the man took shape.

'Bloody hell,' laughed Danny. 'Dick.' Danny immediately leapt to his feet and shook hands with Dick Manning. 'Boys, this is Dick Manning. He was with the RAF.'

'Still with them as far as I know,' laughed the airman.

Introductions made, Manning sat down and filled in Danny on his movements since they'd last met.

'As you correctly surmised, I was sent to Malta last April. Incidentally, you know that Al Bowlly was killed soon after that show?'

'Yes,' said Danny sadly. There was silence for a moment, then the airman continued.

'Malta was quite a show. Not sure how I ever made it through. The Nazis chucked everything at us, Danny, and I mean everything. When I arrived, they slackened a bit. Russia, I think. Well, if that was their idea of slack then I'm jolly glad I wasn't there from the start. It felt like the Messerschmitts were attacking every day. But we were gradually building up our strength. More planes, more men. It meant we could fight back rather than take it on the chin; in fact, soon we were able to have a go at them and their convoys.'

'Thanks,' said Danny and meant it. They had heard of the devastating impact the RAF were having on enemy shipping.

'Of course, those German blighters weren't going to take this lying down and they came back at us. They had better planes than us.'

'Seems to be the way,' said Danny sourly. 'Their tanks are better, too.'

'Really? Well our Hurricanes were badly matched against their Messerschmitts and Stukas. They hit us hard last summer. We were reeling for a while, but when the Spitfires arrived in March, we gave them something to think about. With Spitfires, we're more than a match for Jerry. Unfortunately, they kept bombing the planes on the ground. Thankfully more Spits have arrived. The tide's turning.'

'When did you come over?' asked Danny.

'Yesterday,' laughed Manning. 'I thought I'd relax a little. I think I've earned it.'

'Sounds like you've earned a beer,' pointed out Bert.

'Best idea I've heard in a while,' grinned Manning.

By early evening, Danny was back at the leaguer eight miles north of Bir Hacheim. He was heartened by the arrival of some new tanks. Over a dozen Grants and another ten Stuarts sat proudly waiting for their new owners. The Grants still gave Danny some cause for worry, but they were at least an improvement. He spied Arthur amongst the bunch of men examining them.

'What do you think?' asked Danny, looking at the new arrivals.

'Not much,' said Arthur who was world weary of these things at the best of times. 'I mean, do they think that Jerry just comes at us head on? I'd have loved for one of the eggheads who designs these things to come and spend a day fighting. They'd buck up their ideas pretty sharpish, I suspect.'

The conversation around the tanks suggested the men were of a similar mind. It quietened a little when two officers appeared and then the posture of the men straightened when they realised who it was.

Lieutenant-Colonel 'Pip' Roberts had seen the crews looking around the new arrivals and went over to hear their thoughts. He tapped the front of the first Grant with his stick.

'What do you think, Cyril?' said Roberts to Major Cyril Joly.

'You know what I think,' replied Joly. Danny noticed Joly motion with his eyes towards the men. Roberts smiled and nodded. He turned to the men.

'We'll put these through their paces tomorrow,' he announced to the men. 'I think the enemy will find these a tougher prospect than what they've faced until now.'

Danny had to admire the way the colonel was putting a brave face on some of the obvious limitations. He noticed that Major Joly was less sphinx-like in this regard.

'Any thoughts, men?'

No one wanted to be seen as a bellyacher, so the comments were confined to appreciating that they had, at least, a gun that could match the German Panzer. Joly was studying the men more closely

117

as they spoke. His eyes fixed on Danny. Perhaps it was something on Danny's face but when the men had finished Joly spoke up.

'What do you think…?'

'Shaw, sir.'

'Shaw. Do you share these opinions?'

Danny found himself reddening a little as all eyes turned towards him. Out of the corner of his eye he saw a grin erupt over the face of Arthur. Unseen by the officers, Arthur nudged him in the ribs.

'Well, sir, I think the Grant is an improvement on what we've had. As the men say, the gun means we can take a pop at the Panzers from the same distance. They won't like that. Of course, this assumes that they come at us head on. It's not always the case, though, as we know.'

Joly and Roberts were both nodding thoughtfully.

'But that's not the biggest issue.'

Danny noticed Arthur suddenly spin his head round. This was obviously going to be a new one on him.

'Careful, Danny boy,' said Arthur in a stage whisper so bad that it might have been heard in Cairo. The group laughed at this, including the two officers.

'Go on, Shaw,' said Roberts. 'Don't worry, we need to know these things. It might save lives.'

Danny turned to the Grant and stepped backwards. If Arthur had been surprised by Danny's tone before, he was now close to shock. All eyes followed Danny as he continued stepping backwards and looking along the line of tanks. He pointed to one of the Stuarts further up the line.

'If you look at the Stuart and then compare it to the Grant, you'll see that it's quite a bit shorter. Now that's all very well for me although it'll make no odds to a short arse like Arthur here.'

118

The soldiers and the two officers erupted into laughter at this, none more so than Arthur although not before he had pronounced Danny a 'cheeky git'.

Roberts and Joly glanced at one another.

'I think I see what you're saying, Shaw,' said the lieutenant-colonel. 'You're concerned about our ability to hide hull-down on a ridge.'

'Yes, sir, the top of the Grant is going to stick out like a sore thumb. We'll lose the element of surprise and give the Panzers a nice target to aim at. Don't get me wrong, it's wonderful to be able to lob a few fourteen-pound shells in Jerry's direction but next time can you ask the powers that be to stick the big gun in the turret and have done with it?'

'I shall tell them personally what Private Shaw thinks.'

Danny laughed good-naturedly along with the rest of the men. The two officers departed leaving Danny at the mercy of a dozen berets slapping him around the head, none harder than Arthur. He was laughing too much to care.

The laughing stopped a few moments later as they heard aircraft overhead. Silence fell as a couple of dozen eyes peered up into the sky nervously. Two planes came into view.

'Messerschmitts,' said one man.

The two planes were not accompanied by any others. They posed no threat at the height they were flying. Danny relaxed a little. The two planes were a reminder that the training over the last few weeks was for a purpose. The number of these reconnaissance flights by the enemy had increased. They were coming again. The warmer weather heralded the return of the war. Danny exchanged glances with Arthur. His friend's face was taut.

'Let's get a cup of tea,' said Arthur.

The next day was the 24th of May. Danny was assigned to a new tank. Whether it was because of his comments the previous day or some form of divine retribution, he was in one of the Grants. He smiled ruefully as Arthur cackled away at the news and confirmed his previously well-hidden belief in the existence of the Divine.

The Grant, unlike the Stuart, could host seven people although six could operate it if need be. The larger hull just about managed to incorporate the extra bodies. Danny was handed the role of gunner on the seventy-five-millimetre gun. He and another new arrival, Angus McLeish, walked together to their new tank. They were greeted by the commander, Captain Benson, who introduced them to the crew.

'Men, this is Private Shaw, and Private McLeish. They are joining us from today. As you'll have gathered, this chap is all a bit new for us too,' said Benson, slapping the Grant like it was an old friend he'd just shared a joke with. 'We've been using the Stuart up until now. Shaw will be our gunner on this big chap here.'

Benson put his hand on the seventy-five-millimetre cannon, then added, 'I think, McLeish, it makes sense for you to be the loader.'

McLeish was a year younger than Danny and had arrived the previous month. Taller than Danny he was all skin, bones and acne; he seemed pleased to be on the big gun albeit as a loader.

'This is Wodehouse, no relation to the writer. He's the driver. We call him "PG" although I gather his first name is Sebastian. I think he prefers PG.'

'I do,' confirmed the burly Yorkshireman. His face was round, but he certainly did not seem in any way jolly. Danny recognised this face. It was one worn by the veterans of the last year who'd faced superior weaponry, who'd lost friends and who knew the job was far from over. A cigarette was permanently hung from his lower lip like a swear word. It stayed there from breakfast until bedtime. He smoked like a factory town.

'PG is our mechanic when we're adrift from the echelon. Next up we have Archie Andrews, our gunner who'll be with me in the turret.'

Andrews was a tall, lean corporal. He wore a thin moustache and greeted Danny with a welcoming smile.

'Good to have you on board,' said Andrews. His clipped voice surprised Danny as it was more like that of an officer than a man in the ranks.

'Young Billy Thompson here' – continued Benson indicating a boy who looked like he should have been in a school classroom – 'is a recent arrival to this show. We're showing him the ropes and he is Archie's loader for the thirty-seven-millimetre.'

A young man appeared from behind the Grant. He wore spectacles and Danny suspected, given their thickness, he was as blind as a bat. Loader would be the summit of his roles in this war.

'Finally, we have Sid Gregson who operates communications and is our very own Kit Carson. He can navigate by the stars.'

'When he can see them,' pointed out Andrews, much to everyone's amusement.

Gregson was somewhere between thirty and fifty. Like most young people, Danny's ability to differentiate age for someone older diminished when the person was older than thirty. Gregson seemed friendly but was quite reserved. He was, though, something of an electronics whizz. This, along with an interest in astronomy, were his sole topics of conversation. He kept himself to himself.

Introductions made, everyone climbed into the cabin to familiarise themselves with their new home. This wasn't as novel an experience now for Danny. He'd ridden inside the Grant before, like all the

121

others, and been given instructions on how it operated. They were all the same in Danny's view: cramped, hot and smelly. Having two additional bodies in the hull, albeit a larger one, was unlikely to make things any more comfortable.

It remained to be seen if the new Grant would be safer. The fifty-one-millimetre-thick armour was welcome. It would give good protection from long-range fire. In combination with the bigger gun, it meant that the Panzers would have to get closer to give them trouble. Of course, the more powerful anti-tank guns such as the eighty-eight-millimetre would always be a danger. However, tank on tank, they could now outpunch the enemy.

The men hopped down from the turret and took up their positions. Danny made his way past the driver's seat to the right and settled into the gunner's seat. McLeish pushed past him to his seat.

'Not much room,' commented Danny as he ducked his head slightly to avoid bumping it for a third time. He glanced over at the driver's seat.

'How do you get out if we brew up, PG?'

'I'll climb over you,' came the terse reply.

'How many machine guns does one tank need?' asked Danny. He was looking at the trigger PG was examining and already noted the gun in the turret.

Benson's voice from above answered Danny's question.

'Americans seem to put machine guns everywhere they can as far as I can see. Bloody waste of space if you ask me.'

'Not much of a traverse on this. Let's hope they don't attack us from the side,' said Danny.

McLeish then spoke up. 'Are these shells German?' He was looking at the AP Armour Piercing shells. 'They have German writing.'

Danny laughed as did Benson up in the turret.

'The American AP shells shatter on impact. Total rubbish. We use captured German shells instead. They work better.' At this point Danny was looking through the telescope. 'Don't think much of this scope. How am I supposed to be accurate with five-hundred-yard increments?'

'Best guess then burst and adjust,' responded Archie Andrews laughing.

'I hope Jerry gives us time to do that,' said Danny sourly.

'There's loads of storage for the thirty-seven's shells,' said McLeish. 'Not much for ours, Danny.'

'You're kidding,' replied Danny. He wasn't happy at hearing this.

He heard Archie Andrews chuckle. 'Sorry old boy. Thirty-seven takes precedence still.'

Danny grinned up at Andrews. 'You won't say that when Mark IVs begin pasting us from a thousand yards.'

'Shaw will have taken him out by then, Archie, right?' chipped in Benson. 'Hurry up, PG, and get this crate moving. We'll be late for the exercises.'

The engine kicked into life at first time of asking. Danny raised his eyebrow at this and grinned. He looked up at Andrews who was also smiling. For all their sniffiness about some aspects of the Grant, the one common tribute paid by all who had used it was its reliability. In this regard, it was far superior to what had gone before. In battle, engine reliability was as much a part of their chances of survival as the armour or the weapons; it really could be the difference between life and death.

Benson sat on the cupola and gazed out across the flat plain. Instinct made him look up. A slight disturbance in the atmosphere. Something that could barely be heard. Then a few dark specks appeared in the sky.

'Our friends are back,' he announced on his mic.

'Say "hello" for me, sir,' replied Andrews. 'You know how.'

Benson offered a uniquely British wave to the six Messerschmitts that flew past.

'They're gearing up for something,' he said before murmuring more to himself, 'I just hope we've time to get used to this tin.'

CHAPTER FIFTEEN

Eight miles north of Bir Hacheim, Libya, 26th May 1942

Lieutenant-Colonel 'Pip' Roberts studied the faces of the men in front of him. He was framed by a large map of Libya mounted on a makeshift easel. He'd barely referred to it during the briefing for the simple reason he didn't know where the Germans were at that moment. However, his senses were tingling. Standing alongside him was his adjutant, Captain Peter Burr. Seated in front of him were the senior officers under his command. Looking at the faces of his majors, Joly, Hutton, Strange and Witheridge, he felt some comfort.

All the other captains stood behind the senior officers. Two of them, Shattock and Benson, he noticed, were sharing a joke. He wasn't sure they would be in such a good mood twenty-four hours from now. His skin always prickled when he sensed something in the air. It felt prickly now.

'Bletchley's Ultra unit have been picking up traffic for days now that the Germans are going to spring an attack. We don't know where or when, but they've been saying it could happen any time now. I think they're right. I can feel it. More than that, I have a gut feeling that Jerry will attack tomorrow. Everyone is to be up at one hour before first light and we'll take up the battle formation I reconnoitred a few days ago. Get a good night's sleep. That's all.'

A few hours later, Roberts was shaken gently at first then more forcefully from his sleep. It took a few moments for his eyes to adjust to the harsh light from the torch. Captain Peter Burr, Roberts' adjutant, looked down at his commanding officer.

'Yes, what is it, Burr? Bad news?'

'Yes, sir. You were right; they're on the move.'

'What time is it?'

Burr glanced at his watch. 'After three, sir.' He didn't have to add, 'in the morning'.

Roberts sat up in the bed and rubbed his eyes. He focused on his adjutant and asked, 'Where are they now?'

'Heading south, sir. They've turned off the Trigh Capuzzo and our best guess is they are making for Bir Hacheim.'

'Remind me what we have there?' Roberts was still in the process of waking from his sleep.

'4th Armoured, sir. Not all of it,' came the reply.

'Against?'

'The 15th and 21st Panzer armies, we believe. Basically the whole of the Afrika Korps. Perhaps some Italians, too.'

'How the hell did our intelligence miss a bloody big army moving in this direction? They've had planes flying over us for days now. Even Ultra at Bletchley knew something was in the offing.'

'The men are ready, sir.'

'At least we made sure of that,' replied Roberts jumping out of his camp bed. He was already dressed. Then he stopped for a moment.

Just how ready were they? The answer to this question was barely a few hours away. He cast aside any anxiety he was feeling.

'Very well, let's give Jerry the welcome he deserves.'

If there's one thing less pleasant than having to wake up early when in the middle of a deep sleep, it's waking up early when you've barely managed to sleep at all. It had been one of those nights for Danny and he was distinctly displeased. Just a few weeks of camp and he knew that he'd softened a little.

At least he was no longer the junior member of the crew and therefore designated brew master. That honour went to the Scotsman, McLeish. It was still dark, and the leaguer was alive with the sound of shouting, some laughter and even some engines being tested.

Danny wondered if the earlier start was significant. He'd noticed that Captain Benson had been quite tight-lipped the previous night after the senior staff meeting. No one had asked why but the looks around the crew all suggested they'd also noticed the sombre mood of the commander.

Benson wasn't around for breakfast which added to the sense that something was in the offing. There was just a hint of distant rumbling in the air. Danny felt his skin tingle as he considered the reasons for this.

'What's happening, sir?' asked Danny when he saw Benson finally return. Behind him the regiment was already beginning to depart. What had started off as an early start was unquestionably something more now. Benson's face was grim.

'The enemy has made a long march through the night. We believe they are not very many miles away.'

This revelation, while hardly a surprise, was still enough to provoke a few colourful reactions from the men around the campfire. Benson allowed them to let off steam for a minute before raising his hand for silence.

'I think we can be fairly certain the show is starting again. We'll see action soon. Very soon, I suspect, if that sound in the distance is anything to go by. Just remember a few things. You've been training for this over the last few months. You are ready. We also have something that Jerry is not expecting.'

Benson glanced towards the big Grant.

'No longer are we outmatched by superior armour. This time we're the ones with the better tanks. If we use our advantage, we can inflict a lot of damage on Jerry today. Enough to make him stop and think.'

Danny listened and felt heartened by what he was hearing. The misgivings he'd had about the Grant began to recede as he considered the possibility that it was better than what they were up against. How true this was didn't matter at that moment. Benson had shrewdly guessed that the sudden arrival of the enemy was likely to put the wind up everyone a little. His words not only provided badly needed solace, they instilled, once more, a belief that this time they would be the hunter.

There was a muffled hum in the camp: the sound of men trying not to make too much noise and not quite succeeding. Despite the darkness, everyone was up but there seemed to be no real sense of urgency which confused Danny. He inquired of Benson why they weren't upping sticks and engaging the enemy. Benson held his hands up in the universally recognised symbol of 'search me'.

'Eat your breakfast. We'll be mixing it soon enough. I suspect the powers that be haven't quite decided if this is a feint or the big push.'

Danny nodded. It made sense. Rommel was well known for just this sort of artifice. He spied five men walking away from the camp carrying spades. They came rushing back seconds later when the shouts started. It was just after seven. The mad scramble had begun.

They gulped down their breakfast as they raced for their tents. The sound of engines growing louder in the distance added a certain alacrity to finishing their meal. It made the arrival of three sergeants, shouting at everyone, an irrelevance. Everyone could hear the enemy now. An ominous deep rumbling on the horizon. It sent a chill through Danny. He threw on his overcoat and scarf and rushed to pack up the tents.

The sun was up now, and reports were filtering through from the Light Squadron who'd set off earlier. They were a mile ahead of the main group and had sighted dust on the horizon. A lot of dust. They were barely ten minutes away.

'Talk about leaving it to the last minute,' commented Sid Gregson on the radio.

As there were two radios in the tank, Danny was able to hear much of what was going on thanks to Gregson. They both listened in on the wireless which was now giving a running commentary on events up ahead.

'Jerry has overrun Bir Hacheim,' said Gregson grimly. 'Doesn't sound good.'

'How the hell did they do that?' asked PG, echoing Danny's thoughts. He fought back a wave of nausea. It was always a battle to fight back the sickening thought that the Afrika Korps was just better tank on tank, leader on leader, man on man. They seemed always to be one step ahead. Once more the swiftness of their strike had caught the Allies off guard. Danny's heart began to race as the tank rolled ever closer to this extraordinary army. For the first time in months, he felt fear. His senses were waking up from the torpor of inactivity. Danny now had enough experience to recognise that fear wasn't just an ever-present companion in the desert. It was a friend, too. It gave his survival instincts the impetus to act and the mental, physical and spiritual resources to keep going.

It was now after seven in the morning and more news was coming through. None of it good. The B echelon had been overrun and captured. This meant a lot of fuel and supplies would now be in the enemy's hands.

Roberts' calm voice crackled on the wireless. 'Move to battle position Larwood.' Danny looked over to PG who ignored him. Gregson smiled and mouthed 'south-west'. They trundled on towards a rumbling sound that was no longer just engines. The battle was underway.

Major Hutton's voice came over the radio.

'Sighted the enemy. Must be over one hundred tanks. Three thousand yards away.'

'Definitely not friends?' asked Roberts although he knew the answer.

'No, not friends, sir.'

'I can see them now,' said Roberts. 'Good lord, some of them are sitting outside on top, cool as you please.'

Burr now reported to their column, 'Yes, one hundred tanks. Twenty abreast, at least five rows of them. Make that six. Sorry, no. Bloody hell, there are eight rows of the devils. Must be two hundred of them out there.'

Danny's heart sank at hearing this. Whatever advantage they had with Grant, a new, potentially insurmountable, problem faced them. They were badly outnumbered.

'Do not open fire until they are one zero, zero, zero yards. I think hull-down is out of the question,' warned Roberts. His voice betrayed no nerves.

'Must be two hundred tanks,' said Hutton in a tone that was clearly awed. 'Two thousand yards now and closing.'

'Right, B and C squadrons take up battle line on the ridge three hundred yards in front. B Squadron right, C squadron left. Wait for my order, mind.'

Danny could see what Roberts was thinking. The B and C squadrons were composed of the Grants. They could take a pop at the Panzers from further out.

'That leaves you, A Squadron,' said Roberts. 'Can you move to protect our right flank? And keep in touch with the 8th Hussars whatever you do. They're around there somewhere. I don't want you or them, for that matter, firing at us. Are those blasted twenty-five pounders here yet, by the way?'

Danny looked through his telescope. The Panzers were advancing ominously towards them. He glanced down at PG. He still had his viewing flap opened. He was eating a biscuit.

'Want some tea?' asked Danny.

PG turned around and looked at him. Then he did something that surprised Danny. He grinned. This was the first time he'd seen the Yorkshireman smile in the few days since they'd been thrown together. Cool devil, thought Danny.

Roberts spoke again. 'We will contact our friends on the left. No one fire until I give the order. Off.'

Give the bloody order, thought Danny nervously. He motioned to McLeish to load. He pointed to the AP Armour Piercing shells. Moments later Benson spoke to them on the internal radio.

'Ready, Shaw? Give them all you've got when the order comes through.'

'Yes, sir.' In Danny's mind he could see where the Panzers would be. Their regiment had done exercises over this vast salt plain. He looked through the telescope again. All he could see in the distance was a shimmering haze. Nothing was distinct. Yet they were there. The nerve-shredding rumble of their engines made the lack of visibility even more terrifying. Danny's stomach was now in knots at the ominous rattle of the approaching tanks.

'Bloody hell,' said Benson. He was still sitting on top of the cupola scanning the horizon with his binoculars.

Danny squinted but could see nothing. The sun reflected off the haze and temporarily made his eyes water. He rubbed them and returned his attention to what was in the distance. Then he saw them. His heart lurched. In just the blink of an eye, the dark shapes had emerged as if from a malevolent mirage. They were spread out across three miles of desert like a black cloud. The sight was awe-inspiring and terrifying in equal measure.

A flash caught Danny's eye as he looked through his telescope. Then he heard a series of crumps. All along the line of Panzers there were puffs of black smoke. PG slowly shut his flap as if he was trying to keep out the rain.

'Pick your target, Shaw. Archie, you wait until I give the order. They're still a bit too far,' said Benson slowly. He had now taken the eminently sensible, in Danny's view, precaution of ducking into the turret.

Moments later, the air around the tank was torn apart with explosions. Danny's thumb hovered over the firing button. When would Roberts issue the order to fire? At this rate they would all be...

'Hello Cambrai, Cambrai calling. Fire now!' ordered Roberts.

132

CHAPTER SIXTEEN

South-west of El Cherima, Libya, Night of 26th/27th May 1942

Twelve hours earlier

'Venezia.'

A single instruction saw the two Panzer divisions begin the long march towards battle. Manfred looked at his watch. It was 2030. He was wrapped up in an overcoat and happy to be on the move. Even the short break of a few hours was long enough for the cold to begin slowly infiltrating his bones.

'At last,' he said. The commander, Lieutenant Basler, overheard him. He smiled grimly at his gunner.

'What's your rush?'

'I'm cold,' said Manfred truthfully.

As much to himself as to Manfred, the former SS officer murmured, 'Things will heat up soon, I suspect.'

They were to drive through the night with perhaps one stop.

Manfred glanced down at their driver Horst Klein. His would be the most difficult job. Driving at night was always a fraught affair. The driver could not let his concentration slip for a moment. In front of him, and behind, were tanks. Behind them were the vehicles of the support echelon. Over ten thousand vehicles were on the move. The last thing they needed was a collision. The commander had to keep alert throughout and guide the driver. They worked in tandem to ensure their safe passage through the night.

The march would take them seventy-five kilometres from the Trigh Capuzzo road to their destination. The plan was to circle around the Allied box at Bir Hacheim. Thanks to the sandstorms they had endured over the previous few days, the extent of the attack would be a major surprise for their enemy. It was a comfort of sorts for Manfred who was still itching damnably from the sand that had set up home in his clothing. The element of surprise always came at a cost, reflected Manfred ruefully.

Manfred moved about continually in his seat trying to gain some relief from the prickly feeling of the sand. He noticed Basler smiling grimly at his constant fidgeting. The lieutenant knew exactly what he was experiencing. He was covered in sand himself.

'Be thankful you're not exhausted and in need of a bed,' commented Basler, wryly.

'True, it could be worse,' agreed Manfred in a wearied voice.

Manfred craved sleep. He closed his eyes for a moment then opened them with a start. He would not allow himself the luxury of rest. Beside him, Basler was enduring the cold without complaint and forcing himself to stay alert to the movement of the convoy around him. But both were exhausted in a way that was almost tangible.

'You should sleep if you can,' said Basler. 'Then take over from me after we stop.'

Manfred didn't need to be told twice. Despite the cold, the noise, his discomfort with the sand, sleep came easily. It was over, seemingly, within seconds. In fact, three hours or more had passed, much to Manfred's surprise.

The entire army had stopped for refuelling. This meant a check on all vehicles: air filters, guns and tracks. It allowed time for some food and coffee. Although he'd only had a short sleep, Manfred felt refreshed and alert after his second coffee. The stop lasted close to an hour and a half. He held a light for Horst Klein as he dismantled the filter to clean it. This was a requirement after every fifty kilometres of travel.

By 0230 in the morning they were back on the march. Manfred sat in Basler's position. Any anxiety about the battle ahead was replaced by the very real fear that he would be responsible for an accident. He kept his eyes firmly fixed towards the vehicle ahead and the oil drums at the side of the road in which lights had been placed by the advance party to guide the way of the main convoy. Gerd Kleff, Manfred's loader, was tasked with cleaning the guns. The sand and dust had built up in them at a phenomenal rate. They could not afford for any blockages to impair performance, especially with the possibility of direct contact with infantry and tanks in a matter of hours.

They drove at a speed that would have made a tortoise impatient. For three seemingly endless hours they crawled along. Metre by metre they closed in on the enemy. Reports were coming through of sightings of scout vehicles from the South African Armoured Car Regiment. They had been a frequent companion over the last few months. The memory of their treatment of him when he was captured, as well as the bravery with which they fought against overwhelming odds on Tottensontag, was a cold reminder of the hard fighting that lay ahead.

Manfred was almost happy to see the first signs of light appearing on the horizon. Notwithstanding the proximity to the enemy, he was simply glad to be finished with the disorientating effects of darkness, the wearying need to stay concentrated on the road ahead. Now the tanks ahead were easily visible. With the first light, Basler replaced him in the cupola and Manfred resumed his position beneath him at the gun.

With the arrival of the daylight, the Panzer convoy began to change its formation into one that they employed when they made their frontal attack. Basler stayed up top, much to Manfred's surprise. Contact with the enemy would happen soon. He looked through his periscope. The Panzers were now side by side. Around forty metres separated them. Up ahead, inevitably, was Captain Kummel. Alongside him was their new commander, Lieutenant-Colonel Teege, leading the metal armada over the sand sea. For a moment Manfred wondered what it must be like to be in the enemy's shoes and see such a formidable sight. He didn't envy them.

The heat in the cabin had increased dramatically with the rise of the sun. Visibility began to deteriorate as the horizon became a shimmering mirage which affected the eyes the longer you stared at it. The radio crackled with news that some British positions were being overrun. Clearly, despite the company of the South African scouts, some element of surprise had been gained. The enemy were out there. But where?

Then Manfred heard it.

'Tanks,' warned Kummel. 'Three kilometres ahead.'

Manfred gazed through the lens of his periscope. It took another minute before the dark shapes began to speckle the glistening haze. It was difficult at first to pick out what he was seeing and then he knew. The high turret could only be the new tank they'd been hearing rumours of. It was American, like so many of the British tanks. Basler ducked into the turret and confirmed the suspicion that they were facing a new

136

type of tank. The order to attack would come from Kummel.

A nod from Kleff and a shell was loaded into their fifty-one-millimetre cannon. After what seemed an eternity, the order came.

'Fire.'

Perspiration dripped down Manfred's face as he pressed the button. He scored a hit and was about to celebrate when, with some dismay, he saw that his shell had bounced off the front armour of the Grant. Angered by this and now somewhat closer, he told Kleff to keep loading.

Manfred fired again. Dismay turned to horror when he saw his shell shatter ineffectively once more. Basler had seen the same. His face was grim.

'I don't like this,' said the lieutenant. Nor did Manfred. He wondered why the British weren't firing back. They were now around a kilometre away. Suddenly, the camouflage was discarded and they could see the Grants more clearly. He saw the flashes and then the puffs of smoke emerge from the ridge. If it was true that they had a seventy-five-millimetre gun, then the Panzers would be well within their range.

Shells were striking the ground all around them throwing up plumes of dust and dirt. This was worrying. Previously they hadn't had this sort of range. Moments later a tank just to the left of Manfred exploded. Yet another of Manfred's shells bounced harmlessly off the Grant. Smoke and dust now shrouded Manfred's view, but the radio traffic was intense.

'We need artillery,' called Kummel to Teege.

'I hear you,' came Teege's reply.

'Get closer!' ordered Kummel. The realisation that they were outgunned lent an edge to the captain's voice.

'I'm coming with the 2nd Battalion,' said Teege, realising that they needed to assist Kummel who was drawing most of the enemy fire. The 2nd Battalion, according to Gerhardt, was aiming to hit the Allies from their flank. It sounded like they were finally in position. Not a moment too soon.

The smoke cleared enough for Manfred to see Kummel up ahead. His Mark IV was moving fast but also weaving. Manfred could imagine the effort that Hubbuch was putting in to avoid getting hit. Just to his left he could see Horst Klein twisting his steering like a boxer trying to avoid his opponent's lunges.

Manfred's heart leapt when he saw the first of the British tanks erupt into flames. The 2nd Battalion were beginning to make their presence felt. Emboldened by this success, Manfred redoubled his efforts to score a hit. They were now close enough to do some damage. And he was. His next effort, with an AP Armour Piercing shell, penetrated the tank.

'HE shells,' ordered Manfred. The High Explosive shells would strike panic into the British. Already half a dozen of their Grants were in flames. He didn't want to think about the toll being extracted on the 1st Battalion.

The shelling from the British began to lessen. Initially, Manfred thought this was because the British, aware of the attack on their flanks, were spreading their fire more widely. Then Kummel's voice came over the radio.

'They're pulling back,' said the captain. There was a hint of relief in his voice, thought Manfred. Through the haze and the giant smoke pillars, Manfred could see over half a dozen British tanks motionless. Smoking. Dead.

They slowed down while they passed one crew after another abandoning their smoking Mark IIIs. They hopped onto the front of Manfred's tank. Ahead they could see the last of the Allies escaping.

Kummel ordered a halt. This was unlikely to last long so Manfred took the opportunity to climb out and stretch his legs. The sight that greeted him was shocking.

The British had been on the receiving end of a fearful beating but so too had the Afrika Korps. The field was littered with the smoking hulks of the Panzers. They'd won the initial engagement but at a great cost.

Basler and the other commanders from the 1st Battalion convened around Kummel who was busy reorganising them. Manfred recognised the intense focus of the captain and the urgency with which he was giving directions. They would not let the Allies escape, that much was clear. Basler returned a few minutes later and spoke to the crew.

'We don't know how many we've lost but clearly this new tank of the British is capable of outgunning us. So we must get close. Kummel looked at the new tank. It has a seventy-five-millimetre gun, but it is fixed to the sponson. They can't move side to side. If we attack from the side, they have problems. Our orders are to head north in pursuit of what's left of this regiment.'

Manfred couldn't stop his eyes shifting to the decimated tanks littering the field. Basler glared at Manfred.

'Do you have a problem with this, Brehme?' asked the lieutenant abruptly.

Manfred shifted on his feet and felt like a schoolboy caught out by the teacher.

'No, sir,' said Manfred. He paused then added, 'But next time, can we attack them from the flank?'

All the crew laughed except Basler. There was just a hint of amusement in his eyes. They all recognised that something had changed. The Mark III and even the Mark IV was up against something just as deadly. The Allies were beginning to learn from their mistakes. They had made major strides in narrowing the gap between the respective tanks. Even their tactic of digging in and picking off the Panzers had been more coherent than before. The Panzers had simply overpowered them by sheer weight of numbers. In the first battle this was possible. But a month from now would they still have the men and the armour to do this?

The crew returned to their tanks and the camp echoed to the sounds of engines coughing to life again. Whatever Basler's reaction to Manfred's question, it was clear that the lieutenant had something on his mind. He sat brooding in the cupola without saying anything more to the crew.

'Now you've done it,' whispered Klein. The chubby Rhinelander's features broke into a grin.

Manfred shrugged. He was glad he'd said what he'd said. The world hadn't ended. Basler understood because he would have been smart enough to realise that attacking such tanks head on was suicidal. The early morning sun was turning the cabin into an oven. A long, difficult day lay ahead. Fear gripped him again as they set off in pursuit of the enemy.

CHAPTER SEVENTEEN

Five miles north-east of Bir Hacheim, Libya, 27th May 1942

'Just too many of them,' murmured Benson. He looked shaken but his features hardened quickly as he regained his composure. Danny glanced at the captain. He'd been speaking to himself although he'd voiced the thoughts of every man in the crew. The German advance had been halted temporarily but they risked being picked off by the overwhelming numbers they faced.

'We need to withdraw,' added Benson. 'If we can get them to follow us, we should be able to take them within range of our guns.'

Why aren't these guns used as a screen for the tanks, thought Danny? Have we learned nothing from fighting the Afrika Korps? Instead, the new six-pound guns were dug in at several well-defended boxes in the rear. Fat lot of use they were there. What Danny had seen worried him. The sheer weight of numbers would be like trying to hold back a metal tide.

An hour later the battle was joined again. It was no less ferocious.

Lieutenant-Colonel Pip Roberts was viewing the advance of the Panzers with increasing alarm. Outwardly he remained calm, but he'd been shocked by the intensity of the battle. Wave after wave of enemy tanks was advancing. They were taking many casualties yet still they drove forward. Shell and shot sliced the air around them. Roberts could even hear the twenty-five-pound guns hitting the Germans from some distant box.

But it wasn't going to be enough. The regiment would be wiped out if they stayed where they were. All around him he could see the devastating impact wrought by the Panzers. It was only a small comfort to see a similar tale in the burning hulks impeding the advance of the enemy.

'It's no use,' he said to Peter Burr, his adjutant. 'We knock out one tank and another takes its place. They're still coming. We can only slow them down, but they'll wipe us out at this rate. Tell Brigade that we can't hang on much longer. We'll either have nothing left or we'll be cut off.'

'Yes, sir,' replied Burr and immediately got on the radio to communicate the message.

The commander of 'C' Squadron, Major Cyril Joly, came on the radio to Roberts.

'We need to withdraw, sir. We're almost out of ammo.' Joly neglected to mention that he was wounded, that his tank had sustained around twenty-five hits and was now barely operable.

The air was stained with smoke and the smell of cordite. Roberts knew he couldn't wait much longer. There was no sign of support coming from the Fifth Royal Tank Regiment.

'Yes, understood. Withdraw. Good luck,' replied Roberts.

On the right-hand side of the ridge, the commander of 'B' Squadron, Major George Witheridge, spoke next to Roberts.

'Three tanks still firing, sir. Ammo low. Three others still operable but out of ammo.'

'There must be twenty tanks knocked out over there. Good work. We need to reorganise, George. Withdraw now. Reverse slowly for a quarter of a mile, then we'll dash for the higher ground.'

As he said this, they were rocked by a hit to the front armour. He nodded down to the driver and they, too, began to withdraw. He looked over to Peter Burr. 'Tell Brigade we need ammo. Fast. Get the ammo lorries to meet us at the rallying point.'

A shaken Peter Burr acknowledged the lieutenant-colonel and turned to the radio. His voice remained calm as they received a parting hit from a shell. It bounced off.

Danny glanced towards McLeish. The young man held his arms out. This required no explanation. The young Scot's shirt was like a wet flannel, his face glistening with sweat, fatigue and something else: pride. Danny nodded to him then turned to Benson and said, 'We're out of ammo, sir.'

Benson's body seemed to go limp for a moment, then he straightened and glanced towards Archie Andrews.

'Archie?'

'Three shells left.'

'Hold fire in case we need them. PG, we need to get to the rally point. Fast. Turn around. I can't see any Jerry following us.'

'Can you see anything, McLeish?'

'My periscope is smashed, sir,' replied the young Scotsman.

PG managed to swing them round and they drove forward at nearly fifteen miles per hour towards the rally point. Danny and the others were soaked in sweat. It was mid-morning and the sun was slowly turning their metal home into an oven.

The fear that Danny had felt prior to facing the Germans had evaporated during the fight. His survival instinct had overcome the terror. For the short engagement, his whole being was engaged and mobilised towards one purpose: destroying the approaching enemy. Now he felt some of the nervousness return. The battle had been a whirl. He'd not paused to think. Instead, the training had kicked in: his mind and body had fused with the tank. It wasn't until they were pulling back that he realised how much he'd blocked from his mind.

The scream of the shells, the hits to their armour, the reports of the destroyed tanks, the news of those who had probably been killed. They had all been circulating in the air around Danny. He'd forced them from his mind. But he'd heard everything. His body felt like it had absorbed all the hits they'd received. Somehow, almost against any rational odds, they'd survived. But they'd come so close to suffering the same fate as so many other crews. He began to shake a little. Just ahead of him, McLeish was also shaking. The delayed shock to what they'd undergone finally overcame him. Danny touched McLeish's arm.

'Well done, there,' said Danny to the young Scot.

The Scotsman smiled back and seemed to stop shaking. Danny felt better for having spoken to McLeish.

'Does it get any easier?' asked McLeish.

Danny laughed and said no. If anything, it was worse. The knowledge that you'd survived was a comfort only until you realised that you would soon have to face the same hell all over again. To his credit, McLeish laughed, too. Danny liked him. He was no older in years but much older in experience than the Glaswegian. Danny could see already that he had a genuine grit about him like so many of the Scottish battalions he'd heard about.

They rumbled forward at speed, the tracks crushing the rock into sand. The news from the other squadrons sounded grim. They'd slowed

144

the enemy advance. At a cost. Benson, noted Danny, was quiet. The noise of shelling had receded, and he finally risked putting his head outside the cupola. Within a few seconds he was back inside.

'Bloody hell,' exclaimed the captain. 'There's a band of enemy tanks heading this way. Gregson, tell the CO to avoid the rallying point. We can't fight them without ammo. Archie, traverse right.'

Gregson communicated the sighting of the enemy; then Roberts' calm voice came over the radio of the remaining tanks from the three squadrons.

'Enemy tanks spotted at rallying point. Ignore previous order. Withdraw four miles north-east to pre-arranged point.'

Danny frowned a question to PG which the big driver took to mean, correctly, where are we going?

'Three miles south of El Adem. Brigade HQ has moved there. It's just west of Sidi Rezegh.'

Danny didn't need to be reminded of where El Adem was. His heart sank as he thought of the battle that had been fought over the airfield just a few months previously. They were back there; this time they were on the run. It was demoralising. He thought again of Phil Lawrence, burned alive. His sacrifice had been utterly in vain.

Benson's voice provided a welcome interruption. 'The enemy don't seem to be chasing us, thank God. If only they knew what our ammo situation was, they'd have been over here like a shot.'

Danny looked through his telescope but could see only an expanse of hilly rock and sand. He gave up and sat back against the warm metal wall of the Grant. No one spoke, each lost in their thoughts. Finally, Benson alerted them to the distant brigade HQ.

'Once we've loaded the new shells, give the tracks a check,' said Danny to McLeish.

Danny went up to the top and sat on the cupola with Benson. He could see dozens of vehicles in the distance. Five minutes later they joined the remaining tanks of the regiment. It was a sorry looking sight. Danny climbed down from the hull and made a circuit round to survey the impact made by the German shells. They'd been clanging against the armour like hailstones. The Grant had withstood quite a beating. He counted nearly twenty hits. Benson joined him and both quietly marvelled at the punishment they'd received.

'I'm glad I was in this beast and not one of the 'Honeys',' said Danny after a low whistle.

'Indeed,' agreed Benson who then went off in search of Roberts.

The brigade was full of noise and activity as the regiment went about the job of refuelling and re-arming. Danny helped McLeish load fresh shells into the cabin while Archie Andrews and Billy Thompson did likewise for their gun. Then Danny and McLeish carefully examined the tracks on one side of the tank while Andrews and Thompson inspected the other. At the back PG had his head buried in the engine to check for any damage. He shut the hatch door triumphantly and patted the Grant.

'Not so much as a dent.'

This was welcome news but elsewhere it was a depressing story. Only a handful of tanks remained from the regiment. A few were still operable and needed only re-arming and refuelling. Other tanks limped back and would need repair. One of those was Danny's squadron leader, Major Witheridge. Benson returned to the crew after a hastily convened conference with Witheridge.

'Right men, to the tank. Major Witheridge is taking over the ten remaining Grants. Major Joly is wounded. Captain Upcott-Gill will take over the six remaining Honeys. There's not a lot we can do to help the French at Bir Hacheim I'm afraid, and I think that some of echelon has been captured. The major thinks that Jerry will be fairly stretched now and perhaps there's a job to be done in attacking their supply lines. They'll be running low on fuel, too, and won't want to come too near our guns again. They know what to expect now.'

Danny took a deep breath and steeled himself as he climbed back inside the metal cabin. Increasingly he had to fight the feeling that this would be his coffin. Such thoughts were momentary, but they were also habitual. Once an idea takes root it becomes difficult to excise. To fight it constantly risked it becoming an obsession. Instead, Danny realised he had to live with the knowledge rather than fight it. He knew he shared this feeling with every man who'd ever stepped into a tank, or ever would, from either side. The fear would remain with them, an unwelcome companion, on every patrol, on every engagement, every, bloody, day.

CHAPTER EIGHTEEN

Bir Hacheim, Libya, 27th May 1942

'British Tanks straight ahead,' called Basler from the cupola. The tanks had appeared in view just as they emerged from behind a ridge. It was mid-afternoon and the chase of the British had resumed following a three-hour wait for fuel. Manfred had watched the 'Lion of Capuzzo', Kummel, living up to his name, pacing backwards and forwards like he was in a cage. Refuelling had been completed allowing the squadron to resume the chase. By then, news began to filter through that the British were harassing the supply echelon.

They drove for a few kilometres. A dust cloud in the distance prompted Manfred to check his telescope. Moments later Basler confirmed what Manfred could see: the enemy approaching. Not the new tank with the powerful gun but the less dangerous Stuart and some Crusaders.

'Distance is just under nine zero zero metres,' said Manfred.

'Fire when you're ready,' ordered Basler.

'Gerd, HE shells,' said Manfred to his loader. Kleff's sweat-soaked face made the barest hint of a nod. Manfred fired. And missed.

'Three metres, short. They'll be aware of us now,' said Basler, unworried. Manfred was angry with himself. He hated showing any sign of weakness or incompetence in front of the lieutenant. Kleff loaded another shell and Manfred made sure of his aim. He pressed the trigger. Nothing. He pressed again.

'Fire, Brehme,' pressed Basler, clearly irritated.

'It's not working,' replied Manfred. He looked at Kleff. 'Reload, Gerd.' Kleff removed the shell and threw it back in.

'Ready?' asked Manfred. Kleff nodded.

This time Manfred's aim was unerringly accurate. The Stuart erupted into flames. The hatches kicked open and a couple of crew emerged from the flames. Moments later a machine gun began chattering. It was Keil, the radio operator.

Basler shouted down.

'Cease firing.'

Keil looked up at Basler in confusion. Even Manfred was a little surprised. He, personally, did not believe in firing at enemy escaping from a burning hull. He hadn't expected Basler to be of a similar view. The more time he spent with the former SS lieutenant the more highly he regarded him. Manfred was also beginning to understand why he had not risen further despite his evident abilities.

'Sir?' asked Keil.

Basler glared at Keil. The radio operator released his finger from the trigger. No more was said. The other Panzers had opened fire on the British tanks to devastating effect. Explosion followed explosion. The British returned fire but their shots fell harmlessly short. Then Basler snapped at Manfred.

'Why have you stopped firing at the tanks?'

Manfred motioned to Kleff who opened the breech and loaded another shell. Manfred pressed the firing button. There was no response.

'What is going on down there?' yelled Basler.

Kleff opened the breech and shut it again more firmly. A split second later Manfred fired and hit a second tank.

The British began to withdraw quickly. Manfred fired half a dozen other shells, but the remaining enemy tanks were moving too quickly and avoided any serious damage. Basler ordered a halt to the firing. The guns fell silent. The Panzers moved forward slowly. They reached the burning Crusaders and Stuarts a few minutes later. Nine of them lay in flames following the short engagement. Basler glanced down into the hull and pointed to Kleff and Keil.

'Go and see what we can use from the British tanks. Don't rob the soldiers,' ordered Basler. He seemed to be staring at Keil when he said this.

Kleff and Keil exited the hatch and went in search of anything they could salvage. A few of the other crews were similarly engaged. Once upon a time that had been his job. He still had nightmares of the sights he'd seen inside the destroyed tanks. The scorch-black figures that had once been men and the charcoal smell of the burnt tissue was something he knew he would never forget.

Moments later he heard Basler make a dismissive noise. Manfred shot Basler a glance. The lieutenant smiled grimly.

'See for yourself.'

Manfred climbed up through the cupola. He caught sight of Keil bent double, retching by the side of a Crusader. Perhaps it was the state of the dead in the tanks or, Manfred hoped, it was seeing the dead bodies of the Englishmen he'd gunned down as they escaped from their burning tank. Manfred had heard many stories from the

150

other crews of how the British had not shot at German soldiers as they escaped. Many on both sides had adopted this practice. Of course, it was not always the case. Some, like Keil, continued the killing. It seemed cowardly to Manfred. The look on Basler's face suggested that he'd deliberately wanted Keil to view the result of his own murderous proficiency.

Perhaps Keil would learn from what he'd done. If he did, though, it would come at a cost. The heart might confess but the mind would not forget. Manfred was grateful to Basler that he'd not asked him to go. The thought of seeing what his own accuracy had caused would have killed something inside of him. It might have made him hesitate when required to push the firing button. This would endanger them all. Manfred realised that the shield he had against his own feelings of guilt was the knowledge that he had not solely been following orders. Quite simply, it was self-defence. They were firing at him.

The halt lasted over an hour and then they were off again, until darkness and low fuel forced them to stop. There was no further contact with the enemy. With some relief, they formed a leaguer between Rigel Ridge and Bir Lefa around ten kilometres south of Acroma. They had now lost contact with the rest of the division and would need to refuel if they were to continue the chase.

The evening revealed the toll extracted by the day's fighting. The regiment was down to thirty-nine tanks that could still run. Twenty-three had been destroyed beyond salvage and the others, including Gerhardt's, had broken down or been damaged in the firefight and required repair.

'What happened to you?' asked Manfred when he finally found his friend in the leaguer.

'The engine gave out,' explained Gerhardt. 'I was driving along and then I heard the engine coughing like an old man. Seconds later it stopped completely. Just when we were in the line of fire of the British. We were lucky they took off before any of their shells could do us any damage. I spent the afternoon with Lukas trying to fix things but no luck. When it was dark, we got a lift back here. What about our Bavarian friend, Fischer? Do you think he made it through?'

'I haven't heard. I think his tank was hit but I don't know where he ended up. We're all over the place now.'

After Gerhardt had left, Manfred returned to his crew. The campfire flickered in the light breeze, casting distorted shadows against their battered Mark IV. Basler sat alone, reading. He'd managed to find an old copy of David Copperfield. In English. He sat reading it with a small dictionary beside him which he referred to every so often.

They were joined by Lieutenant Stiefelmayer. His arrival prompted Basler to set his book down and get to his feet.

'Sorry, I appear to be interrupting your Anglophile commander,' said Stiefelmayer, archly. Manfred grinned but made sure that Basler did not see this. Basler ignored his friend, and they went off towards a group including Kummel and Teege.

Manfred slumped to the ground wearily. They were all underneath a makeshift tent attached to the hull. Jentz was snoring like the trooper he was. Kleff was sleeping, too. He was as silent in slumber as he was in the tank. Keil was awake, staring straight up into the night sky. Perhaps he was avoiding sleep, thought Manfred, fearful of seeing the men he'd killed reappear in his dreams. Manfred wanted to say something to him. He started towards him but then stopped. Even in the dim light he could see the tears glistening in the young man's face. Manfred turned away. He didn't want the boy to know he'd seen him. Anyway, what was there to say?

The next few days saw the regiment slowly reconfigure. This required Manfred's tank to go in search of the supply train which they located early afternoon the next day. They were still low on fuel and priority was given to refitting damaged Panzers to bring up the regiment strength. Early morning of the 29th saw the return of Fischer and several of the stranded crews.

'My tank lasted five minutes,' laughed Fischer. 'We were one of the first to be hit. The firing started from the Tommies. We were hit immediately. The tank began to brew up. We were lucky; all of us escaped. Shells raining down on us and you lot heading off into the distance. I don't like that new tank the British have.'

'Have you seen it?' asked Gerhardt. 'Ugly looking thing.'

'Not very practical,' added Manfred draining his coffee. 'The seventy-five can only fire in one direction.'

'Really?' laughed Fischer who had yet to see the new addition to the enemy tank armoury. 'Why did they do that?'

'I'll ask Churchill next time I see him,' replied Gerhardt.

'Do that,' agreed Fischer, 'and tell him to give up while you're at it. You're going to lose.'

Manfred wondered if Fischer really believed they would win. Confronting the new tank had been a reminder that the Allies were only going to grow more powerful. They had the industrial might of the Americans and the manpower of the Commonwealth to support them while Germany was divided between two fronts. No one spoke of the fear they all felt: the war had already been lost.

'Has any mail come?' asked Fischer.

'No. Haven't seen Marseille recently. He usually brings it,' replied Manfred.

'So we're stuck here,' said Gerhardt looking around the camp a little forlornly. 'Has anyone got a football?'

They stayed a week in the assembly areas. Rommel, for once, decided to be patient and use the time to allow the divisions to regain their strength, match up displaced crews with new tanks and strengthen their supply lines for the next stage of their push.

Shelling from enemy artillery was frequent but sounded more menacing than dangerous. It was notice of what they would face in the future when they pushed east. Occasional visits by the RAF posed more of a problem and a few bombing runs on the assembly areas had caused greater damage.

These aerial attacks halted as the khamsin attacked the invaders. Once again North Africa and Mother Nature posted a reminder that the greatest enemy either side faced was not to be found wearing a uniform. The end of May and early June saw both sides enveloped in a hot, dusty wind from the south that made life wretched for all who faced it. The oven-hot airstream scorched and blinded and choked. It infiltrated nostrils, clothing, food and drink. By the time its hateful intensity was abating, most soldiers were ready to sue for peace.

With the weather once more returning to merely intolerable, the 4th of June saw the regiment ready to march again. Orders came through that they had to clear minefields south-west of Bir el Harmat. This would allow the Afrika Korps to outflank the defensive boxes on the Gazala Line which defended the desert route into Tobruk. This was always assuming that the Allies did not attack first.

Manfred sat on the cupola and listened to the nearby eighty-eights pulsing repeatedly to targets somewhere in the distance. Out of curiosity he asked to borrow Basler's binoculars. He stared at them and, just for a moment, he remembered holding a similar pair on a ship. It seemed like a lifetime ago. His chest constricted as the memory of his friend's death returned. A voice behind him snapped him back to the present day.

'Be quick, we'll be leaving soon,' urged Basler making no effort, as usual, to hide his irritation.

The field glasses were even more powerful than the ones he'd used on the ship. Basler must have had good contacts in supply to snaffle these, thought Manfred. No wonder he wanted them back. Manfred moved his view down to look at the artillery ranged a hundred yards in front of them. There were half a dozen guns. But only two of them were firing. He scanned along the line and looked at the gunners. They were all eating. Lunch break in the middle of war. Manfred smiled at the very normality of it. The gunners didn't seem to have any more luxurious food than the crews. It looked like they were drinking *Erbswurst,* a soup made from pellets crushed into boiling water, and *Graubrot,* a grey rye bread that tasted as awful as it looked.

Just then Manfred caught sight of a tall, skinny figure and his heart leapt.

'Oh my God. Matthias,' said Manfred and laughed out loud. The others in his crew looked at him irritably.

'Seen your boyfriend?'

Manfred handed the field glasses back to Basler and shook his head.

'A friend from training has just been blasting the Tommies to hell. I haven't seen him since early last year.'

Basler rolled his eyes and told him to get the others to clear up. Manfred leapt to it, feeling more energised than he could remember in the last few months. He couldn't wait to tell Gerhardt.

'Are you going to finish that?'

The soldier removed his hat to reveal a striking head of red hair. He wiped his forehead and held up a lump of the rye bread. He grimaced and handed it to the other soldier.

'I can't believe you like this rubbish,' said the red-haired soldier.

Matthias Klug stood up to his full six feet five and ran a hand down his exceptionally thin body. A grin lit up his face.

'How do you think I maintain such a physique?'

The other gunners laughed and some bread was thrown in his direction which, much to his own surprise as much as his comrades, Matthias caught and popped into his mouth.

Matthias put his hand to his forehead to shield his eyes from the midday sun. It was hot, not like summer, but still enough to burn. His skin, so white and delicate once, had hardened, like his body, to the rigours of the alien landscape that was now their home.

He sat down again and used the bread to wipe up any remaining soup. He was no less hungry, though. He woke up hungry and went to bed hungry. Back home he'd never thought much about food. Now it filled his waking thoughts. If he got back home, he would dedicate himself to the cause of becoming obese. With such warm thoughts he heard the stir behind him of tank engines.

He wondered if Manfred, Gerhardt and Lothar were out there now. It seemed like a lifetime ago since they were in training. Over a year of his short life had been spent in this horrible place. He'd been in action right from the moment he stepped onto the port side in Tripoli the previous May.

Once again, he offered up a silent prayer of thanks to the heavens that he'd been considered too tall for service in a Panzer. They'd put him in the artillery. The luckiest break of his life. Well, almost. As he lay back against the big anti-tank gun, he heard a voice shouting out orders. He jumped up just in time to come eye to eye with Lieutenant Kessler.

The two men viewed each other with mutual dislike. Everywhere he went. Every time. It didn't matter where; the bullies would follow him. He was tall, skinny and smart. Different. They sensed weakness. Like a bee to pollen they came. Once it had been physical. Now it was verbal. Oddly, he no longer cared. Kessler could say what he wanted and Matthias would smile and salute. After so long in North Africa with these men, he knew where he stood. His comrades liked him. More importantly, they valued him. He took instruction well. He was tireless when digging trenches. And he was intelligent.

'Klug' barked Kessler. 'Lying down again?'

The whole gun crew had been resting but this was immaterial to Kessler.

'Yes, sir,' responded Matthias, eyes straight ahead. He avoided smiling but it was a close-run thing. Best not to poke the beehive.

Kessler glared at Matthias then, with nothing else to say, stalked forward to the next gun placement.

'He loves you,' said Sainz, a corporal and the crew's leader. 'Try not to get him too angry for God's sake. I'll bet you we're the last to pull out.'

An hour later, Sainz's prediction proved accurate. Kessler returned and told them they would stay behind with one tank squadron. The other guns would be moved to a new position a kilometre away to the south-west.

'Might be better for us,' pointed out Matthias to Sainz.

The burly corporal from Leipzig shook his head and looked at Matthias, not without fondness.

'Kessler has it in for you and that means for us also. Trust me. If they're wrong and the Tommies attack again then we're exposed.'

'Let's hope they try and outflank us,' replied Matthias optimistically.

'Hope? My feeling is we're depending on their very predictability.'

CHAPTER NINETEEN

Bir Timer MR 380439, Libya, 5th June 1942

Arthur slapped his cards down on the makeshift table and cackled loudly.

'Read 'em and weep, girls, read 'em and weep.'

This brought a predictable series of groans from the group around the table. Arthur pulled the matchsticks over towards him and pointed out that everyone around the table owed him the equivalent of thousands. Danny led the rest of the table in pointing out that his chances of ever seeing it, irrespective of what Herr Rommel had in store for him, were as likely as finding a virgin in a brothel.

'Only if it's you, son,' pointed out Arthur which produced a prolonged burst of laughing, none louder than Danny's. The winning hand was a pair of aces and eights. Unspoken around the table was a similar thought. This was the 'dead man's' hand, named as such because it was reputed to have been what Wild Bill Hickok was holding when he was shot in the back by 'Broken Nose' Jack McCall. The game was effectively over as the Londoner had all but cleaned out the other players.

'I'll prepare a chit for you boys on what you owe me,' said Arthur.

'Hurry up, Arthur, I need something to clean my backside with now,' said Corporal Alf Lumley, the gunner in Arthur's tank. The group broke up and walked back in the darkness. The moon was blocked out by heavy cloud giving a chill to the air.

Danny walked with Arthur back to his new tank. They looked at the M3 Stuart. For the past year it had been a stalwart of Allied armour. Yet, with the arrival of the larger and more powerful Grant, it somehow looked like a sardine tin with tracks. It had been tested in battle against the Panzers and been proven inferior. Having seen the devastation caused by the Grant, Arthur was less than impressed about returning to battle in this tank. Even in the dark, lit only by the campfires, it was plain that this Stuart had seen better days.

Arthur spotted Danny gazing at the dents and bullet grazes in the armour. Nothing was said. Arthur shrugged and they parted. Danny returned to the makeshift tent that had been erected against their hull. Archie Andrews looked up from his book.

'Did you win?'

'No,' replied Danny with a rueful smile.

'I don't know why you bother. You always lose.'

Danny glanced over the shoulder of Andrews at the book. He was reading *Don Quixote*.

'Is that Spanish?'

'You're quick,' replied Andrews although not unkindly.

'Did you learn it at university?'

'No, I was there for a few years,' said Andrews, setting the book down on his lap.

'The Civil War?' asked Danny in surprise.

'Yes. Arrived a few months after it started. I went with some chums from Cambridge. It seemed the thing to do.'

159

Danny sat down beside Andrews. He was no one's idea of a soldier. The receding hairline, the spectacles and the rather skinny, unathletic body. Yet he'd probably gained more combat experience than anyone in their regiment.

'I'd have thought you'd have had your fill of fighting after that. You might have been able to avoid it at your advanced age,' laughed Danny. Andrews grinned.

'Yes, despite my elderly years – thirty really is quite ancient – it never occurred to me not to join up.'

Andrews was silent for a moment. Danny watched him collect his thoughts, perhaps even his composure. There was no doubt that an old scar had become inflamed in the last few moments. He began to speak once more, but his voice, choked with hatred, became barely a whisper.

'I was in Guernica, Danny,' continued Andrews. He paused again. Danny felt his chest tighten. Whether it was guilt or empathy he didn't know.

'If you'd seen what they did. The bombing by those bastards.' He spat the last word out with feeling. He stopped to regain some control then added, tears glinting in his eyes, 'So many children dead. I never thought humans could be capable of such evil.'

'I'm sorry for bringing it up again, Archie,' replied Danny, honestly.

Andrews smiled and patted him on the back.

'Don't worry. I was just going to say, though, if you'd been there, you'd have realised that to do nothing now would have been, in its own way, a greater crime. To sit back and allow these people to win? No. I couldn't live with myself.'

Danny nodded. His experience of the war and of the Germans had been different. The desert conflict had, in his experience and from listening to others, respected the rules of war. Danny recognised that, despite Andrews' professorial manner, there was a hard glint in his eyes. He doubted the corporal would ever show much mercy where German soldiers were concerned. Neither of them, given their roles in the tank, would be called upon to make those instantaneous life and death decisions. A gunner's target was often half a mile away or further. The lack of proximity to the results of their fire protected them against self-reproach.

The shadow boxing continued throughout the next few days. The main threat came from long-range shelling by the enemy's eighty-eight-millimetre guns. This required the tanks to sidestep continually. It was a siege of sorts. Both sides were poised to strike but not yet prepared to commit. In between this dodging and weaving around artillery shells, there were occasional scuffles with stray tanks from both sides. It was wearying to the body and the spirit.

Then the sky turned from blue to blood red and then, ultimately, to black. The guns from both sides sang their shrill melody. But one thing was increasingly clear to Danny and the men. They were losing.

First it was the death of Lieutenant-Colonel Uniacke of the 5th Royal Tank Regiment. He'd been sharing the load of protecting the series of boxes on the Gazala Line with them. Then, a day later, the commander of the 3 RTR, 'Pip' Roberts, was wounded and narrowly escaped death when his tank was destroyed by a HE shell.

Bir Hacheim fell despite the heroic resistance of the Free French. Then the combined 1st and 6th Royal Tank Regiments were given such a fearful beating by the Germans, it forced their withdrawal on the 12th of June.

Things came to a head for Danny and the regiment on the 13th of June. The day started at 0530 with a sandstorm that initially paralysed both sides. The storms blew intermittently during the day limiting movement from the regiment. Early reports suggested that the artillery was making an impact on the Panzers. But then news came through that tank support was needed to avoid the Rigel Ridge being overrun. Danny and the squadron set off, reaching the ridge soon after five in the afternoon.

Their instructions were simple in theory: delay the enemy armour. Danny wished that the man who'd given this order could see what he was looking at through his telescope. Spread out across half of the horizon was a dark, malevolent wave. A tidal surge that Danny knew was unstoppable. He could scarcely believe that so many enemy tanks could still be operational after all this time. Their own tanks were falling apart. Over the last fortnight they'd been on the receiving end of a battering.

'Do they ever stop?' wondered Andrews as he gazed at the approaching swell of German armour. They made a fearful sound like a throbbing growl. The ground seemed to tremble beneath them.

'Apparently not,' observed Benson. The two men could have been chatting at Simpsons over breakfast. A shell exploded fifty yards in front of them, a gout of sand flying twenty feet into the air. Benson raised one eyebrow and added, 'Looks like the party is starting. Shaw, can you send them a few invitations?'

Danny pressed the firing button a split second later. The firefight began. The tank was rocked time and time again by shells. Explosions ripped the atmosphere all around. After only a few minutes the air was an acrid blue with smoke and cordite.

'C'mon, Danny,' said Andrews. 'They're getting closer. Can't you do something?' He took off his spectacles and polished the mist from them.

'You can have a go if you want,' replied Danny as he squeezed off another shot.

'I see myself as more of a sniper, old chum. I'll leave the wild lunges to you and that big gun of yours.'

A loud explosion to their left told them that one of their squadron had been hit. There wasn't time to see who it was or if anyone had survived. The Germans kept advancing, impervious to the losses they were sustaining.

The quick fire and manoeuvre tactics employed by the Panzers limited the impact of the long-range shelling from Danny and the remaining Grants' seventy-five-millimetre guns.

'They won't stay still,' said Danny through teeth that were rapidly becoming too clenched to speak. 'This bloody gun is useless. I can't move it to hit them.'

'I think Fitz has worked this out,' observed Benson drily. 'Archie, are they in range yet?'

The crump of the thirty-seven-millimetre was Andrews' answer.

'That's a yes then,' said Benson but there was an edge to his voice now. The Germans were closing and with each yard the intensity of fire grew. The radio was ablaze with communications. The messages told one story – the regiment was losing tank after tank.

'I make them five zero zero yards now,' said Benson on his mic. Whether he was providing firing instructions or sending a coded message to withdraw, Danny couldn't decide. Behind them, Allied twenty-five-pounders were making more noise than impact. But Archie Andrews' AP Armour Piercing shells were making their presence felt.

'PG, start to move back. Slowly,' ordered Benson.

Six Grants backed away from the ridge and disappeared into the night that had fallen seemingly without anyone, least of all the Germans, noticing. Danny listened closely to the radio traffic for news of who had been hit. His heart froze when he heard the next message.

'Picked up survivors from Jenkins' crew.'

This was Arthur's tank.

A mute sense of defeat lay heavy in the air. A tacit feeling that it had all been avoidable. The limitless courage of the Eighth Army was simply not enough when confronted by an enemy that was better prepared, better organised and better led.

Danny was not immune from this despair nor silent in his anger as he watched the regiment being disbanded then reformed from one day to the next. The number of working tanks whittled. The men were unable to overcome the challenges posed by the enemy, the desert and by the inept leadership that was endemic from Gazala all the way to Cairo and beyond.

'C'mon, Danny lad, I thought you'd be happy to get out of this hell hole for a while,' said PG as he and the crew discussed the rumour that they would be returning towards Alamein.

'If we leave, then Tobruk will be on its own again,' pointed out Andrews. His round, rimless glasses glowed like two orbs in the lamplight.

'They can hold out for a few weeks. They did it before,' said Gregson.

Danny stared into the distance and replied coldly, 'Weeks? By the time we go back to Alamein and regroup, months will have passed, and you know it. Then our Colonel Blimps will just figure out a new way to fail against the Germans. They've been doing it since World War I and they're still doing it now.'

Andrews glanced towards PG and Gregson to warn them to talk about something else. Although the crew were close and had come through so much together, the subject of Tobruk was invariably guaranteed to stoke tension.

'Well, if it's all the same to you, Danny, I like my skin the way it is. And if we're told to hop it tomorrow, I, for one, will be singing 'Show Me the Way to Go Home' all the way back.'

Even Danny smiled at this but felt a crushing weight descend on his chest. He hated the thought of facing an enemy whose rumbling tanks could still be heard in the distance. He hated abandoning Tom even more. For the last week they'd been involved in a series of scuffles with tanks, artillery and soft-skinned vehicles. It seemed to Danny the Germans were intent on avoiding the fight as much as they were. He suspected the encounter on the first day had been as costly to them as it had been for the Allies.

Tobruk would probably be abandoned to its fate once more. There was nothing he could do except sit and rage at the weak leadership and try to deny the sense of relief he felt inside.

He thought about Tom. A wave of guilt rose and threatened to overwhelm him. He wanted nothing more than to take the tank and join him and the other men in Tobruk; to fight it out side by side. If they were to fall then, at least they'd be together when it happened. Another part of him recognised the lie he was telling himself.

The news on Arthur was only marginally better. He'd escaped but had been badly burned. No one could tell Danny just how badly. His hands gripped one another in knuckle-white frustration. At that moment Captain Benson returned to their bivouac.

'Lights out,' ordered Benson, slumping down to the ground.

'Sorry, sir,' replied PG. 'We got caught up on tactics.'

Benson raised an amused eyebrow at this. He studied PG for a moment and said, 'Will we win?'

'There's a rumour going round that we're going to pull out, sir,' replied PG. Benson looked slightly shocked by this. He saw McLeish, Thompson and Andrews turn towards him and realised everyone was thinking the same. Gregson was snoring away by this stage. He looked at the wireless man and smiled. Then he turned to the other men again. They were clearly expecting him to confirm or deny the rumour. He nodded and replied resignedly, 'Yes. We're heading back east. Night march. We leave at 2200. That gives us an hour to pack up.'

Danny was aware that the captain was looking at him. It was as if he wanted Danny to say what was on his mind. Danny obliged.

'And Tobruk?'

Benson's face was taut with fatigue but also something else. Sympathy.

'I know your brother is there, Shaw. I'm not any happier about this than you are but things are not going our way. The order has come from the very top. We can't let Jerry capture any more prisoners or equipment.'

Once again, they'd been out thought. Danny refused to believe they'd been out fought. Never that. The worn out faces around him bore testimony to the spirit that was being whittled away not by the men of another army, nor by the hellish conditions they were being asked to fight in. Their defeat was solely due to inferior leadership.

'I'm sorry, Shaw. Tobruk will hold out; you'll see.'

Danny doubted even Benson believed that now. There was little point in arguing with him. He was a good man and Danny liked him. He nodded to Benson and rose to his feet on the pretext of taking a spade for a walk. In truth, he wanted to be on his own. He walked away from the leaguer to a spot where he could be alone with his thoughts.

It took a few moments for his eyes to adjust to the darkness. He stared out into the night. The sounds of the enemy moving seemed like distant thunder. It never seemed to let up. There was a relentlessness to the way they waged war. The whole army acted in concert rather than as a collection of groups. No wonder they were winning. Danny was in no doubt that they would capture Tobruk.

Thoughts of Tom lay siege to his mind, landing on him like shells. His fists clenched and he fought back tears of frustration.

But there was another feeling, too. It was the guilt of a man who was secretly relieved that someone had taken a decision that a part of him hoped would be made. The desire to be far away from violence and death, if only for a little while, was as undeniable as it was overpowering. A part of him wanted to believe that Tom and the rest of the men in Tobruk would hold out like they had before. That they would be relieved again. He knew this was an illusion.

They were abandoning the port to its fate. Tom and the others would fight. And they would be defeated. Would they see sense and surrender or keep on fighting to the last? His chest tightened so much that he could barely breathe. His brother's face, then his mother's, filled his mind. What would he say to her? To his father?

He was running away.

CHAPTER TWENTY

South-west of Tobruk, Libya, 19th June 1942

Manfred hadn't felt so tired since the dark days of December when they'd been withdrawing slowly from the Allied onslaught. Then, sleep had been a rare commodity. Every day had been fight then run with the occasional turn around and fight back thrown in to leaven the daily dish of retreat.

This time they had the momentum. They were driving forward and seeing the enemy turn tail. Yet it seemed to Manfred they would soon be in the same situation as the British and the Allies had faced six months previously. A relatively small army would be dominating thousands of kilometres of land, spread out like a fog over the sea. Their supply lines would be stretched to breaking point and targeted by the British whose piratical bent had not changed one iota since the days of Captain Morgan.

But Tobruk would change everything.

Even Manfred could see the importance of capturing the port. At a stroke they would have a place where new men and materiel could land and reinforce their push to rid North Africa of the Allies. The prospect of fighting through the Middle East was only marginally more appealing than struggling through the vast, frozen wilderness of Russia.

At this moment all Manfred craved was to sleep for a week. All around him he saw men sleepwalking. Among them there were a few men who could still find the energy and the motivation to bark out orders. Manfred had long since come to accept he was not like them. They belonged to the next level of man's evolution. Perhaps supermen did exist.

Basler was one such man. Inexhaustible, forever alert, forever committed to the drive for victory. The only thing Manfred was uncertain of was his commitment to the idea that had brought them here in the first place. He suspected this had long since vanished in the face of another idea, infinitely more powerful. This cause was universal within the Afrika Korps and, unfortunately, shared by the enemy, too. The desire to survive. Every day was a battle to endure against the twin enemies they faced: the Allies and North Africa, itself.

Manfred looked at the sores on his leg. There were some mild shrapnel wounds from a few days ago that had barely been treated. They weren't painful or serious enough to prevent him fighting but they irritated him continually. His body could not self-heal because its energy and spirit were waging another war. One that involved the mind.

He looked down with disgust at the food he was eating. This didn't help either. The lack of fresh fruit and vegetables inhibited his body's ability to heal. He knew the sores he had now would be his companion for months if they didn't capture the port that had eluded them for over a year.

Tobruk.

It was so close now. They'd ripped up the defensive boxes surrounding the town. Thousands of prisoners, tonnes of supplies yet it would be all for nothing if they failed, once again, to capture the fortress.

The success in driving the British away from the Gazala Line had, at least, allowed the Afrika Korps to recover stockpiles of food that had been hidden the previous year. Better still, Manfred was now outfitted in British clothes. He'd found a pair of grey corduroy trousers to go with what remained of his uniform. Last year he'd laughed at the German soldiers wearing English dress; now he was one of them. And he wasn't alone. Basler was similarly attired and his transformation to English gent was now complete. Laughter at his new wardrobe was conspicuously contained to behind his back.

'Get some sleep,' ordered Basler returning to the bivouac. 'The attack begins at 0520 tomorrow.'

Of course, even dressed like a country squire, Basler still had the capacity to jolt them from their more childish fancies.

'The minefields?' asked Manfred.

'Paths are being created now. There will be no artillery fire, just an aerial attack. They'll come over from Crete.'

Brief and to the point as ever. Basler rarely wasted even a syllable.

Work on the tanks had stopped now and a strangely expectant silence descended over the leaguer. They had been here before. And failed. This time things felt different. The capitulation of the enemy had renewed belief that the fortress was within their reach. One last effort, thought Manfred, before he swiftly felt coherence ebb away to be replaced by random ideas and memories and then he was falling, falling, falling into darkness.

'They're out there,' observed Bert Gissing, draining yet another brew.

There was going to be little argument from Tom on that. They'd talked of nothing else for a month now. The muffled sounds of the Afrika Korps, although many miles away, still carried through the night to the check post on the inner perimeter manned by the 201st Guards. Bert gazed out into the darkness. Ahead, the minefields and the barbed wire were visible for about fifty yards before they dissolved into the haze of the desert. He shivered despite the slow rise in temperature.

'How much longer?' asked Tom for the seventh time at least.

Bert glanced at his watch. Their stint was due to finish at 0600 and then they would have a well-earned sleep.

'Another five minutes and counting,' replied Bert. He watched Tom fish some cigarettes from his pocket. He took the one offered and put it in his mouth. The two men looked at each other expectantly.

'I've no matches left,' said Tom.

'Me neither,' came the reply.

A series of oaths followed from Tom and chuckles from Bert. Tom left his friend in search of a light for his cigarette. A minute later he returned. A pale orange glow lit his face casting demonic shadows around his eyes. Tom was now profiled against the backdrop of tanks from the 4th Royal Tank Regiment. He stopped suddenly and turned to look at the tanks and then back to Bert. Then he shrugged and said, 'The welcoming committee.'

It was said with a grin but inside he wasn't so sure. For the last few weeks, they'd listened with increasing dismay and no little concern about how the renewed push from the enemy had seemed to sweep aside the defensive boxes around the Gazala Line. One after one they'd fallen like a row of dominoes: Bir Hacheim, the 150th Brigade Box, Knightsbridge.

Tom walked up to Bert and lit his cigarette. There was a distinct rumble in the air now. Tom thought about Danny. He felt his stomach

171

knot at the thought of his brother and what he'd had to face over the last few weeks. He was afraid. There was no use in denying it.

The rumble in the distance was more distinct now. It was getting closer. Bert and Tom exchanged looks. Bert frowned. From somewhere else there was a hum. Tom spun around to face the town and the dark silhouette of the escarpment to the east. He gazed skywards.

Men were emerging now from behind the vehicles. Some were running, others staggering, half asleep. The hum was louder, deeper and more malevolent. Tom and Bert ran to retrieve their helmets.

'Not much warning, was there?' said Bert.

The low hum was transforming into a higher pitch. Tom and Bert stood transfixed as the ack, ack began exploding uselessly in the sky. Now the noise of the planes was changing again into something far more terrifying. The Stukas began to scream as they descended sharply towards the harbour. They began bombing and strafing defensive positions a few miles away on the escarpment.

'Just planes?' asked Bert in a hushed tone.

His question was answered immediately as the first shells began to rain down near them. The accuracy, given the distance, was frightening.

'What was that you said about them being out there?' asked Tom sprinting towards a trench.

For once Manfred was glad that visibility was so poor. Orange smoke obscured his view. It was necessary though to stop the Stukas, the Messerschmitts and the HE-111 bombers blowing up the very attack they were supposed to be supporting. The scream of shells and Stukas vibrated through Manfred's body like a terrified shiver.

Somewhere up ahead, inevitably, was Captain Kummel. He was the first through the ditch and into the alleys carved out in the early hours of the morning through the minefields. The Panzers poured

172

forward before fanning out to avoid the artillery and anti-tank fire emerging from Tobruk and the escarpment.

The air was hot with more than just shell and shot. By mid-morning the cabin was a metal oven which was only made worse by the slow progress towards the port. Thankfully the marksmanship of the Allied artillery did not match the standard of the Afrika Korps. In fact, to Manfred's eyes, it seemed perfunctory. Perhaps their progress had been greater than he'd imagined, and the Allied gun crews were fearful of hitting their own men. Position after position was being overrun. It felt so different to this time last year when they'd been held at bay by pinpoint anti-tank shelling.

By 1000 in the morning, Manfred's Mark IV had run out of orange smoke bombs to mark its position. The dust being thrown up by the bombing made identification of friend or enemy tanks next to impossible for the Luftwaffe. At Manfred's suggestion they resorted to sending up purple flairs to the next wave of Stuka attacks.

The radio spat updates on the progress of the attack. The 2nd Battalion, with Gerhardt, had driven Allied tanks eastwards while Manfred and the 1st Battalion rolled west towards Gabr Gasem. The 21st Panzer division was now winning the battle on the escarpment north of Kings Cross which was being used by the Allies to shell the Axis advance. Bit by bit the defensive ring around Tobruk was being dismantled.

The truck stopped at the edge of the Pilastrano Ridge and the remaining soldiers debouched to the thunderous sound of explosions. Was this the third, fourth or tenth wave of aerial bombing? Tom had lost count. He glanced up briefly at the blue sky and saw the HE-111 bombers flying off having deposited their deadly payload. He didn't doubt others would follow.

Billowing black smoke rose into the cerulean sky. Vehicles and buildings lay ablaze after the latest attack. It seemed the enemy was picking them off area by area in a concerted yet methodical dismantling of their fighting capability and their spirit. Evil smelling smoke laced with tongues of red crackled a malign portent that worse was to come.

The Pilastrano ridge was on the western side of Tobruk. Defensive ditches had been dug but they now looked dangerously exposed when faced with the likely arrival of the tanks as well as the constant threat of aerial attack. Soldiers were dotted along the ridge but how they were meant to fight back was a mystery to Tom. He surveyed the appalling scene and arrived at a rather black conclusion.

'It's like that Errol Flynn movie,' yelled Tom over the noise of the explosions.

'Which one?'

'You know. The one where he plays General Custer.

'*They Died with Their Boots On*?'

'Yes, that one,' shouted Tom as they ran inside the fort to take cover.

'Glad you're so chipper about our chances,' replied Bert. He laughed grimly as he said this.

'I'm not,' admitted Tom watching soldiers streaming to take cover. He looked around him. The fort was becoming more crowded, yet the reason why was unclear to him.

'This is no good. We'll be sitting ducks if we go in there.'

'Any suggestions about where we go?' asked Bert. His eyes darted around looking for somewhere they could move to. The glare of the afternoon sun made him squint. He saw Tom staring up at a bunker sixty yards away. A six-pound gun was peeking out from a gap. No one seemed to be manning it.

'What about there?' asked Tom.

In the distance they heard the rumble of the German advance, but the number of explosions had died down since the last sortie from the Luftwaffe. Bert glanced up to check there were no more planes and then nodded. They clambered over the ridge and made their way to the gun placement.

The reason why it had ceased firing became immediately plain when they arrived. Two dead bodies lay in the small bunker. They dragged the dead men out of the way. There was no time for a eulogy.

'Sorry, mate,' said Tom by way of apology for his rough handling. The hacking sound of tanks and other vehicles was growing louder.

'Can you remember how to fire one of these things?' asked Bert suddenly.

'That's a point,' replied Tom, staring at the breech. Then another more important thought struck him. 'Where's the ammo?'

They looked around. All they could see were spent shells. Their eyes met.

'That's not much bloody good.'

Then the first of the tanks appeared in view. It was German. They ducked down but it was too late – the tank drew to a halt. Tom's breath was coming in short gasps now. He glanced at Bert. His friend was white with fear. Tom peeked over the mound of the bunker and his worst fears were confirmed. ·

The turret was moving.

They trundled along the road at a leisurely pace unimpeded by any hostile fire. Manfred and Basler's eyes were glued to their sights. Ahead they could see soldiers streaming into the fortress. To their right lay a low escarpment. Dug into the ridge were signs of gun placements.

'I see a gun. Ten metres up at two o'clock,' said Manfred, peering through his telescope. 'Traversing right.'

'Hurry,' replied Basler. 'If it's a fifty-seven-millimetre, we're dead at this range.'

'I wonder why it's not firing,' replied Manfred. His movements were rapid, but he was calm. The gun did not seem to be manned.

'I can't see anyone,' responded Basler squinting through his periscope. 'But we need to put it out of action. Fire when you're ready.'

The gun was now in Manfred's sights. He glanced at Kleff. The young loader was tensed but ready to load the shell into the breech.

'HE shell.'

Kleff nodded and quickly opened the breech. The movement was swift and they were ready. Manfred did not want to waste his ammunition. Nor did he want to look foolish by missing. He took a second to confirm the accuracy of his aim. His finger hovered over the firing button.

'It's pointing at us, Bert,' said Tom breathlessly. His heart was racing and he felt faint with fear. 'Have you a white handkerchief?'

'No,' said Bert. He could barely speak. His throat tightened.

Tom uttered an oath then took off his helmet and stuck it on the end of his rifle. He started to hold it up. In a moment of refined cruelty from fate, the helmet fell off.

'Bugger,' said Tom through gritted teeth. He stared at the helmet temporarily paralysed by his stupidity.

'Quick,' said Bert. Panic gripped both for a moment; then Tom scrambled to pick up the helmet. He wrapped the band around the tip of his gun.

Tom's arm was shaking as he carefully raised the rifle up. Nausea choked his throat. His stomach was knotted in fear as he waited for the crump from the gun that would spell the last thing he would ever hear.

176

'When you're ready,' said Basler, irritably. The rest of the regiment was behind him now and he didn't want to be responsible for holding the advance up. The first comments were coming through on the radio telling him to hurry up.

Manfred pressed the firing button.

Nothing.

'Not again,' snarled Basler. 'I thought you'd fixed this.'

Manfred reddened in embarrassment but also anger. He swung around to Kleff who immediately opened the breech and then slammed it shut again. This had worked in the past and there was no reason to suppose it would not do so again.

'Fire, dammit,' roared Basler. His eyes were blazing.

Perspiration matted Manfred's forehead. He wiped his eye and checked his aim once more and then his thumb moved towards the trigger. Easy does it.

'Stop,' shouted Basler suddenly. 'They're surrendering.'

'What?' asked Manfred as he pressed the button.

CHAPTER TWENTY-ONE

Little Gloston, 21st June 1942

Stan Shaw heard a scream from the kitchen followed by the sound of crockery crashing to the floor. Sweat dripped from his face like a broken drainpipe in a rain shower. He wiped his forehead and wondered whether Kate had seen a mouse. He waited a moment and then heard nothing else. He returned his attention to the horseshoe.

It was just after midday and hunger pangs were beginning to make their presence felt in his stomach. He was looking forward to eating the bread he'd smelled coming from the kitchen. He liked it toasted with butter piled onto it like bricks. He pitied the poor city folks with their heavily rationed access to food. This was never a problem in the country. Milk, butter, eggs were currency now. The thought of the butter melting on the toast made his mouth water in anticipation. It would be good to have a rest. His right arm ached from a morning spent trying to get horseshoes ready for the Leddings family. Not just his arm. His shoulder had been giving him trouble for the last year or two. The doctor had said it was the early onset of arthritis. Inevitable, he said, given the type of job he did.

'Stan,' said Kate, arriving at the doorway of the barn that doubled as a forge. Her eyes were red and tears were streaming down her face.

'Tobruk. They say it's fallen.'

Stan dropped the hammer. It hit the ground with a thud. He went to Kate and they hugged one another tightly. How long they stayed like that he didn't know. Kate clung to him in quiet desperation. He wanted to say something to comfort her, but his own heart felt as if it had been smashed into pieces. Then he heard a voice behind him call his name.

Sarah Cavendish tore off her black riding hat and let light reddish hair fall freely over her shoulders. Watching her was Jeffrey, the young stable lad. He was younger by a couple of years and obviously in love with her. She smiled to him but made sure not to encourage his hopes. She let Jeffrey take the reins of the horse; hooves echoed around the yard as he led her towards the stables.

'It's good to have you back, Lady Sarah. The horses have missed you,' said Jeffrey. He wanted to add that he'd missed her, but his courage failed him.

'It's good to be back,' replied Sarah, jumping gracefully to the ground.

She wandered along the path to the kitchen entrance of Cavendish Hall. Curtis, the butler, and his wife, Sarah's old governess, stood up as she entered. Their faces were anguished. Sarah turned to Elsie. There were tears in her eyes. In the background the radio announcer was talking but Sarah ignored what he was saying.

'Good Lord, what's wrong?'

Curtis glanced at his wife and then answered her.

179

'They've taken Tobruk. The Germans have taken Tobruk.'

Sarah felt her chest tighten. A cold fear gripped her and she nodded mutely. She left the kitchen and ran upstairs to the library. Her father, Henry, was on the phone. Standing beside him was her mother, Jane. Henry put the phone down when she entered.

'You've heard?'

'Yes, is it true?'

'I'm afraid so. I've just been trying to find out more from Chubby at the War Office. He doesn't know the full story yet,' replied her father.

'We should go into the village. To the Shaw's and the Gissing's,' said Sarah.

Henry looked at his daughter and felt a swell of pride. She was no longer the spoilt little girl that he'd once feared she would be. Instead, she was growing more like her mother each day. As role models went, Jane Cavendish was without equal.

Yet lurking beneath his delight at the way Sarah was growing up was something else. Fear. The same fear shared by everyone in the land. What would happen if they lost? It was unthinkable and yet, at that moment, nothing else preoccupied him more than the thought of his son growing up and going off to war or his daughter being exposed to Nazi invaders. Irrational, perhaps, but the effort required to stop his mind spiralling downwards was immense.

'Yes, Sarah's quite right,' said Jane looking at Henry. 'We should go.'

They set off immediately towards the village. It was a beautiful afternoon; the sun brightened the green yet all they saw was grey.

The walk to the village was only a matter of minutes. The first stop would be the Shaw household. Jane gripped Henry's arm when they came within sight. At the entrance to the forge were Stan and Kate hugging one another. There could be no question that they'd heard the news. Henry stepped forward through the gate.

'Mr and Mrs Shaw.'

Stan released Kate and turned to greet the visitor. He recognised the voice. Kate's eyes were glistening with tears and Jane went immediately to her. No words were spoken. They embraced one another.

'You've heard the news then,' said Henry. It wasn't a question.

'Aye, sir. It's bad news all right.'

Henry nodded. It was bad news. Bad for the morale of the country and bad for the village. He thought of poor Lottie Gissing who had already lost one of her boys, Hugh. Now they faced the horrible prospect that one or even two had been killed, wounded or captured. At least they knew that Danny had made it out of 'the Cauldron' safely. Stan looked hopefully at Henry and asked, 'Have you heard anything, sir?'

'No. I was on the phone just now. My friend at the War Office has no news yet. I gather the best we may hope for is that he's been taken prisoner.'

'Aye, that's what I was thinking.'

The two men nodded to each other. There seemed little else to say. Sarah joined her mother and embraced Kate. Henry felt oddly moved by the gesture. It was so natural and yet so strange to see. Life was moving so fast now. He felt the fear return. It tightened his chest like a tourniquet. He could barely breathe with the pride and anguish of it all.

CHAPTER TWENTY-TWO

Ladenburg, Germany, 21st June 1942

It was when they started to sing the *Horst Wessel* song that Peter Brehme returned to his office. His office? No longer. He shared it with Ernst Keller. In a moment of madness, that he regretted bitterly now, he'd given up his desk for the young Gestapo officer. Of course, he knew the real reason why he'd offered to do so.

Fear.

Despite having a son on the front line, despite decades of service to the community, these were changed times. The values that had formed him as a child had been the model for his own parenting. These had become corrupted. Perhaps it had always been so. Perhaps the very severity of the discipline that had formed the characters of generation after generation of young men in his country was in itself to blame for the disintegration of decency and respect. The rule of law had been usurped by criminals. Villains were running the show now. The body politic was rotting from the head down.

He looked at the desk that had once been his. A brown folder lay there. Temptation. He glanced at the door and then back to the folder. He leaned over the desk and picked it up. Inside was a thick sheaf of papers. On each was a small biography of key townsfolk. He flicked through it but could not see his own name. It wasn't just adults either. He recognised the faces of some adolescents. Beside the names of the young adults was the phrase 'possible Edelweiss Pirate'. Brehme almost snorted at this.

Ernst Keller had his arm around young Jost Graf as they sang. Graf had just joined the police force. He disliked the boy. No, that wasn't quite what he felt, he realised. He liked him but felt nothing but contempt for what he was. Chubby, bespectacled and balding. There was little about him that proclaimed either Aryan or superman. He was like a puppy. Eager to please, fearful and responsive to discipline as well as praise.

He was useful, though. Graf nominally reported to Brehme, but they both knew who his real boss was. Graf's appointment a month previously had, at last, allowed Keller a chance to keep a watch on the one person he, paradoxically, knew least about. Graf had immediately understood what his role was to be and went about it with enthusiasm.

The file on Brehme had yielded nothing so far; Keller had no reason to believe it would. However, the project he'd been given required absolute certainty about the uprightness and, importantly, the confidence in the zeal with which public officials represented the party and the government. In this regard there were question marks over the chief of police.

It had not gone unnoticed by Keller that Brehme had not joined in with the singing of the *Horst Wessel* song before leaving them to go into his office. It was almost as if he felt that because his son was out there he was above them all. A wave of anger rushed through Keller. Then another thought struck him.

The file.

He'd left the file on the desk. Brehme would not have been aware of the project. If he looked at the file, he would know the true nature of his work in Ladenburg – documenting the names, activities and opinions of all its key citizens. The song finished and he flung the arm of Graf from his shoulder and rushed straight for *his* office. He opened the door.

Brehme was sitting at the desk to the side of the room. He was on the phone. Seeing Keller enter the office he nodded. He thanked the person at the other end of the line and put the phone down.

'No news about Manfred,' said Brehme.

Keller nodded and glanced towards his desk. The file was there, just where he'd left it. He walked over to the file and lifted it. There was no obvious sign that it had been read but Keller could not be sure. He looked over towards Brehme. The policeman was looking at a file which related to a recent spate of shoplifting. Keller glanced down at the folder in his hands. Had Brehme had enough time to see what was in the file? Unquestionably, the answer was yes.

'You must be very proud,' said Keller in the soft voice that Brehme detested. He looked up from the file.

'Naturally. But I'm proud of the whole army. They are magnificent. It's a great victory for them. For Rommel.'

'And for National Socialism.'

'Of course.'

'I'm sorry you couldn't join our spontaneous celebration.'

Brehme felt his nerve endings tighten. The thought of singing any Nazi song sickened him. He realised with each passing day just how much he hated everything and everyone connected with this movement.

'I wanted to hear if there was any news of my son,' explained

184

Brehme after a few moments. He tried to keep his tone neutral but the meaning was all too clear. He is there. He is serving his country. He is putting his life on the line every day.

'We each of us serve in our own way, Peter,' replied Keller with a soulless smile.

'True,' said Brehme. His ability to lie so convincingly was an asset that would have made him as good a politician as a policeman. To close the current topic, he opened the file in his hands and showed it to Keller.

'I'm going to speak to the store again about this.'

Keller, sensing that he'd taken the conversation as far as he could, nodded.

'It's probably young people, Peter. You should send Graf into the store undercover. Tell him to keep an eye on these kids.'

Brehme had to stop himself choking with laughter. Graf was an idiot and could barely catch a cold without instruction. He looked at Keller as if he was seriously considering this idea.

'I'll look at that, Ernst. You may be onto something there.'

Brehme realised that this was an excellent idea just as the thought occurred to Keller that he would no longer have someone to spy on Brehme. Brehme was thinking this, too. He decided to strike immediately. He rose to his feet and went to the door.

'Graf, will you join us please?'

A moment later Graf stumbled into the room. If he'd had a tail, it would have been wagging. He saw Brehme beaming at him.

'Lieutenant Keller has just made a most excellent suggestion. One that I am fully in accord with.'

Brehme looked from Graf to Keller. He could see the eyes of Keller burning with anger which made the moment exquisitely enjoyable. He cautioned himself against laying it on too thick. Turning back to Graf he allowed an air of gravity to descend on him. Then he explained the plan to Graf who was almost overcome with emotion at the prospect of going undercover. It was the very stuff of the books he enjoyed reading so much. Although he would never admit this to anyone outside his family, he'd grown up reading the books of John Buchan. Richard Hannay was a hero to him. Now, at last, he, Jost Graf, would have an opportunity to join the Fatherland's struggle against fifth columnists and the enemy within.

The late afternoon sunshine was warm enough to make Brehme wish he could remove his tie. But he was still on duty. It would not do to be seen so unkempt. He envied the youngsters he saw with their shirts open, able to run around without a care in the world. It made him wonder if the war would still be on when they grew up. He hoped not. Surely the world would see sense.

His destination was Geschäft Ladenburg. He would explain to Arnold Weber that the best way of investigating the recent spate of shoplifting would be to plant a man in the shop. As Graf was still relatively new and unknown, he would fit that role perfectly. It would also get him away from the police station for a while. He didn't trust Graf. His artlessness made him the worst of spies. He was so obvious that it rather endeared him to Brehme although he remained on his guard. He had little doubt that Keller would have been aware that he would see through this subterfuge. The fact that he didn't care if Brehme did was a worry.

He entered the shop and waited for a couple of customers to leave before speaking with the owner.

'Your usual?' asked Weber. A smile was never very far away from his face. 'Or perhaps something a bit stronger? It was great news earlier about Tobruk.'

'Indeed,' said Brehme, trying to look pleased. And failing. This communicated itself to Weber and the smile left the shopkeeper's face. Brehme added, 'I'll be happier when I know Manfred is safe and well.'

Weber nodded. Then he said, 'You're here on business?'

'Yes,' replied Brehme. 'We, that is Herr Keller, has had an idea that I hope you will be amenable to.' As he said this, he looked out of the shop doorway. He could see a young man standing in the square looking in his direction. Further behind the young man was Keller. So, the Gestapo man had followed him.

He pretended not to notice and returned his attention to Weber. It didn't take long to explain the idea and Weber immediately assented. Graf would start work the next morning. Brehme was relieved that this had not been a problem and he came away with something approaching a lightness of heart. If only he knew more about Manfred. He could manage the problems here comfortably. Not knowing his son's fate was agony. For all Keller's suspicions, Brehme had nothing to hide. His opinion was his own. Perhaps he just needed to play the game more; fit in better with the party men. It wouldn't be easy but it just required him to lie. He was good at that.

Brehme left the shop. As he exited through the doors, the young man turned away and began walking towards a group of his friends who were congregated in the square. His name was Robert Sauer. He was in his final year at school. The file belonging to Keller had identified him as a potential member of the Edelweiss Pirates. Sauer stopped to stroke a golden Labrador that looked very much like Felix, Otto Becker's dog. This was confirmed a few moments later when Becker appeared and exchanged a few words with Sauer, no doubt about the dog. He led Felix away.

Brehme ignored both Sauer and Keller and headed in the opposite direction, his mind racing.

The next morning Brehme rose early and made his way towards the school that Manfred had once attended. The sight of it made his heart lurch. He used to take Manfred to school until the boy had reached the point when he no longer wanted his father to accompany him. It was too embarrassing. A crashing sadness descended on him when he realised how relieved he'd been by Manfred's request. No longer having to walk his son to school or collect him had made life a little easier. He remembered how bored he'd been. The unceasing stream of questions the boy would come out with. The constant need to demonstrate to his father what he'd learned. The coldness he'd shown his own boy. The inability to think of anything to say to him. Resentment, even, that he had to drop the boy off in the morning.

Tears stung his eyes as he recalled the mornings when he'd seen him off. Often there was no 'goodbye'. Just two strangers. What he would give to have that time back again. He watched school children walking along in groups or singly towards the school. They looked so young and full of life. How many of their fathers were out in North Africa? Or worse, Russia?

He waited on a bench. His eyes scanned the road along which so many of the pupils were streaming. Finally, he caught sight of the person he'd come to see. Robert Sauer was walking with a couple of his friends. Holding his hand was a girl, perhaps around fifteen and chocolate-box pretty. Brehme recalled how he'd never had much of a way with the opposite sex. He feared Manfred had inherited the same gaucheness that women could so easily see. Then they would disregard you. Brehme shook his head at the memory.

As Sauer neared the school someone must have said something because he glanced in the direction of Brehme. A look of fear crossed Sauer's face which as good as confirmed what was on Brehme's mind. He motioned with his head for Sauer to cross over the road and join him.

The group stopped and, for a moment, it looked like they would all come over. Brehme shook his head and looked Sauer directly in the eye. Then Brehme rose from his seat and moved behind one of the large trees lining the road. Less than a minute later, he was joined by Sauer. Brehme held out a cigarette.

'Light me,' ordered the policeman.

Sauer said nothing but did as he was asked. He looked into the eyes of Brehme. A certain amount of confidence had returned to the young man. Not quite arrogance but he'd regained the composure briefly lost when he'd first seen Brehme.

'They're on to you,' said Brehme. There was little point in pleasantries.

'Who?' asked Sauer, evidently confused. 'They' in his eyes was anyone old, who worked in a government job.

'Don't be stupid, son. The Gestapo. They know about you and your friends. The Pirates or whatever ridiculous name you all go under here.'

Sauer's body stiffened into a defensive pose. A denial was sure to follow. Brehme had no time for this. He held a hand up which silenced Sauer's protest before it had a chance to begin.

'They have a file on you. Stop meeting with your friends; you will put them in danger and' – added Brehme, standing very close to Sauer and looking him directly in the eye – 'stop robbing the store. As of this morning there is a policeman working undercover there. You or your friends will get caught. Stop now. Do you understand?'

Fear returned to the blue eyes of Sauer. Fear and surprise. Like a deer startled moments before the hunter pulls the trigger. Brehme was pleased that he'd caught the boy out. His suspicion had been correct.

He and his friends were the ones responsible for the shoplifting. Sauer nodded sullenly. Not so proud looking now, are you, thought Brehme with some satisfaction. He was rooted to the spot now and unsure of what he should say or do.

'Go,' ordered Brehme. 'Remember, stop stealing. I can't help you any more than this. They're watching me too.'

Sauer nodded and turned to go. He jogged over the road to his friends who were waiting for him at the school gates. They all looked over towards Brehme but the policeman was already on his way back down the road. They watched him cast the cigarette aside.

CHAPTER TWENTY-THREE

Mersa Metruh, Egypt, 29th June 1942

Manfred studied his thumb. There was a blister on it caused by the day-to-day action of pressing the firing button. No one had told him that this would happen. He was in agony every time he fired. And it would only get worse.

It was evening. They'd taken Mersa Metruh. But Manfred couldn't have cared less. It was just another name to him. After they'd taken Tobruk he thought they'd be given time to rest before making a renewed push. How little he knew! Rommel was relentless. A genius as a leader but he cared little for his men, thought Manfred sourly. They were cannon fodder for his surge to glory. It was no longer enough to know that he didn't spare himself either.

Manfred was near collapse. Sunken eyes stared back at him from the hull, none more so than Basler's. The commander was exhausted although he'd never admit it. They'd pushed on from Tobruk over the last week. They'd fought, and beaten, countless attacks from the never-ending supply of enemy armour. Little by little, the war of attrition was whittling them. There were fewer Panzers left now and fewer men who could operate them. The British leaders may not have had the tactical brilliance of the German leader, but they worked along similar principles. Throw men and machines against the advance of the enemy until there was either no enemy left to fight or no soldiers to fight him with.

Kleff was sitting on his own as usual. He was not the most communicative of men. Perhaps he still felt overawed at being with experienced crew like him and Basler. Manfred almost smiled at the thought of being a veteran. He noticed Kleff was holding some beads. They glinted off the lamplight.

'What are those?' asked Manfred.

Kleff turned around. Even in the darkness he could see that he was faintly embarrassed.

'Rosary beads,' replied the young man.

'I didn't know you were a Catholic,' replied Manfred. He realised it was a stupid thing to say. Why would he know? Religion was hardly a regular topic of conversation in the cabin. Kleff smiled and shrugged.

'Not much of a Catholic,' he admitted honestly. 'When you do what we do every day it's hard to have any faith.'

'So why pray?' asked Manfred, moving closer to Kleff. He was genuinely curious.

'Catholic guilt, I suppose. It never leaves you even if your faith does.'

'Try being married,' said a voice just behind them. 'Then you'll know what guilt really is.'

Manfred and the others laughed. They laughed partly because none of them were married but they'd heard the grumbles from other married men. They laughed because they needed to at that moment. More than anything else, they laughed because the comment came from the source least likely to have made a joke.

Basler sat down with them. The flickering lamplight only emphasised the dark shadows under the lieutenant's eyes.

'You're married?' asked Manfred in surprise. It was strange to ask such a question. Particularly strange to ask it of Basler. Manfred realised just how much his relationship with the lieutenant had evolved over the last year. Perhaps it was a sign that he was beginning to find his voice at last. It was something he'd noticed in himself over the last month. He was one of the senior men now and it was a good feeling; a reminder to him of how he'd been at training.

'Was,' responded Basler.

A silence fell on the group. There could be any number of reasons as to why he was no longer married. Basler sensed that the mood had become heavier.

'It's not what you think, although I sometimes wish it were. She wasn't killed or anything like that. We're divorced, or soon will be.'

They were all spellbound by the sudden and unexpected revelations from Basler. He asked for some coffee. Keil quickly poured him a cup and they all leaned forward in that universal manner that implores the speaker to continue. Basler sighed. He'd already said too much. But what the hell? Here they were, several thousand miles from home, facing death daily.

'Last year, while I was over here, she started seeing someone else. An SS man would you believe? A major who'd managed to avoid any fighting for the last three years. I heard from my sister about what was happening. Colonel Cramer gave me compassionate leave. I'll never forget his words. You know how he spoke. That growl. He grabbed me by the arm. He had a strong grip. He said, "You go home and beat the hell out of that guy. Don't worry, Basler. Trust me."'

The group laughed nervously. Then Manfred asked the question on everyone's mind.

'Did you?'

A hard look came into the eyes of the lieutenant. He looked Manfred in the eye and replied, 'Damn right I did. Put him in hospital.'

The crew broke into a spontaneous round of applause. Basler's eyes widened and he told them to quieten down. He didn't seem too angry though.

'The story doesn't quite end there, though.'

The group were hanging on his every word by now. He looked at the fire lit faces of each man.

'When I got back, Cramer called me over. He asked me had I done what he wanted me to do. I said "yes". He said, "Good, son. But your career is over in the SS." Just like that. My career was over.' Basler shook his head and smiled. He looked down at the fire and was silent for a moment. Then he lifted his head and said, 'But you know what?' Utter silence in the tank. Manfred was holding his breath.

'It was worth it.'

They rolled to a halt for what seemed like the tenth time that day. Inside it was as hot and unpleasant as ever. Manfred wasn't sure whether to feel pleased that they were stopping or irritated. It only delayed the inevitable contact with the enemy. His mouth was dry. What he would have given for a drink.

'More minefields?' asked Manfred.

'More minefields,' answered Jentz.

Basler ordered Kleff to make some coffee while they waited for the mines to be cleared.

'Make it quick, though. The British might send over some planes.'

Kleff didn't need reminding of this. The nearer they came to the British position at Alamein, the more frequently they encountered the aerial threat of the RAF. Until the Luftwaffe were reinforced, the

RAF were the dominant force in the air. Manfred jumped down from the hull along with the others, glad to have a break. Up ahead he saw the *pionier* battalion picking their way forward through the rugged stony desert. Manfred once more wondered where all the sand had gone. Could any place on earth have been more godforsaken than this? He doubted it.

Kleff called to them that the coffee was ready. It was then that they heard the drone. Low at first. That was all they needed. Within seconds they were clambering back into the cabin. From somewhere behind they heard guns being fired. The noise grew progressively louder. This wasn't the coughing whine of the fighters but the deeper groan of the bigger aircraft: the Blenheim Bombers.

In less than a few minutes the air was ripped apart by bombs exploding around them. There was nothing that anyone could do except pray that they weren't hit.

They weren't.

Basler's nerve held enough to survey the scene from outside the turret. He laughed grimly.

'I think the RAF may be doing us a favour. They're bombing their own minefield.'

Manfred stared up at the lieutenant and thought him crazy for even risking being outside. Then it occurred to him that he was probably no safer inside the tank if a bomb landed close enough. He decided to join Basler and peek his head through the turret. There was no question that a pathway was emerging through the minefield thanks to the misdirected bombs of the Blenheims. Manfred wasn't sure how grateful he was about this.

The action was brief and they rolled forward again. A few hours later their Mark IV was rocked by a couple of explosions just ahead.

'Mines,' said Jentz, immediately. 'Is there no end to them?'

The tank stopped again. The light was beginning to fade. Manfred suspected this would be it for the day. They couldn't risk going forward without being certain that they weren't wading into yet another minefield. The radio burst into life and Keil confirmed they would be stopping here. The supply echelon was being called forward to make ready for the next day.

They were to attack the enemy positions outside a railway halt called El Alamein. It was the 1st of July.

CHAPTER TWENTY-FOUR

Cairo, Egypt, 2nd July 1942

Moving from the hot, stuffy street to the cool, disinfectant-laced air of the hospital made Danny's head swim. The reception was like a bazaar. Men, women, children, soldiers, nurses and doctors sat, talked, rushed and cried. It was chaos. A fly landed on his face. He swatted it away, somewhat surprised by its presence. He jogged up the stairs, past cracked walls with pastel paint peeling like burned skin.

A couple of flights later he reached the floor he was looking for. A pair of double doors greeted him. Underneath some Arabic writing was an apologetic translation. It read 'Burns Unit'. He went through the door. Muffled screams behind ward doors welcomed him.

Danny's footsteps echoed along the corridor. A nurse appeared from one door carrying a tray. A foul smell rose from the metal basin covered with a cloth. Her starched white nurses cap was clamped to her head, squeezing her hair into place and erasing any smile that had ever been smiled. She frowned at him as he walked along the corridor. He ignored her and then felt a stab of guilt. It was war for them too. He turned around to say something, but she'd entered a room and was gone.

He looked again at the card in his hand and searched for the ward number. He saw it up ahead. A young man emerged from the room. His head was swathed in bandages and he was in a wheelchair being pushed by an orderly. Danny glanced down. He still had all his limbs. Danny didn't dare think about what lay under the bandages.

He reached the door. A quick look through the small windows revealed two rows of beds. All were filled by men hidden behind bandages. It was like a tomb of mummies. They were in the right country for it, he supposed. His heart quickened a little as he pushed the door forward.

A doctor glanced at Danny but said nothing. He was with a nurse and too busy to act as a guide for a visitor in perfect health. Danny stood at the top of the ward and scanned each bed. There was no screaming as he'd heard in some of the other rooms, just a low moan. His heart stopped beating. How can it, when it's broken? He took a deep breath and began to walk along the centre aisle. Above him a ceiling fan sliced the agonised air.

He forced himself to study each man he passed. Some nodded to him. He nodded back. It was distressing to look at them. How must it be for them? One of the men tried to form words with his mouth but his charred vocal cords would never speak again. Danny smiled to him but kept moving slowly forward.

Arthur was in the last bed.

A scanty curtain partially covered him. When Danny reached the bed, he saw him lying with the bedclothes to one side. He looked absurd. From head to foot he was bandaged like Boris Karloff in that movie they'd seen when they first arrived. He almost smiled and then stopped himself. Arthur hadn't moved. In fact, Danny wondered if he could move with all those bandages. He went over to his friend and sat down on a seat by the bed.

'Arthur,' he whispered.

Arthur made no sound. Danny wondered if he was sleeping. It was difficult to tell. The eyes not only had bandages, there was cotton wool on them, too. A chill fell over Danny that had nothing to do with the cool of the ward.

He sat there for a few minutes unsure of what to do. He couldn't touch Arthur; too fearful that it might be agonising for his damaged skin. Arthur remained still. The minutes went by, and he began to feel foolish. A part of him wanted to escape the heart-rending sobs around him. But he knew he would have to stay.

A doctor came over to him. He was Egyptian. Danny wondered why there wasn't a British doctor here to look after the men. The doctor's voice was accented but clipped in a manner of someone who had learned in England.

'Your friend is sleeping. He is a friend, I take it?'

'Yes,' replied Danny. 'We came over together.' The doctor nodded and said nothing. There was sympathy in his eyes.

'Can you tell me what will happen to him?'

'Of course,' said the doctor, a ghost of a smile appearing on his lips. 'His war is, of course, over. A lot of his body has been burned and it's likely he will be blind. Certainly one eye is gone. Perhaps both eyes. He will stay here a bit longer then, I imagine, he will be shipped back to England to recover properly. He will need more surgery on his skin.'

'How bad was he?'

'Very bad,' admitted the doctor. 'But I've seen worse and they survived. He will be in a great deal of pain for a long time. The road ahead will not be easy.'

Danny nodded and felt tears sting his eyes. The doctor put a hand on his shoulder.

'Can I stay?' asked Danny.

'Of course,' replied the doctor. 'Let the nurse know if you need anything.'

Danny shook his head and said that they were busy enough. The doctor left. Danny sat by the bedside, gazing at Arthur through his tears. An hour later there was the first hint of movement. At first it was barely discernible. Then his arm moved slightly, then a leg. A low moan came from beneath the bandages. The moan became a cry. Unsure of what to do, Danny called the nurse over.

The nurse shook her head. There was nothing she could do. Danny turned to Arthur. He was panicking as the crying grew louder and louder.

'Arthur, it's Danny. Can you hear me?'

The sobbing quietened for a second. But only for a second. It started again. More piercing, this time. A new doctor came over.

He shook his head at Danny. 'You should leave. There's nothing that can be done for the moment. I'm sorry.'

'Morphine?' asked Danny.

The doctor frowned and Danny said sorry.

'We give morphine, but we have to be careful on the quantity. You know it brings its own problems.'

Danny nodded. The doctor stood back in a manner that suggested he leave. Danny took the hint and with some relief rose from his chair. He looked down at Arthur. The tears returned to his eyes when he heard the scream of a wounded animal.

He turned and left.

He walked blindly through the streets of Cairo, sometimes bumping into people, apologising, moving on. His cheeks were wet with shattered tears. He felt like a fool. Had he really expected to see his friend sitting up in bed smiling stoically and cracking a few jokes? How naïve. He'd seen what burns were like. Why should Arthur have got off more lightly? Just because he was a friend of the heroically indestructible Danny Shaw did not give him special exemption from the pain of war.

He was at Sisters Street now. How he'd arrived he barely knew. For a moment he wondered if he should avail himself of the women there, such was his loathing for everything to do with the war, this country and himself for being so untouched. The thought repelled him as much as it attracted him. Instead, he found a bar, sat down and ordered a beer. He tried and failed to stop the memory of his times here with Arthur. The beer went quickly, and he ordered another and then another. By the time he left the bar he felt light-headed. And angry.

He stumbled onto the street and realised he was not as drunk as he wanted to be. A few women stood in doorways, and he gazed at them for a moment then turned away. Too scared to do what he didn't want to do anyway.

He went to the hotel, cleared up his belongings and checked out. He'd spent only one day of his leave but he wanted to return to the camp. It was his home now. He went to the train station and sat down in the waiting room. A radio announcer was talking about the latest German push on Alamein. He stood up and walked out of the room, unable to listen to the news of the fighting anymore.

After a day's journey he arrived back at the enormous camp at Tel el Qabir, twenty miles from the Bitter Lakes just north-west of Suez. At another time he would have liked the camp. Thousands of tents dotted the landscape. Intermingled with them were huts for the officers. The camp had cooked meals which offered a change from the usual diet of bully beef they endured when out in the 'blue'. There was fresh water also and, a novelty for Danny, an open-air cinema.

It was late afternoon when he reached his crew. He threw his kit bag into the tent he shared with McLeish and asked for a brew.

'What are we called this week?' asked Danny bitterly.

This was a reference to the ever-changing status of the regiment. One week it was the 3 RTR, the next it was amalgamated with the 5 RTR, his old training regiment, into the 3/5 RTR.

'We're 3/5 RTR still but don't make me swear to it,' said the Scot, handing him a tea.

'Anything good on at the pictures?' asked Danny. He didn't care what was on, he just wanted something to take his mind off Arthur and the war.

'Ziegfeld Follies, but...'

'Don't make me swear to it,' said Danny with something approaching a smile.

McLeish could see that Danny's mood was low. He felt he had to ask though.

'How was your friend?'

Danny shook his head and sat down on the hard ground. He looked at the wisps of grass.

'Awful.'

'Sorry.'

Danny nodded but was in no mood to talk about his friend. He changed the subject.

'Any news about the colonel and Major Joly?'

'Back in a day or two apparently. Major Franklin's still in charge. It's as well you're back as I think we may be heading off again tomorrow.'

'Not to Alamein, surely?' exclaimed Danny. The fighting was, as far

202

as he knew, still going on but the regiment, in Danny's view, was in no fit state to face the Afrika Korps. At that moment he wouldn't have given tuppence for their chances against a sufficiently well-organised and motivated Girl Guide troop.

'No. From what the major says, we'll be off, not sure where, but definitely not Alamein.'

'Poor bastards. I'm glad I'm not there,' said Danny. 'I wonder how they're getting on.'

CHAPTER TWENTY-FIVE

Ruweisat Ridge, south of El Alamein, Egypt, 2nd July 1942

Manfred stared vacantly through the telescope. Clouds of dust obscured his view, but he could just see the turrets of the Panzers peeking through. The view hadn't changed for an hour, yet he'd kept his face pressed against the sight. Once or twice he shut his eyes and found time to rest before the shaking of the tank ripped through his slumber and forced him to concentrate on God knows what. Grime and dust black-bleached his face. Rivulets of sweat streaked down his cheeks. Basler told him he looked like a zebra.

He was bewildered by the obedience with which the Afrika Korps followed a madman such as Rommel. He never stopped. Not for a minute. It was never enough for such a man. Tobruk? Manfred had already forgotten about it. His hopes that they would stop for a while were soon shattered. There was only a brief pause to re-equip, refuel and reinforce. No rest, though. Not even a chance to swim or drink beer with his friends or regain some semblance of strength. That hope was gone. It was simply never going to stop. Rommel would keep pushing on until there were literally no tanks left.

And there weren't many left now. Six working Panzers in the 1st Battalion.

If the Allies had had any idea how screwed they were at that moment, they wouldn't be running away. But that had stopped now, hadn't it? They weren't running anymore. Manfred sensed they'd gone back as far as they were prepared to go. The advantage was, once more, swinging back to the enemy: the Allied supply lines were short, and the RAF owned the skies. The Afrika Korps was a long way from home, whichever way you looked at it. Ladenburg. Tripoli. Bloody hell, even Tobruk.

Manfred glanced over at Basler. He was sleeping. This was not unusual now. Work on their Mark IV often carried on late into the night. Then there were the night bombing raids by the RAF which disrupted sleep. By the time they rose early the next morning, sleep deprivation was acute. Opportunities to nap on marches were grabbed where possible. Poor Jentz. He had to stay awake, though.

'Enemy tanks,' said Jentz.

Well, if anything was going to wake the lieutenant from a deep sleep it was those two words. His eyes sprang open.

'Where?'

Manfred, Basler and Kleff all had their eyes fixed through their viewers searching through the dust and sand for a sign of what Jentz had seen. The shelling started before they could fix on anything with certainty.

'Where are the damn tanks?' said Basler in frustration.

Through the dust and the smoke they could all see a ridge further ahead. Dark shapes suggested there were tanks, hull-down, dug in. Basler didn't have to give any orders. Manfred had already pointed to the HE shells. Kleff reacted immediately. A shell was in the breech before Basler ordered them to fire. Manfred pressed the firing button and felt a stab of pain in his thumb. The sore had not healed and nor would it until he had a break from the blasted war.

'Do you want me to slow down, sir?' asked Jentz.

'No, keep going,' ordered Basler. 'They look like Mathildas. They can't hurt us from there. I'm surprised they still have any of those left. The British probably gave them to the Indians.'

In fact, it was a New Zealand brigade who were holding the ridge and, by the sounds of the radio traffic, were giving the Italian Ariete Division hell.

Forty metres in front, Kummel was leading the charge towards the New Zealanders. The eighty-eights were finding their mark. Basler fixed his eyes on the ridge and said, 'Ruweisat Ridge up ahead.'

The artillery fire from the Panzer was sporadic causing Basler to swear openly. This was a rare occurrence and Manfred glanced at the lieutenant in surprise. But not for long; Kummel was on the radio barking orders. He seemed to be demanding that the intensity of the artillery screen increase.

'We're nearly out of ammo,' came the reply. This was incredible. An officer from the artillery telling them they could not continue shelling.

'Sorry, can you repeat that?' This was Stiefelmayer. It was as if he wanted the artillery man to understand, as publicly as possible, just how ludicrous the statement was.

Basler stared at the radio dumbfounded and yet not surprised. They were making an attack against a well-guarded position and a key group within the division were without ammunition. He shook his head and could imagine Teege, Kummel and Stiefelmayer doing likewise. Their mission was now bordering on suicidal. News came through that the rear areas were under attack from the RAF. Multiple waves of fighters and bombers were holding up the advance of the supply train.

'Break off the attack,' snarled Kummel angrily. Whatever the truth about the attack on the supply echelon, this was an ongoing open wound that was inhibiting the greatest army on the planet from performing its task. The blame for the lack of ammunition, of fuel, of food, of men and materiel lay further afield from North Africa.

That evening back at the leaguer, as tired as he felt, Manfred sensed his spirits lifting. The flyer, Marseille, had brought with him mail and the usual collection of newspapers and magazines from his recent trip back to Germany. It was good to read letters from his father. Manfred felt that he understood him better. He sensed a change in him, too. The letters were tinged with regret for things never said. He seemed more communicative, more open in writing than when face to face.

As much of a lift as the mail gave to everyone there was also a sense of relief. An acknowledgement a disaster had been averted that day. They'd only lost two tanks. This was a miracle of sorts. It was clear to him and surely to Rommel that they were, once again, stretched too thinly with too few working tanks to mount a serious attack against the Allied positions. As if to confirm this, they heard the drone of RAF planes overhead. Would they ever stop?

Rommel's calculation was theoretically correct. The Allies would only stop when they'd been overrun. The reality of Afrika Korps' position was much more precarious. A serious attack from the Allies could very well wipe them out. They had a handful of tanks, held together by glue, and an army that was exhausted.

There were no lights in the camp. All was dark. No one could smoke. The ground seemed to throb at the proximity of the enemy bombers. Manfred felt a vibration pass through his body. The icy claw of fear gripped him. From the corner of his eye he could see Kleff, Jentz and Keil staring worriedly up into the sky. From feeling a certain amount of elation at the thought they would cease fighting, if only for a short spell, possibly the rest of the summer months, his stomach became a knotted jangle of frayed nerves.

A few distant explosions lit up the night. The RAF were bombing empty desert. Let them, thought Manfred. Probably they were letting off a few bombs just to try their luck. Hard on any Jerboas running around, of course. The noise of the drone slowly lessened and the camp began to relax again. Nothing was said though. They'd all been equally scared.

Basler left them to join a meeting with the commanders. He returned an hour later with probably the only man who he considered a friend, Stiefelmayer. The two lieutenants remained on their feet chatting while the crew waited impatiently to hear the news they were hoping for. Stiefelmayer finally left and Basler slumped to the ground wearily. The crew looked at him eager for news. He paused and looked at the exhausted faces and a grim smile broke out over his face.

'The attack will cease for the time being. The Alamein box is too heavily defended for us to make a dent with what we have. We need more air support. There isn't any.'

Basler looked up to the sky and then back down at the crew.

'It doesn't mean that you're on your holidays. We will stay here and wait for the damaged tanks to be repaired. The *pioniers* will be out tomorrow laying a few mines of our own. We're also seeing how we can fix the Allied guns we captured and use them ourselves. So we're not really going anywhere.'

'I hope we're not going to waste time on their bloody tanks. They're useless,' said Jentz, which raised a few smiles amongst the men.

208

'Only against ours,' pointed out Manfred. This earned a nod of approval from Basler.

'Don't worry, we won't be given those things,' smiled Basler. 'Perhaps the infantry will have some. Anyway, get some rest while you can.'

As it was still early evening, Manfred went in search of Gerhardt. The 2nd Battalion were at the opposite end of the leaguer from Manfred. There were far fewer tanks now, so he didn't have to walk too far. Gerhardt seemed to be with a different group of men.

'Have they changed your tank?'

'Yes,' grumbled Gerhardt, throwing his cigarette angrily to the ground. 'I'm with Captain Wahl. He's made me the radio operator would you believe?'

Gerhardt's woes were greeted in time honoured fashion. Manfred burst out laughing. He received a light punch on the arm for his trouble.

'That's good, isn't it?' said Manfred eventually. 'He's the head of the 2nd Battalion. He only wants the best in his tank.'

'So why did Kummel take you then?' sneered Gerhardt but without any real malice.

'He obviously asked for you,' pointed Manfred but couldn't resist another dig. 'I can just see him saying "send me the best knob twiddler we have." You should be proud.'

'Very funny. You're worse than Fischer. Where is he these days? I haven't seen him for a while.'

'Dysentery,' said Manfred.

Gerhardt stopped and stared at Manfred and then the two boys burst out laughing.

'Lucky devil,' said Gerhardt when they'd calmed down.

'Why? It sounds like we won't be doing much for the next week or so.'

'That doesn't mean the Tommies won't,' pointed out Gerhardt. 'We're sitting ducks for the RAF, out here.'

'True,' agreed Manfred. The mood of ebullience at Fischer's misfortune dissipated in a moment as they considered just how exposed they were.

'Still, if I'm going to go, better it's like this,' said Gerhardt using his arms to hold a fake rifle. Manfred looked confused which made Gerhardt grin. 'Firing at the enemy rather than sitting with my trousers round my ankles.'

They both roared with laughter causing a few of the men sitting by the tanks to look up at them in irritation. One or two told them to shut up. But the vision of their friend in the most vulnerable position of all was too vivid. Try as they might, they couldn't stop laughing. It came out as snorts which only made matters worse and further increased their hilarity.

'I can't wait to see him again. I'll give him hell,' said Gerhardt.

This wasn't going to happen, though. War and the enemy have a way of upsetting the best laid plans. Both were aware that this war was a series of actions, of meetings and of partings. Only fate knew where their stories would end. And its decision is final. They returned to their crews in a better humour, blithely unaware that a new story was about to unfold.

CHAPTER TWENTY-SIX

Tahag Camp 30, Quassasin, Egypt, 13th July 1942

It was late afternoon when Lieutenant 'Pip' Roberts walked along the ranks of men. Ostensibly he was there to inspect them. The real purpose was that they inspect him. Badly wounded just prior to the retreat from the Gazala Line, he was back and, if not fully fit, he was ready and able to fight. Accompanying him were the two other senior casualties from the engagement, Major Joly and Captain Burr.

He walked along the line and what he saw worried him. Despite a couple of weeks near Suez to recuperate and rebuild, their return to the front line revealed that they were tottering on the edge. He wondered what sort of state the Afrika Korps were in. How did they keep coming back?

On 4th July they'd called off what looked like a major offensive and now, just over a week later, they were pressing hard again. Where were they finding the men, the machinery and the strength to keep coming back? Roberts had no idea and dwelling on it made little sense. They were not letting up and nor could the Allies. One thing that was helping the Afrika Korps was the strengthening of their aerial threat. The Luftwaffe were once more able to reach the Allied lines. After the inspection he spoke to them in a voice that he hoped seemed stronger than he felt.

'Along the Ruweisat Ridge, our Commonwealth Allies, the New Zealanders and the South Africans, are going toe to toe with the enemy. Every inch of territory is being fought over. And, yes, many are dying. They need our support and that is why we're back in the 'blue'. If the enemy breaks through the ridge they'll have a clear run to Alamein. At that point we may as well roll out a red carpet and direct them on to Cairo. I don't particularly want to do that. Do you?'

'No, sir,' chorused the ranks of men before him.

Roberts smiled and turned to Joly. Speaking just loud enough for the men to hear him but giving the impression that he was only speaking to Joly, he said, 'There Cyril, I told you they were ready.'

Joly smiled and replied, 'I never doubted, sir.'

Most of the men on the front rank smiled dutifully. Danny was standing back in the last rank. He couldn't smile. He was neither tired, angry nor interested. What lay ahead he knew all about. Day after day of attrition. The Allies had finally begun to work out how to stop the German advance. A combination of digging in behind minefields, an artillery screen with big anti-tank twenty-five-pound guns and regular aerial bombardment. All together this had succeeded in halting the Germans in their tracks. They would now proceed to wrestle over every rock, ridge and desert rat.

The agonised eyes of his father as he'd set off to the war swam into his mind. He'd known what would happen. The clash of two mighty armies, no matter how well led or, for that matter, how badly, would always end up in a quagmire. A stalemate. One thing remained constant. Men would die trying to fulfil the ambitions of others.

He was no longer angry at Bob, his friend who'd tried to desert and then damn near killed himself to avoid the war. He was probably in a prison somewhere or what was left of him, after the incident on a train. But he was alive. Beth and the family had moved from Little Gloston, unable to look the other villagers in the eye. Bob would come out of prison eventually. Probably he'd change his name. The world would forget long before it even thought to forgive.

His reverie was broken by the sound of aeroplanes overhead. His heart stopped for a moment until his ears attuned themselves to the sound. Then he relaxed. They were British. He saw half a dozen Hurricanes flying through the white puffs of cloud. They looked as if they were on their way to meet the enemy. Good luck, thought Danny; then he followed the rest of the crew back to the tank.

Dick Manning plunged through the cloud on the last sortie of the day and saw the German minefield with two lines of tape marking the route through. The Panzers were under fire from anti-tank guns although they seemed remarkably untroubled. Then he saw one erupt into flames. Seconds later men came rolling out of the tank. Manning flew through the black smoke belching up from the turret. He ignored the soldiers escaping and pressed ahead towards their target, a supply echelon that had been spotted in an earlier sortie. The Panzers below were too widely spread for the bombs of the Hurricane Fighter to do any damage.

'Red leader, any sign of bogies?'

'No,' replied Manning. 'No sign of the supply train either.'

'Keep an eye out for any Messerschmitts. I'm not really in the mood to face them today.'

Nor me, thought Manning. He disliked the Hurricane fighter-bomber. It did neither job particularly well. Two five-hundred-pound bombs was a payload that made the value of the sortie somewhat limited in Manning's eyes. The sooner he was back in his Spitfire the better.

They pressed on. Each mile brought them closer to confrontation with the increased Luftwaffe presence. And perhaps Marseille. In the months he'd been here, the name of the Luftwaffe pilot cropped up time and again. Such was his reputation that every pilot he'd met since his arrival had professed a desire to take him on, one on one, and show him what for. Manning assumed they were lying. They all did to an extent. They claimed kills that were probably shared; they exaggerated the manoeuvres they'd employed to evade or destroy the enemy. Harmless fun.

Not much had been heard of Marseille in a while. Manning wondered if he'd been killed. But, surely, they would have heard. He edged his plane downwards. The desert was empty below him. He kept descending until he was barely a few hundred feet off the ground. The plane began to rock.

'Bit windy now,' said Manning.

'Club selection will be important. Hit the ball low,' came the reply which made Manning smile. He glanced down and saw sand swirling below. Not quite a sandstorm but enough to make things a bit unpleasant for the folk on the ground. It was difficult to tell friend from foe.

'Bogies sighted,' said another voice over the radio.

Manning looked around him and could see nothing.

'Where?' he asked in exasperation. Then he saw them. His hands reacted faster than his heart. Which was just as well. They were outnumbered at least two to one. It had just taken a split second to see that there were at least a dozen fighters. They were only six.

'Let's get back over the tanks we saw. Drop our bombs and get away,' said Manning.

There was no argument from the others.

'Control to Red Leader, we're sending up support.'

'Tell them to get a move on will you. Over.'

Out of his peripheral vision, Manning saw the lines of Panzers stretching over half a kilometre. There weren't as many as he'd been expecting. They were advancing towards the ridge being held by the New Zealanders. He began banking towards them. It would be a miracle if he hit one, but it was worth a try. It would certainly give the Jerries something to think about. If nothing else, it would lighten the aircraft by the total of the two five-hundred-pound bombs he was carrying. In a race back to the base, this could be the difference between life and death.

He gripped the stick tightly and slowly levelled the plane with the ground. A few puffs of smoke appeared. His stomach was too knotted to dismiss their efforts entirely. He just wanted to get rid of the bombs and clear off.

He picked a row of tanks. They were around fifty metres apart. Three, two, one…

Captain Wolfgang Wahl was not yet thirty but already leading his own battalion. Gerhardt looked at him in a kind of awe. The captain barely blinked at the shells which were hitting the tank like a malevolent hailstorm. Unquestionably it inspired confidence. Or was it a kind of recklessness? The difference between the two was the difference between mist and fog. In Wahl's case it was confidence. You could see when someone was simply mad.

'Keep pressing ahead. The sand will give us cover.'

It doesn't seem to be giving us much cover now, thought Gerhardt. They'd sustained over a dozen hits that day. Somehow the Mark IV's thicker frontal armour had held up against the onslaught. He offered

215

a brief and silent prayer to the German engineers who'd made the Mark IV the most well-protected tank in the war.

Two explosions, louder than the ones they were used to from the six pounders, went off behind them.

'The planes,' said Wahl. They'd seen the planes a few minutes earlier and breathed a collective sigh of relief when they'd ignored the tanks and kept moving. There was no time to feel guilty for being glad that someone else was going to be in the line of fire. They were on the receiving end of it, every day. Two more explosions rent the air nearby throwing up gouts of sand. These were closer than before. Gerhardt wiped the sweat from his eyes and tried to remember how many planes they'd seen. Certainly three. Were there more? He hadn't seen any others but perhaps he'd missed some of them.

Gerhardt sensed it before it happened.

Something changed in the air, split seconds before the detonation. Like inhaling before you let out a sigh. He ducked. So, too, did Wahl. Two giant explosions rocked the tank.

They stopped moving and immediately the cabin began to fill with smoke. Gerhardt heard someone groan and realised, with relief, it wasn't him. His body was already escaping before his mind had time to react. The driver kicked open the hatch and fell out of the hull. Gerhardt was about to follow him when he heard someone shouting. It was Hess.

'Kroos, help me. The captain's been hit.'

Gerhardt glanced up. It was true. Blood streamed down Wahl's face. He was unconscious. Flames were now licking dangerously close to the engine and, more importantly, the shells.

Without hesitating he moved upwards from the wireless position to the turret to help the gunner lift the stricken captain out from the cupola. The heat was burning his breath. He stopped breathing. Within seconds his lungs felt like they were going to explode.

216

Hess was already outside the cupola with his hands underneath the arms of Wahl. Gerhardt grabbed the captain's legs and helped push him upwards. Slowly the captain was hoisted out of the turret. Gerhardt could hear cracking inside the cabin now. The heat was burning his face and he let out a roar of pain. When the captain's leg was through the cupola, Gerhardt gripped the cupola. His legs were in agony from the heat; his hands burned on the metal. He hoisted himself out of the tank.

Below him, Hess was struggling with the unconscious Wahl. Scrambling down from the turret, Gerhardt joined him and grabbed the captain's legs. They carried him away from the tank just as ammunition began to explode like a fireworks display.

'Hurry,' said Hess.

Gerhardt resisted the temptation to point out that he was perfectly aware of the need to hurry. Something exploded nearby. Gerhardt felt a stab of pain in his arm as a splinter of metal sliced his bicep. He collapsed to the ground. Hess continued to drag the captain away from the tank.

His arm was bloodied, his body protesting at the excruciating pain. But he was alive. Gerhardt slowly raised himself to his feet and stumbled over towards Hess.

The three men were now in a natural depression. They kept their heads down while gunfire ripped the air around them. Gerhardt glanced enviously at the retreating Panzers. If he'd sprinted he would have been able to catch one, but that would have meant leaving Wahl and Hess. The thought was momentary then discarded.

'If we stay here, perhaps we can make it back with the captain when it's dark.'

This made sense. The light was poor and made poorer by the sand being lifted by the strong wind. Perhaps there was a chance they could make it after all. Gerhardt glanced down at his arm. His shirt had blood soaking through but he could move his arm. It was painful but the wounds were not serious. His hands were burning from having gripped the metal of the tank as it brewed up. And his skin was tingling from either fear or the singeing it had undergone. It was almost funny. He was a mess.

Wahl was now conscious. His head wound was not so serious and was a result of having been knocked out rather than any shrapnel or effect of the explosion.

'What happened?' asked Wahl. His voice was weak.

Hess told him.

He looked at the two men who had, without doubt, saved his life. He nodded. That was it. No more needed to be said. He glanced up at the sky.

'So we wait here.'

It wasn't a suggestion. His mind was recovering quickly now. Through the flurries of sand, they could see a dozen or so Panzers receding into the distance. The firing was no longer concentrated around them and, instead, was focused on the enemy retreat.

Gerhardt's breath was coming in shallow bursts. It hurt when he inhaled too deeply. He lowered his head to avoid the sand blowing into his eyes. He tried to think of a time when he'd felt in more pain or discomfort. The evening spent running around the parade ground sprang to mind. Yet even that was no comparison to how he felt now. He grimaced in agony.

'Good work, Kroos,' said Hess, looking at Gerhardt. 'I couldn't have done that without you.'

Out of the corner of his eye, he saw Wahl looking at him. Hess was speaking in a low voice into the captain's ear. A moment later Wahl looked at him. There was something in his eyes that he hadn't seen before. It went beyond gratitude, respect even. It was a love that only men who have faced death and worked together to conquer it can feel.

The gunfire was ebbing away with the light. But a new sound was growing louder. The sound of men, on foot, talking to one another. Their voices were not German. The three men in the shallow looked at one another. It was a slim hope that they could stay unobserved. Each passing minute saw the light grow dimmer. The wind was dying and there was less sand being picked up and thrown through the air.

The voices grew louder.

It was difficult to understand them at first. It was English but the accent was too strong to understand. They heard the crack of rifles being fired.

'Idiots,' hissed Wahl. Gerhardt wasn't sure if he was referring to the Allied infantry or any German crew who had decided to fight. The sound of shouts grew louder. The crack of guns grew more insistent.

Gerhardt ducked down further. His heart was racing now and the back of his throat was a torment. The adrenalin that had surged through him following their escape was wearing off and his body was suffering. There was a further crash of gunfire but Gerhardt could not bring himself to look up and see who was firing or where it was happening.

The acrid smell of burning now filled his nostrils. The wind had lightened but it had also shifted. Black smoke from their tanks was drifting lazily over them.

'Can you see them?' whispered Wahl.

Hess shook his head. The gunfire had stopped for a moment along with the shouts. Gerhardt's hopes began to flicker more strongly.

If not dark, then it was certainly going to be night within the next fifteen minutes. Each passing second seemed to stretch endlessly like the sermon of his old pastor. Just ten minutes or more. The Allies would not want to be out in the dark any more than they would.

More gunfire.

It seemed to come from somewhere behind the destroyed tank.

'The bastards had better not be killing our men,' said Wahl in a low growl. Despite his youth, he was of the old school. You did not kill men who had escaped from burning tanks.

The shouts had returned. They couldn't see where they were coming from. The shouts grew louder. Another gunshot. This was very close. You could hear the bolt action on the Lee Enfield.

Gerhardt's chest tightened and he stopped breathing for a moment. He looked up but could see nothing now. The night was filled with disembodied voices shouting. Fear gripped him but he forced himself to look up. He didn't want to be shot, cowering face down.

'Over here,' an English voice shouted. It came from behind them.

A gunshot.

Gerhardt flinched. In fact, the three men flinched at the same moment. They turned around.

Two Allied soldiers were standing near them. They were young. Scared. And pointing rifles right at them. This was a combination that did not bode well.

'Do not shoot,' said Hess slowly. He began to raise his hands. Gerhardt and Wahl did likewise. A couple of other Allied soldiers ran over. They were all pointing their Lee Enfields at Gerhardt and the others. There was silence for a moment. One of the soldiers motioned with his gun for them to rise.

More soldiers arrived.

First Hess and then Wahl rose. They helped Gerhardt up as it was now plain that he was the more badly injured. All had their hands up now. Gerhardt looked at the young men before him. They were all a similar age to him. New Zealanders. He looked into the eyes of the sergeant who'd just arrived.

'Do any of you speak English?'

All three answered 'yes' simultaneously. It would have been funny had it not been so frightening.

'Come with us,' ordered the sergeant.

Gerhardt, Wahl and Hess exchanged brief looks and then nodded.

'Yes, sergeant,' said Wahl.

It was night. The firing had stopped and other soldiers had arrived. Gerhardt could see there were few other prisoners. And then he realised in shock that's that what he was now.

A prisoner of war.

CHAPTER TWENTY-SEVEN

*El Tahag Mobilisation Camp, 40 miles north-east of Cairo,
Egypt, 13th August 1942*

'Who is this Pyman anyway?' asked Danny, looking at Benson. He
was referring to the new lieutenant-colonel who was to replace Pip
Roberts.

Benson smiled and replied. 'Ever seen any paintings of Napoleon?'

Danny smiled and nodded.

'Well, imagine someone like that with similar ambition and energy;
then I think you'll have an idea of what the new CO is like.'

'Have you met him?'

'Only briefly,' replied Benson. He tapped his pipe on a rock and
then put it back in his mouth. 'I think he'll be good. He said to all
of us that there are three things he would not tolerate: drunkenness,
idleness and stupidity.'

Danny turned away and gazed out at the endless sea of tents at
the camp. They would be on the march again soon. Back out into
the blue. They'd had a longer break from the fighting and Danny felt

something of his old self returning. He'd not gone back to see Arthur and so had missed him when he left. He wrote instead. It had felt like an act of cowardice. And he'd admitted as much in the letter. He felt better for having done so. But only a little bit.

Benson was looking at him thoughtfully. A half smile lay on his face. Danny frowned at the captain.

'Sir?' he asked.

Benson grinned and said nothing. His attention was diverted by the appearance of a sergeant.

'At last,' said Benson. 'Come this way, Shaw.'

Benson stood up and Danny followed suit. He followed the captain towards the sergeant.

'Major Crisp asked to see you both,' said the sergeant.

The three men went to a tent at the far end of a row of newly arrived Grants. They were not the new Shermans from America that Danny had heard so much about, but at least they were better than the Crusaders.

Major Bob Crisp was a tall, athletic South African. A former test cricketer, he was something of a legend in the regiment. Decorated and promoted as often as he'd been wounded, he ran the squadron like Captain Blood running pirate missions on the Spanish Main.

'Shaw, I have some news for you. Take a seat.'

Danny looked at the serious face of the Major and felt every part of his body tense. There had been no word about Tom since Tobruk had fallen. He waited for the body blow to land.

'Don't look so serious, Shaw,' said Crisp, and a smile creased his tanned face. 'It's about your brother. I know that you've been worried about him since Tobruk fell. I have just received word that he's alive. It's not all good, of course. He was taken captive by the Germans. He's somewhere in Italy now.'

223

Danny had to stop himself crying with relief. Not only on the fact that he was alive but that, in all probability, he might survive the war. At least one of them would return to the village.

'Thank you, sir,' said Danny. He felt Benson clap him on the shoulder. He was saying something, but Danny could barely take it in. There was silence for a moment and Danny made to stand up.

'Not so fast, Shaw. There's one other thing,' said Crisp. His eyes were lit by the knowledge that, for once, he was the bringer of good news rather than bad. 'Take a look inside that box.'

Throughout the meeting, Danny had been aware of a small flat box sitting on the table between him and the major. He knew what was inside. He picked up the box and opened it.

There were stripes inside.

'Congratulations, Corporal Shaw.'

That was one more than he'd expected. He nodded stupidly; such was his shock. Benson chuckled just behind him. Danny turned to him and smiled.

'I might be giving you orders soon at this rate, sir.'

Crisp and Benson both burst out laughing at this. For a second Danny felt a surge of happiness. The news that Tom was alive and that he'd been promoted would eventually find its way back home. One would be a source of great comfort; the other would bring pride.

It was only after he'd departed from Crisp and Benson that the darkness descended on him again. It had been his companion since the end of May and now, despite the news, it had barely lightened. He tried not to think of Arthur, but guilt has a way of piercing any armour you wear. His father had lived with survivor's guilt and it was his now, too. Just for a moment he smiled darkly as he reminded himself of the one truth that accompanied this self-reproach.

He might not survive.

Two days passed. Danny stared at the stripes and tried to find the motivation to sew them onto his shirt. He sensed Benson was becoming irritated by the fact that he'd not yet done so. He put them back inside the box and went for a walk. It was early afternoon in the camp. Training exercises had finished because of the heat. It was well over one hundred now. It felt like he was walking into a solid wall of heat. The sweat sizzled on his skin like frying fat.

Ahead he could see a few hardy souls playing cricket. Others were watching in groups offering good-natured advice to the players on their manifest inadequacies. The players were responding in kind. By the sound of the accents, it was England versus New Zealand.

Five groups of six planes buzzed overhead. Danny watched them descend and fly low over the desert. He wondered if Dick Manning was among them. He'd seen him again a week ago. Manning offered his sympathy on hearing about Arthur.

He was beginning to regret not joining the others from the crew who were going for a swim. In the distance he saw the barbed wire fencing demarcating the prisoner of war camp. Several hundred Germans and Italians were housed there waiting, like most of the Allies, to be transferred.

Every day he saw new arrivals at the camp. Some were coming back from the desert. There were also new arrivals fresh from home. The three-ton trucks deposited them in the middle of the camp. Danny could see a small convoy drawing up in the large square in the middle.

He ignored them and went to a makeshift NAAFI for a tea and a biscuit. Even a short walk in the sun felt like he was turning into a Sunday roast. The large tent offered shade and he was glad of a seat. As he was drinking his tea, he spotted Captain Benson entering the tent. It occurred to him that he really should put the stripes on. It was beginning to seem disrespectful. Benson had spotted him now. His face turned stony as he noted the absence of stripes. He came over to the table. Danny rose but one look at Benson's face and he sat down again. He braced himself for the worst. Benson sat down in the manner of someone who had little time for seats.

'I don't know what you think you're playing at, Shaw, but if you don't put those bloody stripes on by the time I'm back, I'll recommend to the major that they're taken from you.'

Benson didn't wait for a reply. He was on his feet immediately and away. Danny stared angrily out into the square. He was cross with himself for not doing as he'd been told. There was anger, too, for Benson. A few other men had seen his humiliation. He scowled at them and clutched the mug tightly. He drained the tea in a gulp. It burned his throat though he hardly noticed.

Rising from his table he walked forwards without thinking about where he was going. The square in the middle of the camp was crowded like a city. He wanted to lose himself in the noise, the shouting and the truck engines coughing and spluttering like old men. Almost at once though, he realised he hated being with people. Rather than stay with the throng he decided to cross the square and head back to the tank. A voice shouting in his ear got an earful back. The soldier looked at Danny somewhat hurt as well as surprised, but he was already pushing through the crowd of soldiers.

He weaved out of the way of a bunch of men jumping off a truck. What had possessed him to come this way? It was mobbed and madness in a tiny space. Anger at himself for yet another act of stupidity bubbled to the surface. Could he do nothing right? Utter idiot. He felt himself jostled or perhaps it was him doing the jostling. He needed to get away from here, that much was certain.

He went past one truck with soldiers fresh from England. You could always tell. They were fair, fat and full of good humour. They'd learn soon enough. He brushed past one and then, unseeingly, banged into another.

'Watch it, mate,' said the soldier. Danny knew the man had been within rights to complain and turned to apologise. He hadn't been looking where he was going. It was difficult to see through the red mist.

'Leave him, Sid. Looks like Rommel's beaten him already,' said another voice.

The apology died on Danny's lips. Instead, they curled into a snarl, his face a mask of hatred. He threw the first man out of the way and made for the second man who'd mocked him. There were shouts now as the soldiers realised, too late, his intention. Danny could see fear in the eyes of the second man and that drove him more. He could also see that he had put his hands up in a manner which suggested not self-defence, but an apology was about to come his way. But Danny could only hear his heart racing and the voices of hate in his head. His first punch landed in the solar plexus of the soldier. His second, a wild swing, thankfully missed as the man collapsed to the ground.

Arms grabbed Danny and he struggled manically to free himself. He was snarling like an animal. And then the mist cleared, and he realised what he'd done. He immediately stopped struggling. He heard a voice near him.

A voice he knew.

'Well, Shaw. Looks like the boot's on the other foot.'

Danny turned and stared into the clear blue eyes of Captain Edmund Aston. There was little sympathy in the eyes, only the usual mocking humour. The captain put the cheroot back in his mouth and turned his attention behind Danny.

'Let him go,' he ordered the men holding Danny.

227

Danny's eyes were wide with horror at what he'd done. He looked at the man he'd hit. His friends were helping him up from the ground. He stepped forward and the two men faced one another. Danny shook his head. He wanted to apologise but no words came. Instead, he looked away and strode off through a parting in the crowd. He could barely breathe in the hot air. Too many people around. He started to run.

He ran for half a mile, to the farthest point of the camp where he would be alone. He dropped to the ground on his knees and began to sob. His body heaved as he fought to draw in air. His eyes lost focus as they filled with tears. For five minutes he stayed there full of despair at what he'd done. A wave of self-loathing overcame him. What had he become? He sat staring ahead for several minutes. Finally, he picked out a letter from his breast pocket. It was damp with his sweat. The ink on the envelope had long since faded. The ink on the letter was beginning to fade, too.

Then, aware that some men were coming over to him, he stood up and dusted himself down. He took a deep breath and started to walk in their direction.

'Everything all right?' asked one of the men as he walked towards him. They could see Danny's red-rimmed eyes.

Danny nodded, not trusting himself to say anything. He kept going. It took five minutes to return to the tank. Benson was sitting there alone. They looked at one another. He didn't know.

The box containing the stripes was sitting on top of his kit bag. Danny picked it up and handed it to Benson.

'I can't take this, sir.'

Benson looked astounded at first. Then angry. He was just about to speak when Danny held his hand up.

'Permission to speak, sir.'

228

This stopped Benson and he nodded curtly. Danny told him what had happened. Benson said nothing while Danny spoke. He put his pipe in his mouth and listened intently.

'There was no damage done?'

'I don't think so, sir.'

'What were you thinking?' pressed the captain.

'I don't know, sir. After what happened to Arthur, Phil Lawrence, Sergeant Reed. All of them. It was too much.'

Benson nodded and took the box containing the stripes away from Danny.

'Go and find the man you hit. Apologise to him. I'll speak to Captain Aston.'

It took an hour to find the man he'd hit. He was at the far end of the camp from where the regiment was stationed. Danny saw him standing with a group of men. One of them was the man he'd pushed out of the way initially.

They watched him warily as he came over. Danny wanted to smile but knew it was a forlorn hope. He decided to get straight to the point.

'I'm sorry. I feel terrible about what I did. It was cowardly,' said Danny. He held his hand out.

The soldier nodded to Danny and shook his hand.

'It was m…'

'No, please, it was my fault,' said Danny interrupting the apology that was about to come his way. 'Don't argue with me,' added Danny with a smile.

The group burst out in a relieved sort of laugh.

'What do you boys do?' asked Danny.

'We're sappers,' said the soldier he'd hit. His name was Ian. He sounded like he was from the south-west.

'Mines?' asked Danny. He saw the heads nod around him. 'Well, you're in the right place here. If it's not us, then it's them. They're everywhere.'

'Thanks for the good news,' replied Ian and the group laughed again. 'What's the bad news?'

'I'm with tanks. You'll be laying out the red carpet for me and my mates,' laughed Danny. The sappers responded good-naturedly with a very specific suggestion on what he could do with his tank.

He chatted with them for ten minutes giving a highly coloured version of his time in North Africa. There seemed little point in scaring them senseless, so he made his way back. The late afternoon sun was not as hatefully hot as earlier. The flies were still awake, though, and as militant as ever. They attacked with their usual frenzied determination. Yet despite their aggravating attentions, Danny's mood had lifted somewhat.

The area around the tank was empty. The crew were still bathing probably, and Benson was nowhere to be seen. Something on his kit bag caught Danny's attention. There were several letters that had obviously just arrived. Sitting on top of them was the box containing his stripes. He opened it. They were still there. There was also a folded note. Danny read the note and found tears stinging his eyes.

He sat down and fished inside a bag belonging to McLeish. It took a few moments but he found what he was looking for. The small sewing kit was contained in a leather pouch. He took off his shirt and unrolled his shirt sleeve. Placing the first set of stripes on his arm, he began to sew.

CHAPTER TWENTY-EIGHT

Alam el Halfa Ridge, 15km south-east of El Alamein, Egypt, 31st August 1942

It was almost beautiful. The night sky was lit up by parachute flares that twinkled wickedly down at the large force of Panzers advancing slowly like dark ink on a blotter.

The going was much too slow. Any element of surprise was being lost with each passing minute and every mile closer to the enemy positions along the Alam Halfa Ridge. The atmosphere in Manfred's tank was tense. Invariably the mood was dictated by the commander. Basler was intense at the best of times. On this occasion he'd made things worse for himself by emphasising the previous evening that speed was of the essence. The Allies were likely to be dug in with land mines in front and an artillery shield behind. If they could reach them during the night, they might just catch them unawares.

That hope was lying in tatters as they saw the sun rise on a regiment that had barely made half of the fifty kilometres they had been tasked to march. The proof of this lay ahead. The German *pioniers* and infantry were being shelled by the Allied guns. The reception committee was up and ready to greet them. As ever, the calculation was that many would die but some would get through. Their lives only had value as a stepping stone for others, reflected Manfred.

Sweat poured from the bodies of the men while they sat silently listening to the grind and whine of the wheels. Jentz was driving; his eyes fixed on the tank ahead. He flinched as an explosion sent rock into the air. One could never become inured to the explosions. Especially as they grew louder. Nausea and panic were Manfred's constant companions at the moments just before battle. As soon as he was able to shoot back then a curtain descended on him. Every particle of his being was focused on one thing: survival. This could not be decided by him, of course. All he could do was to keep firing and hope. The minutes until he could start firing were a sick agony for him.

He looked at Basler and could see anger in the lieutenant's eyes. A comment earlier had revealed the source of his anger.

'Why didn't we know about this minefield?'

The stop-starting, always weaving progress was likely to play hell with their petrol reserves. The rising sun would improve the accuracy of artillery fire and open them to aerial attack. The closer to the ridge they came, the further it was for the Luftwaffe to travel to protect them. It didn't take a mathematician to work out they would soon be on their own. By 1030 they were mired in soft sand and fuel was running low.

'We'll have to halt and wait for fuel trucks,' said Basler who had moved to Jentz's shoulder to gaze down at the petrol gauge.

Kummel was of a similar mind and the march was halted. Manfred and Jentz took the opportunity to check the engine while Keil made the coffee. The veteran driver could barely hide the shaking of his hands as he lit a cigarette. He smiled at Manfred in embarrassment.

'This is going to be hell. I can feel it. We're at our best when we're moving fast.'

Manfred and Jentz listened to the battle raging a few kilometres ahead. They continued their checks on the tracks until Keil called that their coffee was ready. They joined the others. Manfred looked around at the dull eyes of his comrades. There was little sense of heroic ambition there. Nor was there obvious fear or, indeed, the indifference that assails you when you realise there really is no hope. In its place the training and experience of countless encounters was beginning to prevail. The noises around them were not just the sounds of battle but the shouts of soldiers preparing for what lay ahead. They did this by checking machinery, testing weapons, challenging one another to their jobs. It worked in a strange way. Your thoughts turned outward from the terror you were feeling and towards what you were there to do.

'What's that?' asked Jentz, three hours later, soon after they had set off again. Visibility had begun to deteriorate and, for once, it was nothing to do with the midday heat haze which turned the horizon into a glinting blur. Manfred joined Basler outside the turret.

'Sandstorm,' said Manfred simply.

'At least it will blow into the faces of Tommy,' added Basler with a hint of a smile. The two men dived back into the hot, stinking safety of the interior. The thought of what the sand would do to the enemy gave both Manfred and Basler a lift. Then Kummel's voice came loud and clear on the radio.

'We are to push to the western side of the Alam el Halfa ridge. Trieste and Ariete are caught up in the minefields.'

'Of course they're caught up in them. They weren't told about them in the first place,' snapped Basler angrily.

They trundled forward behind a dozen other Mark IIIs. As they were in No Man's Land, the regiment was ordered to fan out to present a wider target for the inevitable bombardment they would face.

The combination of coffee and the likely discomfort of the enemy had energised Manfred. The sandstorm was better than a smokescreen for the attack. It would prevent aerial reconnaissance and bombing. It would delay the moment when they'd begin to face the long-range shelling from the enemy twenty-five pounders. Perhaps things might just go their way.

A couple of miles further ahead, directly in their path, was the Alam el Halfa ridge. This was the southern underbelly to the Allied stronghold at El Alamein. The rocky ridge was an undulating series of very highly defensible positions that had been created by the Allies.

Standing at the top of the ridge was one Lieutenant James Carruthers. He held his binoculars to his eyes and surveyed the Deir el Agram depression, or at least what he could see of it. This wasn't much. They would have to come this way, he thought. Pity he couldn't see anything. He cast aside his binoculars. There was little point in looking while the sand was blowing with such anger. He looked around him. There were six-pounder guns lined up waiting to give Jerry the welcome he most assuredly deserved. A young man, a sergeant, came over to him.

'Tea, sir?'

Carruthers glanced at the young man and smiled. 'Yes, thank you, McMillan. That would be very nice.'

How surreal, thought Carruthers. Two years ago, he'd been a manager of a shoe factory. Now he was running a battalion of gunners. Class always tells, he reflected. They could see he was officer material from the off. He surveyed the faces of his men. Most were sitting smoking cigarettes. Their battle would start soon. Carruthers was happy for them to grab a few minutes of peace. The big guns were firing from a position further back. The noise was more sporadic since the sandstorm had started to blow in their faces. Carruthers crouched down to avoid the full intensity of its blast.

McMillan arrived a few minutes later with a mug of tea. He'd covered the top with a card. After eighteen months in this godforsaken land he'd grown used to sand in his tea. It usually sank to the bottom. With his back to the sand, Carruthers positioned the card at the top in such a way as to allow him to drink. He took his first sip when he heard the shout from one of his men.

'Tanks, sir. Loads of them.'

Carruthers remained seated and sipped his tea.

'How many is that exactly, Finch? And how far?'

A few moments passed.

'At least eighty, sir. Must be two thousand yards.'

'Very well,' replied Carruthers. He rose to his feet and drank another large mouthful. The remainder of the mug was emptied. A ghastly mixture of tea and sand fell like treacle to the rocky ground. Carruthers glanced down at it distastefully. 'McMillan, where are you? Can you take this?'

The young gunner appeared and took the lieutenant's cup. Carruthers returned his attention to the dark shapes appearing through the blowing sand.

'How far are they now?' He could have been asking someone's opinion on the weather.

'Fifteen hundred yards, sir,' replied a sergeant. Half a minute later he added, 'A thousand yards.'

Carruthers picked up his binoculars to see for himself and said calmly, 'Perhaps we should start shooting.'

Manfred's first view of the Alam el Halfa ridge was when he saw the puffs of white smoke. Moments later the air was split apart by the sound of explosions. It was too far away to return fire. They had to keep going in the face of this almighty barrage. But not every tank was so limited. They now had many more Mark IVs which had a seventy-five-millimetre gun. This was going to be a nasty surprise for the British.

'Enemy tanks one thousand metres,' reported Kummel over the radio. 'Mark IVs commence firing. The rest of you wait until we're within range.'

In a moment of jubilation, he saw clouds of smoke being thrown skyward along the ridge as the new Mark IVs began to exact a toll. British tanks were in flames, too. Manfred motioned to Kleff to make ready.

'HE shells.'

Basler looked at Manfred and nodded. 'Aim for the artillery on the ridge. We'll let the Mark IVs deal with the tanks.'

The six pounders were beginning to inflict casualties though. The radio was sizzling with messages for help that would be ignored as they pressed forward; they were making progress. Within a few minutes the Panzers were past the first line of guns. Prisoners were being taken. Guns captured. Kummel came on the radio again.

'British tanks retreating. Pursue.'

Jentz turned the tank eastwards in a direction parallel to the northern ridge. They followed a group of the 1st Battalion tanks led by Kummel. Manfred could not see the enemy tanks such was the dust being thrown up by the lead tanks and the remnants of the earlier sandstorm. The pursuit, at least, took them away from the direct line of fire they'd endured. As the light began to fade, so did their hopes of engaging the remnants of the enemy tank regiment. By 1930 it was clear they'd escaped. They were in an advanced position on the edge of the Alam el Halfa ridge but without infantry support. Kummel gave the order to withdraw.

They were reunited with the rest of the division at 2100 just south of the Deir el Agram depression. A very tired crew staggered out of the tank and collapsed on the ground.

'Ten minutes to do what you have to do,' ordered Basler. 'Then, Kleff, get the food ready. No fires. Keil, examine the tracks. Brehme, check the guns and organise the ammo. Jentz, check the engine.'

It took over an hour to check their vehicle, by which time it was too late to go in search of Fischer for a chat and a cigarette. Instead, Manfred sank onto his bedding and was asleep before his eyes shut.

So ended the first day of the battle of Alam el Halfa.

CHAPTER TWENTY-NINE

Alam el Halfa, Egypt, 1st September 1942

Just after four in the morning, Danny sat with the rest of the crew listening to Benson. He'd just returned from a conference with the senior commanders. For once the mood was upbeat. They'd had a few weeks of rest at the Canal and now they were refreshed if not exactly raring to fight. No sane person was ever raring to fight but they would be more prepared this time. Danny had sensed a change in the mood of the regiment since the arrival of the new commander in North Africa, General Bernard Montgomery. He had taken command in the previous month.

His coming brought with it more reinforcements and the first Shermans. Danny had not seen one, but the rumours were strong that it addressed the major problems with the Grant. It was all good news and Benson quoted the words of Pip Roberts on why the advantage was now, at long last, likely to swing their way.

'I spoke to Major Joly. He told me that the colonel thinks this could be like Gazala again but with a crucial difference. We'll be sitting in the path of the Panzer Divisions supported by a whole brigade. That means infantry and artillery will be backing us up. And let's not forget the RAF. They'll be taking pot shots at Jerry, too. We repulsed their first attack yesterday. We expect them to come back hard today.'

Major Crisp came by as Benson was speaking. The South African stopped for a moment and listened to Benson. Then he chipped in at the end.

'I think we can count on them coming back hard. I gather they've got some new toys, too. The new Mark IVs are carrying seventy-five-millimetre guns. Don't get caught out thinking you can outreach them. We don't know how many they have. Don't take chances. Our job is to take over from the Notts Yeomanry at point 89. We may be required to support the next push. Is everyone ready?' said the South African with a grin.

'Yes, sir,' chorused Danny and the other crew members.

They set off in confident spirits.

It lasted two hours.

By eight they were confronted by thirty Panzers supported by anti-tank guns.

'Looks like they've learned their lesson,' said Benson, viewing with some dismay the sight of the assembled armour less than a couple of miles away. 'They've brought in the big boys.'

A year spent fighting in a tank had taught Danny that the deadliest weapon they faced was the eighty-eight-millimetre gun. When that hit you, it was over. Their guns could only inflict damage at relatively close range, although the Grants were changing things.

The mood of confidence was now drenched in the cold sweat of fear. Then he heard what, for a tank man, was the equivalent of the

US cavalry. Overhead came the hum of Allied bombers. Somewhere up ahead, life was about to become somewhat uncomfortable for the enemy.

'Careful, careful, Marseille is in the air.'

Manning felt a momentary wave pass through him and then something else. Excitement. He'd heard so much about the German flyer but had not, yet, faced him. He looked around at the other planes. There were a dozen fighters accompanying the bombers. The arid light-brown land stretched endlessly below. Manning glanced at his altimeter. He was at 20,000 feet. Signs of the battle ahead at the Alam el Halfa ridge were visible. Plumes of smoke rose ominously into the sky.

The radio began to crackle with responses to the prospect of encountering Marseille. Manning decided not to add his voice to the growing hubris. He glanced across at Thompson. His mouth was moving in a dramatic fashion. He was an Al Bowlly fan. Probably 'Goodnight Sweetheart' if memory served. He'd once treated the squadron to a rather raucous version of it while flying back from a sortie.

'Red Leader, any sighting of Jerry?' asked Manning, hoping there was no trace of nervousness in his voice.

They ran into them two minutes later.

Manning could see the yellow tipped BF 109s massed like a swarm of wasps. His heart began to beat faster and adrenalin coursed through his body. He was ready. A babble of voices could be heard on the radio. German voices. This happened from time to time.

'*Halts Maul*,' shouted Manning into his radio with a grin.

'Tallyho,' came the reply in a distinctly German accent.

They were around 1,000 feet below the Spitfires and they formed a protective circle. The Spitfires began to fan out, then, one after another, started to dive. The numbers were very much in favour of the Allies. Manning could only count eight Messerschmitts. Seeing the attack coming, one of the enemy BF 109s peeled away and seemed to fall behind the others. Manning wondered if it was running scared. Then he saw it describe the most extraordinary arc and accelerate. Within seconds it had hit one of the Spitfires. This could only be Marseille.

Manning didn't have time to think about this anymore. The sky was now a mass of dogfights. It looked like the Spitfires outnumbered the Messerschmitts almost two to one. But this advantage was not telling. One of the Germans was running amok within the Spitfire lines.

Sweat poured down Manning's face. Then the sickening realisation hit him. A German fighter was on his tail. He pushed forward on his stick then executed a half roll. Within seconds he now had the Messerschmitt in his sights. He kicked his rudder left to allow him a right-angle attack and turned the gun button to fire. A four second burst followed. The tracers from the eight guns hit their mark. Smoke began to pour from the stricken German fighter. It began to spiral downwards. Then it was out of view and out of Manning's mind.

He peeled away, relieved to have bested the German in this encounter. His mind turned to the small matter of helping his squadron. It was bedlam and they were having the worst of it. And it was not hard to guess why. One man flew with urgency and venom. For all the reports of his conduct when the fighting stopped, there was no question that Marseille was a killer.

The British had lost over half of the squadron at a cost of only a couple of the Messerschmitts. Battle smoke, thick with death, filled the sky. A BF 109 appeared in Manning's sights. It had just hit a Spitfire. The tail was on fire.

'Red Leader here, Red Two, you're on fire. Eject.'

There was no response. The plane turned sharply and went into a headlong descent. Manning felt his heart lurch. There would be no more singing from Thompson. Manning turned hunter once more.

The Messerschmitt was unaware of Manning. This gave the Spitfire vital seconds to dive towards him. He closed to within one hundred and fifty yards. It was practically impossible to miss. Manning let go a three second burst with full deflection and spun away as he saw a jet of red flame coming from the engine of the fighter.

He climbed up steeply, his eyes sinking to the back of his skull. At this point it was every man for himself. The battle was spread out over miles of sky. As his eyes searched for a friend or foe, he felt his plane shudder.

The plane had been hit.

In a split second he realised two things. The bullets had not hit anything of consequence: he still had control of the aircraft, but he was in the sights of the enemy. Manning swore out loud but also acted instinctively. He thrust the stick forward and then kicked the rudder right. He heard another burst of gunfire. It missed.

Fear gripped Manning as he looked around wildly to see where the attack was coming from. Then he realised it was underneath him. He didn't panic. He spun left in anticipation of his enemy firing at him but the man he was up against was more calculating. He'd held off until he was certain.

For one glorious moment he thought he was clear of his assailant. The sky around him seemed clear. Perhaps he'd broken off the encounter because ammunition or fuel was low. All his senses were on highest alert. It had been a close call. Up ahead he saw a lone fighter. He saw the yellow tip before he saw the swastika. The German plane seemed unaware of Manning's approach.

Closing in, he lined up the aircraft in his sights. Four hundred feet away, three hundred then suddenly, the BF 109 swung viciously upwards. Within a matter of seconds it had arced tightly. Manning knew what would happen next. They'd talked about Marseille's technique often yet here he was about to fall victim to it. The high deflection firing from short range, immediate, instinctive, and probably executed without the aid of gun sights. Manning was already opening his hood when the plane ran into the bullets and the engine burst into flame. The control stick was wrenched from his other hand.

Moments later Manning was out of the plane and falling from the sky. Remarkably he was uninjured. The plane was in a tailspin and he chased it down through the air. He felt for the rip cord of his parachute and tugged. The speed of his descent was immediately arrested. He was falling faster than he would have liked. In truth he didn't know what to expect. The ground was coming towards him quickly. He braced himself for the inevitable impact and tried to remember to roll.

He hit the ground with a thud and a grunt. His roll mitigated the impact but the wind had been knocked out of him. He lay there for several minutes and stared up at the sky. It was blue. This was hardly news, but it told him that he'd strayed quite some distance from the dogfight. The question was, where exactly was he? He could hear plainly the sound of fighting, muffled explosions, the crack of guns. None of this gave him a clue as to which side of the divide he'd fallen. The sky was empty.

He hoisted himself up and scanned the horizon. Ribbons of black smoke floated gently upwards. Five planes had certainly bought it. He wondered how many of them were Spitfires.

The buzz of an engine woke him from this reverie. He quickly got rid of the parachute and tried to stand up. He gave up. He'd rest a little longer. It didn't feel as if anything was broken. Nor did it feel as if everything was in perfect running order. A faintness overcame him. He wasn't sure if this was the sun or, more likely, shock.

The buzz of the plane grew louder.

He rolled away from the parachute and faced in the direction of the plane. It seemed to be heading this direction. It was also flying rather low. The final observation was the most chilling. If his eyes weren't deceiving him, its front was tipped with yellow.

He lay on the ground and waited for the enemy plane to come. The pilot was flying parallel with the ground, perhaps one hundred feet. Should he play dead? It was probably too late for that now. Manning wondered idly if that had been a tactical mistake. There was little for it now but to take his medicine. He sat up from his flat position.

He'd look the beggar in the eye.

The plane was a few hundred yards away now. And loud. Very loud in fact. Manning braced himself for the bullets that would strafe him into the next world.

They didn't come.

He saw the pilot looking at him. He saluted then he was away. The enemy plane was riddled with bullets, yet it had survived. Such was the margin between life, death and everything in between. Marseille, for Manning was in no doubt it was he, lived a charmed life. The plane ascended quickly into the blue sky and within minutes was no more than a dark speck.

Manning tried to stand again. He rose gingerly to his feet. Nothing was broken. He wondered about the pain in his side. If it was a busted rib, then he'd got off lightly. He sat down again and considered his options. They weren't great. He didn't know how far inside his own lines or, indeed, enemy's, he was. He didn't know how far he would need to walk. It would be night within an hour or two. This was a consideration, too.

The sun was beginning to burn him. He pulled the parachute over his head and sat underneath the white silk listening to the sound of battle. It was horrible and hypnotic. Oddly, he felt sorry for the poor devils caught in the middle of it all.

He stayed like that for an hour.

Then he heard a vehicle. It grew louder. If it were the Germans, he would be a prisoner of war if he were lucky. They may decide to dispense a more immediate form of justice. He threw back the parachute and rose slowly once more.

The jeep approached him at speed and drew up a few feet away. A sergeant jumped out and looked Manning up and down.

'Lost your kite?' asked a very English voice.

'It seems to have lost me.'

'Hop in,' suggested the sergeant.

Manning didn't need to be asked twice and he hobbled over to the jeep. The sergeant helped him in, and they set off in a north-east direction.

'We're just two miles up this way,' said the sergeant.

'How did you know I was here?' asked Manning although he already knew the answer.

'Your men contacted us. Apparently, some chap called Marseille had dropped a message telling them where they could find you. Probably too close to our lines to risk sending someone from their side. Jerry gave our boys a bit of a pasting up there I gather. You're the third one we've picked up today.'

The battle continued to thunder somewhere in the vast nothingness. Manning could think of nothing else to say. He looked in the direction of the fighting. It rumbled and raged in the dying light.

CHAPTER THIRTY

Alam el Halfa, Egypt, 2nd September 1942

Manfred gazed up at the sky and looked forlornly at the bombers. They had been coming in twelves and eighteens for the last twenty-four hours. It was a tidal surge from which there was no escape. He and the rest of the crew looked up at the approaching waves and did not move. They couldn't.

They were out of fuel.

Some far-off spot would be obliterated by their evil cargo. The ack, ack seemed perfunctory as if they were going through the motions. By now Manfred and, he suspected, Basler, accepted that they were losing. There was no way past the wall of fire they'd encountered. Surely Rommel could see this. Surely he could see that without petrol it was academic anyway. They were stuck; at the merciless mercy of an enemy that knew they had them where they wanted.

Basler and Manfred exchanged glances; an unspoken acknowledgement that there was no point in wasting ammunition. It was just after ten in the morning and Manfred hadn't fired a shell.

Another shell landed in a proximity sufficient to raise heart rates more than a beat or two.

'So what do we do, sir? Throw rocks at them?' asked Manfred sourly.

There was more than a hint of amusement in Basler's eyes, but his mouth was fixed. Here they were, attacking an enemy that hadn't so much dug in as merged with the evil landscape and laid trap upon trap for their quarry. But worst of all, they'd hardly any ammo to shoot back. All in all, the boy was entitled to grouse a bit. Basler turned to Keil on the wireless.

'Where are the damn ammunition trucks?'

The young wireless operator got to work. A few minutes later he turned to Basler, a look of disbelief on his face.

'Another hour, maybe less.'

Manfred sat back and made himself comfortable as Basler duly exploded in fury. He poured forth an eloquently oath-laden rant on the murderous stupidity of those running the war. If ever this was a testimony to Basler's renunciation of the creed of National Socialism, this was it. His conclusion had the rest of the cabin nodding in agreement.

'Those fools couldn't run a pissing contest at Oktoberfest.'

The supply train arrived just before eleven. By then the tank was punch drunk with fear. Had the Allied shooting been directed towards them then they would have been ripped to shreds. But they weren't the target. A dozen ink-black ribbons of smoke rising into the cerulean blue sky told of the devastating effect of the RAF bombing on the fuel and ammunition supply columns. Manfred gazed at the smoke in rapt fascination. He wasn't alone. The crew was silent. Then it woke from this terrible thrall and began to function as a unit.

Manfred and Kleff were to load the ammunition while Keil and Jentz took care of the fuel. They exited the tank just as the Allied artillery fire began to target them. Explosions began sending jets of sand skywards. Their eardrums were bursting at the noise. The eye-watering stench of burning was suffocating. Panic-stricken supply drivers screamed at them to hurry up and load what they could. Everyone was shouting. It was bedlam.

Manfred ducked as he hauled the new shells towards the tank. He ducked as the whhfft of a shell split the sky nearby. It would have been funny had it not been so terrifying; as if in ducking he could, in some way, avoid the random obliteration promised by artillery fire. After a few minutes the supply drivers had had enough.

Manfred screamed at them in frustration. Yet he couldn't blame them. What sane person would want to be in the middle of this pandemonium. He certainly didn't. He saw Basler emerge from the tank, eyes ablaze.

'Where are they going?'

Manfred shook his head and replied sourly, 'Same place we should be, sir. Safety.'

Basler glared at Manfred then spun around and snarled, 'Back to the tank.'

Flashes erupted all around the Panzers but miraculously none were hit. Manfred settled into his seat and waited for the instruction to move. He didn't have to wait long. Kummel's voice on the radio announced the attack they'd been expecting.

'Fifty or sixty tanks heading this way. Move forward and engage.'

Forward?

Manfred exchanged looks with Jentz; then the veteran grinned and shook his head. It was an insane way to spend a morning. A life, even. Jentz returned his focus to the job in hand. The tank lurched forward sending Manfred off balance. He reddened in embarrassment, but no one had noticed.

248

Evening fell.

Manfred looked at the empty eyes of the crew and knew that there would not be another day like today. The attack was as good as finished. There was nothing left to give. He watched Basler return to their bivouac from his conference with Kummel and the other battalion leader, whoever it was now. Zugner? No, he'd been wounded the day before. The 2nd Battalion didn't have much luck with their commanders. This thought brought a stab of pain with it as he thought about Gerhardt. Had he been captured? No news had come through yet.

Basler hit the ground like Schmeling in the second Louis fight. He remembered how his father had turned the radio off after the first knockdown. He recognised a lost cause.

'Just the five Mark IIIs. We think around thirty of theirs destroyed,' announced Basler, wearily. It didn't seem a cause for celebration at that moment.

'Five destroyed or five out of action?' asked Manfred.

'Destroyed.'

Manfred and the others nodded. They'd survived another day, but a few hadn't. Manfred wondered about Fischer but then caught a glimpse of the Bavarian at the far end of the hedgehog position they'd adopted. Out in the darkness they could hear motor vehicles buzzing around. It felt oppressive; different somehow compared to when they were near Tripoli. There it felt as if they were the home team. Now, they were very much the away side. The crowd, the referee, everything was against them.

Planes overhead now. Did they ever stop? The drone was followed by the inevitable parachute flares that lit up the night and then the thunder of bombs. It felt so one-sided that Manfred was amazed that

Rommel could not see what was plain to the soldiers whose lives were being sacrificed so cheaply.

They could not win.

The Allied defences were too strong. The air superiority overwhelming. Surely someone with common sense would say 'enough'. They were all too exhausted to feel any triumph at the damage they'd inflicted on the Allies. It didn't matter. More tanks would come. It was a never-ending conveyor belt that the Allies had access to. It was different for Germany. They could only patch up their damaged Panzers and, in some cases, those of the enemy. Good luck to the poor buggers that had to drive in those death traps, thought Manfred. Give them to the Italians.

The enemy motor vehicles sounded louder now. They were haunting the leaguer like malign spirits. The distant thunder persisted but this was not the sort that brought rain. Only hellfire.

'Are they ours?' asked Keil, edgily. His eyes were fixed at a point somewhere in the night. Manfred would have asked the same question a minute or two earlier but hadn't trusted himself to sound anything other than what he was, skirting at the edge of panic. The sound of the vehicles had attracted the interest of several Panzer crews. A few were on their feet and walking towards spaces where they could see better. This seemed a damn fool thing to do, thought Manfred, and he remained seated. Basler was more interested in eating, but the sound of the engines was louder.

He looked up; irritation burned on his face. It had been a nightmarish day without all this. Manfred watched the head of the battalion's fourth company pick up a machine gun and walk out of the leaguer followed by a few other similarly armed crew members. They obviously felt something was afoot.

The others in the crew fell silent and stared warily out into the darkness. Manfred's heart was beating fast again. Would the Allies dare launch a night raid on a Panzer leaguer? Without tanks it would be suicidal. But then wasn't war the suicide business on an industrial scale? What else would make a man drive at speed towards gunfire?

These thoughts raced through Manfred's mind as his eyes tried to focus on the blackness around them. He could see nothing but could almost hear sand scraping over more sand in the gentle breeze, so heightened were his senses.

The crack of rifle fire startled Manfred but he was quick to react. He fell forward and crawled towards a machine gun. Basler was on his feet and over by the tank to pick up another gun.

The Panzer crew began firing shots randomly into the darkness but it was difficult to see their target. More gunfire was exchanged.

'Over there,' came a shout.

They began to concentrate their attack on the area identified. Soon the gunfire abated as they realised that the enemy had driven off. Manfred sank wearily to the ground and knew that this would only be the first of a few harassing confrontations. It was going to be a long night and an even longer day tomorrow.

Later that night the news came from Basler that they'd all been expecting.

'We're pulling back.'

CHAPTER THIRTY-ONE

Ladenburg, Germany, 5th September 1942

Peter Brehme watched Keller arrive at the station. The Gestapo man was silhouetted against dark grey cloud. It had got to the point where Brehme no longer disguised his contempt for him. Keller was equally disinclined to hide his feelings. Gone was the veneer of insincere flattery used by each. It was a war without arms. The choice of weapons was nuance, tone of voice and facial expression. Outwardly, their relations seemed courteous. But some knew the real story. Even those exposed to the two men each day could barely gauge the level of mutual loathing.

Each day was a battle for Brehme. The daily trek into the office. The daily humiliation of sitting at a small desk while Keller lorded over him at his antique oak table. Caught in the middle was Jost Graf. It was cold comfort for Brehme to see the daily degradation the little man experienced at the hands of the Gestapo man. He had become a weapon for Keller to use against Brehme. So much so that Brehme was inclined to forgive the little man's role as a spy.

This morning was as typical as any in confirming Brehme's belief in the decay at the heart of Nazism. Their interests lay not with the future of the Fatherland or the welfare of the people. The only thing that mattered, Brehme now realised, was the process by which they were enriching themselves. As chief of police, even he was powerless to stop the biggest criminal gang of them all.

The atmosphere in the office was invariably dictated by the mood of Keller. Brehme could see when he arrived that it was going to be a long day. No one smiled anymore except when Keller did. And then it was counterfeit. A mere imitation of a sentiment that they were gradually losing the ability to feel.

The early morning pleasantries usually marked the end of anything like civil interaction. The poison soon began to leak from the pores. As ever, it was Keller who started things off.

'Have you seen, Graf? Our brave boys are having to turn tail. Rommel has failed yet again.'

The remark might have been taken solely as a slight on the leadership qualities of Field Marshall Rommel. However, Keller was adept at making jibes against Manfred and the Afrika Korps through various guises. Rommel was a favourite Trojan Horse for his real intent. Graf glanced at Brehme and then back to Keller. Even he could read the signs by now.

'Perhaps he is regrouping,' smiled the hapless policeman.

'Regrouping you think? He's spent the last three months regrouping since we took Tobruk.'

Brehme noted sourly that it was always 'we' when things were going well.

'Rommel has to go. And examples need to be made of the men who are running away like rabble. What do you think, Peter?' Keller said this with a smile that would have done justice to a fox reviewing dinner options in a chicken coop.

'I think you're right, Ernst. I would love nothing more than to see these men forced to make a real contribution to winning the war.'

Keller's smile faded slightly. He suspected Brehme was not finished. The insolence of the policeman was growing by the week.

'Yes, a spell working in the Gestapo would show them what it really takes to defeat our enemies.'

Brehme was studying a report as he said this so could not see the hatred burning in the eyes of the Gestapo man. He, too, had become proficient in land mining his flattery with insults.

'Where are we going, sir?' asked Graf, nervously. They were driving out of town into the country. Brehme glanced at Graf and decided to take him into his confidence. If Graf reported back to Keller, it was of no consequence to him.

'We're going to the Kramer farm.'

Graf looked perplexed for a moment, grasping to connect the name to something he knew. Brehme waited.

'The cattle farmer?'

'The big cattle farmer,' smiled Brehme.

'Why?'

'Black market,' said Brehme, simply. He enjoyed the look of shock on Graf's face. Oddly, he quite liked the little man. He was not a bad sort. Not stupid but unquestionably naïve. And weak. Sadly, very weak. But could he really be blamed for this? He'd avoided active service because of his eyesight. He was married with a child on the way. What a world to bring a baby into.

Of course, Graf was going to live in fear of Keller. If he thought about it long enough, he realised that he was living in fear of the Gestapo man, too. So what if Graf was reporting on Brehme's activities? There was nothing to reveal except an honest policeman doing his duty. It might work to his favour. After all, he'd see what good police work looked like. There could be no shame in what he did, unlike Keller. But people like Keller were beyond shame.

They drove past enormous fields filled with cattle. The green pastures dazzled in the morning sunshine. It filled Brehme with sadness to think of such beauty being turned into a muddy graveyard for the youth of his country. The Kramer farmhouse finally appeared in view. It was an enormous building and dated from a time before Luther. The Kramer family had owned this land just as long.

They drove down a driveway that was a quarter of a kilometre long. Even in Weimar, even during this period of Hitler, some were making money. But to do so there was probably a price to pay. In America, they called it 'protection'. It was the Mafia who ran such rackets. It didn't feel much different over here.

They pulled up outside the house and saw a servant open the door. He was in his seventies and could probably count his service to the Kramer family in decades rather than years. The presence of a police car did not seem to surprise the old servant unduly. This was unusual. Brehme was used to seeing fear and suspicion on the faces of people he met in everyday life. Even those who had little to fear. Or perhaps they did. Everyone has secrets. The man bowed to Brehme.

'How may I help you?'

'Is Herr Kramer in?' asked Brehme.

The answer was yes, and the servant led the two policemen inside. He asked them to wait in a large hallway while he went to fetch the landowner. The hallway, once again, made Brehme feel that he'd chosen the wrong career. *Objets d'art* decorated side tables and a large painting hung at the top of the stairs. It looked like a Lovis Corinth self-portrait. Expertly done, thought Brehme, but hideous. He was staring up at it when Herr Kramer arrived.

Kramer was in his forties. He was clearly a working farmer as his clothes looked old and there were traces of mud on the cuffs of his trousers. His face was tanned, and the blue eyes suggested both intelligence and impatience.

'I see you're looking at the Corinth. My father knew him. How can I help you?'

The greeting was courteous but cold. It was clear that neither he nor Graf was welcome. Brehme nodded and got straight to the point.

'The police in Heidelberg have asked me to look into a black-market case. It involves the smuggling and sale of beef. Have any of your cattle been stolen lately?'

It was there just for a split second. A frown. The hesitation. Then the lie.

'No, Brehme. Is someone suggesting that my livestock is involved?'

'No, Herr Kramer. I am making the rounds of local farmers to find out if they are aware of or have heard anything about this illicit trade.'

'I fear you have made a wasted trip, Brehme. I know nothing.'

Once more Brehme's senses were screaming at him that this was not the case. But another thought was now stirring in his mind. An idea as unwelcome as it was so obvious. There was little more to be gained by taking up Kramer's time and both knew it.

'Of course, if you should hear anything about this, you will let me know?'

'Of course,' said Kramer leading Brehme and Graf to the door. Graf moved on towards the car but Brehme stayed for a moment. He and Kramer studied one another, then Brehme spoke.

'I'm sorry for troubling you. I think I understand the situation better. These are terrible times.'

'Indeed,' said Kramer. There was a hint of a frown on his face. Brehme nodded to him then turned towards the car. As he was climbing in, he glanced back towards the farm. The owner was standing at the doorway, uncertainty etched over his features. Graf climbed in beside him, but Brehme's eyes never left the farm owner. His heart was racing now. Barely able to believe what he was about to do, Brehme climbed out of the car and walked back to Kramer.

'I'm not with them,' said Brehme, simply. Kramer's eyes widened slightly but he remained tight-lipped. Brehme returned to the car. With one last look towards Kramer he turned and ducked inside the car.

He started the engine and took a deep breath. Graf glanced nervously towards Brehme; curiosity bled from his eyes. What had happened between the two men? He was shocked by what he saw: Brehme's eyes were blazing, his lips were set in a semi-snarl of anger. Graf said nothing. Even he could see the riot of emotions raging under the surface. They drove off and it was only when they were halfway up the driveway of the farm that Brehme gave vent to his feelings.

He hit the steering wheel of the car with the heel of his palm. A volley of oaths poured forth. Graf looked on in shock. When the storm passed, Graf found his courage and enquired, 'Sir, what is wrong?'

Brehme looked at his not so young protégé, or was he merely Keller's apprentice? What could he say to him? The fact was that he was getting old and stupid. Where once there was an insightful wariness, an ability to see around the corner, there was now only naivety. A year of virtual inactivity had left him mentally obese. He was not fit for this role now.

'No, Graf, I should have prepared better for that interview. There is nothing to worry about. Kramer is not a black marketeer.'

He believed this, too. Kramer was rich. Why would he or any other farmer in his situation sully his hands with such a trade? The simple answer was that they would only do so if they were being forced to trade this way. There was only one criminal group with this level of power. He thought of Keller again. When the criminals were in charge of policing and justice, it was probably time to quit.

For the rest of the journey back into town, Brehme engaged Graf in general conversation about his family and what his ambitions were. He wanted to signal to his subordinate that the time would soon come when he would take over. The tone was light, but the meaning was clear, even to Graf.

They spoke all the way back to town, but Brehme's mind was elsewhere. The thought of retirement had only been one he'd considered in those moments when he felt the greatest hatred towards Keller. What was the point, though? He was being paid a good salary to do next to nothing. Even the daily weight of being near Keller was bearable given the lifestyle that his role afforded him. What would he do in retirement?

They drove slowly through the Market Platz. It was crowded with townsfolk of all ages milling around. Once again, he reflected on how few Hitler Youth there were now. Some elderly women caught his eye. One was the wife of Otto Becker, Agatha. Like her husband, she appeared to be weighed down by her food shopping. Brehme smiled at this. There were only two of them in the house. Neither was particularly big. They clearly had healthy appetites. He drove on towards the police station.

And then it hit him.

The bags of food. The words spoken by Becker to the schoolboy, Robert Sauer. Brehme could barely breathe. It had been there in front of him all this time and he'd missed it. There was no question of him quitting now.

None whatsoever.

PART 3: EL ALAMEIN

Sept 1942–November 1942

Lieutenant-General Bernard Montgomery replaced General Claude Auchinleck as Commander-in-Chief of the Eighth Army. Montgomery decreed that the Allies would retreat no further than their current position: El Alamein, a small coastal railway halt, one hundred kilometres from Alexandria. Preparations for the forthcoming battle began. Reinforcements arrived, training began and both sides commenced the laying of enormous minefields in the narrow strip between the coast and the impassable Qattara Depression.

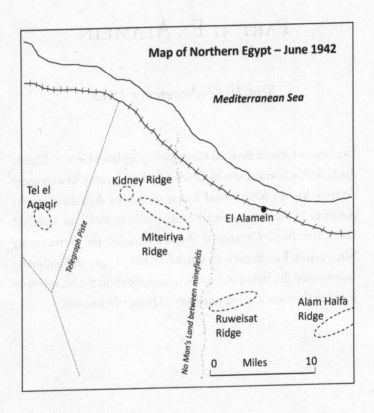

Map of Northern Egypt – June 1942

Mediterranean Sea

Tel el Aqaqir

Kidney Ridge

El Alamein

Telegraph Piste

Miteiriya Ridge

No Man's Land between minefields

Ruweisat Ridge

Alam Haifa Ridge

0   Miles   10

CHAPTER THIRTY-TWO

Training Camp near El Alamein, 20th September 1942

'You're kidding,' said Danny, clearly unable to hide his disbelief. This was met by a glare from Captain Benson. The news that they would not have the new Sherman for the expected confrontation with the Germans was a body blow. Evidently this applied as much to the other members of the crew as it did to Danny.

'I'm afraid so,' replied Benson sternly before adding, 'And there's no use in bellyaching about it either. We must accept it and move on. The Grant is a fine tank. Tad unwieldy, I agree. Jerry would give his right arm to have a gun like this.'

To emphasise the point, Benson placed his hand on the seventy-five-millimetre cannon.

The news, if not shattering, was a major disappointment. The new Shermans had begun to arrive in the training area. The 3 RTR hoped it would have its fair share of the new vehicles which boasted both superior armoured protection and a bigger gun in the turret. It had a lower profile as well, which made it a smaller target, although not so small as the Crusader.

The regiment had been given ten Shermans. All of these were with 'B' Squadron. The Grants were all with 'C' Squadron. The crew went to inspect their new Grant with a degree of suspicion.

'The Shermans and the Grants will be the battering ram, I suspect,' said Danny unenthusiastically. PG glanced at him and nodded grimly. Tanks like these were not designed to bring up the rear.

'I suspect you're right, Danny,' said Andrews as they walked away from the Sherman.

'Do you know much about this new chap?' asked Danny, referring to Montgomery.

'No, not come across him before,' admitted Andrews. 'I daresay we'll find out soon enough what he's made of.'

'We're all just flesh and blood, Archie, flesh and blood,' said PG adding his usual glum perspective on anything and everything.

Towards the end of September, training was in full swing. The arrival of General Montgomery had sent a current through the whole of the Eighth Army. The preparation for the autumn campaign was as much physical as it was strategic. This did not go down well with everyone.

'Route march?' exclaimed PG.

Benson grinned and ordered PG and the rest of the crew to get ready. The whole battalion had to do it. The smile widened as the burly Yorkshireman gazed up at the cloudless blue sky. His usual glum demeanour took on an even more hangdog expression.

'How far?' asked PG in a voice that was as much a desperate appeal to sanity as it was a request for information.

'Seven miles,' replied Benson, enjoying the misery of his driver immensely. As much as Danny was not looking forward to the march either, it was made more inviting by the thought that PG would have to haul his unathletic body over a distance that it was ill designed to cover. The march was relatively easy for Danny given his youth as well as a level of conditioning that was the equal of anyone in the regiment. 'We'll be back before midnight if you don't hold us up too much.'

Danny, McLeish and Gregson looked on in great amusement at the evident misery of their big driver. Archie Andrews did not seem any happier than PG.

'Can't I stay behind and read Herodotus?' asked Andrews plaintively. PG had more practical concerns to deal with.

'I better be off to t' bog then,' said PG morosely. 'Can you give me some of King Herod to wipe my backside, Archie?'

Andrews succinctly suggested that help would not be forthcoming. Then Danny piped up with his tuppence worth.

'Good idea, big boy, it'll help you lose some of that weight,' said Danny helpfully.

PG replied, 'Why don't you go lose your virginity with your sister, country boy,' before trooping off to relieve himself before the march.

A couple of days later the crew spent several hours on the firing range, firstly with rifles and then with the tank. Understanding the effective range of their gun would be critical in the upcoming battles. It could launch shells to distances up to five thousand yards but against armour the range reduced to a little over one thousand yards or less when confronted by the Panzer Mark IVs.

'Good shooting,' commented Benson at the end of the day. 'You seem to have your eye in there.'

'It'll be more than cricket balls coming our direction soon, though,' replied Danny, acknowledging the cricket reference from Benson. That raised a smile.

'I'm sure you'll still hit them for six, Shaw. You'll need to.'

Life at the camp allowed them to catch up on the latest Hollywood films. This gave a sense of normality that felt unreal, such was the change to their lives over the last year. The films and their stars were a frequent source of conversation amongst the men, particularly the female leads.

'Betty Grable, she'll do,' announced PG.

'She says the same about you,' replied Danny.

'She would'n'all. They want something they can get hold of.'

Danny spent a few seconds appraising the ample form of PG who helped him by turning sideways and then towards him.

'You could be right, there,' said Danny. 'What about you, Sid?'

'Gary Cooper,' interjected PG before guffawing at his own joke.

'Garbo.'

'Makes sense,' said PG. 'You *vont* to be alone.'

'Away from you anyway, dreamboat,' laughed Gregson. 'What about you, Danny?'

'Well tonight, Sidney, I shall be accompanying Maureen O'Sullivan in my dreams.'

'Lucky girl,' said PG. 'If she needs a real man, you know where to find me.'

'I'll bear it in mind,' nodded Danny in a serious manner. 'What's on tonight?'

'*They Died with Their Boots On,*' said McLeish.

'There's a cheery thought,' said PG sourly. 'Didn't end well for them, did it?'

'Maybe you could be Sitting Bull, PG. You certainly look like one from here, big boy,' said Danny, rising quickly to avoid items from PG's tool kit that were being hurled in his direction.

The rumours became fact when the commanding officer of the regiment, Lieutenant-Colonel Pyman, arrived to speak to them flanked by his squadron leaders and other senior officers. Beside him were Major Robert Crisp, who commanded Danny's 'A' Squadron; Major Upcott-Gill, the commanding officer of 'B' Squadron and Major Colin Franklin who led 'C' Squadron. Other senior officers were also present as Pyman briefed the men about the forthcoming operation. His slight figure was dwarfed by the enormous map of the area around El Alamein; it seemed like a metaphor for the war in the North African desert.

'Well, I'm sure you'll have gathered that I'm not here to talk about the weather.'

This was greeted by laughter among the ranks of the men just in front of him.

'It is bloody hot, though,' continued Pyman glancing up at the late afternoon sun. 'Behind me you'll see a board showing the layout of the Alamein halt and the surrounding areas. The coloured sections represent our best guess at the minefields Jerry has laid. We're constantly monitoring this through aerial photography but as you can see, it's pretty extensive.'

Pyman used a stick to indicate the areas he was talking about. He turned back to the men.

'Over the next few weeks, we're going to train as we've never trained before. Nothing will be left to chance. This time we're going to chase Rommel and the Afrika Korps all the way back to Tripoli and then Germany. We're kicking them out for good. We have the men. We have the guns and, as you'll have seen with these new Shermans, we have the tanks. This time there can be no excuses. We have to win.'

'The detailed plan is still being worked out so, you'll understand, I can only speak in general terms. It's going to be a night attack.'

Pyman paused while the ranks of men took this in. With each passing day it had become clear that a big push was in the offing.

The news that it was to commence at night was a shock. Although many of the crews had been involved in some night-time firefights, this was the first time an attack on such a scale had been considered. There was a moment of silence and then a low mumble from some of the men. Pyman held his hand up to quieten the talking.

'Yes, I know. If it's a surprise for you, can you imagine how Jerry will feel?'

This was greeted with a ripple of laughter.

'Yes, it's going to be a night attack and we're going to train for this. Now, doubtless a few of you will have considered one slight problem with this idea. Anyone care to guess what that might be?'

Danny raised his hand.

Pyman pointed to Danny and smiled.

'Brave man. What's your name?'

'Shaw, sir.'

'Go on,' replied Pyman.

'Well, sir, you pointed to the problem a minute ago. How are we supposed to get through a minefield at night?'

Pyman smiled. He'd been hoping this would be the question that was asked. He turned to his adjutant Captain Barker.

'Would you care to show them, Barker?'

Captain Barker held up a strange metal device. It had a long arm like a broom handle with a disc at its head that looked like a film can.

'This,' explained Pyman, 'is a mine detector. Basically, our boffins have come up with a way of finding mines without giving the game away to Jerry. Now I had to study this bit, but it works through these metal coils.' Pyman indicated the coils on the underside of the disc-like shape. 'They oscillate when they encounter a metal object underground. The Sapper will have earphones and hear a "ping". Invented by two Polish officers, apparently. It's going to save thousands of lives because we can work at night, avoid prodding the earth with a bayonet, and hopefully catch the enemy unawares. I was going to say asleep but I gather they'll be wide awake, trust me. From what I hear we'll be shelling them all night. I shall let Major Crisp explain in more detail about the attack.'

Crisp stepped forward and smiled. His teeth seemed to gleam against the deep tan of his skin. Danny was used to hearing his squadron leader's South African accent, but he was amused to see a few straining to understand what was being said.

'There will be two gaps. One north and one south.'

Crisp indicated on the board where these would be.

'We will be located at the Miteiriya Ridge and will proceed through the northern gap. Now these lanes will be created by the Sapper chaps using this metal detector. There will be about forty sappers per gap led by a couple of officers. They'll have infantry support, of course. When they reach the minefield, they will put a blue pinpoint light to indicate where it starts. A second blue light will indicate when we believe we're through the mine belt. The lanes themselves will be at least two tank widths or more. Around twenty-four feet wide. There will be three teams of sappers. The first will find the mines and place a white cone cut out of a petrol can over them; the third group will pick them up. The middle group will run white tape along the sides of the lane with green and orange lights telling you which side you should be on. Do I need to tell you to stay on the green side?'

This was greeted with laughter.

'Thought not. You'll need these lights. Visibility won't be great with all the sand the tanks kick up.' Crisp then took some white tape and unrolled a foot, holding it aloft. 'This will be reeled out in eight-foot strips with lights showing you the way. There will also be

269

T-lights in the middle of the lane. It'll be like driving up Regent Street at Christmas. Anyway, I hope that's clear. Any questions?'

'When are we going?' shouted a voice from the back.

'No idea,' replied Crisp with a grin. 'Any others?'

'Can I go home?' shouted another. Crisp joined in the laughter and suggested succinctly that this was unlikely any time soon.

The crews and the support personnel filed away from the meeting. Benson walked alongside Danny and PG.

'So what do you think, chaps?'

Before Danny could answer, PG replied glumly, 'I'm with the lad that wanted to go home.'

'Good to see you're as positive as ever, PG,' smiled Benson. 'What about you, Shaw?'

Danny was silent for a moment and then replied, 'It feels more considered this time. No more cavalry charges.'

Benson stopped and looked at Danny; then he nodded.

'I'd forgotten you were at Sidi Rezegh.'

Danny fought to control his emotions as the faces of his former crew mates swam into his mind. It had been a mess. A regiment virtually wiped out over a single day. Yet he'd hardly been alone in experiencing this. Every regiment, every battalion, every man had faced or would face unimaginable terror over the course of this war. They walked towards their tank in silence. Each wondering when the call to action would come.

From that day, the crews began practising movement through minefields. The initial training took place during daylight hours, but this was soon to switch to night. The crews and the soldiers were all to practise night marches repeatedly. Nothing was to be left to chance.

The regiment would be called upon to tow guns and, on occasion, one another, to replicate both initial attack and actual combat situations when tanks were knocked out but reparable. The success of the Germans in recovering their Panzers had forced the Allies to raise their game in this field.

Day and night began to merge. There was no slackening in the preparations for the next battle. For it was always the next battle. Danny had long since given up hoping the next one would be the decisive one. This time he sensed an air of purposefulness that he'd not seen before. This was partly due to the insistence by Montgomery that the men be kept aware of the plans.

Everyone had a sense of what their job was and how it fitted into the overall scheme. Just the knowing made the plan feel more solid. This sense of purpose cascaded through the ranks. It was not hubristic. They'd lost too many friends and comrades for that. But it was there. A tacit hope, an unspoken commitment to those around them and those who had fallen that this time they would prevail.

CHAPTER THIRTY-THREE

Sidi abd el Rhaman, 28km from El Alamein, Egypt, 28th September 1942

'Any mail today?' asked Manfred, looking up at the sky. There were a few planes buzzing overhead either returning or heading out on a sortie. Otherwise, the sky was clear and blue.

Fischer shrugged and said he hadn't received any mail. Such an admission was invariably a cue for abuse from Manfred on the unpopularity of the Bavarian. They went for a stroll away from the leaguer. The late afternoon sun was tolerable but still hot enough to burn. They found a shaded spot on the other side of a rocky ridge which descended into a flat-bottomed wadi with soft sand. They were far enough away from the leaguer now to talk with complete freedom or just enjoy the motionless silence of the desert.

'How do you find Stiefelmayer?' asked Manfred. Fischer had recently been assigned to a new tank. He was finally a gunner but, true to form, disappointed that he'd not yet been given his own tank.

'He's good. Up there with Kummel.'

'And Basler.'

'And Basler,' agreed Fischer. Manfred glanced at his friend's newly earned stripes. Fischer saw this and added, sourly, 'I've been here a year and a half and all I have to show for it is being a lousy corporal and the proud owner of a sore shoulder.'

Manfred grinned sympathetically and pointed out the obvious. 'Could have been worse.'

Had it really been ten months since Manfred rescued the wounded Fischer on that terrible Sunday, *Totensonntag*? Fischer dismissed the point with a wave of his hand and they stared out at the flat, rocky landscape.

'How is your family?' asked Manfred.

'They barely notice the war. Aside from me being here and the SS wandering around Munich like they own the city, then life is normal for them. My sister is training to be a teacher now.'

Manfred's ears pricked up at this. The memory of a very attractive girl in a photograph held by Fischer sprang into his mind. Fischer glanced at Manfred and read his mind in an instant.

'Don't you dare even think about my sister. I'll stick your head inside one of those eighty-eights.'

'Tell me about your shoulder again?' asked Manfred.

He earned a punch in the arm for this less-than-subtle reminder that Fischer owed him his life. It's an odd comment on the psyche of the male that such a reaction to bravery displayed was not only considered acceptable but was embraced. Anything else would have been as embarrassing for the speaker as it would have been for the listener. War was nothing more than the natural extension of man's inability to communicate meaningfully.

'How is your father?' asked Fischer. This was an area where the two boys had shared an almost identical upbringing. A patriarchal household ruled by fear and discipline. It bred the society that had arisen in the Fatherland. Obedience was demanded and brutally achieved.

'My father cannot say too much because he has the Gestapo in the office. They probably read his letters.'

Manfred stopped for a moment to ponder this thought. *The Gestapo read my father's letters.* He shook his head and the two boys exchanged looks.

'This is what we're fighting for,' said Fischer bitterly, giving voice to the thought in both their minds.

Manfred laughed but without any real humour. 'So it seems. I don't think I care who wins. As long as I survive that's all that matters.'

'I wonder what will be left if we lose,' said Fischer, reflectively.

'Your sister,' laughed Manfred, rolling over to avoid the blows that were certain to rain down on him.

A few days later Manfred and Basler were out on morning patrol. They sat atop of the Panzer looking at the *pioniers* working on the minefield. There were dozens of soldiers stretched out as far as the eye could see. They were all stooping like old men planting mines and booby traps for the expected assault by the Allies.

'They're calling it the Devil's Gardens,' said Basler. He said it quietly and, for a moment, Manfred wondered if there was a lurking sympathy for the poor men that would be caught in this mesh and obliterated without trace. 'Five kilometres long, maybe six kilometres deep. I don't envy anyone going through that.'

Manfred looked at the horseshoe shape the *pioniers* had adopted. It looked as if they were creating entry points past the wire for the Allied soldiers; lulling them into a false sense of security on the location of the mines before they sprang the booby traps and touched the mines. Some of the booby traps looked horrifically treacherous. Some as big as the 250-pound bombs used by bombers. They were being laid out in a chessboard fashion with trip wires set carefully nearby.

The sight of the operation left Manfred spellbound. This was broken only by the sound of a lone plane overhead. The two men looked up at it.

'Maybe we have some mail,' said Basler simply. Manfred wondered who would be writing to the lieutenant. He'd never mentioned any family aside from the wife who'd left him. They watched the plane descend and land near to the leaguer before returning their attention to the desert and the sky. It occurred to Manfred that the Allies could have done significant damage to them if they'd launched an attack on the belts that were being mined. Perhaps the Allies were doing likewise.

'Captain Kummel is returning to Germany,' said Basler after a few minutes had passed. He smiled at the surprised look on Manfred's face.

'Why?' said Manfred. This seemed extraordinary to him. 'The Lion of Capuzzo' leaving just before the anticipated Allied offensive.

'He deserves to, Brehme. It makes sense,' was Basler's reply. 'Think about it. We have thousands of men out here battling forwards, then backwards, then forwards again. It seems like it will never end unless you are killed, maimed or captured. The men will see that there is a way back home. It suits our leaders to have real-life heroes coming home and inspiring, teaching the next wave of men who come out. I wonder how long it will be before our friend up there returns home.'

They both looked up and saw a plane rising into the sky. There was no question in Manfred's mind that Basler was referring to Marseille. One hundred and fifty confirmed kills, they said.

275

The two men followed the aircraft as it rose into the clear blue sky. He had been joined by other Messerschmitt fighters. There was now half a dozen of them heading towards enemy lines. They watched silently as they flew out of sight.

Half an hour later they saw five planes return and land. Such was war. There was a momentary sadness, then they returned to scanning the endless nothingness.

Manfred felt a touch on his arm from Basler a few minutes later. The sixth plane was returning. It was trailing black smoke. There was not the usual buzz of the engine. It was coughing and spluttering like a bronchial old man. At a certain point the engine stopped. The pilot was gliding back towards the German lines. All around them, activity stopped. The *pioniers* looked up at the sky along with the men on the other Panzers. The plane was around four hundred metres from the ground. It seemed impossible that it could land in such a condition. Red flames were pouring from the plane.

'Come on,' said Manfred to himself. 'Bail out you fool.'

The engine started again as the pilot decided he was too high to glide down quickly enough. Then a figure emerged from the plane. He seemed to hit against the wing and then he was falling. No parachute opened. The figure fell four hundred metres and hit the desert sand watched by the soldiers in silent shock.

Two hours later they returned to the leaguer. The memory of what they'd seen was still scored on their minds, muting conversation. Later that evening one of the supply drivers came past clutching the post. Manfred looked up at the red-rimmed eyes of the young man. He frowned a question as he took the post from him.

'Haven't you heard?' asked the driver.

'Heard what?' asked Manfred.

'It was Captain Marseille that was killed today,' said the young man.

Manfred glanced down and saw the shocked expression on Basler's face. Then the lieutenant nodded. Nothing else was said. Manfred sat down and read the letter from his father in a daze. The war felt terribly close again. Like the mythical Kraken he'd read about as a child, its tentacles stretched everywhere, bringing death and destruction to everything within its reach.

A week later Dick Manning sauntered into the headquarters of his squadron. In this case, the headquarters was a large tent with half a dozen tables and two large upright boards. A large map was pinned to the first board. On the other was a list of pilots. In the centre of the tent were half a dozen tables set together with an enormous map laid out flat on top. Sitting on the map were model planes, tanks and guns. A few officers milled around the table chatting and occasionally gesturing towards the map.

'Hi, Dick, when did you get back?' said a man behind a desk at the entrance to the tent.

'Last night. I think I need another break,' replied the airman.

The man laughed and offered up a few salacious reasons for the evident fatigue of their flyer. Manning was never a man to forgo the opportunity to imply that he'd satisfied every craving of his female admirers over the last few days in Cairo.

'Who's up today?'

The man consulted the roster.

'Looks like Jarvis, Heathcott and Wilkins will be accompanying the reconnaissance boys.'

'I'll speak with Wilkins. Put my name down, will you?'

The man looked quizzical but shrugged his shoulders.

'I'm sure Wilko won't object to an afternoon nap. Very well, Dick.' He paused. 'What's that in your hand? Is that what I think it is?'

Manning looked down at his hand. He was carrying a wreath. A small card was taped on it. There were three words.

R.I.P. Hauptmann Marseille.

278

CHAPTER THIRTY-FOUR

Heidelberg, Germany, 21st October 1942

Sammy Schneider was a career criminal. Or at least he had been. After his third spell in prison and with the arrival of war he took the very wise decision to retire from felonious activities. What was the point? He was merely an amateur. The true professionals were running the country. He lacked their vision, their ambition.

So Sammy became a window cleaner. He often wondered about the wisdom of such a profession as it offered so much temptation. How many times had that open window beckoned him, pleaded with him, begged him to nip in and fill a swag bag?

But Sammy said no. He'd made a promise to his wife.

Heike Schneider had spent ten of their twenty-seven married years bringing up their children single-handedly. She'd known what he was from the start, but love blinded her to the very real risks of matrimony with a man likely to spend enforced time away from the family home.

When Heike Schneider saw Peter Brehme standing at the door, her face fell. Brehme was used to seeing some degree of suspicion and caution when he arrived on doorsteps. Such was the nature of his job. Heike Schneider's reaction was one he would remember.

In the space of a few seconds her face ran a gamut of emotions from fear to anger and then back to fear. The anger part was the most fun as she considered the very real possibility that Sammy had once more lapsed into his old ways. It struck Brehme that, if he had, he would never have made it to prison for his rather impressively made wife would have squashed her more diminutive husband like a rhino sitting on a fly.

So amusing was the reaction, Brehme, in a moment of humour that had certainly not been a thread through his life, genuinely considered keeping up the pretence that Sammy was in trouble with the law again. He didn't have the heart. He'd done enough to Sammy over the years. Anyway, Brehme's stock-in-trade humour was exceptionally dry and almost wholly reliant on the hubristic folly of others rather than the improvisation required here. Brehme held his hands up as he saw murder in the eyes of Frau Schneider.

'Please, I am not here to arrest Sammy. Quite the opposite. I need a favour, would you believe?'

One look at the face of Sammy's wife told Brehme that she certainly did not believe it and that he was walking on thin ice. Unfortunately, Brehme had little time for negotiating the tortuously Byzantine emotional state of a middle-aged married woman. He went direct.

'I need to see Sammy now. Where is he?'

Even a woman as forceful as Heike Schneider knows where the power lies. She climbed down from the high horse that she was threatening to mount and yelled into the corridor, 'Sammy, there's someone here to see you.'

This was never going to be an easy reunion, accepted Brehme. After all, he'd arrested Sammy. Twice. On both occasions he'd been jailed for a couple of years. Oddly, though, he didn't dislike the little burglar. He was just professionally obliged to discourage his activities.

When Sammy appeared in the corridor, it was no surprise that his face fell at the first sight of their visitor. Guilt clouded his face like a child caught stealing Berliners from the pantry.

Brehme smiled by way of appeasement although even he would have been the first to acknowledge his natural lack of warmth might have made the rictus grin even less welcoming than a frown.

'Good morning, Chief. What brings you here?' asked Sammy cautiously.

'Good morning, Sammy,' replied Brehme. He glanced at Frau Schneider and then back to Sammy. 'Is there somewhere we can talk?'

Sammy looked at Brehme in utter shock. The two men were sitting on a park bench. This was just as well as Sammy might well have collapsed otherwise. It was clear from what the chief of police had said to him, and by the tone of his voice, that he was completely serious. He shook his head. Fearfully at first and then energetically.

'Absolutely not. I left all that behind me.'

'I know, Sammy, I know. And if you don't want to do it, fine. I will walk away and you will never see me again.'

Sammy was appalled. The idea of returning to the trade that had cost him ten years of his life behind bars and, to add insult to injury, at the request of a man who'd been responsible for much of that incarceration seemed like a horrible joke. He stared at the chief of police. There was no question he was being serious. The question was...

'Why? And why me?'

Brehme looked away and sighed. He knew that what he was asking would have been too much of a friend, never mind someone who owed him nothing and had every reason to despise him.

'There's a filing cabinet I need you to break into. It belongs to the Gestapo.'

If the original request had been a shock, this put Sammy into a state of apoplexy.

'Gestapo?' he exclaimed. He rose to his feet which, sadly, didn't mean very much in Sammy's case and therefore undermined the impact he wanted to generate. 'You want me to break into the Gestapo's private files? Are you insane? These people are evil. I want nothing to do with them. Why should I help you?'

Brehme's answer was quiet and resigned.

'You answered your own question, Sammy. These people are evil. Don't worry, I understand, Sammy. I'm asking too much.'

Brehme stood up. He couldn't look at Sammy. Not because he was angry. Far from it. He appreciated the fear the little man was feeling. Brehme was close to tears now and this made him incredulous. Once he had prided himself on his stoic nature, his iron discipline and his sternness. What had caused this change? Renata's death? No, it had begun the moment he'd said goodbye to his son as he left for a war that Germany should not have started. He fought hard to regain his composure then, finally, looked at Sammy.

'I'm sorry. I shouldn't have come.'

He started to walk back towards the Schneider household. But Sammy hadn't moved. Brehme wasn't aware of this initially and then he turned around, surprised. He frowned at Sammy.

'You haven't told me why you want this. Why now?' asked the former burglar.

Brehme shrugged. What could he say? A feeling? A sense of something about to explode? The changes happening all around him? More Gestapo had arrived at the police station. SS, too. Manfred's old friend Erich was a regular visitor. There was an air of expectancy.

They were planning something. A raid.

'I think a lot of innocent people are going to suffer, Sammy. I'd like to stop that,' replied Brehme sadly.

Sammy Schneider stared at Brehme. By rights he should have hated this man but, oddly, he didn't. They stood on opposite sides of a divide professionally. Or, at least, they had. Because of Brehme, Sammy had missed seeing his son grow up. But this had always been a risk irrespective of the arresting officer. He hadn't taken it personally. Brehme was not a person one could like. He was too serious, too virtuous. While he, Sammy, had a more flexible moral compass. Yet, he sensed that Brehme was no Nazi acolyte. He was straight. Sammy suspected strongly that Brehme did not equate his role with the objectives of the ruling party, the men who had pulled the country into a war. He could respect that.

'I can't, Chief. I have to think of my family,' said Sammy. There was a tinge of regret in his voice.

Brehme nodded. He exhaled and started to move again, followed by Sammy. They walked in silence; then Brehme asked Sammy, 'You had a boy, I remember. How is he?'

It was Sammy's turn to exhale loudly and none too happily.

'He's in North Africa.'

Brehme paused for a moment and the two fathers looked at one another. Then he started to move again.

'Mine, too.'

283

CHAPTER THIRTY-FIVE

El Alamein, Egypt, 22nd October 1942

There were three letters for Danny. This was unusual. He normally expected one and sometimes, deliriously, he would receive two. The third was a worry. He didn't recognise the writing. A sense of foreboding assailed him as he held the letter and debated whether to open it first or last. He decided to wait. Better he should savour the other two letters first.

His mother's letter was full of the usual questions about his health, what he was eating but, mercifully, stopped short of any enquiry as to his bowel movements. Danny smiled at this thought as he was pretty sure she'd wanted to ask. They still hadn't heard anything from Tom, but they'd had it confirmed he was alive and in Italy somewhere. He was probably safe now but, knowing Tom, he'd be trying to escape. They'd shoot him if they caught him. Danny felt a chill descend as he thought about the risks his brother would face even as a prisoner of war.

The second letter was thick. Inside was a letter and a photograph. It was a pity it was black and white. One couldn't see those extraordinary green eyes. She was smiling embarrassedly. Probably she felt foolish trying to take a picture of herself. He wondered how many she'd had to take before choosing the least mortifying. It took his breath away to think that she was writing to him. Not just writing, in fact revealing herself, her thoughts, her emotions and her feelings towards him.

He was so lucky. The sound of a plane overhead shattered the reverie of his good fortune. A thought occurred to him that was difficult to deny. Perhaps her feelings towards him were tied up in the situation they were in. The idea of a young man going off to fight for his country had a certain romance to it for a girl of an impressionable age. Would that romance have been sustainable had Danny been the apprentice 'smithy'? He tried not to think of the answer to this question.

He stared at the third letter for a few moments and then opened it. A quick glance at the top right-hand corner told him that it was from Edith Perry. Anxiety seized him. He began to read.

Dear Danny,

I wanted to write to you to let you know how Arthur is. I'm sure you will want to know. He is alive and, if not quite well, he is with us and that is the main thing. He's in great pain. We all suffer for him. I cry every night at seeing how he is. They say he will have to have a lot of operations. I don't think he'll ever work again. His hands. I can't describe them, but they are in a bad way. The girls are wonderful. Without them I don't know how I'd have managed. We talk about you often. Arthur remembers you fondly. I hope when all this is finished, you'll remember us and visit. Thanks for being such a friend to Arthur over the last year.

Danny put the letter down. Tears stung his eyes as he thought of his friend again. The memory of the hospital, the screams of men suffering, the smell of the disinfectant, became real to him again. He wiped the tears away with the heel of his palm and folded the letter. He put it in his knapsack along with the others he'd kept from home. He returned to them often. The connection they provided was more than just with family or love even. They represented the best of him, and he wanted to preserve something of this amid the brutality, the violence and the chivalry that surrounded him.

He looked around. The tanks were mostly camouflaged under canvas. This was to make them look like lorries for any aerial reconnaissance by the Luftwaffe. Men were sitting in the shade, engrossed in reading letters from home. It was as if they knew something was in the air. And it was. All around them there was a look in the eyes of the senior officers. An edginess that had been building throughout October. A fact picked up by PG.

'You noticed they're all a bit grim-faced these days.'

Danny looked at the Yorkshireman who was every bit as dour as men from that wonderful part of the world are reputed to be. He made a show of looking PG up and down.

'Get out of it you, cheeky tyke. Some folks are serious. Not kids like you,' said PG defensively. He ignored Danny's laughter. Finally, Danny responded to the original thought.

'I agree. Do you think they're going to give us the orders soon?' asked Danny.

'Aye. I do. It's a full moon on the 23rd. Makes sense to do it when we can all see each other.'

'They can see us, too, n'all,' remarked Danny moodily.

Later that morning the rumour became fact. It was Major Robert

Crisp who broke the news to them. They all assembled in front of the South African. There was little of the usual banter that Crisp enjoyed so much. He went straight to it.

'Men, Colonel Pyman has just given us our orders. They come all the way from Monty. It's happening tomorrow night. We're finally going in. As you know, it'll be a night attack. There will be two phases. The first phase is named "Lightfoot". The Sapper chaps will go in and remove those bloody mines. We'll follow soon after that. This is the break-in phase. Two lanes will be cleared. One north and one south. The southern lane will be a feint. The real attack will occur in the northern lane. That's where we'll be. In both cases, the infantry will clear a path for the armour to storm the citadel, so to speak. Following this will be "Supercharge". This phase will take place over a narrower front of around two to three miles and will involve two infantry brigades plus the armour. The good news is that we are going to be used in almost all the phases.'

He paused for a moment and regarded the men in front of him.

'I know we've heard all this before, but I think this time it really will be different. I will read out to you the thoughts of our Commander-in-Chief.'

Crisp took a piece of paper out of his pocket and unfolded it. Then he began to read. 'When I assumed command of the Eighth Army, I said that the mandate was to destroy Rommel and his army, and that it would be done as soon as we are ready. We are ready now. The battle which is now about to begin will be one of the decisive battles of history. It will be the turning point of the war. The eyes of the whole world will be on us, watching anxiously which way the battle will swing. We can give them their answer at once: "It will swing our way". We have first-class equipment; good tanks;

287

good anti-tank guns; plenty of artillery and plenty of ammunition; and we are backed up by the finest air striking force in the world. All that is necessary is that each one of us, every officer and man, should enter this battle with the determination to see it through – to fight and to kill – and finally, to win. If we all do this there can be only one result – together we will hit the enemy for "six", right out of North Africa. The sooner we win this battle, which will be the turning point of the war, the sooner we shall all get back home to our families. Therefore, let every officer and man enter the battle with a stout heart, and the determination to do his duty as long as he has breath in his body. And let no man surrender so long as he is unwounded and can fight. Let us all pray that "The Lord mighty in battle" will give us victory.'

When he'd finished, he looked up at the men who were sitting in rapt attention.

'Tomorrow night, Jerry will be on the receiving end of one almighty shellacking from our artillery boys. This will buy us time for the initial move through the minefields. Are there any questions?'

There were none.

'Very well, I will brief the commanders now on specific details as it applies to them. But this is the one we've been waiting for. Probably for the first time, we have the men, the equipment and, most importantly, a sound strategy. We can deal the Afrika Korps a body blow and I can tell you there isn't a senior officer who has spent time with Monty who doesn't believe that this is it. This is our time.'

It rang true. Danny could see the belief radiating from Crisp, or perhaps he was just a good salesman. Unquestionably, though, Danny felt his spirit lift. For once the plan didn't seem the blindly optimistic cavalry charge of old. Instead, it was a combined effort across all the services bar Navy and, critically, they were not playing cricket. It would happen at night. It seemed, at long last, the Allies had learned the lesson of past failure. Danny certainly hoped so. For the first time, he thought so, too.

CHAPTER THIRTY-SIX

Ladenburg, Germany, 22nd October 1942

'I can't believe I'm doing this,' hissed Sammy for what seemed like the twentieth time. Sammy accompanied Brehme into the police station, looking around him like a schoolboy visiting the headmaster.

It was eleven at night and the station was empty except for a policeman at the reception. Brehme nodded to the man behind the counter, Kaltz. He was new, young and rich, and utterly uninterested in the job. It served one purpose – to keep him away from the front line. Brehme understood this all too well. Had he not done the same? Indolent the young man may have been, but he was not entirely stupid.

'I'm just interrogating a suspect,' explained Brehme to the young policeman. He might as well have said he was marrying a horse. The boy acknowledged him briefly before returning to his newspaper.

They went through into the office Brehme shared with Keller. Brehme showed him the large metal filing cabinet that was used to store the Gestapo files. Sammy nodded then extracted from his pocket a leather wallet.

'What's that?' asked Brehme stupidly. Sammy raised his eyebrows but didn't answer. Tools of the trade realised Brehme. He went over to his desk and sat down. 'I'll leave you to it.'

And Sammy went to it. The leather pouch, from the quick glance by Brehme, seemed to contain a variety of metal implements. Brehme looked at Sammy's hands as he picked out a couple of the metal lock picks. His fingers were long and slender, very much at odds with the rest of Sammy, which was neither.

He selected a couple of metal picks and went to work. Brehme turned away rather like a gentleman when confronted with a woman undressing. He felt it oddly inappropriate to watch the act of breaking in.

Seconds later he heard the filing cabinet drawers open. He spun around to Sammy, in shock.

'Already?'

'I was good, you know,' smiled Sammy.

'Still practising?' asked Brehme grimly but there was a twinkle in his eye.

'Only when I lock myself out,' explained Sammy.

Brehme was over to the cabinet in the blink of an eye. He fished through a couple of the drawers before he found what he was looking for.

'Can you keep watch?' asked Brehme.

Sammy went to the door and opened it just wide enough to allow him a view of the corridor.

Brehme carefully flicked through the file he'd first seen a month previously. There was still no mention of him, but the rest of the file was full of biographical information about key town officials. Nothing in them seemed suspicious. Businessmen, too, were included. A number were suspected of having helped Jewish people escape abroad. This

291

was based on past political allegiances rather than anything tangible. After a few minutes Brehme replaced the file, slightly dissatisfied.

He searched through the other drawers and removed another file. This one was thinner. His eyes widened when he saw the abstract.

'*Information pertaining to the provision of sanctuary to Jews.*'

He flicked through the file. A number of the men and women mentioned in the previous file also appeared here. This was not unexpected but it appeared that there was an operation being planned to conduct surprise searches on a mass scale. Brehme had noticed the build-up of SS personnel in recent days. He looked for a date.

There was nothing else in the file that could confirm when the operation would start. Nor was there any detail on who would conduct the searches. Given the number of SS he'd seen arrive in the previous few days, two things were clear to Brehme: the operation was imminent and likely would involve simultaneous searches to avoid news spreading.

He sat back in his old chair and shook his head. The country was at war, not just with half the world but also with itself. It made sense, of course. These people had created an enemy within to justify their own enrichment as well as their continued presence while others went off to fight. He thought of Erich Sammer again, a boy who represented everything he detested about the country. He'd avoided being sent to the front line because of his connections. While Manfred risked his life in a desert, this piece of excrescence was pretending to play policeman.

'Hurry up,' said Sammy nervously.

'Relax,' replied Brehme. 'The station is quiet these nights.'

Sammy smiled nervously. 'Why? Have you sent all the criminals to fight?'

'No, Sammy. They're running the country now.'

If Sammy was surprised to hear this, he hid it well. In fact, it only confirmed his view that he'd been right to help his old nemesis. In an odd way, and certainly for the first time, they were on the same side.

Sammy performed his magic in shutting the filing cabinet. Then he turned to Brehme and said with a smile, 'Can we go now?'

'No,' replied Brehme. 'One more thing?'

Sammy glanced outside the window.

'We don't have time. I can see people coming into the station.'

Brehme shook his head and pointed at the table. 'Quickly, this drawer.'

Sammy paused for a moment. His face was apoplectic. Then he did as he was ordered. It took a couple of seconds, then the drawer was open. He stood back and let Brehme look. While the police of chief did this, Sammy glanced out the window. The long raincoats suggested only one thing. The men outside were almost certainly Gestapo. And they were now rushing into the station.

Brehme made an exclamation. He motioned for Sammy to come over and lock the desk drawer. A couple of agonising seconds passed as Sammy struggled to do this.

'Hurry,' hissed Brehme.

'You're the one that wanted the bloody thing open with the Gestapo outside,' snarled Sammy.

They heard the click with relief and then immediately Sammy and Brehme darted over to the other desk. Moments later the door burst open. Ernst Keller stood in the entrance with another man that Brehme did not recognise, although he appeared to be cut from the same cloth. Keller looked from Brehme to Sammy and then back again.

'I saw the light on in the office,' said Keller carefully.

'Strange time to be passing the office,' replied Brehme, coolly. The pup behind the desk was obviously under orders to report if he ever came to the office at an unusual time. After what he'd seen in the memo he'd found, Brehme could understand why.

Keller looked once more at Sammy which made the little burglar feel distinctly like a fish staring at a hungry shark. Brehme noted Keller's interest and decided introductions were in order.

'Lieutenant Keller, may I introduce an informant of mine, Sammy Schneider. Sammy was once on the wrong side of the law but has thankfully seen the error of his ways and helped me on occasion with useful information.'

'What were you discussing tonight at such a late hour?' asked Keller. He was staring directly at Sammy. He also sensed the unease in the little man. This made him certain something was afoot. He stepped into the office accompanied by the other Gestapo officer and walked right up to Sammy, ignoring Brehme.

'I heard something in a bar yesterday. I thought that the chief should know.'

'What did you hear?'

'Black market things. Cattle,' replied Sammy. Brehme was looking at Sammy. He hoped that Keller hadn't noticed that he was holding his breath. The mention of cattle made Keller's face turn a shade or three paler.

'What things?' asked Keller. His throat had tightened, making his voice a malevolent whisper.

Sammy noted this and relaxed. Brehme had been right. These crooks were running their own black-market operation.

'I couldn't see who was speaking and they were heading out anyway. He said something about being under the noses of the police but that's as much as I could hear before he was out the door.'

Keller nodded, seemingly relieved. He quizzed Sammy a little more on where this had taken place and seemed satisfied the little man was speaking the truth.

'I'm sorry to have interrupted you,' said Keller, edging towards his desk. He sat down and glanced at the drawer. He introduced the other man but Brehme spotted him testing the drawer to see if it was still locked. He seemed satisfied that nothing untoward had happened. Kaltz would have told them that they'd been there only a few minutes. This was not enough time to have conducted any search.

'That's quite all right,' replied Brehme expansively. 'Sammy was just leaving anyway.'

Keller stood up and shook hands with Sammy. The grip was cold and clammy. Sammy nodded to the other man and then, accompanied by Brehme, escaped out of the office with more than a sigh of relief.

'Well remembered,' said Brehme to the burglar. He'd briefed him in the car coming over for just such an eventuality. They reached the exit of the police station. 'I'll drive you back to Heidelberg.'

Sammy shook his head. There was a shrewd look in his eyes.

'I don't think that would be a good idea. Best I leave you here. Did you find what you wanted?'

'I did, Sammy,' replied Brehme. He held out his hand. Sammy looked down at the proffered hand and gripped it. They parted without another word.

Brehme watched him walk away and then he started towards his car. He stopped and thought better of it. He had one more place to go. He couldn't draw attention to himself with a police car. Instead, he trudged through town in the cold night air, his mind spinning with what he'd read. It wasn't just the raids planned by the Gestapo and the SS. He knew he was about to walk off the edge of a precipice.

Just ahead he saw the house he wanted. A look around told him that he was not being followed but he couldn't take chances. He

295

ducked down an alley way and remained there for five minutes. No one appeared on the street. It was nearly midnight so there was no reason why anyone should be there on a night like this.

Moving around the back, he clambered over a garden fence and approached the back door. There were no lights on inside. This was a problem. They had probably gone to bed. The last thing he wanted to do was attract attention by banging on the door but there was nothing else for it. He rapped the door. Softly at first, then harder. This produced the effect he'd sought. A dog started to bark. A few minutes later a light came on and a figure appeared at the door. Brehme could hear the man muttering darkly on the other side of the door.

'Open up, Otto,' demanded Brehme in a loud whisper. The door opened slowly.

Otto Becker's face fell in shock when he saw who it was. In a better light Brehme would have seen him turn pale. Behind him, Felix was barking the bark of a dog that doesn't know if it should be happy or warning of an intruder.

'Herr Brehme, what are you doing here at this time of night?' replied Becker before turning to the excited Labrador. 'Enough, Felix.'

'Let me in, Otto. I need to speak to you.'

Agatha Becker appeared just behind her husband demanding to know who was calling. Becker opened the door wider. Rather like her husband, she was shocked to see the chief of police standing in their doorway. Felix moved forward and jumped up on Brehme. At least someone was glad to see him, thought Brehme grimly. He stepped forward into the kitchen. The elderly couple were too much in shock to object. But they also felt fear.

'What brings you here?' asked Becker nervously. Gone was the irritation.

Brehme stared at Becker and decided to get to the point.

296

'You are both in grave danger. You and the people you are harbouring.'

Agatha Becker's hand went to her mouth. Her husband was speechless for a few moments. Then he began what sounded like a denial before being silenced by Brehme. There was no time for this.

'Take me to them,' ordered Brehme. 'Now.'

The elderly couple looked at one another and then Agatha nodded. In silence, they led Brehme outside to a small doorway. Becker unlocked it and they descended a wooden flight of stairs to a cellar. Becker gave the door a knock and a few moments later it opened. A face peeked through the crack.

'It's me,' said Becker.

The door opened reluctantly and they entered. Inside was a small cold room lit by a couple of candles. It housed an elderly man and woman. With them was a young girl. She couldn't have been older than five. There was a straw mattress that acted as a bed, a table with two chairs, some books and a few toys. Who could live in such an awful space? Yet Brehme recognised them.

'Doctor Glickman,' said Brehme, looking at the man who had once been his dentist. 'You and Frau Glickman are both in danger. The Gestapo are going to raid a dozen houses they suspect of harbouring Jews. The Beckers have been identified as one such household. The raid will happen tomorrow night. You have to leave, now.'

Even in the candlelight Brehme could see the fear etched into the deep lines of the elderly couple. Brehme glanced down at the child. He knelt and said, 'What's your name?'

'Eliana,' responded the little girl. She was clutching a doll and a teddy tightly to her chest.

'Well, you will have to be a brave girl and help your grandparents. Do you understand?'

She nodded. Glickman finally found his voice and asked, 'How do you know this?'

Brehme shook his head. 'There's no time to explain. Collect your belongings and meet me at the alleyway in twenty minutes. Otto, you and Agatha must make this place look like no one has been living here. Then you must reach anyone else who is harbouring Jewish people and let them know of the raid. Do you understand?'

'Yes, but what can they do? Where can they go?'

Brehme had been thinking of this for the last twenty minutes since he'd uncovered the plan for the raid. There was one possibility. It was a risk, but they were fresh out of alternatives.

'I need to use your phone. I will organise this.'

Glickman looked at Brehme. There was gratitude in his eyes but also something else.

'Why are you doing this? You are putting your life in danger.'

Brehme had no answer for this. It was certainly unusual. He'd spent a lifetime avoiding danger. He shook his head and pointed upstairs to Becker. His heart was pounding. The next few minutes would either be a moment of release, or it would condemn them all to death.

They returned through the backyard back to the house where Felix was eager to greet them again. At any other time, this would have been welcome but there was simply too much to do. A disappointed Labrador watched his master and the visitor disappear into another room.

Becker pointed to the phone in the study. Brehme took a deep breath and looked at the little man whose life he was about to endanger.

'This may not work. He may say no. He may tell the Gestapo. You understand this?'

Becker nodded. Then a thought struck him.

'How did you know?'

'The bags of food, Otto. The bags of food. I've watched you this year. Always carrying food for the five thousand. I didn't realise initially and then…' He left the rest of the sentence unfinished.

Becker nodded. He watched as Brehme picked up the phone. After a year living in fear, Becker felt peace descend on him. He had acted with the best of intentions. If this meant breaking the law, then so be it. The Nazis represented no form of authority that he would ever accept. He hated them and what they stood for. His chest began to swell with emotion. It wasn't much, but he'd stood up against thuggery, hatred and brutality. Whatever will be, will be, he thought.

Brehme fought to control the anxiety in his voice. He'd already stepped forward into an unknown world. The most dangerous moment for him had now arrived. He would now declare what he had done, if not to the world, then to someone who could conceivably give him up to the Nazis. This was the one man in the area who had more reason to hate the Gestapo than most.

'Hello, can you put me through to Lucas Kramer, please? Yes, Kramer farm.'

299

CHAPTER THIRTY-SEVEN

El Alamein, Egypt, 23rd October 1942

'What time is it?' asked Danny. He wasn't even trying to hide the edge in his voice now.

PG looked up and replied irritably, 'Ten minutes from the last time you asked.'

They were sitting outside the tank. Waiting. Benson joined them a few minutes later and they sat silently gazing up at the silver-shining full moon set amid a billion pin pricks of light. It gave the desert a strange pale blue glow before the darkness enveloped it fully.

'What a place,' said PG. 'You spend half the day with your backside boiling and the other half frozen. But what a sky. I'll miss this place.'

'Are you off anywhere then?' asked Benson, an amused smile creasing his face.

'Who knows?' replied the Yorkshireman but there wasn't much belief in it.

'Why?' asked Danny, genuinely curious.

PG shook his head and replied, 'Try spending a day down a pit. It's black, dark and feels like you are within touching distance of hell itself. Then do it day in, day out. Breathing in that dust. No, Danny boy, I'll take my chances here.'

Danny was surprised by this. His life had been so free by comparison. The countryside, fresh air, fresh food. It all seemed so different from the blackness described by PG.

'You know what I miss most?'

The silence that followed Danny's comment was its own question so he continued. 'Sitting under a tree eating an apple. A stolen apple tastes like no apple you've ever had. My pals and I used to mitch off from school and raid the farms in the area for anything we could lay our hands on.'

'I'm surprised they didn't shoot you,' said Benson. 'You were a smithy, weren't you?'

'Yes, sir,' said Danny. He felt a lump in his throat as he thought of his father by the forge.

'Won't be much call for them soon,' pointed out PG. 'Do they have factories where you are?'

Danny smiled but what PG said hit home. He worked with metals, with iron. They had spent the last year in a metal cabin, firing metal shells and being hit by bullets and bombs. This ammunition had been produced on a mammoth scale. The plain fact was PG was right. His world was finished. He thought of the other boys, of the old school in Little Gloston and the terrifying violence of Mrs Grout, of mitching off to swim in the forest, of pinching apples from the local orchards.

'A few of the lads we stole from came here.'

PG and Benson waited for Danny to continue. He said nothing, his mind lost to an image of Bert Gissing waving his fist at him all those years ago. He thought of poor Hugh. Killed during the Crusader operation. Bob was in prison. The others were in prison, too, now. Prisoners of war in Italy.

Tobruk. Greece. There was no escaping this enemy. He was the only one from the village still actively engaged on a front line. A half a dozen or so of them from Little Gloston. He stopped for a second and thought of the other side. People just like him probably. Only they weren't. They'd allowed the Nazis to lead them to war. What sort of people would want to be here doing this?

'You lost your friends?' asked Benson

Danny turned to the captain and shrugged.

'Some. Well, you know my brother and one of the other blokes got captured at Tobruk. They're in Italy now.'

'At least that's something,' said Benson.

Danny nodded but said nothing more. They sat in silence for a few minutes until they were disturbed by the arrival of McLeish carrying some tea. He handed it round to the others.

'How much longer?' asked McLeish. He received a slap round the head with PG's beret.

'Another hour,' replied Benson. The captain stared into the black. Somewhere out in the darkness were men just like them, sitting nervously, waiting for battle.

The night air felt almost tangible. The wet, cold air bathed Danny's face like a damp rag. His hands cupped the warmth of the metal mug and he sipped the tea. It tasted bitter but he was used to it by now. A far cry from crunching through a fresh apple, underneath a tree on a bright spring day. His grip tightened on the mug.

Nearby someone was listening to the Forces radio. Al Bowlly's voice cut through the silence and Danny felt the warmth of the voice envelop and comfort him.

'I love his voice,' said the girl in the bed next to Sarah Cavendish. The dormitory housed eight girls. They were all listening to Forces Radio from the BBC. The station was playing a recording of the late Al Bowlly. He was singing, appropriately, 'Goodnight Sweetheart'. The girls in the dorm grinned conspiratorially. It wasn't quite bedtime yet, but this was their free time and they often listened to the radio for a little while, imagining a boy somewhere, many miles away, who would be listening to this and thinking of them.

Sarah listened to the song and glanced occasionally at a battered photograph of a bunch of men posing in army uniform. Danny and his brother were at the front. Both were smiling as if someone had just told a joke.

Still my love will guide you…

She wondered when she would see him again. It was never if. The idea that he would die seemed inconceivable. Not him. Not Danny.

Dreams enfold you, in each one I'll hold you…

The girls had begun chatting about something or other, but Sarah wished they would keep quiet. She wanted to hear the rest of the song. They could talk over the announcer if they wanted to. Never mind.

Goodnight sweetheart, goodnight.

The door to the dorm opened. Sarah looked up and grimaced as she saw the angry face of the head of form.

Keller walked into the office with an unmistakably triumphant look on his face. Brehme was impassive although he felt like laughing. Keller had asked him to return to the station around seven but without giving a reason. Brehme had, of course, pressed him as hard as he could on why, although he already knew. He also knew that the satisfaction on Keller's face would not last the hour.

Outside the office he heard a lot of noise. It was like a football crowd. This did surprise him, and he noted Keller's evident enjoyment at his confusion. At the end of the corridor there were a lot of black-shirted soldiers. Brehme turned to Keller and raised his eyebrows for an explanation that he didn't need.

'You'll see,' said Keller opaquely.

So will you, thought Brehme. At this point he wasn't sure how far to push taking offence.

'Very well, play your games, Ernst.'

The two men headed down the corridor. The reception area of the station was full of SS men. There were a few of the Gestapo officers who'd become regular visitors to the station. Graf stood alone like a child without friends while big boys milled around him laughing. It was like a party or worse; they were going on a hunt. Brehme looked at them and felt anger rise inside him. They were like an invading force in his police station, his town, his country.

Outside, night had fallen although it was still only early evening. Rain was falling steadily now. He could see people trooping home on the rain-washed streets. A tug on his arm forced him to turn around. He found himself staring into the face of Erich Sammer.

'Hello, Peter,' said Erich. Brehme wondered at what point he'd ceased to be Herr Brehme. Probably when the damn black shirt had been taken out of its packaging.

Brehme nodded and replied carefully, 'Hello, Erich, it's been a while. Where have you been?' He wanted to add 'avoiding the war' but he decided against it. Their humiliation would come anyway. He hoped. Nothing in life was guaranteed. The risk remained great. One mistake, just one slip up and the whole shaky construct would collapse. Something small, something no one realised had been left behind. That would be enough. The owners would be taken away, questioned, tortured probably. All would be revealed. All.

A voice interrupted Erich before he could speak. It was Keller calling everyone to attention.

'Gentlemen,' said Keller, much to Brehme's amusement. 'We are about to embark on a mission of utmost importance. Our country has many enemies. These enemies are not just across sea and ocean. They exist within our own borders.'

Brehme thought of the little girl clutching her teddy bear. He shook his head and then stopped himself lest he be seen.

'To the vehicles, men. Let us cleanse this town of our enemies. Let us make Ladenburg safe for the German people. Heil Hitler.'

There were close to forty men inside the reception area and more outside. Their heels clicked like a round of thunder and they chorused *Heil Hitler* in unison.

Brehme and Erich walked out into the cold night air. Rain was falling gently, and the sky was black as death. The air tingled with electricity. It felt like a storm was coming.

Erich smiled a little embarrassedly at Brehme. It wasn't hard to guess why. Perhaps, somewhere inside lurked a sense of shame or, at least, an acknowledgement of his cowardice. You might be able to fool the world into believing your patriotism and your desire to fight for the Fatherland, thought Brehme, but deep down you know what you are. So do I. I was like you, once. He stared unflinchingly at Erich.

Go on. Ask me.

'How is Manfred?' said Erich. His voice sounded brittle.

'The last I heard from him, he was well,' replied Brehme carefully. 'He's still in Egypt. They're near where the British are holding out. A place called El Alamein.'

305

The waiting was not the worst. It was preferable to fighting and dying, that much was clear. It brought home the unreality of it all for Manfred. Being stuck in an alien environment, fighting for a cause he no longer believed in. Any certainty he'd had about ultimate victory was gone now.

The truth was evident to every soldier that had come up against the storm of violence that the Allies could mete out. The enemy had finally discovered a truth that had been the lynchpin of the Afrika Korps success: integrating and unifying the strengths of the individual services towards specific objectives. No longer did the enemy operate so inefficiently and disparately. Manfred could see that the recent defeats, or strategic withdrawals to give them their proper due, were a portent of the future. A bigger, stronger enemy had finally worked out how to play the game. The result was inevitable. It might take years. Many would die. The outcome would be the same.

Not everyone shared Manfred's view. This astonished him. The man who had taken over from Kummel, Lieutenant-Colonel Teege for one. He and Fischer called him 'Willi' when they chatted each evening. Fischer still believed victory was possible but he was more qualified in his view than previously. The wounding had certainly disabused him of his aura of invincibility, but the arrogance remained untouched. Manfred was glad of this. It was entertaining to listen to on the cold nights.

The day of the 23rd of October was like so many of the others in the last few weeks. Sporadic shelling was ignored. It seemed the Allies were going through the motions as much as they were. This was unfathomable to Manfred. If they'd any idea how exhausted the Afrika Korps were, they'd have attacked and thrown them out of Africa long ago. Now, gradually, they'd seen their strength recover.

Not just personal physical and spiritual reserves but also additions in the form of reinforcements, tanks refitted and repaired. They were still outnumbered but that had never stopped them in the past. Perhaps Fischer was right to feel some confidence.

They were on patrol several kilometres from the leaguer. Every so often they would spot the armoured cars of the enemy but there was little they could do about it. By the time they had a fix on where they were, they were gone. Often, they passed the deathly, blackened hulks of their comrades and, sometimes, their enemy.

The three wrecked tanks they passed now were all Panzers. The holes in the front told a story of a horrifying death. Shrapnel mincing the men inside. Someone had dug graves. Each was only two feet long and probably quite shallow. Not much more was needed for the parts of the men that had been found. Manfred felt a momentary nausea as he imagined the brutalising experience not just for those who had died but the poor men whose job it had been to bury what was left of them. Basler was silent, too, as they passed the graves. But there was no prayer for the dead.

They drove back to the leaguer.

Fischer was reading a book when Manfred arrived at his tank. Books were highly prized items in the leaguer.

'What are you reading?' asked Manfred.

Fischer held it up.

The Interpretation of Dreams by Sigmund Freud.

Not all books were prized equally, though.

Manfred laughed when he saw it and asked, 'Who did it? The butler or the husband?'

Fischer grinned. 'You'll have to work it out for yourself. But the candle is an important clue.'

'Symbolic, I would have thought.'

'Very. Tell me, Manfred, do you think of candles much?'

'No. Caves, mostly,' replied Manfred before continuing slowly in a deep, awed voice. 'Caves in the middle of deep, dark forests.'

'I think I know what your problem is, Manfred,' concluded Fischer holding his index finger up as if he was teaching in class.

'All our problems, my friend. I don't think you've earned your Nobel Prize quite yet.'

Having mined this seam of all its innuendo potential they were quiet for a few moments. The desert remained an implacable, mute presence: the ultimate enemy. They both stared out at it.

'You're looking in the wrong direction,' said Fischer at last.

'How do you mean?'

'The enemy is that way,' replied Fischer pointing east.

'Why don't you stick to Freud and manipulating your genitals?'

Fischer erupted into laughter at this, joined by Manfred seconds later. It felt like they were the only ones making noise in the leaguer. The wave of hilarity passed soon and they were silent once more.

'What time is it?' asked Fischer, setting the book down and sitting up.

Manfred glanced at his watch and said, '2140 almost.' He shivered as he said this. The nights were getting colder now. He pulled his coat around him.

There was a dull sound of a crump in the distance. Manfred frowned.

'What was that?'

308

CHAPTER THIRTY-EIGHT

The cold night air was charged with anticipation. He shivered in the chill. There were so many other things a civilised man could be doing at this time. He looked around him. The ranks of guns and men were bathed in the light of the full moon overhead. He shivered again, this time at the thought of what these guns would do. Soon they would make quite a noise. He looked at his watch. Very soon, in fact.

He stared out into the darkness. Just ahead were the infantry and their sappers making ready to enter the minefields. Further ahead of them were the Germans sitting snuggly confident in the impassability of their minefields. And here he was, Lieutenant James Carruthers, former manager of a shoe factory, seconds away from unleashing the greatest artillery barrage experienced on the planet in nearly twenty-five years. Several miles of guns were to operate like one battery.

A curtain of shells would descend upon the enemy. Then it would move progressively forward by one hundred yards as the infantry advanced. While it had been light, they had used slide rules to derive where their shells would land on the map. Adjustments had been made to take account of the wind, the temperature, the barometric pressure and, of course, the shells themselves. A former shoe factory manager he may have been, but now James Carruthers was a professional and highly experienced artillery man. There was a swell of pride in his chest as he breathed in the cold air.

He looked again at his guns. All were in small pits, underneath camouflage nets. Not that anyone would be looking at this hour. The next day would be a different matter, but the RAF would deal with anyone nosey or stupid enough wanting to check their position.

As Command Post Officer he oversaw the two troops of four guns. He nodded towards the two Gun Position Officers to make ready. He heard one of them say 'Take Post.'

A few seconds later their No.1 ordered, 'HE, 117, charge 3, load.'

It was just like running a factory. Order, process. Leadership. It came so naturally to him. He watched as the twenty-five-pound explosive with 117 fuse was slipped into the breech and rammed home. The metallic clang indicated the breech block was shut. This process would repeat itself at every gun, all along the line. It reoccurred six hundred times that night for almost every gun on the line. Over eight hundred guns were pointed at the enemy. Yes, Carruthers didn't envy Jerry one bit.

He glanced at his watch.

The gun position officer, a sergeant nearby said, 'Zero one five degrees.'

The gunner made a final adjustment of his sight and then nodded to the GPO. Carruthers glanced at his watch and wished he'd lit his pipe.

'Troop rest,' ordered the GPO.

The men either side of the gun relaxed. But this would only be for a few moments. The work would begin soon. The silence that followed prickled like a fire just beginning to burn.

The watch said forty seconds to go. He nodded to the two GPOs. The nearest one ordered his troop to take post. Carruthers stared at

310

the watch ticking down when, suddenly, he heard the crump of one of his guns.

He glared angrily at his sergeant.

'Was that you, McMillan?' hissed Carruthers angrily. What he said next was thankfully drowned out by the sound of a storm bursting over the Axis lines.

The Battle of El Alamein was underway.

Danny watched the sky light up. As far as the eye could see there were brilliant, blinding flashes followed split seconds later by thunderous explosions. His body vibrated as the terrible onslaught shook the earth. It felt like the world was tearing itself apart which, in a sense, it was.

The guns crashed incessantly while the crew watched the proceedings as if they were at a fireworks display. The horizon flickered and the earth shuddered in fear. It was relentless.

'That's the starter's pistol,' said Benson.

'Poor sods,' said PG. He was talking about the sappers and infantry men who would soon be marching forward into the minefields but, just for a moment, Danny wondered if there was thought there, too, for the men on the other side of the minefield.

It seemed strange to even consider sympathy. It was their fault that they were all here. Yet what little direct contact he'd had with the Afrika Korps and what he'd heard, suggested that, in the harsh context they found themselves in, humanity was still able to win some battles. The story of how Rommel, upon overrunning an Allied military hospital treating both sides at Mersa Metruh during the summer, had refused to take the doctors as prisoners of war. Instead, they were asked to stay on to treat the wounded before being allowed safe passage to Switzerland once German doctors could replace them. Danny suspected that many were back in North Africa now.

The response from the enemy seemed perfunctory. The odd shell slicing the air and screaming impotently in the night. PG said as much. McLeish said nothing very much at all and Benson smoked his pipe thoughtfully.

'They must be lying doggo,' concluded PG.

'I suspect they are. Why would anyone be out on a night like this?' replied Benson, like he was talking about a rainy evening in Piccadilly.

Danny tried not to think of that. All he could do was wait for the signal to advance. Sooner would be better. Not just to get it over with, either. The darkness made him feel safe. It seemed odd that something he would have feared as a child was now his protection. Daylight would change things for everyone. If the sappers and the infantry were unable to forge a sufficient path through the minefields, then they would be sitting ducks for the Germans.

The moon glimmered like a halo over the hellish scene below. Its luminous purity was in mute contrast to the astonishing testimony to man's ceaseless quest to find new, more effective ways to kill and destroy. Danny looked on, mesmerised by the wall of white light and the scream of shells. It stopped briefly and then, as if they could not be tamed, the guns started again. Overhead was the throbbing drone of bombers who were about to unleash yet more misery on the enemy.

PG was right. They were dug in. Waiting. It's not as if they hadn't done this before. It's not as if this tactic hadn't been tried before. It didn't work then. Why should it be any more successful now? Danny tried to ignore the voices in his head but even the bludgeoning bellows of the guns could not drown out the sound of his fears.

'What do you think, Shaw?' asked Benson, as they gazed at the angry horizon.

'I think,' replied Danny, 'that I need some more tea, sir.'

'Excellent idea, Shaw.'

312

Danny turned to McLeish who made no secret at his displeasure at being asked to brew up at this time. His sullen expression made Danny forget his fears for a moment and made him feel a bit better.

'Well done, Danny,' said Andrews. 'Leadership is all about the art of delegation.'

The radio burst into life seconds after the barrage started. Manfred was more interested in listening to what was being said on the radio than what he was seeing and hearing. It all seemed so far away to him. Then the radio went dead. Keil and Kleff both took turns at it. They turned to Basler. The lieutenant looked from them to the radio and then pointed to the horizon that was lit with a blinding light.

'I think it's safe to say that our friends have decided enough is enough.'

It was an unusual reflection on the commencement of battle. Manfred turned his attention to the horizon and the flashing and the distant screams of shells. Panzer Regiment 8 was, relatively speaking, a long way from the desperate shelling that was raining down on the forward positions. There, in the line of fire, were the anti-tank guns and the German and Italian infantry arrayed in front of the minefields. They were situated near the Alarm Piste, just in front of the headquarters.

'What will happen now?' asked Keil. He was fidgeting with a cup.

'Let them fire,' snapped Basler. He seemed irritated, but not at Keil. 'If they want to waste their ammunition on rocks and sand, let them. When the sun comes up, we'll see them all before us, stuck in the middle of a minefield trying to reach Kidney Ridge. We'll pick them off. They never learn.'

They had talked about the two ridges in front of them endlessly. Kidney Ridge and Miteiriya Ridge to its south were both of strategic importance to the Allies. For this reason, tens of thousands of mines had been planted in the areas surrounding them; guns were trained on them. Any attempt to take them would be met by a hail of fire that no one could survive.

The Miteiriya Ridge ran parallel to the coast, twenty kilometres inland. It was around five kilometres long and extended in a series of features forming another low ridge that was shaped like a kidney. These two points were held by the Germans and were certain to be targets for the expected Allied assault.

Basler, although dismissive of the likely tactics that the Allies were to use, was distinctly on edge. Manfred knew why. They had been talking the previous day about the anticipated advance from the enemy.

'They will be stuck in the minefields. We'll shoot at them until our ammunition runs out.'

Manfred asked the question he already knew the answer to.

'What happens then?'

'They'll just send more men to attack. They'll climb over the dead bodies of their comrades and we shall fall back as far as our petrol will allow us to.'

Basler eyed Manfred closely as he said this. It felt strange to have been given such an insight into Basler's mood. Yet, increasingly, Basler was less able to disguise his state of mind. It stood in marked contrast to so many around them. There had been an air of unreality about the period leading up to the beginning of the barrage. So much so that Manfred now avoided conversation with anyone except Fischer about what lay ahead.

The simple fact was that no one knew the extent of, or at least was willing to acknowledge, the obvious disparity between the two sides in terms of men and materiel. To a man they knew they were better soldiers. They had proved this time and again. But this was not an equal fight.

Manfred listened to the barrage in silence. Light flickered on the faces of his fellow crew like they were watching a film at the cinema. It wasn't fear they were experiencing at that moment; they were all too numbed by cold and hunger. Nor was it resignation, for, despite everything, there was still a flicker of hope that they could win. Rather it was the sense of living in a dream. The noise and the pyrotechnics of what had been unleashed by the Allies was hypnotic and horribly beautiful. But the initial awe gave way, once more, to realisation that soon they would all be in the middle of this storm. Manfred and the others trembled in the cold of the night and waited. It was not shelling they had to fear but the silence that followed. That's when the enemy would come. That's when the fighting would start.

CHAPTER THIRTY-NINE

Ladenburg, Germany, 23rd October 1942

The first rumble of thunder came as Peter Brehme waited for Keller to emerge from the station. The Gestapo man loped over towards him like a Labrador about to go for a walk. His face split with a triumphant grin. It seemed like he was about to burst into song. He took his hands from his pocket and handed a piece of paper to Brehme.

'These are the homes we are going to visit.'

Visit? Brehme could have laughed. As it happened, he already knew the list. Keller couldn't know this of course. Brehme studied the list with a frown. He was no actor but he did a nice line in impassivity and neutrality when he had to.

'Becker?' he exclaimed but not too dismissively. He turned his eyes towards Keller in disbelief. 'They are an old couple. Are you really telling me they are harbouring Jews?'

Keller nodded exultantly.

'What proof do you have?' pressed Brehme. It would look odd if he, at least, didn't demand this. In truth, he just wanted it all over

316

with. The rain was getting heavier now and the ink on the paper was running. The two men started to move towards Brehme's police car.

'Do you want to come with me?' asked Brehme.

'Yes,' replied Keller, starting to trot, his shoes splashing on the pavement.

They reached the car and climbed in. Just as he was about to start the motor, Brehme saw Graf running towards them. He nearly slipped on the wet road. Around him the other police cars and military vehicles were departing.

Graf fell into the back seat and apologised. Brehme felt like shaking his head but decided not to humiliate the policeman in front of Keller. He started the engine and soon they were off.

'I want to go to Becker's house. If I'm wrong, I'm wrong. I need to see with my own eyes, Ernst. This is extraordinary.'

'I quite understand. To answer your question, we have testimony from Herr Weber at the grocery store that Becker and some of the others on that list are buying unusually large quantities of food.'

'They have a dog,' pointed out Brehme. It sounded weak, even to him. The Gestapo man laughed sardonically.

'This dog obviously likes potatoes,' replied Keller. He made little attempt to hide his contempt.

The first flashes of lightning were now visible, and the thunder crashed more loudly. It felt like a portent. But for who? Brehme felt his chest tighten. The Jewish families had all been spirited away to the Kramer farm. Robert Sauer, a mere schoolboy, had confirmed that they would be moved within twenty-four hours. How he knew, Brehme did not inquire.

The rain was falling heavily now, the wipers fighting a losing battle against its intensity. Behind him was another car. At least eight policemen and Gestapo would overpower an elderly couple. It

317

was almost laughable, yet his insides were churning. If they found some sign that there had been other people in the house, then it was all over. They wouldn't take long to break the Beckers. They knew nothing of Kramer. But Robert Sauer did. And so did he. They would be questioned and slowly the whole house of cards would crumble.

The Becker house was up ahead. He could see the lights on in the front room. Perhaps they would be sitting down to their evening meal, able to relax for perhaps the first time in over a year. Except they knew there would be visitors. Brehme wondered how they would react. So much depended on them.

The car pulled to a stop and they got out. Keller silently ordered the other policemen around the back of the house. A few people on the street had seen what was happening and were milling towards them.

Brehme and Graf followed the Gestapo man to the front door. Keller was about to batter the front door with the heel of his fist when Brehme held a hand up. Inside a dog began to bark.

'Let me,' he said and stepped forward in front of Keller. He knocked on the door. It wasn't a loud knock and Keller was visibly irritated at having this part of his show ruined. He'd wanted noise and fear. In its place was polite restraint. He was about to take over proceedings when he heard the door being unlatched then opened.

Otto Becker stood there staring stupidly at Brehme and then Keller. It was quite a performance, thought Brehme. He really looked like he had no idea of what was going on.

'Herr Brehme,' said Becker after a few moments. 'What are you doing here?' He didn't need to add, 'with all these policemen'? That was evident from the glance he shot Keller and Graf. Felix the Labrador had come to see what was going on. His tail was wagging in a welcoming manner. He started to bark.

'Shush, Felix,' said Becker.

318

'Herr Becker, we have reason to believe you are harbouring foreign nationals. Let us in.'

Foreign nationals? Brehme glanced at Keller in surprise. He'd known Dr Glickman all his life. Now he was an enemy of the state. A fifth columnist of sorts. Brehme almost snorted in disgust.

Keller stepped forward; his patience was wearing thin. He pushed Becker to one side. Felix realised that this was not a friendly visitor and began to growl. Keller turned to Becker as he passed. 'Control that dog or I will shoot it.'

There was no question he meant it. Becker bent down and tried to calm Felix. He glanced up at Brehme as he entered. Brehme merely shrugged at Becker and followed Keller into the house along with Graf. The other policemen were in the kitchen now. One of them was Erich but he stood back a little to let his senior colleagues take the lead. There was a look of excitement on his face. Brehme felt his hatred for the boy rise. This was his war. The only one he was qualified to wage: against old men and women.

'Start searching,' ordered Keller.

Becker had found his voice, or at least pretended to.

'This is an outrage. Who are you? Herr Brehme, what is the meaning of this?'

Brehme turned to Keller and raised his eyebrows. He had no intention of justifying the unjustifiable. This was Keller's show. He would let the Gestapo man explain. Keller ignored the complaints and shouted to the policemen to turn the place inside out. Then he spun around to Becker.

'Do you have an attic?' demanded Keller.

'Or cellar?' added Brehme. This thought impressed Keller as much as it surprised him.

'Or cellar,' added Keller unnecessarily.

'We don't have an attic,' said Becker in a more resigned voice. 'We do have a cellar.'

'Show me,' said Keller. Becker led Brehme, Keller and Graf out the back door and towards the door leading to the cellar.

By this stage Brehme was marvelling at the performance of Becker. He was walking the fine line between defeat and anger with aplomb. His business at the door was worthy of Chaplin. A brief explanation that the cellar was rarely used was emphasised by a slight struggle to open the door. He turned to Brehme and smiled with embarrassment. Rain dripped off his hat but there was no mistaking the anger in the eyes of Keller.

'It's a little stuck,' said Becker with a shrug.

'Let me try,' said Brehme, pretending impatience. Much to his surprise it was. There had been no such problems the previous evening. Becker had obviously done something with the key. Finally, after a few shakes, the key managed to do its job. The door dragged along the ground. Another nice touch, thought Brehme.

'There's no electricity down here,' said Becker as they stepped forward into a dark stairwell. Keller took out a torch and lit up the stairs. It was bitterly cold. This would have been uninhabitable. The first glimmerings of doom were already puncturing the confidence Keller had felt on the way here.

They reached the bottom of the stairs and opened the door. The room was empty now save for some junk and furniture partially covered by dusty bedsheets. This was turning into a bravura performance. Brehme glanced at Becker. The little man remained impassive, but he gave another shrug of his shoulders. The resignation mixed with confusion was beginning to wear away the confidence of Keller.

'Any other rooms?' demanded Keller. His voice was almost shrill with anger. Or perhaps fear. There was nothing to suggest that this room had been used in recent months.

'No,' said Becker simply.

They trooped back upstairs to the backyard. Thunder crashed overhead and the rain seemed to intensify. Their feet splashed through puddles as they made their way back to the kitchen. They met with the other policemen inside. Brehme saw one give a shake of his head.

It was clear that the old couple could not possibly have been harbouring anyone. Raging eyes turned on Becker. Felix was barking for all his worth. This served only to increase Brehme's anxiety. He suspected Keller was not far away from violence. Keller's temperature gauge was rising rapidly. He recognised the signs. They had reached a danger point.

Keller turned to the dog. His hand went to his pocket. Brehme knew what would happen now. He stepped in front of Keller blocking out his view of Felix. He motioned with his eyes to Agatha Becker to remove Felix just as Keller screamed in his ear, 'Get that dog out of here.'

Agatha Becker immediately grabbed Felix's collar and led him into the adjoining living room. This seemed to mollify the Labrador a little. She knelt and stroked him, but all the time kept her eyes on Keller.

Denied the chance to inflict violence, Keller spun around to Becker and snarled at him, 'If I find anything that proves you've been lying to me then you and your wife will face the direst of consequences.'

Brehme silently prayed that Becker kept his council. This was not the time for grandstanding. Evidently Becker was of a like mind for he looked fearful. Of course, this may not have been acting, reflected Brehme. He was still feeling tense.

Felix began barking but Agatha Becker remained with him and spoke soothingly. This seemed to have an effect.

'I can assure you that we would never do such a thing,' said Becker fearfully.

Felix stopped barking now which, perhaps, only irritated Keller further. He wanted to act. Hurt someone or something. He glared at Becker, impotent with rage, but could not think of anything else to say. His face was burning red now. His humiliation was complete. Brehme remained silent and scanned the room just in case there was anything incriminating.

Then he felt his stomach lurch.

Lying by one of the chairs was an old, battered teddy bear. He couldn't breathe. His heart began to accelerate. The toy was out in the open. He wanted to leap over the table and hide it. Instead, he could do nothing but stand there, powerless. Thunder rumbled outside once more as they stood there looking at one another wondering what to do next. A flash of lightning and the back door blew open bringing rain into the kitchen. Erich shut the door. Finally, Keller turned to the other uniformed men.

'You're sure there was nothing?' asked Keller through gritted teeth.

A curt nod followed. The other Gestapo man was clearly irritated by their failure and particularly by Keller's hubris. In the nod Brehme suspected there was little love lost between the two men. But they were not safe yet. One of the SS men was standing just a few feet away from the teddy bear.

Brehme held his breath. Just then Felix left the kitchen area and moved towards the chair where the teddy was lying. He began to sniff the toy. Brehme couldn't look. By doing so, he feared he'd draw attention to what was so obvious to him. There lay the evidence that Keller sought.

Erich went over to the dog and began to stroke it. Brehme felt faint. How could he not see what the dog was sniffing? Was he a complete idiot? The answer, Brehme realised, was 'yes'. But one of the other men might see what was happening.

Then Felix picked the teddy up and trotted into the kitchen holding it in his mouth. Brehme wanted to die right then. It was over now, surely. He looked at Becker. His face was white. He'd seen it, too.

And so had Graf.

Brehme looked at Graf. The little man's face was impassive, but he could not miss the panic in the eyes of his chief. Keller was muttering angrily to himself beside Brehme. Graf and Brehme continued to stare at one another. Then Graf bent down to the dog.

He grabbed one end of the teddy and began to pull it. The dog pulled back. Growling. But not angrily. It was a game to him.

Graf continued pulling at the teddy, but he was also doing something else. He was leading the dog out of the kitchen into the adjoining living room. The Labrador's tail was wagging furiously.

Keller shouted at Graf.

'Stop doing that, you idiot. Let's go.'

He spun around and stalked out of the kitchen towards the front door followed by his men. Graf stood up and returned to the kitchen, his eyes never leaving those of Brehme.

Soon it was only Brehme and the Beckers in the kitchen. No one could speak. It's difficult to chat when you can't breathe. Brehme's heart was still racing. With a nod to the householders, Brehme followed the others out of the front door. The rain was lashing down outside yet a small crowd of onlookers were there to add a further layer of humiliation to Keller's evening. He ignored Brehme who was standing by his car waiting and joined his men who were milling together like a wolf pack.

Brehme and Graf walked towards the police car in silence. Beside the car was Robert Sauer. The young man was soaked to the skin.

323

He and Brehme exchanged looks. There was a barely perceptible nod from the young man and relief coursed through the veins of Brehme.

Just ahead of Brehme walked Erich. Brehme felt a wave of anger course through him.

'Hey, Erich,' said Brehme.

Erich turned around. He looked like an evil little bully dressed up in a uniform. Brehme felt utter revulsion.

'Keep fighting the good fight,' said Brehme witheringly before climbing into the car and shutting the door to any reply. Graf climbed into the passenger seat a few seconds later. The two men sat for a moment and watched the rain batter the front window of the car. Finally, when at last Brehme was capable of speech, he turned to Graf.

'Can I buy you a beer, Jost?'

'Two, sir. I think you owe me at least two.'

Brehme nodded and then they both broke into smiles.

'Two it is, then.'

CHAPTER FORTY

El Alamein, Egypt, 24th October 1942

The order came to start moving. Benson nodded to PG. The engine burst into life. Outside the tank, the shelling continued unabated. Danny tensed up again. They rolled forward and the tightness slowly eased. They were on their way. Within minutes the Yorkshireman was already complaining.

'Can't see nowt.'

'What's that in English?' asked Danny, which brought a smile to Benson's face. This widened further when PG responded in typically robust fashion.

The rumbling clanking screech of the wheels over the tracks seemed to drown out the sound of the distant explosions in the German lines. As yet the response from the Germans was low key. This astounded Danny. It worried him, too. There had to be a reason. Benson also looked perturbed by the lack of response.

'Why aren't they firing at us?' murmured Benson. His head was outside the turret, but he could see little beyond the immediate tanks in front.

Danny peered through McLeish's periscope. Clouds of dust were being thrown up by the tanks. Visibility was barely a few yards. Danny shivered a little while McLeish's knee moved up and down rapidly. Just ahead lay the entrance to the British minefield. Much further ahead was the passage created by the sappers through the enemy minefield. Three soldiers, looking weary, stood by the entrance waving them through. White tape marked out the route. Lights flickered behind the blanket of sand being thrown up by the tanks.

Breeching the minefield brought it home to Danny that they were now fully committed. There was no turning back. They were in the middle of an endless line of traffic. One by one the regiment rolled forward followed by infantry, artillery, and Uncle Tom Cobley, commented PG.

Progress was paralysingly slow. With each passing minute the tension grew inside. No one wanted to be stuck in the minefield when the sun came up. Then it would be target practice for the eighty-eights which were arrayed in front of them.

They stopped around midnight to refuel. PG took care of this while McLeish and Danny inspected the tank. By this stage they had still not reached the enemy minefields. The word up ahead was that the depth of the enemy minefield belt was greater than first anticipated. At two in the morning, they began their movement forward again. The firing had not ceased from the Allied guns.

'I can't believe there'll be anything left of them at the other side,' said McLeish. It did seem incredible that anyone could survive such a horrifying torrent of shelling, yet Danny remembered the words of his father shortly before he'd left. It was one of the few times he'd spoken about his experiences twenty-five years before on the Western Front.

'Our guns blew half the country away and yet they came out of their holes and their trenches and mowed our boys down.'

Archie Andrews smiled grimly at McLeish.

'Don't get your hopes up, son. They've had a lot of experience in digging in against that sort of bombardment.'

Danny was sorry to see the young Scot's face fall but it was better he was forewarned. There was no question there would be a welcome for them soon. The order came to move. An exchange of looks but no one said, 'good luck'. They scrambled back inside the tank.

'Forward,' said Benson.

The tank didn't move.

Benson ducked down and glared at PG. 'Did you hear what I said?' PG was pressing the starter but the response from the engine was a whine and then silence. He shook his head and turned to Benson. The captain climbed down into the hull and knelt by PG.

'Shall I give it one more try?'

'Choke?' suggested Benson.

'Already on. Anyway, I don't want to flood the bloody thing.'

The engine whined a little but refused to start. PG and Benson looked outwardly calm but Danny could feel the tension rise. Outside there were shouts as the other tanks realised they were now stuck. Benson clambered back into the cupola and waved his arms for the others to move around them.

He went out of the hull hatch to inspect the engine. Danny joined him. He wasn't sure what he could do as PG was more of an expert but, on the principle that two heads were better than one, he thought he might be of some use.

'Hold the light,' said PG, opening the hatch to reveal the engine. He went straight to the plugs. Removing one after another he gave them a wipe and then replaced them. Then he looked around for any sign of damage. He slammed the hatch shut and indicated to Danny that they return.

327

There was an air of expectancy inside as PG tried the engine again. It whined a little then finally rumbled into life. PG waited for a minute, listening intently to the sound. At last he seemed satisfied and nodded to Benson. They set off towards the enemy minefields once more.

The tank did not clear the Allied minefields until after three thirty and by four they were on the outskirts of the enemy's fields. No one spoke. Even PG's frequent rants at the pace of progress had died away to be replaced by sullen silence. Danny was bathed in sweat. Benson lit a pipe and then proceeded to ignore it. McLeish's leg was still juddering. The silence felt oppressive. Radio contact had been banned until the morning. Their world existed solely within the confines of the cabin. Archie Andrews had the glazed eyes of a man lost in his own dark memories.

The incessant noise of the Allied barrage came to a halt around four in the morning. It was a strange silence broken only by the screeching of the tank wheels. It also heightened their sense of vulnerability. If the barrage had served one purpose it was to discourage the enemy from putting their head above the parapet. Now they not only had lost their covering fire, but they were also becoming nicely silhouetted against the rising sun.

By five it was clear to everyone they would not escape the minefield by first light. Danny avoided looking outside now. Light would become their enemy. And still they crawled forward. It seemed impossible that any vehicle could move so slowly. Yet forward they inched. The first machine gun fire became audible as the sky lightened. Then they heard the first crumps of German anti-tank fire.

'It's started,' said Benson. He was sitting with his head and body outside the cupola. 'They'll want us to disperse soon.'

'I hope they've cleared the minefields then. I don't fancy taking any bloody chances in them,' pointed out PG. There was apprehension in his voice but the rest of the crew grinned.

'Let's hope,' replied Benson who did not believe they were going to escape the minefield by the time they were within range of the anti-tank fire. 'I've a feeling it's going to be pretty sticky for a while, chaps.'

It was.

Later that morning they passed the first signs that the Germans were finding their range. A few tanks from other regiments sat at the side, burning. Black smoke twisted up into the sky providing further help to the enemy on distance and direction. They couldn't stop though. Their orders were to keep pouring forward. The noise of German shelling was louder now which was enough to start PG off.

'Bloody sitting targets we are. They can see us clear as day,' said the Yorkshireman.

'You forget one thing, PG,' said Danny.

'What's that?'

'We can see them. Difficult to hide one of those big eighty-eights, even in a desert.'

'Good point, young Shaw. Start bloody firing at them then.'

By seven in the morning, they had reached battle positions on a ridge. All the tanks from 3 RTR had made it through, dispersed, and were hull-down on the upslope of a ridge. This made it more difficult for the German gunners. Over the course of the day Danny witnessed the extraordinary start to the battle.

The lane that they'd driven through was packed nose to tail with Allied men and armour. The congestion and the dust cloud it caused was astonishing. It seemed to Danny that one well-targeted German attack from air or gun could have ended the war there and then, such was the concentration of Allied men streaming through the narrow lane.

Sappers were busy trying to widen the lane while engineers were rolling communication lines. Danny's mind was spinning at the logistical endeavour required. But reassured, too. The memory of the confusion of Operation Crusader was still too vivid. Then, they had made an uncoordinated attack and fought blind for the first week or so. The lesson had been learned. Now he could see infantry and armour side by side. Each had its role to play. Together they presented a greater threat to the enemy than they would individually.

All along the ridge there were soldiers and tanks from other regiments. The Nottingham Yeomanry on one side, the Staffordshire Yeomanry on the other. And still they surged forward through the narrow lane created by the sappers. Military policemen directed traffic like it was a busy high street. But the firing from the Germans was hitting its mark too. Benson gave the order and soon Danny was exchanging fire with the enemy shot for shot.

Montgomery, according to Benson, had predicted a war of attrition akin to the fighting a few decades previously. It looked to Danny like this was going to prove correct. This would not be a single knockout blow. It would be fought inch by inch, sometimes at a distance, like two boxers wary of each other; probing and jabbing, looking for an opening or a moment of lapsed concentration. Other times the confrontation would be resolved by a bayonet.

There they sat, unable to move. Both sides had one another pinned down now. Anyone unwise enough to move around was swiftly disabused of this notion by the chatter of machine gun fire. To this was added the growing heat of the day and the flies to torment them further.

'What happens now?' asked PG. He already knew but wanted to hear it, either as a punishment or reassurance.

'We're still short of where we should be,' explained Benson. 'They'll want us to move forward again tonight. Our job is not to get involved with long-range duels. They want us in amongst them.'

PG and Danny exchanged looks.

'Can't wait,' said the Yorkshireman sourly.

'Shaw, kick Wodehouse,' said Benson. 'That's an order.'

CHAPTER FORTY-ONE

The order came through at 0630 to move forward. Basler nodded to Jentz. The driver started the engine and they began to advance. Outside they could hear the sporadic chatter of machine gun fire and explosions, but the barrage had ended a couple of hours earlier. They were all groggy from lack of sleep. Manfred felt a weight behind his eyes. His mind and his movements felt heavy. He sensed a long day lay ahead.

Keil was on the radio constantly, keeping the crew informed of the attack as it developed. It was now apparent that the Allies had made a major push across a wide front. Elements of the 21st Panzers and the Italian Folgore and Pavia regiments were facing a concerted attack to the south.

'The Allies are mired in the minefield,' said Stiefelmayer over the radio. 'We can kill this attack off before it begins.'

As highly as Manfred regarded Kummel's replacement, he'd always found him a little too gung-ho for his liking. He and Willi Teege, the regiment commander, were very alike in this regard. Teege had chosen to situate himself with Stiefelmayer for the start of this engagement. Manfred, with a sinking heart, anticipated cavalry charges towards the stranded Allied tanks. It made sense but, as ever, it risked high losses. This was something that they could ill afford. Unlike the Allies, their reinforcement capacity was finite. It seemed an obvious point to him, and he found their utter conviction in the efficacy of this style of attack unfathomable.

It was not long before the first Allied tanks appeared in their view. Manfred recognised the distinctive shape of the Grants immediately. Basler's eyes were fixed on his binoculars.

'Incredible,' said the lieutenant. He sounded shocked. Manfred wasn't sure if this was fear or something else.

'What's wrong?' asked Manfred, hoping he'd kept the worry from his voice.

'There's too many of them trying to get through a small space,' said Basler. 'What are they thinking?'

Manfred could now see what Basler had seen. The congestion on the Allied side made them an easy target.

'Fire,' ordered Basler.

Manfred pressed the firing button and his battle started. A few stray shots and then he found his distance. The initial hits bounced off the heavy frontal armour but, as they closed in, the impacts began to tell. One after another of the Grants brewed up.

Then they heard Stiefelmayer exclaim, 'What the hell is that?'

Basler pinned his binoculars to his eyes to see what had caused the battalion leader's surprise. Then he saw it. The new Sherman was distinctive from the Grant, with its big gun in the turret rather than the side.

'They have a new tank,' said Basler.

Manfred looked through his gun sights and saw it for the first time. A feeling of desolation overwhelmed him. The enemy would not stop evolving their armour. They had the resources to create, produce and send out these new machines while the Panzer regiments existed inside machines that were held together by hardly anything more than glue and limitless courage.

But the Shermans were stuck like the other tanks in the Devil's Garden. A few of the enemy tanks tried to disperse but they drove into the mines which began to wreak another type of hell on them. Tank after tank was destroyed. Barely a couple of the Panzers had suffered any damage. The attack was halted and the enemy withdrew until they were around three kilometres back.

But Manfred sensed that they were facing a greater threat than they'd ever faced before. The opening encounter had set the tone for the next few days. Every night the Allies would bombard the German and Italian positions denying them any opportunity to sleep except in short bursts. The next morning, they would throw tanks forward in attack all along the line. Time and again the Panzers would absorb this attack and inflict far more casualties than they suffered themselves. But day by day they were being worn down. Lack of sleep was one thing but soon they would, once more, run out of petrol and ammunition.

The war of attrition had begun. The wrestling over every ridge and wadi. The death toll rose like mercury in the hot African sun. Day and night blurred for the combatants because the fighting during the day and the shelling at night developed its own shocking routine.

Three nights later, Manfred stood with Fischer and gazed at the horizon.

'They should start anytime…'

The first crumps confirmed Fischer's view and the whole of the horizon was lit up by the thousand guns they were facing.

'… soon,' completed Fischer. 'Persistent, aren't they. I'll give them that.'

The two young men glanced at one another and a sense of unease descended on them. Even Fischer's normal certainty appeared to be eroding in the face of the overwhelming opposition they were facing. The previous evening he'd admitted his doubts. Now he repeated the same phrase again.

'They just keep coming. Whatever we throw at them, more come. It's like they want us to use up all of our ammo, fuel, men.'

'You heard about the convoy from Sicily?'

'Yes, it was sunk yesterday. We needed those supplies.'

'We're low on our HE shells now. I don't know what they expect us to fight with. Those new tanks of theirs, too. It feels like we're hitting them with tennis balls,' said Fischer ruefully.

Manfred's smile widened when he saw Fischer's frown deepen.

'I just knew you played tennis. Dancing around the court in your whites.'

Manfred then began to mimic a ballet dancer playing tennis which was so ridiculous even Fischer had to laugh.

'I don't know what's so wrong about tennis.'

'I'm building a picture of your privileged life.'

The smile faded a little and Fischer stretched his arms out. 'Not so privileged now.' Then he made a show of patting away the layer of dust that caked his uniform. 'My family were friends with Gottfried von Cramm. Well, up until he was arrested. After that it was difficult, although my father probably stayed in contact. We were at Wimbledon with him when he lost to Perry.'

'He lost every time,' said Manfred. 'I listened to the last one on the radio with my father.'

'He won in Paris,' pointed out Fischer, a little defensively.

Manfred made a face to suggest that Paris didn't count much. Then a thought struck him.

335

'I wonder where he is now.'

'They sent him to Russia, I heard.'

'What about Schmeling? Did you know him, too?'

Fischer grinned at the hint of sarcasm in Manfred's voice.

'I met him. Twice, actually. I liked him. Wasn't he wounded in Crete?'

'Yes,' exclaimed Manfred. 'You're right. I heard that, too.'

They were silent for a few moments listening to the barrage. The shells seemed to be falling elsewhere but the call would come for them to return to the tanks. They'd tried to grab some sleep in their tanks for the previous three nights. Despite the bombardment, an hour or two had been managed. One shell landed a lot closer to the leaguer. They looked at one another and with a nod, parted.

Manfred trotted back towards the others. All around him the crews were quickly clearing up and leaping into the tanks for protection from the fire. Although sporadic, no one wanted to risk being hit by shrapnel or being obliterated by a chance shell landing nearby. He saw Basler glaring at him from the turret. He could be like a mother hen sometimes yet, in an odd way, Manfred cared about him. Sometimes the chinks would appear in the walls he'd built around himself. Everyone did this, of course. They dressed their fears in bravado, their insecurity in composure, their lack of knowledge in knowing silence. Basler was unusual insofar as his demeanour was one of permanent irritation. Even when he was pleased with how the crew had acted, it was expressed through dissatisfaction. It took a moment before Manfred realised this could have been his father.

'Where have you been? The warning came minutes ago,' snarled Basler as Manfred climbed into the cabin.

Manfred contented himself with an apology as both knew Basler was not interested in the answer to the question.

336

Basler looked at Jentz. He asked, 'All checks have been made?'

'Yes, sir.'

'The steering linkage? You said it was rattling.'

Jentz nodded wearily. He'd spent the afternoon fixing it. He flinched as an explosion rocked the tanks. Most of them were falling apart. Their operational strength was gradually being whittled away.

Somewhere in the night a machine gun was firing. The only damage it was likely to inflict on the leaguer was to deprive the crews of sleep. But even then, it was doomed to failure. Everyone was exhausted. Sleep was no longer an issue. They sat silently listening to the sound of the gunfire.

'Do they take turns?' asked Keil.

Basler smiled mirthlessly.

'That's the strategy. The Allies are taking it in turns to push forward at us. Then they retire and someone new comes along. They're still fighting the Great War again only this time there's no one new going to come and replace us. They'll keep chipping away until we either fall back or there's nothing left to hit.'

'Will Rommel withdraw?' asked Manfred. Saying 'retreat' was *verboten*.

Basler studied Manfred for a moment. Perhaps he'd said too much. His face betrayed little anxiety. Then he frowned and replied, 'We nearly had them a day or two ago. The field marshall is a gambler. He'll roll the dice one more time. Back them up against our minefield and blast them into the next world.'

CHAPTER FORTY-TWO

El Alamein, Egypt, 1st November 1942

Evening brought its usual bite in the air. Danny wrapped his coat more tightly around him, not that it made much difference. The cold air could creep through the layers with ease. He felt for the infantrymen at the front who did not have the luxury of a campfire or overcoats.

'How long has Benson been away?' asked PG returning with his spade from a walk in the night.

'Not long. He thinks we'll be moving back up to the front tomorrow,' replied Danny, not looking up from his tea. He missed PG rolling his eyes.

'Can't wait,' said the Yorkshireman collapsing to the ground.

Danny finally turned to him.

'Have you sorted out the engine?'

PG nodded and said, 'Yes, it was the plugs. Just a little condensation.'

'You didn't need to change them?' asked Danny. The answer had been a little too easy. PG shot Danny a look but did not answer. The tank had refused to start on a couple of occasions in the last few days, both times during the night march. PG had simply dried the plugs and they'd started again. The unspoken question was what would happen if it should occur during the day, mid-battle. Any further conversation on the subject ended with the return of Benson. Archie Andrews set down his book and joined the others.

'Gather round,' ordered the captain.

The crew turned to face the captain. Benson drew out the tension a little longer as he fumbled with his pipe. Finally, he looked up and began to speak.

'We move out around dawn tomorrow. There's going to be a major push towards the enemy base at Tel el Aqqaqir. Their base is roughly three miles north-west of Kidney. Freyburg and the New Zealanders will go in first. This will be a night attack. Their infantry will look to break through followed by the second, eighth and ninth Armoured Brigades. The attack will be concentrated across a two-mile strip. The artillery and the RAF will start to hit them tonight, then the Kiwis move in. Our turn will come around dawn. We'll be accompanied, once more, by the Notts on the left, Staffs in the centre with us on the right. Any questions?'

It wasn't a question, but Danny voiced the thought on everyone's mind.

'The New Zealanders will be hit hard. So will the armoured boys when the eighty-eights get a sight of them at first light.'

Benson's face was grim but he made no reply. The words of Pyman, quoting Freyburg, echoed in his mind.

'For armour to attack a wall of guns sounds like another Balaclava.'

They would be shelled, gunned and bombed from all sides. The casualties were likely to be shocking. And the 3 RTR was expected to follow them into the hellhole and no doubt others would follow them. The body count would rise and rise until the Afrika Korps had run out of men or ammo.

'Try and rest if you can. It'll be a long day tomorrow,' warned Benson.

Danny glanced towards PG. He wondered what the Yorkshireman was thinking. The solemn face had a different character than usual. Resignation rather than cynicism lurked behind his eyes. This was likely to be a cauldron in every sense.

They climbed into the hull to try and grab some sleep, but Danny found it impossible. There was too much nervous energy in his body, too many thoughts racing through his mind. In the end he re-read letters from home for the hundredth time. None of the others were sleeping either. It was as if they sensed that tomorrow would be momentous.

Oddly, Danny was in no doubt that they would break though. The slugging match of the previous few days was surely beginning to tell on the enemy. They were crumbling, as the plan had suggested they would. The calculations of high command were essentially correct. Less comforting was the thought that they were built on such high attrition. It was difficult to avoid the bitter conclusion that Montgomery was prepared to win at all costs. What was the loss of a brigade or two when set against the overall objective of defeating the enemy? The answer of course depended on which end of the gun sight you were standing at.

McLeish's leg started juddering again. He reddened a little when he realised Danny had noticed it.

'Don't worry,' said Danny. 'We're all bricking it.'

McLeish's grin widened when PG said from the driver's seat, 'Speak for yourself, soft lad. Some of us real men can't wait to get back at the Hun.'

Danny arched his eyebrows and leaned forward.

'Do you know, there's an idea in there somewhere, sir. I think we should send PG in first,' said Danny. 'Perhaps he could talk cricket at them. If we can't bomb them into submission, we could try boring them instead.'

Even Benson was chuckling at the exchange while puffing on his pipe.

'You've no culture, country boy. Pair of wellies and a friendly sheep, and you're happy.'

'You forgot sweeping up horse droppings,' pointed out Danny, grinning.

'That's bath time for your lot,' replied PG. Some of his spirit seemed to have returned.

Planes flew overhead but no one batted an eyelid. They recognised the low growl of the bombers heading in the direction of the Axis lines. The aerial bombardment would continue for hours. By now, no one expected it to do any more damage to the enemy than interrupt their sleep. Days of bombing by the planes and big guns had done little, seemingly, to dent either the enemy spirit or the intensity of the fighting.

If anything, the unending assault threatened to hurt the morale of the Allies more if only because it raised hopes during the night that were dashed the next morning. Nothing seemed to stop the Afrika Korps. They were having everything thrown at them, yet they kept coming back for more: undeterred, unbroken and undefeated.

CHAPTER FORTY-THREE

Tel el Aqqaqir, 30km east of El Alamein, 1st–2nd November 1942

Less than twenty kilometres away from Danny, Manfred sat with his head propped against the side of the tank, thinking not dissimilar thoughts. Night after night they had been pounded by Allied artillery and bombers. The surprise wasn't so much that there was anything left alive in the desert as that there were any shells left to launch. It was relentless.

He was beyond fear now. They all were. Unspoken but shared was the belief that sooner or later they would die. It was there in the gallows humour, the enervation, the hollow-eyed grins that masked their hunger, their fatigue and their resignation. The joke amongst the crews was that if Montgomery had been using the Afrika Korps rather than his own army, the job would have been completed by now.

Manfred shivered in the metal fridge that was protecting them. Kleff's body was shaking, and it may have been fear, but Manfred suspected it was just the cold. Keil was reading the Bible. Basler slept.

342

How the lieutenant was able to, Manfred did not know. He was too tired to sleep. He thought about leaving the tank and going in search of Fischer but realised that he might wake up Basler. He'd see him tomorrow. Perhaps.

Overhead, the never-ending sound of the Allied bombers caused the tank to vibrate. Manfred glanced up, although what he expected to see given that he was inside the tank was debatable. He grinned at his stupidity and glanced round to see if anyone had noticed. No one had. Each lost in their own world. Jentz was snoring like a bull with a cold. Manfred stared at him. The driver's head was tilted back and he seemed to be sucking in every particle of the rank air in the hull before expelling it noisily through his open mouth.

The bombing had begun somewhere in the distance. Keil and Manfred exchanged glances, then Keil returned to read his Bible. For three hours Manfred listened, hypnotised by the rumble of explosions. Then, towards midnight, just as he was finally drifting off to sleep, there was an almighty bang followed by more explosions. It was loud enough to wake both Basler and Jentz.

'What was that?' asked Basler groggily.

Manfred shrugged. Then a thought occurred to him.

'My guess would be they hit either our fuel or the ammo.'

'Great,' growled Basler. 'So tomorrow we'll be fighting with rocks then walking back to camp.'

More minor explosions followed but Manfred had already drifted off to sleep. It didn't last long. The Allied artillery barrage began. Manfred's eyes opened slowly. His head was heavy, and it took a moment for his focus to adjust sufficiently to see his watch. It was just after one in the morning. He shut his eyes again but it was too late. He knew the bombardment would last the night. Another hour went by before sleep finally overcame him.

Around four in the morning he was shaken awake by Kleff. His head was swimming in lethargy. Basler was telling him something but he couldn't hear him. The barrage continued unabated. He was aware that the tank itself was shaking. They were on the move. Then he finally heard what Basler was saying.

'They've overrun our forward positions.'

Manfred nodded and then listened closely to the explosions in the distance. They seemed different. He looked at Basler, a frown on his face.

'The bombers started with the forward area earlier. They're bombing the rear now.'

'And we're stuck in the middle,' said Manfred sourly.

It took a moment for him to realise that this would soon no longer be true. They'd avoided the heavy bombing by luck. Soon they'd meet the Allied attack head on. This was confirmed moments later when Keil turned to Manfred.

'Captain Stiefelmayer is ordering us forward. Otto Piste has been taken and they're threatening the HQ. The 21st is moving up now. They think this is the big push. It's all going to go through the north. The counter-attack begins at dawn.'

Manfred glanced through his telescope. The first signs of light were visible with the fringe of purple developing on the horizon. Soon the sun would begin to bleach the sky. The shapes of their attacker would become visible.

As the dawn broke, the heat inside the cabin grew and the atmosphere became more oppressive. Sweat dripped from Manfred's face. Then he heard Basler make a sound that sounded like, 'ahh.'

They finally were able to see the enemy in the distance. Dozens of dark shapes stood out like molehills on the eastern horizon. Lots of molehills. The rising sun silhouetted them. It was an open invitation to start shelling them. As if a switch had been thrown, the deafening crump of dozens of eighty-eights sprang to life.

'How many?' asked Manfred.

Basler was silent for a moment as he peered through the hatch of the cupola with his binoculars. He was silently totting up the number while the eighty-eights greeted the new arrivals in deadly fashion.

'At least sixty,' said Basler.

They slowed to a halt to allow first the anti-tank guns to engage the enemy and then the Italian Littorio tank battalion. Manfred gazed through his sight in silence. What had been, just moments earlier, a clear horizon was now full of smoke and shells.

'My God, they are taking a beating,' said Basler in a hushed whisper. Yet still they came, headlong into the hail of fire from the well-sighted positions. Even without the benefit of Basler's powerful binoculars, Manfred could see that the Allies were on the receiving end of a fearful hammering. But some of the tanks were breaking through. The Allied tactics weren't clever, but they would work if they had overwhelming numbers of men and armour.

'British tanks have reached the Rahman track,' said Keil breathlessly. He was listening to the busy radio traffic. The Rahman track, lined with telegraph poles, was a pivotal point for both sides. It ran diagonally in front of Aqqaqir Ridge. The German and Italian defences were deployed in a wide crescent along the track. A couple of dozen eighty-eights acted as a screen. If the Allies overran them then the game was as good as over for the Afrika Korps.

The idea that the Allies were now within killing range of such a heavily defended area came as a shock to Manfred. This was not because he believed they would overcome the Axis position. Rather he was dismayed that men could be thrown forward so callously and forfeited on such a suicidal mission. Yet, their sacrifice would act as a bridgehead for those that followed. Eventually they would either overrun the position or the Afrika Korps and the Italians would have to withdraw.

Manfred's thoughts were interrupted by the first sounds of explosions nearing them. The Allied tanks were getting closer.

'Forward, Jentz. We are to engage,' said Basler simply.

Manfred listened closely to the engine as it coughed in protest before firing to life. They set off slowly, jerking forward and hurling Manfred backwards. He looked through his sight but could see very little laterally. Frustrated at the limited view, he edged over towards Kleff and looked through his periscope.

On the left was Willi Teege, the head of the Panzer Regiment 8. To their right he saw the 1st Battalion leader, Captain Stiefelmayer's tank. He had to acknowledge that both men led from the front. The captain seemed to be taking a risk by having so much of his torso outside the cupola. Just below him would be Fischer, waiting, like Manfred, for the order to start firing. At the clip they were moving, that would not be long in coming. Manfred hoped that the enemy tanks were not the big Grants or Shermans with the seventy-five-millimetre guns.

The clank of the tracks filled the air, initially blocking out the distant blasts. But within minutes the sound of battle grew louder.

'How far?' asked Manfred.

'Two thousand metres,' replied Basler calmly. But this was rapidly shrinking. Within seconds it would be eighteen hundred and then fifteen hundred. Jentz was already zigzagging to make it difficult for any enemy gunners who'd lock on to them.

A nod to Kleff and the first shell was loaded into the breech. It was AP Armour Piercing. Manfred's eyes were glued to the sight making calculations on his aim. Basler held the binoculars to his eyes and began counting down the distance to the first wave of enemy ahead. There had to be more than sixty tanks thought Manfred. They were getting hit though. Many were already in flames. But still they came.

Basler told Jentz to straighten up. There was little point in trying to zigzag if they were also trying to shoot. This was when they were most at risk. A direct target. Manfred held his breath waiting for the order to fire. He realised that they were not yet getting hit by the enemy. This meant they were not yet within the range of the enemy's big guns.

'Twelve hundred metres,' said Basler. 'One thousand. Nine hundred… fire.'

Manfred pressed the button. Seconds later Kleff rammed another shell into the breech. Manfred's first shot had missed, short and right. The next hit the target full on the turret just as it returned fire. A shell bounced harmlessly off the front of the Panzer Mark III. The British tank was not so fortunate. It erupted into flame. One man escaped from a hatch, then another. Basler left them.

The next target was less than six hundred metres away. They were now within the deadly range of the enemy guns. Manfred pressed the trigger again. Another hit. The tracks of the enemy tank crumpled inwards, stopping it dead. Seconds later a shell went screaming over the head of Manfred's tank.

Manfred's next shot took out the tank. He didn't see anyone emerge before turning his attention to the next tank. They were now like medieval jousters. The Allies were closing in, but the smoke and the dust obscured just how close they were. Manfred was firing blind.

And then they were among the enemy tanks.

It was difficult to detect friend from foe.

'Traverse left,' said Basler. 'Fire immediately.'

Manfred responded instantaneously and let off a round. Seconds later a loud explosion split the air inside the cabin causing it and the crew to vibrate. The heat of the blast could be felt even inside the hull.

Through his sight, Manfred saw Stiefelmayer's tank on the right engaging with two approaching Crusaders.

'Traverse left,' ordered Basler.

'Sir, Captain Stiefelmayer is being attacked,' shouted Manfred. There was a note of desperation in his voice. One on one the Panzer had the beating of most enemy tanks. Taking on two was another matter.

'So are we,' snarled Basler angrily. Manfred was already doing as he was told. Less than fifty metres ahead he saw a British tank emerge from behind a screen of black smoke and sand. Manfred fired. He signalled to Kleff to load another shell and leased it off immediately. Something hit their armour and bounced off. The second British tank erupted into flames.

'Traverse right,' ordered Basler.

Manfred rapidly wheeled the turret round as quickly as he could just in time to see the tank with Fischer and Stiefelmayer explode. One of the British tanks that had attacked them was in flames. Manfred had the second tank in his sights. He fired off one shell and then another. Jentz continued to move forward. There was no time to see if anyone had survived from Fischer's tank.

The enemy was streaming towards them. Some were blocked by the smoking wrecks of other British tanks. Kleff kept loading and Manfred kept firing. Around them explosions were concussing the tank but miraculously they had not been hit. The sheer confusion became their friend. The smoke and the dust obscured so much that aimless firing risked hitting their own side.

Keil shook his head. Manfred didn't know if that meant they were dead or that he simply did not know. There was no time for any further questions. Basler was speaking on their internal radio.

348

'There's another wave of tanks coming. My God, will they ever stop?'

Manfred already knew the answer to that question. He peered through his sight and saw the menacing dark shapes in the distance.

'Jentz, reverse,' ordered Basler.

Jentz brought them to a halt and hit the reverse gear. British tanks were moving laterally but Manfred couldn't get any shots off as they were shielded by the burning metal hulks, mostly British, that littered the battlefield.

Other Panzers appeared to be of a like mind and were withdrawing slowly. Manfred could see British infantry abandoning slit trenches as the metal giants threatened to crush them under their tracks.

'Lieutenant,' shouted Keil, 'I can see Captain Stiefelmayer.'

'Where?' shouted Basler before answering his own question. 'No, I see him.'

Manfred could just about see Fischer and another crewman dragging the stricken captain into a slit trench to avoid the tracks of a British tank. The enemy vehicle resisted the opportunity to gun them down. Instead, it moved on, passing a couple of burned-out Panzers. Fischer's head popped up along with the other crewman and then they were dragging Stiefelmayer out from the trench. Manfred lost sight of them at that point as his sight was straight ahead with limited lateral vision.

'Slow down,' ordered Basler. Then he opened the turret hatch wider and shouted down to Fischer.

Manfred returned to his sight while Keil search frantically to see if there were any other enemy tanks near them. Their position was horribly exposed now.

'Hurry,' shouted Basler. Manfred glanced up and then realised he was addressing himself to the men outside. This was a relief. It meant that Fischer was climbing onto the hull with the fallen captain.

Moments later Basler ordered them to speed up. Jentz put his foot to the pedal and they jerked backwards. The tank was rocked by an explosion nearby.

'Can't you go any faster?' shouted Basler over the intercom.

'Not unless I turn around,' shouted Jentz irritably. The lieutenant knew this but he, along with everyone else, was caught up in the fear of being hit.

'Move left,' ordered Basler. 'Now right.'

As they slalomed backwards, the full horror of the battle was unfolding before Manfred. Dozens of tanks, many still glowing red, had been abandoned. Crewmen from both sides darted between trenches and tanks. It was mayhem. Worryingly, the further they withdrew, the more tanks he could see that were either from the Italian Littorio Battalion or Panzers. The number of destroyed British tanks was clearly much larger but it had come at a price. He could no longer see very far ahead but Kleff kept them informed of the attack building in front. Distant booms spoke of the bombardment that the eighty-eights were raining down on the new wave.

But many would get through. This battle was only just beginning.

CHAPTER FORTY-FOUR

North-east of Kidney Ridge, El Alamein, 2nd November 1942

It was nearly eight in the morning. Danny glanced down at PG. His hands were on the steering sticks. He was whistling. This was the only sound in the cabin aside from the engine idling. Outside, the rest of the 3 RTR formed, standing ready like cavalry before a charge. Thoughts of what lay ahead were unavoidable. The sound of the battle taking place barely a few miles ahead of them had reduced them to silence.

For once there was an honesty in the communications about what they were to face. The words 'extreme casualties' had been mentioned. The implication was clear. The defeat of the Afrika Korps was likely to come at a great cost. The confidence they felt that victory was now within their grasp in no way allayed the fear at the back of everyone's mind; this time it could be them.

The radio crackled to life. Sid Gregson listened and then spoke to Benson. Danny heard him say, 'The attack has reached the Rahman track. They've knocked out lots of guns.'

'Well done to them,' said Benson. 'That was the plan.'

At what cost, wondered Danny? They'd sacrificed themselves on the gun line. Danny fought to control his emotions. Not fear this time but sadness for those that had fallen. It could so easily have been them who'd been asked to make the initial, suicidally dangerous, assault. Instead, it had been Wilts and Warwickshire Yeomanry. Any other thoughts were interrupted by Benson. He was standing with his head and chest outside the turret. Over the intercom he said, 'Make ready.'

Danny tested his traverse for the fiftieth time that morning. It was still working. PG was similarly occupied with the steering sticks. McLeish's leg was juddering again. Of the crew, Gregson seemed the most at ease. Every so often he would test the internal radio with a rather risqué joke. The laughter usually confirmed that everything was in working order. Andrews remained tight-lipped. Benson was lost in another world. Smoking a pipe made someone look more reflective, thought Danny. By comparison, cigarettes seemed like a nervous tic, at least the way soldiers like PG smoked them. Allowances could be made for movie stars, of course. They smoked with a certain elan. There was no question Benson and the smoke from his pipe radiated a sense of calm that slowly permeated through the tank, bringing with it memories of home, of family and friends. Danny closed his eyes and all at once he was transported back to his kitchen, his father puffing away while reading a newspaper or listening to the radio.

Voices outside the tank grew in number and volume. Somewhere a sergeant-major was yelling orders, for it could only be a sergeant-major. What a pair of lungs. Was that a hunting horn in the distance? Danny and a few of the others broke into a grin. How could the Nazis seriously expect to defeat a nation that had men who thought it entirely sensible to carry a hunting horn into battle? Naïve, really, on the part of the enemy.

The noise of the idling engines soon became more full throated. Radio chatter ceased. The shouts outside grew louder, as did the sound of Danny's heart. He felt himself tense. The sound of shouting was drowned out by the noise of the engines. Then, they heard the command in their earphones from Benson. 'PG, Advance.'

The tank lurched forward catching McLeish, as ever, by surprise. Every time, thought Danny with a grin. McLeish rubbed his head and reddened. This was no mean feat for the young, once fair-skinned Scot, who'd turned a rather unattractive pink red in the North African sun.

The screeching clank of the tanks must have been audible in Tripoli. Benson sat on the cupola allowing the cold morning air to cool the rising heat inside the turret and hull. This flow brought tiny particles which soon covered everyone in a thin film of dust as they shuddered their way forward towards the sound of gunfire and shelling. Within minutes, plumes of sand being thrown up by the 3 RTR obscured Danny's view and he wondered how it must have felt for the poor infantry blokes following or, in some cases, riding on the tanks.

The pace of the advance was slightly above that of paralysis. Barely one hundred yards covered in three minutes. At this rate it would be darkness by the time they reached the enemy despite the fact they were only a matter of a few miles away. PG worked the steering leavers furiously, still trying to test their manoeuvrability. Danny had never seen him so intent before. Benson remained standing with his chest and head exposed through the hatch; binoculars were fixed to his eyes.

Danny caught sight of a couple of infantry men walking alongside them. They overtook the tank unthinkingly. Both were smoking and chatting like they were on their way to the factory to clock in.

Further forward, the sound of battle continued unabated. The aerial bombardment made the loudest sound. Heavy bombs were landing on the Axis positions, distant earthquakes renting the desert apart.

The two infantry men continued their morning walk, oblivious to the hell they were heading towards. Then they stopped. The tank drew towards them. Danny wondered if this was a realisation that it was time to take cover behind the tank. No, apparently. They were just stopping to light another couple of cigarettes; then they resumed their morning stroll.

Smoke and dust became heavier now and Danny lost sight of the two men. The smoke and the growing volume of battle made Danny's skin prickle with anticipation. A fluttery feeling in the pit of his stomach was not solely due to the vibration of explosions. It wasn't quite fear, more a heightened alertness and, perhaps, excitement.

They gradually became immersed in the coiling black smoke. The smell of cordite permeated the cabin. The two soldiers were out of sight now, probably electing to march behind the tank screen rather than out in the open.

Benson ducked inside and rubbed his eyes. He shook his head but said nothing. He didn't need to. Up ahead Danny could see the first charred evidence of the onslaught suffered by the first tanks breaking through. The smell was no longer just petrol and cordite. The smell of burnt skin has a special quality all its own. The charcoal-like stench seemed to cut through all the odours, sickening everyone inside the hull.

'Bloody hell,' said PG. He was the only one who could speak as they passed burned-out tank after burned-out tank.

Bloody hell indeed.

CHAPTER FORTY-FIVE

Tel el Aqqaqir, 2nd November 1942

Manfred did not know how they managed to evade the shells and the shot pouring around them. Such was the intensity of fire, it put out of his head the fact that Fischer and the wounded captain, Stiefelmayer, were riding outside. Even more astonishing was the sight of so much twisted metal and men retreating.

The mayhem and the obstructions saved Manfred's Panzer. That and the fact that almost all the Allied tanks had been destroyed. Under darkness they had penetrated deeply and overrun so many German positions. The arrival of daylight had turned the tide for the moment in favour of the Germans and Italians. They now had a visible target. The combined efforts of the eighty-eights and the Panzers had halted the first attack. The second wave had already begun though.

'How far?' shouted Jentz. He was effectively driving blind.

'Half a kilometre. Swing left,' ordered Basler, who was acting as Jentz's eyes as the tank retreated back towards the supply echelon.

Basler gazed down at Stiefelmayer and the other two soldiers. All of them were wounded but Stiefelmayer looked in a bad way.

'Hurry, Jentz,' shouted Basler but he knew the veteran driver was going as fast as he could. And it was probably too late anyway for his friend.

They arrived a few minutes later. Manfred climbed down from the hull to chaotic scenes around him. Explosions were splitting the air nearby. Manfred and Basler jumped onto the hull to assist Stiefelmayer, Fischer and another crew member from the tank. Of the three, Fischer's injuries were evidently the least serious. He had a head wound and perhaps some burns. It was hard to tell. The other crewman's face was blackened and there was a lot of blood. But that may have come from the unconscious Stiefelmayer.

Fischer nodded to Manfred as he was helped down. Basler was shouting for stretcher bearers to come over to them. None were available. Around them, the cost of halting the assault was all too plain. Dozens of men lay dead or dying, tended by men who needed medical attention themselves.

Along with Fischer, Manfred and Basler carefully lifted the captain down and carried him over to the nearest doctor they could find.

'Doctor,' shouted Basler, 'Over here. Captain Stiefelmayer is hurt.'

A young doctor spun around. He was amid half a dozen badly injured men. He glared at Basler in a manner of someone who wondered exactly what he was meant to do about that. Manfred had more than a little sympathy for the medics. They were all faced with impossible choices on who to see first. The doctor glanced over and recognised the captain. He started towards them.

Stiefelmayer was unconscious but Manfred could see an ugly wound and some signs of burns to his face and hands. The doctor quickly but with great care examined him.

'Bring him over there,' said the doctor pointing to a group of men lying down on a flat piece of ground.

'I don't see any medics over there,' pointed out Basler, irritably.

The doctor glared at him and replied in barely a whisper, 'He's not going there to be treated, lieutenant. There's nothing we can do except reduce the pain.' Then he turned to Fischer and the other wounded man. 'Go over to that truck; you will be seen there.'

Fischer and the other crewman shook their heads.

'No, doctor. We stay with him.'

Then they knelt by Stiefelmayer and hooked their arms underneath the captain's legs and arms. Manfred and Basler helped lift the dying man. They carried him over to the row of men in silence. Fischer sat down beside the captain and ordered the other crewman to find some morphine. Manfred put his hand out.

'Let me. You stay there.'

It took a few minutes as the truck with the medical supplies was overrun by other men like him. As Manfred trotted back to the group, the sounds of battle still rumbling close by, he knew that the Afrika Korps were near defeat. He was neither surprised nor saddened by this. A wave of resignation, which had been building for some time, assailed him now. Yet he knew he would have to go back and try and staunch the gaping wound the Allies had inflicted on them. Like Stiefelmayer, it would kill them. Kill them all.

He handed a sachet of sulphanilamide to Fischer. This would disinfect the wound. One sachet seemed barely enough but that was all they could spare. The field dressing he handed to the other crewman.

'Morphine?' asked Fischer.

Manfred's face fell.

'None left. Some may come up later.'

Fischer's eyes blazed angrily but not at Manfred. Men that had been wrenched from their homes, families and sent to a faraway land lay dying all around. Yet the very things that could bring them victory or ease the pain of the fallen were in short supply. Manfred understood Fischer's despair and felt the anger growing within him, too.

'The bastards.'

Fischer and Manfred turned in surprise to Basler. His eyes were filled with tears of frustration. Basler had few friends within the regiment. His taciturnity, his intensity, militated against close personal connections. But Stiefelmayer had probably been as close as anyone. The knowledge that he would die was made unbearable by the knowledge that it would be in great pain. All around a similar story was being played out. Men knelt beside fallen comrades with nothing to offer them other than company in their final hours, final minutes, final seconds. The injustice of it all was agonising, the hell unutterable. If any nobility could be unearthed from such desolation, then it was the knowledge that the dying was amongst men who were closer than brothers.

They stayed with Stiefelmayer; they watched him fight for life, as the remainder of the Panzer 8 Regiment 1st Battalion limped back, battered and bruised, to re-arm and refuel. Nearby Kleff was checking over the battered armour while Jentz refuelled. Keil was on the point of collapse such was his exhaustion. He was struggling to carry box after box of shells. A nod from Basler and Manfred rose to help him. Manfred went over to the supply truck to grab more shells only to be met with his second rejection of the day.

'Sorry, we have to ration them now. There are other tanks returning.'

Manfred stared at the soldier in disbelief. There was little he could say that a dozen other soldiers had probably not already said to the poor man. The final insult from their leaders. No more ammunition. Or petrol if the shouts nearby were any guide. Manfred trotted over to Keil to help load the ammunition into the tank.

They had taken a pounding. Manfred had never seen so many dents before. They'd been lucky, no question. Kleff completed his checks on the tracks while Jentz attended to the engine. Manfred turned around and saw many other crews similarly engaged.

Colonel Teege appeared from the turret then clambered down. Manfred watched him speak to a medic and then look around at the terrible scene. Then he spotted Stiefelmayer and went straight over to the head of his 1st Battalion. He knelt and spoke with Basler and Fischer. He remained impassive as he listened to the two men. Then anger burned in his eyes, and he looked around him. Basler's hand fell on his arm. The anger burned quickly to be replaced by sadness, a shake of the head and even tears, if Manfred was not mistaken.

Teege stood up and pointed to the remaining tanks of the regiment. There weren't many. He seemed to be relaying orders. Another attack probably. Basler stood up and spied Manfred. He came over to their vehicle and looked it over.

'The colonel says that there is to be a counter-attack. General von Thoma has ordered that we and the 21st are to attack the northern and southern flanks of the enemy.'

Manfred gave the briefest nod of his head and turned to Kleff and Keil who were standing nearby. There was no sign of fear in their eyes, just resignation.

Manfred returned his gaze to Teege. He was still with Stiefelmayer. It was difficult to think of him as 'Willi' at that moment. His manner was too dignified, his sorrow too profound. Manfred felt touched by the tenderness of the feeling he was witnessing. There was no question that Stiefelmayer would not survive the day.

Within hours, Teege would be dead, too.

CHAPTER FORTY-SIX

East of the Rahman Track, 2nd November 1942

'Poor buggers,' said PG solemnly.

It wasn't much of a eulogy but it matched the sombre mood in the cabin. Outside amid the smoke lay the charred evidence of the earlier onslaught. Derelict hulks that had once been Stuarts or Grants or Shermans littered the landscape like piles of coal. Parts of their armour were glowing like a light bulb.

There were dead bodies around the tanks; the implication was clear to all the men. There wouldn't be much time to escape if they were hit. This thought lay as heavily in the air as the smell of cordite and charcoal. Just ahead, Danny saw a soldier kneeling in a crater. There was a dead body beside him. The boy, for he was no older than Danny, was crying.

'Eighty-eights,' said Danny as he surveyed the carnage.

'Aye,' agreed PG. 'Eighty-eights. Must have caught them at dawn.'

'Certainly looks that way,' Benson, speaking for the first time since they'd entered the first few hundred yards of the battle zone. The sound of shelling up ahead was a reminder that they, too, would soon be encountering those same eighty-eights that had wrought such terror on the crews a few hours earlier. 'We can't let their deaths be in vain, men. We have to break through.'

Danny nodded. What else could the captain say? It was clear that the resolve of the crew had been shaken by witnessing the carnage of earlier.

Danny put his eyes to the viewer. The haze on the horizon was making it difficult to see very much except for the tanks ahead and the black smoke rising skyward. What lateral vision he did have revealed an impressive sight. Left and right, there were tanks on the march. Some were 3 RTR, others were attached to other regiments like the Staffs and the Notts.

PG began to test the steering causing them to zig left then zag right. A nod from Benson was Archie Andrews' cue to test the traverse of the turret. He wheeled left causing the turret to turn several degrees before reversing this and restoring the gun and the turret to its original position.

Progress was slow. They had travelled for over an hour yet still remained over three miles away from the fighting. The odd effect of this was to increase the desire of the men to just get on with it. The sound of battle was unquestionably growing louder. They were in a No Man's Land now. The first signs of German dead were visible, along with some Italian and even some German soldiers marching towards the Allied lines to become prisoners of war. This gave them all renewed heart. PG began to whistle 'Deutschland Uber Alles' much to the amusement of the rest of the crew.

Danny smiled but was reluctant to join in. Whistling is difficult when your throat is tighter than a hangman's noose. His eyes remained

361

fixed to his viewer, but the heat haze was stronger now. Then, for the first time, he saw the telegraph poles. They were nearing the Rahman track. On the other side lay the Afrika Korps.

Every second brought them closer to their destiny.

Basler didn't have to give Jentz a verbal order. He pointed ahead. Jentz responded immediately and they were off. It was nearing eleven in the morning. Only another five hours until dusk, thought Manfred wearily. He joined Basler in standing outside the turret. They looked around at the battered remnants of the Regiment 8.

'How many tanks do we have left?' asked Manfred.

'I don't know. Five perhaps. The other regiments haven't been hit so badly. The 21st Panzers are at full strength. Who knows how many the Italians have left?'

'Enough to hold off the British?'

The answer was 'probably yes' but they both knew that the Afrika Korps was on borrowed time. The wave after wave of attacks from the Allies was sapping their strength like a leak in an engine.

The dust thrown up by the regiment made it difficult to ascertain their strength but, by the sound of their engines, Manfred thought it was less than fifty.

Basler looked around him and said to himself, 'With this we must halt a division?' He shook his head.

'Who takes over from the captain?' asked Manfred suddenly.

Basler glanced at Manfred. Oddly, he seemed amused by the question. Manfred shrugged. He was curious.

'Not me, if that's what you are asking.'

'It was,' replied Manfred.

'Lieutenant Lindner,' said Basler, putting the field glasses back up to his eyes. Manfred wondered if he was hurt at being overlooked.

'I thought he'd been wounded,' responded Manfred after a few minutes of silence.

'He was. Mustn't have been too bad.'

They sat in silence listening to the sound of battle: the crump of anti-tank guns, the chatter of machine guns, the crack of rifle fire. Then, with a nod, Basler indicated that Manfred should return to his position. The explosions were growing louder. The smoke thicker. It hung like a shroud in the air, obscuring the enemy ahead. The smell of death was everywhere now.

'Did you see anything?' asked Kleff, indicating towards the east with his eyes.

'Not yet. Can certainly hear it,' said Manfred. The distant booms were increasingly less distant.

The tank moved ahead cautiously. Within minutes they would be within range of the enemy anti-tank shells. That would be Jentz's signal to speed up and the column would disperse.

Manfred felt his stomach begin to churn once more. The brutal reality of what they were about to face was made even more acute by seeing the seemingly indestructible Stiefelmayer fall.

Shells began to rain down on them. Danny, in fact the whole tank, flinched as a loud explosion to their right destroyed one of the Shermans. PG was still manoeuvring the tank left and right. In this he was helped by the crippled or destroyed tanks acting as slalom posts.

The concussive impact of the shells was physical. The earth was shaking at the barrage they were going through. If this is what it was like now with many guns disabled, what must it have been like earlier for the first assault, wondered Danny. Bullets began to ping uselessly against the armour like hail on a window.

363

McLeish, who had access to a periscope, began to update Danny on what he could see a few minutes into the onslaught.

'Must be half a dozen tanks down already. I can see four fires.'

'Anyone getting out?' asked Danny.

'Some, not many,' answered McLeish ominously.

An explosion close by rocked them, throwing Danny backwards into the Scotsman. The sooner they could get out of this barrage of anti-tank fire the better. There was no response they could offer. Danny preferred to take his chances against the Panzers than face this. And when the shelling stopped would be the moment they came face to face with the enemy Panzers. That much was certain. The low hum overhead of bombers had been a continual accompaniment to the noise of battle. If there was any comfort to be drawn, it was the knowledge that the enemy would also be on the receiving end of a similar bombardment.

They pushed on for another couple of minutes. Danny glanced down at PG. He was tapping at the dashboard repeatedly.

'What's wrong, PG?' asked Danny.

PG was not a man known to worry about things. Any nervousness was hidden behind his normally grim expression. The face that turned around to Danny was white.

'I don't know,' said PG. His voice was tight. 'We seem to have lost a lot of fuel.'

'What's wrong down there?' This was Benson. He ducked his head inside the turret and glared at PG.

'Our fuel, sir. It's disappearing. I don't know if it's the dashboard or if we've been hit.'

Manfred gazed ahead through his viewer. The horizon was black and red with fire and smoke. They would soon be within range of the Allied anti-tank guns. It was a case of hold your breath and hope for the best. The tanks were widely dispersed and driving hard towards the chaos and destruction ahead. On the other side of it lay the Panzers in wait.

Manfred glanced down at Jentz. He willed for them to go faster but this was hardly one of Mercedes Benz's Silver Arrows and Jentz was no von Brauchitsch. No one wanted to endure the hellish rain of shells for one second longer than necessary.

Manfred gripped the wheel that traversed the turret tightly; his muscles tensed for the moment when the tank would be rocked like a boat in a storm. For this was surely a storm towards which they were heading.

Basler was rigid; he kept half a head out of the turret. He was a man who seemed to exist only in the present. This was why Manfred admired him so much. By comparison, he felt like an old man, weighed down by his memory of past times at the Hitler Youth and regret for not realising what it had cost him.

They forged ahead and soon the first shattering screams of shells shredded the air around them. The tank was filled with the foul-smelling stench of war. More and more derelict tanks cluttered the landscape. Every second brought them closer to the other side of this hellish bombardment. There they would hopefully hit the sides of the British tanks with the wedge formation they'd adopted.

The first evidence of the destroyed gun placements dotted the landscape. Dead men and body parts were strewn like flower petals in early autumn. But this was no Eden. They cleared the ridge and had first sight of the enemy in the distance.

Danny noticed the shelling had eased. They seemed to have reached a No Man's Land of blackened metal acting as tombstones to the fallen. PG slowed down at Benson's request. The captain was, once more, with his head outside the turret gazing at the heat haze in the distance. Shots pinged off the sides of the tank.

'Careful, sir,' warned Danny. 'Jerry's still out there.'

'Thank you, Shaw, I'm quite aware of that,' replied Benson, remaining where he was.

Danny gazed through his viewer but could see nothing in the shimmering silver and black horizon. Plumes of smoke were still rising. Distant bombing was visible as the Allied twenty-five pounders and RAF gave the Afrika Korps a taste of what the tanks had just been through. Dense black smoke with orange flames, some twenty feet high, provided a guard of honour for the newly arriving Allied tanks.

'Ahh,' said Benson after some moments. 'I think I see our friends now.'

Andrews glanced up at Benson then met Danny's eyes. The look on his face was clear. Time to get ready.

'Distance three zero zero zero yards.'

The radio crackled to life.

'Ready, Shaw?' asked Benson.

'Yes, sir, High Explosive HE.'

Danny looked through his viewer. He saw the dark shapes moving in the distance. They reminded him of the Errol Flynn movie he'd seen a few months back when Custer first sees the Sioux warriors in the distance. The wide ridge, as far as Danny could see, was filled with dark shapes. In between lay the remains of what had been and what would be.

A tank graveyard.

His finger hovered over the button.

'Fire.'

CHAPTER FORTY-SEVEN

'How far do you think?' asked Manfred.

'Three kilometres and closing,' said Basler without taking his eyes away from his binoculars.

Still too far for them to do any real damage but they would soon be within range of the new Allied tanks. Some of the Mark IVs opened fire. They were similarly equipped with a seventy-five-millimetre gun. This gave them some chance, at least. Manfred gripped his wheel and began to work it left then right to test the traverse.

Jentz was steering in a sharp zigzag too, aware that the Allied High Explosive HE rounds would soon be landing near them. Manfred's left arm was already chaffing against the turret ring. The amount of room wasn't enough for someone of his height. The rapid swings being performed by Jentz added to his discomfort.

The horizon erupted into a series of white puffs of smoke. The enemy had commenced firing. Basler confirmed this but added nothing else. What was there to say? Within minutes, if they survived that long, they'd be in a melee with the enemy. Manfred glanced down at Keil. The loader nodded and used his eyes to indicate the HE shell had been loaded.

The first set of shells exploded around a hundred metres in front of them. Rock and dust flew twenty metres up into the air.

Jentz moved in line behind a derelict Stuart some five hundred metres ahead. Good idea, thought Manfred. It wasn't much but it might persuade the gunners on the other side to choose another target they could see.

'Brehme,' said Basler.

Manfred gazed through his telescopic sight. Basler confirmed his own calculation that there were now two and a half thousand metres separating the two sides. More explosions split the air around them. One after another the Panzers were hit. One erupted into flame. Bits of plate exploded outwards.

More blasts ripped around them like a firework display. The tank rocked back and forth. The sound deafened them. Manfred ducked instinctively then the shelling stopped momentarily. Manfred looked around. Keil was staring up at them. There was a strange look on his face. Manfred frowned, then turned to Basler.

'Sir?' said Manfred. He looked up. Basler was no longer standing. He seemed to be half slumped against the hatch. Manfred leapt up and pulled Basler down. Half his lower jaw was missing.

He was dead.

Manfred and Kleff stared at the dead body. Jentz, unaware of what had happened, was shouting to them.

'Why aren't we firing at them?'

Keil turned around. His eyes widened in shock. He touched Jentz's arm. The driver frowned and then followed the wild eyes of Keil towards the fallen lieutenant.

'My God,' said Jentz.

'Kleff, you take over at the gun. Keil, you load,' said Manfred immediately. There wasn't time to mourn the lieutenant. Manfred took Basler's position at the hatch. He put his head through just as another explosion nearby rocked the tank. They were now past another destroyed Sherman. Less than a couple of kilometres away, he could see a hundred or more enemy tanks. He crouched back inside and removed something from Basler's hand. He stared at the binoculars. A wave of sadness passed through him.

They were wet with Basler's blood.

'Was that you?' asked Benson, watching one of the approaching Panzers erupt into flame.

'Yes, sir,' replied Danny. The shot had been a direct hit from nearly two thousand yards.

'Good shot,' said Benson. 'It's going to get sticky…'

The first explosions began to crash around them, drowning out the captain's chance to finish the sentence. Gouts of desert shot upwards like malign fountains. The intensity of machine gun fire increased. It felt like they were in the middle of a hail hurricane.

'They're on our flanks, too,' warned Benson but noted Danny was already traversing right to deal with the fire coming from that direction. This was possible even on the side gun, but the degree of traverse was severely limited.

Green and red tracer fire split the air between the two sides. Much of it harmlessly bouncing off the armour. But the Panzers were beginning to find their range with the big guns.

Danny saw one Stuart split in two as the turret flew upwards: a horrible reminder of the death of Sergeant Reed and Lieutenant Turner. PG pushed forward, past the destroyed tank. There could be no stopping. No one would have survived such an explosion. Just ahead, another Stuart erupted into flames but a couple of men escaped from the hatch at the side. They were gunned down. Danny's eyes widened in shock. This was the first time he'd seen this. Rage gripped him. The Germans would pay.

'Armour piercing,' ordered Danny.

Benson was back on the intercom, this time to the second gunner, Archie Andrews. 'Eight hundred yards, Andrews, get ready to fire.'

Archie Andrews fired his first round just as Danny launched the first of his AP shells.

'Both short,' said Benson. There was a trace of irritation in his voice. Fear, too. In a matter of minutes the two cavalry charges would meet. The more of the enemy they could kill the better chance they would have to survive this battle.

PG was now slaloming around destroyed tanks. This made life a little more difficult for Danny and Andrews. Danny could understand the natural inclination of anyone to avoid being hit. The constant twisting and turning was interfering with their ability to damage the wave of death approaching them.

Benson saw the problem immediately and said, 'Wodehouse, straight ahead. Give Andrews and Shaw a chance.'

The crash of explosions and the screech of tanks was now deafening. They were seconds away from chaotic intermingling. In fact, they were being hit from three sides. Panzers were on their left flank as well as their right. Ahead lay the big anti-tank guns and field artillery.

How was anyone supposed to get through this?

It was Manfred's tank now. Thoughts of Basler were gone. He looked at the scene ahead. Utter carnage and the battle had barely begun. Begun? Restarted. It had been going on for hours. But this was the critical point now. The Afrika Korps were throwing everything at the Allies. Both the 15th and the 21st Panzer divisions were fighting to halt the Allied advance: all remaining operable tanks. If this didn't halt them, then it was over.

Oily black smoke drifted in front of him; its harsh smell made him feel nauseous. His eyes caught two Allied crew rolling around on the sand trying to extinguish flames. It was horribly compelling and, for the men concerned, utterly futile.

Kleff was pumping out shells at a regular clip.

'Aim for tanks in the second and third rows,' ordered Manfred. They would be through the first row in under a minute now. Just in front he saw a large crater that may have been the result of several anti-tank shell explosions.

'Jentz, do you see the crater?'

'Heading for it now,' replied the driver, who immediately began to downshift and slow the tank.

'Kleff, lower elevation when we dig in.'

'Yes, sir,' said Kleff instinctively.

The tide of Allied tanks had turned to face the flank attack. It was pressing inexorably towards them.

'We'll need cover to our right,' said Manfred. 'Aim for the Grant at two o'clock but hold fire until it looks like it's going to fire at us. I want it closer.'

Kleff glanced up at Manfred. This was a risky game for a young man to be playing. It also left them exposed to the enemy on their left. But the other Panzers could deal with them.

Hopefully.

Kleff knew that hope was not a great strategy in battle but something in Manfred's swift assumption of command boded well. The crater provided some level of protection as only the top of the turret and the gun were visible. The British tide rolled forward.

'Five hundred metres,' said Manfred. His voice was calm. He'd left fear behind now. 'Four hundred metres. Keep an eye out for your second target, Kleff. Three hundred metres.'

Explosions ruptured the ground around them. Then the Grant that they were targeting seemed to realise that they were lying in wait. The big seventy-five-millimetre gun was unable to traverse much but the smaller gun in the turret was turning towards them. They were three hundred metres away now.

'Fire.'

The Grant in front of Danny exploded into flames. No one would have survived. The Panzer's turret began to turn towards Danny's tank.

'Enemy one o'clock, Andrews,' said Benson. There was urgency in his voice.

Andrews fired off a shot but at another tank.

'Shaw?' shouted Benson. They had seconds to react.

'I can't,' responded Danny. The Grant was facing the wrong way. Danny knew he didn't have the lateral flexibility of the turret gun.

The tank surged forward as PG recognised the danger. A puff of white smoke from the Panzer. They heard the shell scream past them. Seconds later they were shielded by the destroyed British tank. The Panzer was fifty yards on the other side. Benson, momentarily, had been struck dumb by the near miss.

'Stop, PG!' shouted Danny as the tank threatened to keep going past their shield and leave them open to another round from the Panzer.

'Traversing right,' said Andrews in the turret.

'Archie, they're expecting us to go forward. We'll reverse and catch them out.'

'Good idea, Shaw,' interjected Benson. 'Ready, Andrews?'

Andrews nodded.

'Reverse,' ordered Benson.

The tank jerked backwards. Andrews leached off a shot with the fifty-seven-millimetre gun.

The AP shell burst through the front of the Panzer. Nobody tried to exit through the hatches. Danny tried not to think of the carnage inside the cabin.

'Bullseye!' exclaimed Benson. 'Edge forward, Wodehouse. We can use this dead tank as cover. Andrews, keep an eye on things to our left.'

Danny's frustration with the Grant was at its peak now. His position on the right of the tank limited his peripheral vision. He felt exposed. This feeling was now acute as a realisation had dawned on him.

Benson had frozen. It was Danny who'd shouted the warning to PG. For the first time he doubted his captain's ability to make the right decisions. He wondered if the others had picked up on this, too. There was no time to discuss it though. Benson was speaking on the intercom.

'Mark III at ten o'clock. Three zero zero yards.'

To the right Danny saw another Mark III appear, straight ahead.

'Twelve o'clock, sir, too,' said Danny, lining up his shot. Andrews fired seconds later. A shell exploded nearby, rocking the tank. Danny's head bounced off the metal. For a second he was disoriented, then he pressed the fire button. Benson and Andrews shouted in unison as they saw the tank on their left explode.

Danny's shot hit the tracks of the Panzer ahead of him. Ominously the turret was turning in their direction.

'HE. Hurry,' shouted Danny to McLeish.

The young Scot loaded the cartridge within a few seconds. Danny had already made a minor adjustment. Through his telescopic view he saw that the gun of the enemy tank was now aimed at them. One or two of the crew were already abandoning the tank. Danny hit the fire button. Seconds later the turret of the enemy tank leapt twenty feet into the air.

There was no time to celebrate surviving their close call. The tank was rocked by a loud crash. Danny flinched. When he opened his eyes, he realised he was covered in blood.

'What the hell was that?' shouted Benson, frantically. 'Wodehouse, move. Enemy tank approaching three zero zero yards, four o'clock.'

The tank did not move.

'Wodehouse,' shouted Benson, ducking inside. 'Why the hell aren't we moving?'

There was smoke inside the cabin. Danny's eyes cleared and he glanced down to his left and saw why there had been no reply from the driver. An armour piercing shell had hit them from the front side of the hull. It took a second for Danny to take in the scene a few feet in front of him.

PG and Sid Gregson were dead.

'We'll have to move,' said Manfred.

'Which way?' asked Jentz. A reasonable question. They had destroyed nearly half a dozen Mark IIIs at least but the enemy kept coming.

Manfred paused a second and then replied, 'I think they're shifting direction, trying to move out of range. My God, there are still so many of them. We need to advance.'

Jentz duly obliged and, after a few false starts, they finally climbed out from the crater. It was welcomed by a shell bouncing off the front

374

armour. It occurred to Manfred that had they waited a minute longer the shell might have caught him.

'They're probing further south,' said Colonel Teege over the radio. 'Report to me who is in pursuit.'

Manfred was shocked by how many of the Regiment 8's tanks had been destroyed now. They had lost at least nineteen from his own battalion. So many familiar names gone. He hoped that his comrades had been able to evacuate their metal homes. He feared the worst and it was not yet midday. An afternoon of fighting lay ahead. He felt an emptiness inside. Who would be left when the day's fighting was over?

Then he felt a swell of anger. He wanted to avenge the death of the lieutenant. He wanted to make the enemy pay. Finally, it was his turn to report.

'It's Brehme, sir. 1st Battalion, second company. Lieutenant Basler has fallen, sir.'

This was greeted by a long silence. Then they heard a sigh before Teege spoke again. In a voice that was barely audible he said, 'Very well, Brehme. You're in command of the tank now. Fall in with the advance.'

And that was it. He was a commander now. It was the role he'd wanted sixteen months ago when he left for North Africa. Back then he never imagined the sense of desolation with which he would greet such news. Yet, as quickly as the sadness swept over him it disappeared and was replaced by something else that was both instinctive and a result of his training: a sense of responsibility towards his men. *His* crew.

'Yes, sir,' replied Manfred, saluting.

They set off in pursuit of the Allied tanks. The signs of battle were everywhere. Dozens of wrecks littered the battlefield, destroyed, derelict and reeking of death. A few of the surviving British crews were scattered around, unable to move for their wounds. Manfred and the other Panzers ignored them and pushed ahead.

'Faster, Jentz, we need to catch up with the others,' said Manfred. It was true. By occupying the crater they'd fallen behind the general advance.

They began to pick up speed. Manfred risked putting more of his body outside the cupola now as the British had swerved away in a different direction. The stench of cordite and burnt charcoal assaulted him. He knew that he would never forget the sights and smells of this day for as long as he lived, however long that might be. Each battle they fought did not feel like one step closer to victory. Quite the opposite. The Allies had taken a fearful battering, yet they would not stop. His own regiment, in fact the whole division, was hanging together by threads now. It was not sustainable.

They were making up ground on the main body of the regiment when something caught Manfred's eye. He looked left, past half a dozen wrecks and then he saw it. A hundred metres away, one of the Grants had started moving. He'd noticed it earlier. It was not blackened or smoking. At first Manfred thought it had been abandoned. Now he could see it was still operable and it was moving to intercept them.

His eyes hardened. A chance to avenge the lieutenant.

'Jentz, turn left, eight o'clock. Kleff, traverse left. Enemy tank, one hundred metres. AP Armour Piercing. Quickly. It's heading this way.'

'They're dead, sir,' said Danny climbing down towards the driver's seat. He motioned for McLeish to take over at the gun. The seat and the dashboard were covered with blood and something that Danny tried not to think about. His stomach heaved as he brushed away the remains of PG from the panel and the seat. Flesh and bone spilled onto the metal floor.

'Hurry, Shaw,' shouted Benson, unaware of the extent of devastation below, or perhaps trying to ignore it. There was more than a trace of panic in his voice now.

Tears blinded Danny's vision. He sat down having cleared away the distorted, twisted remains of what had once been a man. He couldn't bring himself to look in Gregson's direction.

Air was coming through a hole in the side of the tank. The shell had passed through, killing both men, and exited the other side. Had the shot happened further away, it would have stopped within the cabin and ricocheted around, probably killing everyone.

Danny fought back the nausea as he took control of the steering sticks and pushed his foot on the accelerator.

'Move,' screamed Benson.

The tank lurched forward and they headed directly towards the rear guard of the Panzer advance. There was a Mark III directly ahead of them, moving at speed. It was less than one hundred and fifty yards away and had obviously not seen them. The commander's shoulders and the side of his head were visible. Suddenly the German commander turned in their direction and held his binoculars up to his eyes. His mouth fell open and he ducked down into the tank.

The Panzer was now obscured by a destroyed Grant but it was facing in the wrong direction. They had a few vital seconds of advantage now.

'Traverse left,' ordered Benson to Andrews. The gunner was furiously twisting the wheel to get the turret round. Danny steered towards the derelict Grant to provide some cover. He wanted Andrews to fire off a round and then he would duck behind the destroyed tank in front. There would be split seconds between the two tanks firing at one another.

The German tank had reacted more quickly than they'd have thought possible. It seemed to swivel. Within seconds it was almost facing them.

'Fire, dammit,' shouted Benson to Andrews.

Andrews fired.

The shell entered the left side of Manfred's tank. It went through the thirty-millimetre armour like a fist through wet paper. The fragments of the armour encountered Jentz first, shredding him instantly. The shell continued its journey, encountering the right leg of Kleff, removing if from below the knee. But Kleff had died already when a lump of armour embedded itself in his chest.

Keil, beside Jentz, disintegrated in a shower of metal from tank and shell. The dead body of Basler evaporated as thousands of metal shards sliced him apart.

It was only by a miracle that Manfred was not eviscerated. Just as the enemy tank had locked onto the Panzer, Manfred had realised that the British tank would get the first shot in. There was no avoiding the impact of the shell. In those split seconds, as his life hung in the balance, he knew that it would either be an AP Armour Piercing shell or a HE High Explosive one. The latter spelt certain death. The former gave him the merest half chance of survival. He lifted his legs up just as the Grant fired.

At that moment all became a blur. He saw the flash from the mouth of the gun. The tank rocked as the shell penetrated the hull. This was followed by a stab of pain in his shins and feet as the shrapnel ripped through the body of Kleff that had temporarily shielded him, before continuing its journey towards the next soft obstruction.

He screamed in agony and fell into the hull, clutching his bloodied legs. He screamed again when he saw what he'd fallen into. The blood and the tissue and the bones of his comrades had washed the inside of the Panzer a dripping red.

Just above his head, through the tears of pain in his eyes, he could see the fire button. Instinctively, he reached up. His hand felt around for the button. Then his thumb found it. He pressed.

Danny saw the front of the Panzer fold inwards as the shell ripped through the hull. Archie had hit a bullseye. From one hundred and fifty yards, nothing would survive. Shouts of exultation from above. Benson was delighted. He was laughing but there was a hysterical edge to his joy.

'You did it, Archie.'

McLeish reached up and shook Andrews' hand. The fear and the nausea and the grief for the deaths of PG and Gregson were forgotten in the instant that they realised they'd won the duel. Danny stared at the enemy tank and wondered if he should move. He started to roll forward.

'Halt,' shouted Benson.

Danny put his foot on the brake immediately and looked up. He was confused. Why were they stopping?

'Sir, we should move,' said Danny. His foot slipped onto the accelerator in readiness.

'Nonsense, Shaw,' said Benson. A moment later the words died on his lips as they all heard the crump of a gun. Danny automatically ducked down and made himself small. The tank was hit by the shell at the point where the turret meets the hull. At such close range, the projectile passed through the fifty-one-millimetre armour, through the engine, shattering everything in its wake: man, metal and shell. Hot splinters burst into flame in the remains of the fuel.

The noise of tearing metal and screams were deafening. And Danny heard them all. He could hear them as they died. Then he heard something else.

The first crackle of flames.

CHAPTER FORTY-EIGHT

Manfred slumped against the wall of the tank. It was wet. He felt as if he would black out. He couldn't. There was every chance they could be shot at again. Then he heard an almighty crash. He'd hit the other tank. He gave a silent thanks to Kleff who'd obviously been on the point of firing. The thought of Kleff, then the others, stabbed Manfred's heart. There was no other noise in the tank apart from a fizzing sound of flesh, blood and water frying on the hot metal. The crew, his friends even, were all dead.

He steeled himself to look around. No one, nothing, was recognisable anymore. The shower of shrapnel and splinters had made an horrific mess of flesh and bone and organs. Manfred began to retch. He was on all fours now. Adrenalin coursed through his body. It numbed the stinging sore pain in his legs.

He had to move.

He drew himself up and tried to stand. It hurt but he could put his weight on each foot. The fizzing sound was growing louder. There was smoke. His eyes were watering from more than just sadness. The smell of burnt flesh was overpowering his senses and making him weak.

He gripped the edge of the cupola and hauled himself up. The tank began to pop. The flames were reaching the ammunition. Soon the popping would become small explosions. More ammunition would start to heat up, then explode, further obliterating the lumps of human flesh that were the sole remaining evidence that humans had been inside the tank.

It took an enormous effort of will but Manfred managed to push his body through the hatch of the cupola. He fell onto the front of the hull and rolled off onto the hard rocky desert with a thump that knocked the air from him.

Screams ripped through the air.

They weren't his.

God it was hot.

Rivers of sweat flowed from his forehead, or was it blood? He couldn't see. All around him was a blur. The smoke, the sweat, the watery images caused by the heat stopped his eyes from focusing. His arm seemed to be stuck. He wanted to wipe his eyes. He tried to free his hand. No joy. The air seemed to be draining from the cabin. Each breath he took fried his lungs. His legs also seemed to be locked into a position. Something was holding them down. He needed to wipe his eyes.

The coughing started. Breathe, cough, breathe again. The pain seared his throat like acid. The heat was no longer murmuring now; it was crackling. All around him the metal of the cabin seemed to be melting. The sound of the fire was intoxicating, like immersive percussion. He was drowning in its indiscriminate beat. His eyes closed. The temperature was overwhelming him now.

He heard music. His father floated into view and then he saw her. He looked into her green eyes. They smiled invitingly. So much he wanted to say, but how could he? And then they slowly disappeared like dissolving morning mist. He tried to reach out to her. There was a loud rumbling. Like thunder in the distance.

Danny's eyes opened again. The sound of crackling was louder. Getting nearer. Still, he felt weighed down. With a struggle he freed one arm and wiped his eyes. He wished he hadn't. A body was lying over him. It was PG or what remained of his crew mate. He levered him away, freeing up his other arm. The skin on his hand was burning.

Lifeless eyes nearby gazed mockingly at him. It would be his turn next. Death was all around him. It would soon slowly enfold him in its arms and carry him away from the pain, the heat and the hate. He closed his eyes.

A series of explosions outside. He woke with a start. Another explosion, more distant. He roused himself once more. Every breath was a struggle now.

Another body lay over his feet. He tried to kick free. Pain knifed his chest as he tried to rise, he flopped back. It was useless. And the crackling fire grew louder and edged closer. He felt like crying. This is how it would be then. The immensity of the moment was too much. The indignity of it. Absurd almost. He was in despair. Panic rose in him, drowning his spirit, his will to live. The cabin seemed airless now. He cried out a name. Her name.

The shapes in the cabin grew indistinct again and the crackling grew dimmer, like a murmur. And then he woke again. And he began to scream for help. Not like this. It couldn't be like this. He screamed again. He screamed until the pain in his throat threatened to overcome him and then he kept screaming.

The animal screams gave him strength. Somehow, he freed himself from the crushed metal, scraping his leg as he did so, and fell onto the floor of the tank. It was awash with blood. He pulled himself forward towards the escape hatch.

Manfred heard more of the ammunition explode. He crawled away from the tank and fell into an abandoned slit trench. The screams from the British tank were ripping through his head like hot shrapnel. He climbed to his feet and staggered over towards the British tank. The tank *he'd* destroyed.

He could see the twisted metal around the hole that the shell had made. There could be no doubt of the destruction inside. Yet someone had lived; to be more accurate, someone was dying. Dying in a manner that was shocking and terrifying.

Manfred stopped and listened for a second; then he limped around to the side. He stared at the hatch. The last thing he wanted to do was open it. This was war; he'd done what they had done to him. Nothing more, nothing less. It was his duty to kill the enemy. He had done so before. Not like Keil mowing down defenceless men evacuating a tank. He'd killed them when they'd been trying to kill him. It was barbaric but fair. There was no reason why he should pull open the hatch. None whatsoever. The men inside had killed his crewmates.

A louder scream scythed through the wall of the tank and through his mind.

He pulled open the hatch.

The last thing he needed to see was the result of his own handiwork. He knew that the sight inside the tank would stay with him night and day; a nightmare to accompany him for the rest of his life.

The hatch door came away easily just as the screaming reached a crescendo and then stopped. Smoke wafted into his face and blinded him for a moment. Then he saw the lumps of flesh strewn around the interior like rags in a sewing basket. He turned away from the tank, bent over and threw up.

The pain was excruciating. Danny felt as if he would pass out. He shut his eyes. Then the blackness became red. There was sunlight. He opened his eyes and squinted. It took a few moments for him to focus. He could hear someone outside although his ears were still ringing from the shell.

A face appeared at the hatch. He could barely see the features. Soon the face became more distinct. Danny pulled himself closer to the hatch. Daggers of pain raced up through his leg. He grimaced and whispered one word.

'Help.'

The young man at the hatch frowned. His face was covered in blood and grime. The hair was blonde. Danny realised this was a German soldier. Tears of pain welled up in his eyes. He struggled forward to get a better look. To his right he could hear popping. The bullets were beginning to burn. Soon they would catch fire and that would set off a chain reaction with the remaining shells that would result in an explosion.

Danny met the eyes of the young soldier. The fire near the engine was growing stronger now. There was nothing Danny could say. He wasn't going to beg. Nor was he just going to stay there. He inched forward. The heat inside the hull was growing more intense by the second. His blackened hands were smoking.

Manfred looked at the young man. He couldn't have been any older than him. His dark hair was matted with blood and sweat and other things that he couldn't bring himself to think about. He was badly injured. And the tank was beginning to brew up. It was a miracle that it hadn't gone up already.

Manfred wanted to say something but no sound came. He wanted to tell the young man he couldn't help him. His arms fell by his side.

His hand touched the knife he'd taken all those months ago. He took it out of its sheath and stared at it.

He looked back to the young man. The heat rising from the tank was burning his face. Manfred stepped back from the hatch. Out of the corner of his eye he saw the young man crawling towards him. Manfred glanced back at him for a moment. You're going to die anyway, he thought.

Danny watched the young soldier staring mutely at him. He wasn't going to help him, that was clear. Pop, pop, pop went the ammunition. The fire was crackling louder now. He watched as the soldier stepped back from the hatch. Then...

He walked away.

Danny felt like begging. But he would not do that. He couldn't let the German hear his agony, his terror. Death was preferable. And it was imminent. The fire was spreading, the heat unendurable.

Outside the tank he heard a noise. It was difficult to discern what. Something was striking against metal. Moments later he heard a fizz like the sound water makes when it is thrown onto a frying pan. He heard water splashing against metal. Smoke filled the hull and Danny began to cough. But the cracking of flames licking towards the ammunition had stopped.

Manfred lifted the last jerrican and set it down over the engine. He struck the can with his sgian-dubh. Its sharp metal ripped through the thin walls of the jerrican and the water fell into the engine, evaporating immediately while also extinguishing the flame.

Somewhere in the distance he heard the rumble of battle. He stepped back from the tank. The fire seemed to be out. His leg was hurting like hell. Very slowly he walked away from the tank and looked around him. He was alone amidst a scene of shocking brutality. All around him, as far as he could see, were destroyed,

386

blackened, red-glowing tanks and trucks. The stench of death lay thick in the air.

He limped back towards his own tank. The hatch had blown open. Forcing himself to look inside, he confirmed that no one else had survived. He collapsed to the ground and began to sob. But he couldn't stay down long.

Manfred rose once more and pulled a jerrican of water from the side of the tank. It was heavy but he would need it. He had a long walk back in the afternoon sun. With a final look towards his own tank, he turned in the direction from which they'd come and began to walk, slowly, home.

Danny had pulled himself up to the hatch. His shirt was soddened with blood and tissue. His strength was draining away. With a final effort he pulled himself up to the hatch and threw himself out of the hull. He collapsed heavily onto the ground but was too tired to scream in pain. He looked down at his legs, arms and body. He was covered in red. He had no idea how much of the blood was his and how much belonged to the others.

He lay against the wheels. His hands were black causing him agony; his legs and body were burning not just from the pain of the flames but the stinging barbs of the hot shrapnel. Wounds covered him; his life blood slowly seeping onto the sand. He knew he was dying. His body felt like a thousand hot thorns were prodding him repeatedly. The desert was a blur now. He wanted a drink but had no strength left to stand. Alone, propped up against a tank, he would die.

His mind began to wander. He heard voices from his past. He saw the faces of his mother and father swim before him. Then Sarah's face materialised just before the blackness came. He fell to the side, his cheek half turned into the hard, crusty desert.

A few hours passed and the sounds of battle receded like waves on a beach. A Stuart came rumbling through the graveyard of blackened, twisted metal. Then another tank appeared, and then another. The crews looked on in shocked silence at the extraordinary scene of destruction around them.

'Halt,' ordered the captain sitting on the cupola of one tank. He put a cheroot to his mouth and then lifted his binoculars. He could see a body, covered with blood, lying against a tank. Probably dead, he thought. Best to check anyway. Then get the hell out of this bloody place. He ordered the driver to move closer.

'Bennett, go and take a look,' drawled the captain.

The hatch opened and Dave Bennett jumped out of the tank and strolled over to the body. The head was covered in blood yet there was something about the young soldier that seemed familiar. Then it hit him.

'Bloody hell, sir. It's Shaw.'

'Shaw?' said Captain Aston. He paused for a moment and gazed at the bloodied uniform. 'Is he dead?'

Bennett knelt and put two fingers into the groove of the neck near the windpipe. He seemed to take a long time about it, much to Aston's irritation.

'Anything?'

'No, sir.'

Bennett stood up. He looked down at the young man that had been, briefly, his crew mate. He'd liked Shaw. A good sort. He was a mess now. Dried blood caked his hair. His cheek was a paste of dry sand and blood. He seemed to be sleeping.

'What shall we do, sir?' asked Bennett, kneeling again. He lifted Danny's arm and pressed his finger against the underside of his wrist. He held it there for a minute.

'Well?' asked Aston, keen to move on.

'Nothing.'

Bennett stood up and felt a sadness at the death of the young man he'd known briefly. Then a thought struck him. Why wasn't the body cold? Aston was frowning at him. He was never the most patient of captains.

'What's wrong?'

Bennett knelt and felt once more for a pulse.

'It's weak, but there's something there.'

Bennett looked up towards Aston. The captain was already ordering Stone, the gunner, out of the hull to help Bennett. A few seconds later Stone appeared and trotted over to Bennett.

'Bloody hell, not so good-looking now, is he?' said Stone. This was an understatement, thought Bennett.

'Carry him over. Probably too late, anyway, by the looks of him,' said Aston, staring down at Danny.

They crouched down, one at either end, hoisted the limp body up and carried it to the Stuart. They set Danny carefully down on the front. He looked a mess. The whole front of the uniform was red. Aston removed the cheroot and told Stone to get back inside the tank. He surveyed the devastation around him and shook his head. Then he pointed to Danny.

'Wash his head wound, Bennett, see what it's like underneath,' ordered Aston. 'He looks a goner, but we'll do what we can.'

ACKNOWLEDGEMENTS

It is not possible to write a book on your own. There are contributions from so many people either directly or indirectly over many years. Listing them all would be an impossible task.

Special mention, therefore, should be made to my wife and family who have been patient and put up with my occasional grumpiness when working on this project.

This trilogy would not have been possible without my nephew Jack. It was his passion for tanks and his telling me of the Tank Fest at Bovington that sowed the seed of an idea.

I have had wonderful editorial support from my brother Edward, Kathy Lance as well as Sharon and Marina at Lume Books. Thanks!

My late father and mother both loved books and they passed this on to me.

Following writing, comes the business of publishing. My thanks to Mark Hodgson and Sophia Kyriacou for their advice on this important area. Additionally, my thanks to the wonderful folk on 20Booksto50k for contributing so selflessly ideas on how to reach more people and, more importantly, sell books. Thanks to Charles Gray who combines the legal skills of Perry Mason with the football skills of Billy McNeill.

Finally, thanks to all at Lume Books for their support and encouragement.

ABOUT THE AUTHORS

Jack Murray

Jack Murray lives just outside London with his family. Born in Ireland he has spent most of his adult life in England. Jack has written a series of books set in the post WWI period involving a fictional detective Lord Kit Aston. Several characters from this series appear in smaller parts in this book. A spin off series featuring Kit's Aunt Agatha is proving to be equally popular.

J Murray

Jack Murray is the nephew of the author. Jack is currently at Portsmouth University studying Software Engineering. He is also an avid student of World War II and tanks, in particular. Jack has provided research and contributed ideas to the development of this story.